CASE FILE

COMPENDIUM

Bing An Ben

2

CASE FILE

COMPENDIUM

Bing An Ben

WRITTEN BY

ROU BAO BU CHI ROU

COVER ILLUSTRATION BY

BOKI

INTERIOR ILLUSTRATIONS BY

DANKE

TRANSLATED BY

BEN BINGHAM

Seven Seas Entertainment

CASE FILE COMPENDIUM: BING AN BEN VOL. 2

Published originally under the title of《病案本》(Bing An Ben)
Author © 肉包不吃肉 (Rou Bao Bu Chi Rou)
US English edition rights under license granted by 北京晋江原创网络科技有限公司
(Beijing Jinjiang Original Network Technology Co., Ltd.)

Cover Illustration: Boki
Interior Illustrations: DanKe

Seven Seas press and purchase enquiries can be sent
to Marketing Manager Lauren Hill at press@gomanga.com.
Information regarding the distribution and purchase of digital editions is available
from Digital Manager CK Russell at digital@gomanga.com.

TRANSLATION: Ben Bingham
ADAPTATION: Kayce Teo
COVER DESIGN: M. A. Lewife
INTERIOR DESIGN: Clay Gardner
INTERIOR LAYOUT: Karis Page
COPY EDITOR: Rebecca Scoble
PROOFREADER: Jade Gardner, Hnä
EDITOR: Harry Catlin
PREPRESS TECHNICIAN: Melanie Ujimori, Jules Valera
MANAGING EDITOR: Alyssa Scavetta
EDITOR-IN-CHIEF: Julie Davis
PUBLISHER: Lianne Sentar
VICE PRESIDENT: Adam Arnold
PRESIDENT: Jason DeAngelis

ISBN: 978-1-68579-773-7
Printed in Canada
First Printing: June 2024
10 9 8 7 6 5 4 3 2 1

TABLE OF CONTENTS

30

WHO SAID I WANTED MILK?

A WEEK PASSED in the blink of an eye.

Instead of staying at the medical school over the weekend, Xie Qingcheng headed back to the old house in downtown Huzhou to take a look.

It had fallen into disuse shortly after the Xie siblings started attending university. After all, men and women required a degree of separation for decorum's sake, and that tiny space of roughly a hundred square meters made life for both Xie Qingcheng and Xie Xue rather awkward.

But they had formed close bonds with all their neighbors, including Auntie Li, who cherished them as if they were her own children. The Xie siblings returned for a few days at a time every now and then to have dinner with her.

Xie Qingcheng had been very busy recently, so it had been ages since he'd gone home. It just so happened that he was free that week, so he gave Xie Xue a call.

"We're visiting Auntie Li this weekend. I'll come pick you up in my car."

To his surprise, Xie Xue replied, "I passed through there a few days ago. I've already been to visit her."

"...Why didn't you tell me?"

"I—" Xie Xue changed the subject clumsily. "I was just wandering around."

"You need to take three different subway lines to get from Huzhou University to Moyu Alley, and there aren't any major shopping malls nearby. You wandered all the way there by accident?"

"Th-that's right."

"Xie Xue, don't lie to me." Xie Qingcheng's voice turned abruptly chilly. "Have you been keeping something from me lately?"

Xie Xue hemmed and hawed but couldn't come up with any excuse. In the end, she simply exclaimed, "Ge, my phone's battery is dying."

"Xie Xue!"

"It's really dying—I'm hanging up, okay? Ge, I'm busy this weekend, so you can go by yourself. Remember to say hi to Auntie Li for me! Bye-bye!"

Xie Qingcheng was about to protest, but all he got in response was a string of no-connection beeps. He hung up and tossed his phone onto his desk with an icy expression. Then, he walked to his dorm's balcony and smoked an entire cigarette in frustration.

Even if Xie Xue didn't come along, he still had to go back to visit Auntie Li and tidy up the house. Even though they rarely stayed there, it was still his and Xie Xue's real home.

So, on Friday evening after class, Xie Qingcheng packed a few personal belongings and took the subway back to Moyu Alley.

It was one of the few dilapidated longtangs[1] in the city that still hadn't been demolished. Built back in the era of foreign concessions, the edifice had dark red bricks and powdery white edging. The government allocated funds to spruce up the exteriors every year,

---

1 *A style of architecture characteristic of old Shanghai, the term "longtang" can refer to either a network of lanes flanked by two- or three-story terraced houses or a group of such houses connected by a lane.*

but it couldn't change the fate of the building, like a beauty that had passed its prime. With overlapping clotheslines like wrinkles that makeup couldn't conceal and peeling paint that resembled faded lipstick, the sight of these short, squat buildings interspersed between the city's stylish, spacious modern high-rises brought to mind a group photo of old grandmothers alongside young people—very characteristic of their time.

As Xie Qingcheng walked into the alley, the aunts and uncles who were busy taking in the laundry greeted him.

"Professor Xie, you're back?"

"Have you eaten yet, Doctor Xie? I have some extra corn that I can't finish; I'll bring it over later."

After acknowledging them, Xie Qingcheng turned toward the doorway of the building with worn-out bicycles scattered in front and stepped through the gate of his own residence.

The neighbors used to call him "Xiao-Xie" until Xie Xue grew up and started spending more time around them than he did. She also spoke much more sweetly, which was why the neighbors gave the affectionate nickname to her but addressed him politely as "Professor Xie" or "Doctor Xie."

Auntie Li was the only elder who didn't use these honorifics.

Her unit was in the same apartment block as Xie Qingcheng's house, so after he got home and put away his change of clothes, he went to knock on her little red door. No one answered, even after he had knocked for a while.

"Who's making a racket? Do you wanna die? It's the middle of the night—" cursed the old uncle who lived in the attic upstairs. He had opened his window and just barely managed to stick out his balding head. When he saw Xie Qingcheng, he stopped sputtering and cursing. "Oh, Doctor Xie's back."

"Uncle, where's Auntie Li?"

"Ah, she saw Xiao-Xie a couple of days ago and thought that you wouldn't come back so soon, so she went to her friend's place this morning."

"To her friend's place?" Xie Qingcheng frowned.

"That's right. Aiyo, you know what she's like. She gets so hyper around others. Apparently, she's doing some crazy qipao fashion show with her little friends, despite her age. She loves doing those sorts of things, so I'm guessing she won't be back for a few days."

Xie Qingcheng didn't know how to respond.

"Doctor Xie, have you eaten yet?" Done with his idle chattering, the uncle said, "If you haven't, come on up and eat with me."

Xie Qingcheng had never bothered with niceties with his neighbors. "What are you having?"

"Mangoes." The uncle reached his old and wrinkled hand, which looked like tree bark, out of the window and offered Xie Qingcheng a large, peeled mango.

Xie Qingcheng stared.

With his sparse strands of hair blowing wildly in the wind, the old rascal cackled when he saw Xie Qingcheng's expression. "Look at you, look at you. So serious, frowning like that," he said, laughing hysterically. "So funny!"

"...Forget it. You can eat on your own. I'm going home." With that, Xie Qingcheng entered his house, slamming the door behind him.

The apartment was divided into two halves by a simple blue curtain. Xie Xue's space was next to the window that overlooked the scenery outside. Although it was narrow and small, there were several pots of cute succulents and roses in full bloom. The princess bed, which Xie Qingcheng had gotten for her when she was in junior high, was covered in colorful dolls and cushions. Faded celebrity posters were taped to the wall next to it.

Xie Qingcheng tossed his coat onto his own bed and slid his slender fingers into the knot of his tie, pulling it loose with a sigh of relief.

His bed was on the side near the door and separated from the rest of the room by a sheer curtain. He wasn't very picky about this kind of thing, so his bed was an old-fashioned wooden one passed down from his parents. Old furniture was built to last, and it was still very reliable and durable even after more than thirty years dutifully by their side.

After a busy work week, Xie Qingcheng was exhausted. He poured a glass of water and took some medicine, then took a nap on his bed. By the time he woke up, the sky was already completely dark.

Since Auntie Li wasn't around, he was too lazy to have a proper meal, so he dug out his phone and randomly ordered some food for delivery.

A WeChat notification popped up before he could close the app. It was a message from He Yu.

"Where are you?"

Xie Qingcheng couldn't be bothered to reply.

A second message popped up.

"I came to the medical school to look for you, but I didn't see you."

Xie Qingcheng was so tired he didn't feel like typing, so he replied using a minimal number of keystrokes. *"Home."*

In contrast, He Yu wasn't stingy with his words at all. *"You're home? You went home? Is Xie Xue there too?"*

When someone who was constantly tense returned to the place where they felt at ease and could let themselves relax completely, it was very hard to wind them back up again.

That was exactly how Xie Qingcheng felt right now. Lying flat on his old-fashioned bed with his tie loosened and the top two buttons of his shirt undone, his entire body had sunk into lethargy, and he could barely stand to move even the tips of his fingers. He tapped the voice message button and said in a voice hoarse with exhaustion, "Why are you so annoying? She's not with me. It's the weekend. Why are you looking for me? I don't have any milk for you. Don't you know how to order takeout by yourself?"

Xie Qingcheng didn't usually speak to He Yu so harshly. But he found it rather humiliating that He Yu had caught him cheating on their bet. He had yet to figure out how to recover his dignity, so he hadn't gone looking for the little devil all week.

Now that He Yu had found him of his own accord, however, Xie Qingcheng was starting to get angry—he wanted to rest, not worry over this nutcase.

Sure enough, the nutcase fell silent.

A good long while passed before another text message arrived.

"I'm bored."

Xie Qingcheng shot back another stony voice message. "Go play with your classmates."

"I want to come find you."

"Do you not understand what I'm saying, He Yu? It's the weekend. I want to rest and I'm at home. You only came a few times when you were little anyway, so it's not like you'd remember how to get here." Xie Qingcheng shut him down impatiently, but perhaps because he was tired and lying down in bed, there was inevitably a soft nasal tone to his voice.

He Yu replied, *"Don't worry, I remember very well."*

Xie Qingcheng was rendered speechless.

Of course He Yu remembered—how else could he be a xueba?

"Don't come. I don't have the energy to entertain you. Unless you're sick. Are you sick?"

"I'm not sick."

"Then don't come."

But He Yu was undeterred. *"You lost to me last time, but I haven't made my demands yet, have I?"*

Xie Qingcheng stared listlessly at the ceiling. In the bluish glow of the cell phone screen, his face seemed even more overcast.

"...He Yu, just what exactly is it you want?"

This time, He Yu's reply didn't come right away, as if he was pondering what to say.

Just as Xie Qingcheng was about to run out of patience and toss his phone aside so that he could go back to sleep, He Yu sent another message. Surprisingly, it was a voice message this time. The young man's voice was in excellent condition, and he sounded reserved, like a deep pool of warmth.

But the words that he uttered were completely shameless.

"My illness isn't flaring up, but my mood isn't very good. I have to fake it in front of other people, and it's very tiring. But I don't have to do that when I'm with you, so I want to come find you to distract myself and relax."

"...Am I some kind of playground for you to come and distract yourself when you have nothing better to do?" Xie Qingcheng raged at that pleasant voice. "He Yu, what kind of mental problem is this? You used to run away from me faster than a dog from a beating, but now that you've gotten a taste of power, you keep coming back to me on your own? Are you addicted?"

He Yu had no idea what was going on with himself either.

Maybe it was because he'd constantly chased after Xie Xue in the past, so he always had something to look forward to. Now, there was nothing left for him to hang his hopes on, and he didn't want Xie Xue to notice that he had his attention fixed on her, so he could only choose to shift his gaze elsewhere.

Amidst this helpless confusion, he finally realized that Xie Qingcheng was the most suitable distraction. Xie Qingcheng understood him very well, and also...if nothing else, his eyes resembled Xie Xue's.

He Yu knew that they weren't the real deal, but at least they could bring him a bit of comfort. Not to mention, the feeling of having Xie Qingcheng lose to him was very interesting—it was something he had never expected nor imagined before.

Perhaps Xie Qingcheng was right—He Yu *was* a bit addicted.

He'd waited and waited for Xie Qingcheng to order him around again—only for the order to never come. After an entire week of waiting, he felt a bit irritable, so he'd finally stooped to texting Xie Qingcheng himself tonight. Now, with Xie Qingcheng shutting him down repeatedly, he couldn't help but switch from text messages to voice messages with a cold expression on his face, hoping that the other man would be able to hear the displeasure in his voice.

"I'm coming over right now."

Xie Qingcheng was so annoyed that he threw his phone at the wall. He Yu's voice, which was just asking to be spanked, continued uninterrupted in the cramped old room. "You haven't come to find me for an entire week, Professor. You're not scared, are you?"

Xie Qingcheng sighed. "Like hell I'd be fucking scared of you."

He Yu was a man of action; if he said he was coming, he'd definitely show up. Xie Qingcheng hoped that He Yu would take a wrong turn and end up at someone else's house, but when a series of steady knocks sounded on the shabby old security door, Xie Qingcheng knew that hoping for He Yu's IQ to drop was less realistic than hoping he would fall through a manhole cover on his way through a construction site.

The relentless knocking continued.

Lying on the bed, Xie Qingcheng twitched his fingers slightly. He was so tired, it was like the power supply to his body had been cut off. He had no desire to get up at all.

He Yu embodied the fine ethos of a modern university student by displaying the civilized and respectful attitude of someone who honored the old and cherished the young. He didn't hurry Xie Qingcheng, but he didn't leave either. He simply continued to rap on the door with his knuckles from time to time, his strikes measured, even as Xie Qingcheng lay on his bed.

He Yu wasn't impatient at all.

But however patient He Yu might have been, the energetic and sharp-eared old uncle upstairs was getting tetchy. He pushed open the attic window and yelled, "Knocking on and on—shouldn't you ask if anyone's home before you keep knocking for so long?! Huh? I don't know you, young man. Who are you looking for? Are you here for community service, to show goodwill to lonely senior citizens?"

How fucking embarrassing.

Xie Qingcheng, the lonely senior citizen playing dead on the bed, was forced to get up and yank open the security door. "It's fine, Uncle," he yelled upstairs. "It's someone I know."

Xie Qingcheng grabbed the young man standing outside his half-open door by the collar and pulled him into the house.

"Get in here." The dingy door closed behind them with a bang, and the excessive force caused the "good fortune" sign on the door to tremble and slip into a crooked position.

Xie Qingcheng shoved He Yu against the wall with a dark expression on his face.

"What the hell are you doing?"

He Yu leaned back against the wall, giving off the mild fragrance of laundry detergent alongside the vigorously youthful scent of a young man who had spent too much time basking in the sun. That scent wafted into Xie Qingcheng's room, mingling with the cold and dreary smell of tobacco that hung in the air.

He Yu raised an eyebrow and pointed upward. "Didn't that uncle say so already? I'm here to show goodwill to lonely senior citizens." He maneuvered around Xie Qingcheng as he spoke and turned on the room's main light with a click. He moved extremely smoothly, with absolutely none of the reservation a real volunteer would have; he was practically acting like he lived here.

The most irritating thing of all was that, after wandering through the house, this volunteer turned back to politely make demands on the "lonely senior citizen" he was here to console.

"Xie-ge, I'm a little hungry. Can you give me something to eat?"

Xie Qingcheng was so peeved he was about to lose it. Raking his fingers through his hair to push back his bangs, he said, "Why don't you go and drink some milk."

"You have milk for me?"

Speechless, Xie Qingcheng irately rummaged through a cardboard box and threw a carton of Shuhua milk[2] at He Yu.

He Yu glanced at it. "This milk isn't pure enough. I never drink this brand."

Glaring daggers, with his lips set in a thin, frosty line, Xie Qingcheng said, "Then, Young Master, what would you like to drink? Would you like me to find someone to produce milk for you on the spot?"

---

2 *A popular brand of lactose-free milk.*

31

He Was Truly Shameless

THE IMPURE MILK was rejected.

Meanwhile, the takeout that Xie Qingcheng had ordered consisted of only two steamed buns—one meat and one veggie.

He Yu didn't like to eat meat buns because he found them too greasy, but if you gave him a veggie bun, he would feel that the vegetable leaves hadn't been washed thoroughly enough—his attitude was exactly like that of a rich old Republican-era landlord's concubine. In the end, Bossman Xie opened the refrigerator with a cold expression and, with considerable effort, dug out a bag of wontons from the depths of the freezer.

Bossman Xie asked Concubine He, "My next-door neighbor made these. This is the last bag. They're all-natural and preservative-free—this is the only food I have left. Do you want them or not?"

Glancing at Bossman Xie's eyes, Concubine He could tell that this manly patriarch's last shreds of patience had been worn out. He Yu had come here to relax, so it wouldn't do him any good to truly piss Xie Qingcheng off.

So he smiled, unexpectedly showing some reserve with that pretty, handsome face of his—even though it was fake. "In that case, I'll have to trouble you."

The scene that followed seemed like an absurdist parody of volunteerism. Doctor Xie, the lonely senior citizen who was supposed to be the subject of consolation, wore a gloomy expression with lips tightly pursed as he watched over a pot of water boiling on the electric stove, holding a wood-handled ladle. Meanwhile He Yu, the university student volunteer who had come to dole out the consolation, very conscientiously stood as far out of Xie Qingcheng's line of sight as possible. A gentleman's place was not in the kitchen, so he examined the room with calm indifference, as if he were doing exactly what he ought to do.

When He Yu was in junior high, he had come here on several occasions with Xie Xue. Li Ruoqiu had still been around at that time, and the photos from her wedding to Xie Qingcheng had been displayed in this room.

Those photos were all gone now.

But it seemed like it wasn't just Li Ruoqiu's photos that had disappeared. There were several other places that showed marks left by old pictures that had evidently been removed even earlier. It wasn't obvious unless he examined them closely, so He Yu thought that perhaps those photos had already been gone when he visited during his junior high years. However, his attention at the time had been focused on Xie Xue, so he hadn't been very observant.

"Do you want vinegar?" Xie Qingcheng asked.

"Yeah," He Yu said. "I'll add it myself."

It was dead silent inside the room, but snippets of sounds from the neighbors' cramped houses in Moyu Alley could be heard from beyond the walls. Humans on earth were like cells in the body, their movements charmingly out of sync with each other—cells replicated at different times, and people lived according to their own rhythms. When the household to the east was washing dishes and scrubbing chopsticks, the one to the west was only just lighting their stove with an audible spark.

Leaning against the window frame, He Yu saw a chameleon crawling over the sill. He reached out a hand. Surprisingly, the chameleon wasn't afraid of him and allowed him to stroke its head. This was just how He Yu's aura was—cold-blooded animals always had a close affinity to him and never ran away; perhaps it was because they saw him as kin.

But Xie Xue's favorite animals were the fuzzy, warm-blooded ones; she was terrified of creatures like insects and reptiles. If Xie Xue saw this chameleon, she would definitely scream in fright and chase it away.

As He Yu stroked the chameleon's head, it narrowed its eyes in enjoyment.

Perhaps he and Xie Xue really were too different in some respects, he thought. Maybe that was why she liked Wei Dongheng.

Right now, as he stood in the place where Xie Xue had spent her childhood and adolescence, the traces of her life here that would have once eased his mood became a luxuriant thicket of thorns instead, their roots burrowing deep in the earth and their branches piercing high into the sky.

If a field of brambles grew in someone's heart, the world around them would only bring them pain.

He Yu started to feel somewhat unwell, so he quietly bid goodbye to the chameleon and stepped away from Xie Xue's windowsill.

When Xie Qingcheng scooped up the wontons, he turned around to discover that at some point, unbeknownst to him, university student volunteer He Yu had lain down on his bed and covered his face with his pillow.

"...What are you doing? Did you even take a shower before you decided to lie down on my bed?" Xie Qingcheng asked.

He Yu didn't respond. He kept the pillow over his face, as though trying to hide himself like a chameleon.

Xie Qingcheng asked again. "You're not gonna answer?"

He Yu kept quiet.

"If you don't move, I'll assume you've been smothered to death and call the morgue to have you taken away."

After a few seconds of silence, perhaps because he wanted to avoid the misfortune of getting sent to the morgue, He Yu finally lifted a hand and tugged the pillow down slightly to reveal his profile. His almond eyes were filled with disdain. "Your bed reeks of tobacco."

Xie Qingcheng set the bowl down. "If you don't like the smell, then stop lying there and come eat. The sooner you finish eating, the sooner you can leave. I want to rest."

"The smell wasn't so strong the last time I was here."

"That was ages ago."

Indeed it was, He Yu thought.

Back when whatshername—Li Ruoqiu—was still around, Xie Qingcheng didn't smoke. Saozi probably didn't let him. Xie Qingcheng was a rather cold person, but he had a strong sense of responsibility, especially when it came to his duties as a man. If his wife didn't like something, he would definitely find a way to accommodate her.

As He Yu lay on Xie Qingcheng's bed looking at his indifferent side profile, he couldn't help but remember the first time he visited Xie Qingcheng's home. Li Ruoqiu had gone to prepare snacks and tea for him, all smiles, and while he waited for her, he had inadvertently glanced at the large bed half-hidden behind the gauze curtains. At the time, He Yu had found it rather strange because he couldn't really visualize Xie Qingcheng sleeping with a woman.

Were there really times when Xie Qingcheng's stern, solemn face was stained by desire?

Xie Qingcheng frowned. "What are you thinking about?"

"The mysteries of life," He Yu said in a gentle, refined voice.

Xie Qingcheng had nothing to say to that.

"Xie-ge, did you go on any other matchmaking dates after that last one?"

"I don't intend to remarry."

"You're only in your thirties," He Yu said slowly. "Aren't you lonely?"

Xie Qingcheng glanced at him, unconcerned. "Your line of questioning sure is broad, Doctor Busybody."

He Yu smiled. It was probably because Xie Qingcheng had no sex drive.

"Are you eating the wontons? If not, I'm tossing them."

He Yu was actually hungry, so he finally followed Xie Qingcheng's prompting and got up to sit at the small table. The chair Xie Qingcheng had him sit in was the same one that Xie Xue had used as a child. It was small, low, and very uncomfortable for the 189-centimeter-tall He Yu. Xie Qingcheng tossed the little kid a bottle of vinegar and a spoon before asking frostily, "Would you like a bib?"

He Yu didn't bother bickering with him. He turned his face and smiled slightly, looking very obedient. However, the harshness burning in his eyes betrayed his hostile intentions. "In that case, why not feed me yourself, Doctor?"

Xie Qingcheng didn't humor him with a response.

"Here." He Yu handed the silver spoon back to Xie Qingcheng.

"Scram and eat on your own," Xie Qingcheng said coldly.

But the wontons were indeed a bit too hot. He Yu wanted to let them cool down first, so he picked up his phone and tapped away at it for a while.

Xie Qingcheng couldn't hold back his paternal impulses. "If you're going to eat, then eat. Don't play games on your phone."

He Yu didn't even raise his head as his fingers flew over the screen. "This isn't a game."

Xie Qingcheng looked down at the screen to find that it indeed wasn't a game but rather some sort of rapidly scrolling code.

"What is it?"

"I'm practicing. These are hacking commands."

"Don't hackers use computers?"

"I set it up myself," He Yu said calmly. "My phone can do everything a computer can."

Xie Qingcheng wasn't really interested in this sort of thing, nor did he understand it very well, but he had a vague idea of He Yu's skill, and he guessed he was very competent. Still, He Yu just treated attacking other people's firewalls as a game of heightened concentration; he'd never truly crossed the line.

"Two minutes."

He Yu finally hit the enter button and the data froze on the bypass screen of a well-known website. He checked his watch. "My speed was pretty good this time—maybe it's because I'm in a rush to eat wontons."

He closed the page with a smile. He had no interest whatsoever in their data, he just wanted to play with their firewall—like an eccentric thief who liked opening all sorts of advanced locks, but who didn't bother stealing anything once the locks had been cracked.

Xie Qingcheng looked on in silence as He Yu put down his phone. At this point, the wontons were at the perfect temperature, so He Yu bent his head and slowly began to eat.

Handmade wontons were rarely available in stores; He Yu quietly finished the entire bowl but still felt unsatisfied, so he turned to Xie Qingcheng.

"What are you looking at me for? There isn't any code on my face."

"I'd like another bowl."

"Do you think this is a prize-unboxing game? Another bowl? A neighbor made those and gave them to me, and what you just ate was the last bag. There's no more."

"Then do you know how to make them?"

Xie Qingcheng took out a cigarette and held it in his mouth, mumbling, "Even if I did, I wouldn't make them for you." With that, he clicked his lighter on and turned his head slightly to light the cigarette held between his teeth.

He Yu frowned deeply. "Xie Qingcheng, when exactly did you wind up with such a serious tobacco addiction? Can't you stop? This room is tiny to begin with, and now that you've filled it with smoke, I can barely breathe."

"Is this your house or mine?" Xie Qingcheng took a drag and exhaled it in He Yu's direction without the slightest hint of courtesy, then gazed at him through the faint gray fog. "You come into *my* house, eat the wontons that I cooked, sit in my chair, and lie in my bed with my pillow on your face. You keep making demands, but you act like you're being so polite the whole time. If you can't breathe, you can go home. Your family's villa is surrounded by greenery; the air must be very fresh. The door's that way."

He Yu was rendered speechless.

Xie Qingcheng flicked away some ash from his cigarette. "Are you leaving?"

He was met by silence.

"If you're not, then make sure to wash your dishes. You're quite courteous when you're at other people's houses. Don't get all lazy now that you're here."

Fine, it was just a simple chore. This young master had lived abroad, after all, so it wasn't as if he didn't know how to do dishes.

With the sound of running water as accompaniment, Xie Qingcheng smoked an entire cigarette while leaning against the window. He'd been quite tired before, but after that disagreement with He Yu, he'd gradually lost that sense of exhaustion. The cigarette he smoked once the fatigue passed had left him feeling more awake now.

He examined the way He Yu looked washing dishes before the sink. He had no bangs, and he looked refreshing with his handsome forehead exposed—though at the moment, with his head bent as he scrubbed the dishes, a few wisps of hair were hanging down over his brow. His skin was supple and smooth, and despite the dim lighting, his profile seemed to emit a soft glow.

He looked extremely youthful and delicate. And he was intelligent to boot. You had to get very close indeed to catch a whiff of his bestial degeneracy.

Looking at him, Xie Qingcheng thought, *If it wasn't for his mental illness, he'd be completely invincible; he could get any girl he wanted. I wonder what kind of girl it was who found him lacking.*

"You should replace this faucet; there's barely enough water coming out."

After Young Master He condescended to wash the wonton bowl, he turned off the water, let down the sleeves he'd rolled up, and wiped his hands dry.

"We don't come back very often these days," Xie Qingcheng responded. "Changing it isn't worth the hassle."

The young master thought this was no big deal and said, "Then next time I'll have Lao-Zhao find someone to replace it along with this light..."

Xie Qingcheng's expression soured. "What's wrong with the light?"

"It's way too dim. It makes this place feel like a haunted house. If the room gets any darker, you won't even be able to tell who's standing in front of you."

Xie Qingcheng grew angry at He Yu's disdainful tone—what kind of person started nitpicking the moment they put down their chopsticks after eating? "I'm pretty sure this isn't your house," he scoffed. "Besides, you're the one who struggles to identify the person in front of him, aren't you, He Yu?"

He Yu didn't know what to say to that. It was true that he was having a hard time accepting what had happened at the Hangshi hotel—that he'd mistaken Xie Qingcheng for a woman, pinned him down, and kissed him from the table all the way to the bed. He immediately dropped his voice. "You said you wouldn't bring that up again..."

Xie Qingcheng rolled his eyes. "Do you think I wanted to? It's only because I can't get you to shut your mouth."

Just as the awkwardness was beginning to set in, there came a knock at the door.

Concubine He saw it as an opportunity to escape this uncomfortable topic, so he cleared his throat and managed to force a rather deferential tone. "I'll get the door."

"Hello, I'm with Shunfeng Express Shipping. Is this Mr. Xie's address?" someone called from the outside.

He Yu opened the door to see a young man mopping his sweat.

"Um, are you Mr. Xie? You booked an appointment today to have something shipped and asked me to come pick it up at your door."

He Yu turned back and said rather courteously, "Mr. Xie, Shunfeng's here to pick up your package."

"That's right, I do have something that needs to be shipped," Xie Qingcheng recalled. He retrieved a box from the belongings he'd brought home and walked over. "It's a basic daily necessity to be shipped to Sushi. Please check the order slip."

"All righty, no problem!"

After the delivery boy had checked that everything was in order and was about to pack it up, He Yu, who was standing nearby with his arms crossed, suddenly had the feeling that something was off. "Hold on." He stopped the delivery worker from sealing the box, opened it, and took out the article of clothing inside.

A beat of deathly silence followed.

He Yu, who moments ago had been servile and deferential, emanated a dark aura as he lifted the shirt and slowly turned his head. "Xie Qingcheng."

Without any change in expression, Xie Qingcheng asked, "What is it?"

"...You resold the T-shirt I lent you on Xianyu?"[3]

"You said yourself that you don't want it anymore. Even as second-hand apparel, this shirt of yours is being fought over at the high price of five thousand yuan. If I were to keep it, it'd only become a cleaning rag," Xie Qingcheng admitted calmly. "What's the problem?"

"What do you mean, what's the problem? Don't you know that I have mental germaphobia? I'd rather ruin my things than give them to strangers."

Xie Qingcheng was unmoved. "That's one of the ways your mental illness manifests. This is the perfect opportunity for you to overcome it."

As he spoke, he grabbed the box and shoved it into the bewildered delivery boy's hands. "Ship it. The buyer said they'll pay the delivery fee when it arrives."

---

3 *An online platform for the resale of luxury goods. The real-life app is called 闲鱼, "idle fish" (referring to the unused, "idle" goods), but the name is written here as 咸鱼, "salted fish," a slang term for someone lazy or unambitious. Both are pronounced "Xianyu."*

"Xie Qingcheng!"

The delivery boy hesitated and looked to either side. "Then...do I ship it or not?"

The concubine: "Don't ship it."

The patriarch: "Ship it."

The delivery boy wiped his brow. "Wh-why don't you two take some more time to discuss it with each other?"

"There's nothing to discuss. If I say ship it, then ship it." Xie Qingcheng's authoritarianism reared its head once more. He shot the delivery boy a glare. "Hurry up. I'm the one who placed the order."

Not many people could handle the daggers in Xie Qingcheng's eyes, so the delivery boy obediently accepted the order and hurried on his way. That left He Yu, who looked like he had a dense cloud hanging over him because his personal belongings had been sold, and Xie Qingcheng, who was in a great mood because he had just made five thousand yuan.

"You're unhappy?" asked Xie Qingcheng. "Then I'll treat you to a midnight snack. Let's go."

He Yu stood there for a while, but he couldn't bear it anymore. Face blank, he picked up his messenger bag from the bed, shoved Xie Qingcheng out of the way with his shoulder, and walked out the door without a backward glance. "You can eat on your own!" he hissed through gritted teeth. "Careful you don't eat through the five thousand yuan you made from selling my shirt all in one go. Save it! And if you don't have enough to eat, give me a call and I'll personally come and feed you myself!"

Hatefully hurling these harsh words in his wake, the young man left Xie Qingcheng's home with his bag slung over his back.

His driver had been waiting outside the alley for a long while. With a cloudy expression on his face, He Yu tucked his long legs inside the car and instructed the driver to close the window. He didn't spare so much as a glance for the bustling scenes of everyday life outside.

"Young Master, are you feeling unwell?" the driver asked. "Do you need me to take you to the hospital?"

"No need." He Yu leaned back against the seat sullenly. "I don't want to see anyone wearing a white lab coat today."

His phone vibrated as a man who wore a white lab coat sent him a message.

"Next Monday, come to my office for work."

With a long face, Young Master He promptly turned off his phone.

32

I Really Was Wrongly Accused

REGARDLESS OF HOW UPSET he was, He Yu still went over to the medical school next door on the following Monday, messenger bag slung over his shoulder, and knocked on the door.

The teacher nearest to the door said, "Come in."

"Hello, I'm looking for Professor Xie," He Yu said in a refined and courteous manner.

"Xie Qingcheng, your student's here."

Xie Qingcheng stepped out of the inner room of the office. To He Yu's slight surprise, he was wearing a pair of glasses today. Xie Qingcheng hadn't been nearsighted before.

"You've come at just the right time," Xie Qingcheng said crisply. "Come in."

He Yu couldn't help but sneak a few more glances at him. He was pretty handsome in those glasses—they made him look less stern and more scholarly, and He Yu felt less annoyed when he looked at him.

Unfortunately, when Xie Qingcheng opened his mouth and began to talk, his unbearable attitude returned in full force. "I want you to use these course materials to make some PowerPoint presentations for my class. Also, there are some documents here that need to be digitized. A lot of it is medical information, but I don't trust the accuracy of OCR since it's easy for mistakes to happen when images are being converted to text. Make sure to double-check your work after you type it in manually, got it?"

He Yu looked at the thick medical texts stacked on his desk. Most of them were large enough that they could have been used as blunt-force murder weapons. "Professor Xie, don't you know that technology can liberate mankind?" he asked.

Xie Qingcheng slammed one copy each of *General Psychology* and *Social Psychology* down in front of He Yu, making the table quake and the computer screen tremble. "I do. But I also know that humans shouldn't become overly reliant on technology. Now get to work, starting with the content in these books that I've marked in red."

Staring at the two brick-like books, both stuffed with so many sheets of annotations that they had practically doubled in thickness, He Yu tried his best to maintain his composure. After all, he was sitting in Xie Qingcheng's office, and there were still several other professors here who had yet to leave. He whispered to Xie Qingcheng, "Are you trying to kill me?"

Standing beside him, Xie Qingcheng took a sip of his coffee. "No. I'm trying to train your patience and willpower."

He Yu was speechless.

"I don't ask for much. Just do your work carefully." Xie Qingcheng tossed him a Red Bull, then turned back to take care of his own business.

He Yu narrowed his almond eyes slightly. He opened Xie Qingcheng's computer and hovered the cursor over the Word icon, his eyes dark behind the cage of his long lashes.

"Let's see..."

When dealing with the personal computer or mobile phone of a man in his thirties like Xie Qingcheng, it was only natural for it to contain content that wasn't suitable for polite company. Of course, to avoid death by social embarrassment, such a gentleman would carefully set a password for his device, create hidden folders, and refrain from lending it out.

But Xie Qingcheng didn't care.

He had given He Yu his own personal computer to use in his office. With the wicked intention of finding some leverage he could use against Xie Qingcheng, He Yu brought all his skills as a top hacker to bear searching the computer's contents. He'd originally thought that he'd at least be able to find a risqué video or two, but by the time He Yu had polished off an entire can of Red Bull, nothing had turned up.

He couldn't believe it. He changed the code and searched again—but the result was the same.

Xie Qingcheng's personal computer was spotless and pristine; there was nothing in there but academic files and salary reports. The entire device was so clean that it was almost unnerving.

He Yu frowned and leaned back in the office chair as he fiddled with the empty can with his slender fingers. After thinking for a moment, he changed the code and added another section, then hit enter to search.

This time, he found a folder that Xie Qingcheng often used when he was off work. Furthermore, the folder's name, "Happiness," was also suspicious.

With Xie Qingcheng's straightforward, male chauvinist personality, his folder naming system was simple: important files were edited to indicate "Course Materials #1" and "Course Materials #2" while unimportant files retained the default names that the computer had assigned them. He couldn't even be bothered to move his fingers to fix the titles. As such, the "New Folder" naming scheme had already reached #23.

This "Happiness" folder didn't quite fit Xie Qingcheng's personality; when it appeared, He Yu's eyes brightened at once. His energy shot up and his back straightened as he focused all his attention on the screen. He moved the cursor over the pale-yellow file folder and double-clicked.

The folder opened.

Skimming through it quickly, He Yu's expression immediately changed from excited to calm. Then, he frowned, thinking that Xie Qingcheng was completely incomprehensible.

Inside that folder labeled "Happiness," all he saw were a handful of photos of freshwater jellyfish and a couple of videos. He Yu clicked open the clips and found only more jellyfish. Videos of sea jellies from all over the world, from moon jellyfish to flame jellyfish, from every angle that you could possibly imagine. One of the videos was over an hour long—He Yu dragged the progress bar several times, but it really only featured footage of sea jellies floating about like wisps of smoke.

He Yu was baffled.

So, Xie Qingcheng's happiness was watching these jellyfish videos?

They were quite pretty—ancient lifeforms floating in the ocean like sinking mist or moonlight spilling into the water—but even so, He Yu couldn't understand this old man's taste, so he closed the video and exited the screen.

A bit dissatisfied with his discovery, He Yu propped his chin in one hand and changed his troubleshooting methods a few more times, but Xie Qingcheng's personal computer really was just like the world after a snowfall—pure white and perfectly pristine. He tossed the mouse aside and gave up.

He Yu toyed with his empty can, lost in deep thought. If Xie Qingcheng was a normal man, he should still have some semblance of desire...

He turned his gaze back toward the computer screen, coming to the conclusion that Xie Qingcheng was really much too frigid—he was definitely, without a doubt, hyposexual. If that was the case, He Yu needed to change his methods.

He abandoned his plan of looking for porn videos on Xie Qingcheng's computer. Running his tongue gently over his teeth, he regathered his focus as another idea came to him.

Xie Qingcheng had a lecture the next day, in the afternoon. Coincidentally, He Yu was free then, and since he was the one charged with digitizing the class files for Xie Qingcheng, he decided he might as well head over to the medical school and sit in the last row of the multimedia classroom to listen to a free lecture.

Xie Qingcheng hadn't wanted him to come at first. "Why is a screenwriting and directing student trying to sit in on a psychiatry class?"

He Yu politely responded, "Ge, I'm a psychiatric patient."

Xie Qingcheng gave him a look.

"Besides, I'm the one who made your presentation slides last night. If anything goes wrong, I can solve it right away, right?"

Xie Qingcheng thought it over. He supposed He Yu had a point, so he let him do as he pleased.

But the moment He Yu entered the classroom, Xie Qingcheng began to regret it—he had forgotten about their bet. He Yu had spoken closely with all the female students on that list of names he'd given him. Those eleven girls, who were taking psychiatry as an elective, widened their eyes when they saw He Yu walk in, rare smiles of infatuation immediately appearing on their faces.

One of them called out to He Yu. "Hey there, handsome. What are you doing here?"

He Yu waved at her, but then made a silencing gesture and pointed to where Xie Qingcheng was standing before the lectern.

"Oohhh!" The girl immediately lowered her voice and nodded. Then, she very cooperatively turned her head and looked attentively toward the lectern to prepare for class.

He Yu sat down in the last row of seats, next to the window. He tossed his messenger bag down beside him, leaned back with his arms crossed, and took out the earbuds he had been wearing the whole way here as he looked toward Xie Qingcheng.

His message couldn't be clearer: *Look at me, aren't I very polite? Even though your lecture is gibberish to me, I'll listen attentively to everything you say out of respect.*

Unfortunately, his facade only garnered an eye roll from Xie Qingcheng.

Xie Qingcheng placed his textbook on the table with an air of indifference. After his gaze circled back from He Yu, he asked with an overcast expression, "What are you all looking at him for? Have you never seen someone from the neighboring school sit in on a class before?"

All the students were cowed into silence under the pressure exerted by Professor Xie, but they surreptitiously exchanged glances with each other. They really hadn't seen this kind of thing before. Not unless you counted idol dramas about cross-campus romances.

Some of the female students, especially the ones who had already met He Yu, began to indulge in this fantasy. Those whose neurons fired the most quickly had already decided on a maternity hospital for their future children. One after another, they adjusted their posture to look as elegant as they could, hoping that this handsome young man would notice them from his seat in the last row.

It was impossible for Xie Qingcheng not to take note of this scene as he stood at the lectern. This prim and proper professor who was afflicted with sexual apathy found it all abhorrent, but because of his chauvinistic personality, he wasn't the type to blame such behavior on his female students. Instead, he held He Yu responsible. After glaring at He Yu for several more seconds, he finally said in a very cold voice, "Class is starting, so open your books. For today's lecture, you are all forbidden from looking backward. Those incapable of keeping their necks from turning will have six points deducted from their final grade. Consider the consequences on your own."

The students all fell silent.

Meanwhile, He Yu, the subject of all this, couldn't help but lower his head and smile. Previously, he had found Xie Xue's attempt at intimidating her students pretty silly. Now, he had finally discovered the source of this foolishness: of course, she had learned it from Xie Qingcheng.

Xie Qingcheng began the class by going through yesterday's post-lecture exercise questions with the students.

"...According to the CCMD-3, mental disorders include manic episodes, depressive episodes, bipolar disorders, cyclothymia, dysthymia..."

Although most university students spent four years of their youth in the dormitories sleeping on simple wooden beds, relaxing and taking it easy after their college entry exams, medical students definitely did not belong within this category of undergraduates who lived with the leisure of immortals. Instead, they might spend a minimum of five years reliving their miserable "senior year of high school" lifestyle.

Case in point, Xie Qingcheng spent half the class going over an ordinary homework assignment—a testament to its length.

As for He Yu, the student sitting in on the lecture, he at least had the self-awareness of someone who'd shown up uninvited and was actually pretty quiet. He sat in his corner in the back row with his arms crossed, watching Xie Qingcheng.

He discovered that although the way Xie Qingcheng and Xie Xue threatened their students was identical, their teaching methods were completely different. Xie Xue did her utmost to rouse the energy in the room, trying to make all the material she described come to life. In contrast, Xie Qingcheng practically ignored his entire classroom of students.

He stood ramrod straight behind the lectern, looking as though he didn't even belong to this world. Reality had nothing to do with him; it was as if half of him had sunken into some illusory space where knowledge and data acquired material forms that drifted through the air behind him.

It was clear that he belonged to the pure scholarship faction of professors. He didn't want to patiently and systematically guide his students while imparting knowledge, nor did he intend to waste his time and effort coaxing them to learn and study. Instead, Xie Qingcheng was like a lofty messiah who had strolled out of the hallowed temple of knowledge with his long, slender fingertips stained with ink, exhaling the scent of books from between his thin lips. With an expression that was focused and self-aware to the point of recognizing the impermanence of self, he exuded an air of extreme nobility.

It seemed like he didn't care whether you learned or even looked at him, but his bearing at the lectern was in and of itself the most perfect representation of his devotion to the ideal of knowledge.

He Yu genuinely suspected that, at any moment, he would say something along the lines of, "This Exalted One has descended to the world of mortals to bestow knowledge upon you students. All present should kneel in gratitude for this divine favor." As He Yu turned this over in his mind, he gazed at the man at the lectern with the indifferent expression. He was still fully immersed in the world of medicine.

"All right, that's all for yesterday's questions. Now, turn your attention to this presentation."

These words pulled He Yu out of his thoughts. He lifted his eyes as he relaxed the arms that he had kept crossed over his chest. Interlacing his fingers, he set his hands on the table and leaned forward slightly in his seat.

It was a posture that denoted anticipation—and there was certainly no reason He Yu should have been feeling any keen anticipation in Xie Qingcheng's class. But unfortunately, Professor Xie had grown used to being dismissive of others and felt even more disinterested in dumbfucks like He Yu who sat in on classes in their leisure time, so he didn't notice the sudden flicker of tension on his guest's face.

He opened his laptop, connected to the internet, and adjusted the projector. Under the watchful eyes of the students, the cursor moved over to the presentation that He Yu had named "Class Material #1."

With a double-click, the presentation opened.

Xie Qingcheng didn't even look at the screen before lifting his head. "Today we will be discussing hallucinations. Proprioceptive hallucinations, true hallucinations, pseudohallucinations..."

He talked for a long while, completely absorbed in his own lecture. It was only when a male student sitting in the front row

finally couldn't help but lower his head with a sputter of laughter that Xie Qingcheng finally realized that something was off. However, he didn't look back at his presentation. He only furrowed his brow and asked that fearless student, "What is it?"

This time, the male student was no longer the only one who couldn't resist laughing.

"Professor Xie, your PowerPoint..."

Only then did Xie Qingcheng look back at his screen.

Out of concern for students' learning, the president of the university had made great efforts to upgrade the school's hardware facilities. The newly replaced multimedia classroom projector was very bright and clear, and it projected the PowerPoint slide in fine detail.

On the screen was a group of cute, digitally rendered baby sea jellies, their shapes somewhat reminiscent of chibified moon jellyfish. The image was even a fucking animated gif, with the baby sea jellies adorably going through a series of repeated motions with the captions "baby is so mad," "baby has fainted," and "baby is done playing with you, goodbye."

The impact of this sickeningly childish animation was so strong it caused Xie Qingcheng's breath to stutter to a stop. Without thinking, he tried to draw a cigarette to suppress his shock.

He Yu couldn't help but turn his face away, his shoulders trembling as he ducked his head in laughter. Xie Qingcheng whipped around angrily and spotted the culprit leaning comfortably back against his chair with his lashes lowered. Sensing his gaze, He Yu raised his head to reveal the thin, completely undisguised hint of a smile curving the corners of his lips.

This little devil...

Xie Qingcheng's stare was about to pierce through He Yu and nail him to his seat.

He Yu was certain Xie Qingcheng wouldn't admit that he'd conscripted an able-bodied man into making his presentation slides for him in front of a crowd. So, He Yu unfolded his fingers, lifted a hand with a smile and a slightly raised brow, and tapped lightly on his cell phone where it lay on the desk.

His gesture was self-explanatory—he was hinting that Xie Qingcheng should check his notifications.

Xie Qingcheng returned to his lectern and closed the presentation with an extremely dark expression. "There's something wrong with the class materials. Please wait a moment."

It was exceedingly rare for the students to see Professor Xie make a mistake, much less such a silly one. If not for Xie Qingcheng's prestigious reputation, they would have long since burst into hysterical laughter. Everyone did their utmost to suppress it, but it wasn't easy. Who could possibly have the mind to notice the tumultuous tension between their professor and the student from the neighboring university who had come to listen in on their class?

Xie Qingcheng seized the opportunity to swipe open his cell phone, his face overcast. As expected, there was a message from He Yu sent two minutes prior:

"Would you like the real PowerPoint?"

"What do you want?"

He Yu is typing...

A beat passed.

The chat window still said, *"He Yu is typing..."*

Unable to bear it any longer, Xie Qingcheng looked up once more, his eyes skimming past the students choking on their laughter to glare at that gently refined youth reclining casually in his chair and typing ever so unhurriedly.

It was as if He Yu was set on grating over Xie Qingcheng's sore spot, dragging out this awkward scene that could cause Professor Xie to die of embarrassment. He Yu didn't even look at Xie Qingcheng as he extended a single slender finger and slid it across the screen, entering several words, then deleting them, and then repeating the motions, as though he was earnestly pondering the conditions for their exchange.

It was a pity that He Yu's happy mood hidden beneath his mask of civility was exposed when he raised his brows in self-satisfaction at the success of his evil plan.

Just as Xie Qingcheng was about to lose it and walk over to where He Yu was seated to slam a hand onto his table, the message finally arrived.

Xie Qingcheng immediately unlocked his vibrating cell phone.

"Do you remember that shirt of mine that you sold?"

Xie Qingcheng stared.

"Send me 5000 yuan and I'll come help you fix your PowerPoint."

Then, after another long silence.

"While I'm here, a word of warning: if you carry on ignoring me, in ten minutes, your laptop will automatically download and play some rather vulgar videos. Even if you try to force it to shut down, it will be useless. So, Professor, please make the call yourself. I might up my price in a few minutes, who knows?"

Once he finished typing, the hacker set down this tool that he had used to privately communicate with Xie Qingcheng in full view of everyone. Then he slung one of his arms behind him, propped his elbow over the back of his chair, and tipped his chin upward toward the projector at an angle that couldn't be seen by bystanders. He raised his other hand to casually tug at his collar, revealing an innocent-yet-dark smile to Xie Qingcheng.

Xie Qingcheng glared at He Yu with a malevolent expression as he slowly picked up his cell phone. Opening the funds transfer page in the Alipay app, he gritted his teeth and inputted the amount that He Yu had demanded.

A second later, He Yu's phone buzzed on the desk.

He looked down, his lashes obscuring his almond eyes, and saw that five thousand yuan had been deposited into his Alipay account. Then, he got to his feet. As expected of an actor who had been featured in a shitty little drama, He Yu's skills were no longer those of a beginner. He ably feigned concern for Xie Qingcheng as he walked up to the lectern. "Sorry about that, Professor Xie. Seems like I clicked on your course materials by accident when I was backing up your sister's files to your computer yesterday. I'm really very sorry."

As the profiteer of his misfortune, Student He Yu very courteously collected the scraps of Professor Xie's dignity from the ground, then bent down to begin setting things up on Xie Qingcheng's laptop.

Soon after, He Yu dug the real PowerPoint that he had prepared out of his files.

He raised a hand and retreated respectfully and genteelly to the side, offering his spot back to Xie Qingcheng. "Here you go, Professor."

And just like that, the disruption was smoothed over, with He Yu emerging victorious once again.

Still, Xie Qingcheng's expression was gloomier than the dark clouds on Doomsday for the rest of the class, like the calm before a storm. His eyes were colder than ever, as though they were embedded with shards of ice. He Yu didn't doubt for a second that, if "glaring daggers" was a physical phenomenon, he would have long since been perforated so thoroughly he could be used as a sieve.

But this theoretical supposition was clearly not tenable, so he smiled and accepted every single dagger with a roguishness that went undetected by onlookers.

"...That's it for today's lecture." Finally, Xie Qingcheng ended the damned presentation portion of the class with five minutes to spare, extremely relieved to have brought this matter to a close.

"I'll be posting the homework for this week on the school's Intranet, so make sure to download all of it." The relaxed Professor Xie exited the PowerPoint and opened the internet browser. After entering the school's web address, he pressed enter with a decisive click.

A few seconds later...

"UNLIMITED ADULT VIDEOS FREE TO DOWNLOAD, HOT BUSTY BABES IN YOUR AREA, 1,000,000+ SEXY PORN VIDEOS, CLICK HERE: dontbothertypingthisintoyourbrowseryou-dummy.com/nothingtoseehere"

A pop-up advertisement window blew up on the projector screen. A scantily clad woman posed coquettishly as she gazed out at the flabbergasted class.

All the students fell deathly silent.

Xie Qingcheng's eyes shot to He Yu immediately.

He Yu gaped.

It was just his damned luck.

He really had nothing to do with it this time...

33

HE WALKED RIGHT INTO A TRAP

AFTER THE INCIDENT with the course materials, He Yu explained himself to Xie Qingcheng over and over.

But Xie Qingcheng wasn't just overly paternal. He was also a professor. He might be able to let other mishaps go, but there was no way he could put this matter behind him. For a long while, Xie Qingcheng was reluctant to acknowledge He Yu at all.

Helping He Yu manage his mental state was one thing, but He Yu provoking him was another entirely. He Yu had stomped on Xie Qingcheng's minefield—Xie Qingcheng could only bare his teeth in turn.

Justice was not blind; the opportunity for him to put He Yu in his place came very quickly.

On this day, Xie Xue phoned Xie Qingcheng.

"Ge, Huzhou University and Huzhou Medical School are having a centennial celebration of their founding, did you hear?"

"What are they doing?"

"Oh, one of the items on the agenda is for our two schools to collaborate on filming a movie—not the kind that gets aired, but it'll be posted on the university website, and they're gonna organize a celebratory viewing."

Her brother didn't cut her off, so Xie Xue rambled on, "It's just a practice piece being filmed for fun, but because it's the centennial anniversary of both Huzhou University and Huzhou School of Medicine, the admins are taking it pretty seriously and providing a lot of funding. They want the teachers to organize the filming with students from the appropriate majors. It's a super rare opportunity, so I've already started working on the script. Can you come and act as a medical consultant?"

Xie Qingcheng had no interest in this. But since Xie Xue was the one who made the request, he said, "Send me the proposal; I'll take a look."

"Oooh, sure! Of course! You have to cheer me on!"

Not long after she hung up, Xie Xue sent Xie Qingcheng the files for the planned proposal. The staff and students of Huzhou University already had a rough idea as to the general direction of the film. Because it was a collaboration with the neighboring medical school, the working title of this anniversary project in their drafted plan was *The Many Faces of Malady*: an anthology series on the experiences of various patients and other marginalized groups.

Xie Qingcheng was in his office drinking black coffee. After roughly skimming through the file, he found that the project required a considerable number of actors. Xie Xue had already noted the roles that students had volunteered for, but there were still a dozen or so parts left unassigned.

This was the kind of lively production that students would generally be interested in being a part of. Thus, the roles that went unclaimed were probably the kind that weren't very pleasant.

Xie Qingcheng took a look, and it was just as he expected.

Among the roles that no one had shown interest in, some were caretakers who had to deal with patients' bedpans, some were pregnant women experiencing strong physical symptoms, and some were homosexuals who had to have intimate interactions with their scene partners.

With Huzhou University's attitude, as long as the school had their name on it, they would require the students to act out their roles for real even though this was just a practice film. This meant that those acting as caretakers would have to handle bedpans for real, those acting as pregnant women would have to vomit for real, and those acting as homosexuals would have to kiss and embrace their scene partners for real. Plus, this was for the centennial anniversary of the founding of both schools, so everything absolutely had to be just right.

If no one volunteered for these difficult roles, students would end up being forcibly conscripted.

After carefully looking over the plan, Xie Qingcheng suddenly recalled what He Yu had done to his course materials. He couldn't help but narrow his eyes... Then, after a moment's contemplation, he picked up his phone and called Xie Xue back.

"I've finished reading your email."

He leaned back against his office chair, spinning his pen as he spoke in a measured tone. "I can act as your medical consultant, but I have one request."

"What request? Ge, just let me know!"

The character profile of a certain gay role that had been pulled up on the screen reflected in Xie Qingcheng's peach-blossom eyes. He swept his gaze indifferently over the rows of text that made up the entire PowerPoint slide. "I think there's a role here that you should have He Yu try."

Even though Xie Xue was completely baffled to see Xie Qingcheng pulling strings to get He Yu into the role, she assumed it was probably because her brother and He Yu got along well. After all,

Xie Qingcheng had watched He Yu grow up since he was just eight years old—maybe he wanted to give the kid a chance to train himself.

Besides, He Yu was a student in one of the related fields of study. And, on top of being handsome, he had also stepped in to act in that garbage drama. He was studying screenwriting and directing at the moment, but there was no saying which side of the camera he would end up working on in the future.

Thus, Xie Xue cheerfully agreed to Xie Qingcheng's request.

Since the teachers had selected him personally as a "volunteer," He Yu was hard-pressed to refuse the role. So, a few days later, after leaving his evening self-study session, He Yu joined the cast and crew of *The Many Faces of Malady* anthology series for rehearsal.

He was to act in *The Malady of Love,* a short film reflecting the current lived realities of gay men.

When Xie Qingcheng arrived, He Yu was in the midst of rehearsing with the other lead actor. He Yu was a new student to begin with, and he wasn't a drama major. He didn't usually need to attend morning warm-ups, and he hadn't taken many drama classes. Though he had stepped in as the fifth male supporting character in that broke-ass little production, that character had resonated with him personally, so playing him had been easy. But now that he had landed himself a homosexual character to play, it was seriously torture.

Xie Qingcheng leaned against a wall off to the side and watched for a while. Comparing this to when he'd visited the film set in Hangshi, He Yu's acting ability had basically taken a dive off a cliff. On second thought, that was being overly generous—it would be more accurate to say that He Yu's acting had taken a nosedive off the Great Rift Valley of East Africa.

What the hell was he doing? The script described a sweet, private date between the male lead and his sweetheart—both of them had to display youthful and inexperienced love and desire. But after observing for a long while, Xie Qingcheng couldn't see even a hint of love in He Yu's performance. Even an AI would have done a better job.

"How much do you love me? What would you give up for me?" The male student who was acting opposite He Yu was quite talented, pouring emotion into his performance as he questioned He Yu with his arms looped around his neck.

He Yu said blandly, "I love you a lot. I can give up anything if you just ask."

"Then look into my eyes."

A beat of awkward silence followed.

He Yu was supposed to stare into his first love's eyes for a long spell and then, with a sudden surge of passion, lose control and lean down to kiss him. However, as He Yu stared at the other student, his expression turned extremely unpleasant, as if his co-star wasn't his first love but the archnemesis who'd killed his father.

Because they were just practicing, they didn't need to worry about the continuity of the scene too much. Seeing the way He Yu had turned silent and still, the male student who was hugging him around the neck swung his arms slightly and spoke up in a soft voice. "Ge, kiss me."

It would've been fine if the student hadn't used that gentle tone, but as soon as he softened his voice, He Yu shoved him away. He truly couldn't bear it anymore. Face pale, he asked the director, "I'm sorry, can we use an angled shot?"

The person in charge of this short film was a second-year graduate student who was top in the directing major and an extremely stubborn, cool xuejie. She shook her head mercilessly. "You might be able to negotiate this with someone else, but not with me. I said it clearly when I stated my requirements for my actors. I never use angled shots."

He Yu was speechless.

"Granted, we're only rehearsing right now, so you don't have to kiss him for real." The director xuejie turned to the other male student once more and said, "And, you, don't go overboard. You have to let He Yu overcome his mental block, okay? After all, he's not you. You're our school's renowned homo, while he's the renowned straight guy."

The young man was actually fine being referred to as a homo. He was different from his fellow closeted comrades, but he was a bit on the extreme side, believing that everyone had to accept LGBT people, and that those who didn't ought to be buried alongside good ol' Empress Dowager Cixi in the catacombs of history as heretics.

He Yu was a relatively restrained person, so although he was homophobic, he didn't express it openly. Thus, believing that his partner was the type who could be converted by force, the young man had acted with unbridled enthusiasm.

Deliberately forcing He Yu into this role was an extremely effective means of bullying him, striking him precisely where it hurt. Xie Qingcheng finally felt his irritation ease as he watched He Yu beginning to appear almost carsick, his face green enough to rival a sour plum dangling on a branch in May.

He Yu used to be an unfussy child, but ever since their reunion, both his ambitions and physical stature kept scaling newer heights. He no longer held Xie Qingcheng in any regard and even dared to challenge him.

It was only now, as Xie Qingcheng sneeringly watched how helpless He Yu became in the face of crisis, that he finally remembered how it felt to crush the boy in the past. His coldly solemn face, with its sharply defined features, softened at the thought.

It really was quite amusing.

"Oh, Professor Xie." The director spotted the medical consultant for *The Many Faces of Malady*. It just so happened to be break time, which gave He Yu some time to adjust his mindset, so she struck up a conversation with Xie Qingcheng.

"He Yu's really no good. He's done a terrible job in this role."

"Is that so?"

"Hey, why don't you talk to him? Tell him that gay people are exactly the same as ordinary people, and that there's really no difference when it comes to love. Just look at the way he's acting—it's like he's a zombie. I really can't with him..."

Lighting a cigarette, Xie Qingcheng said, "Very well, tell him to come over here." He walked behind the heavy curtain of the rehearsal room's stage to wait, as he found the area in front too noisy.

After a while, an ashen-faced He Yu swept aside the hanging cloth and walked through. The velvety red curtains closed behind him. There was no one else here, and as soon as the curtains hid him from potential onlookers' line of sight, He Yu shoved Xie Qingcheng against the wall with a *bang*, hard enough that ash tumbled from Xie Qingcheng's cigarette.

"Xie Qingcheng, do you want me to wreck you?" he demanded. "Is that it?"

Xie Qingcheng was also very tall, so even though He Yu was pinning him tightly against the ice-cold wall, he didn't seem weak at all. He looked He Yu up and down with those apathetic peach-blossom eyes. "I told you that you must remain calm under any and all circumstances."

He Yu glared.

Soft mockery perfumed with the scent of tobacco drifted between their breaths. Xie Qingcheng asked in a low voice, "Do you not understand?"

He Yu made no response.

"Let go of me."

A few seconds later, figuring that he couldn't *really* strangle Xie Qingcheng to death, He Yu shoved him away viciously.

"You're making me play this role even though you know that I despise homosexuality."

"So?" Xie Qingcheng took his cigarette into his mouth. From this angle, He Yu could vaguely make out his delicate white teeth. "If you can't control your emotions when it comes to something so insignificant, then what more is there to be said about anything else?"

"You're abusing your power to get even."

Xie Qingcheng's smile was mildly derisive. "You can certainly say so... But what can you do about it?"

He Yu couldn't figure out what to say.

"Go and play your part properly." Xie Qingcheng straightened out He Yu's collar. In the darkness cast by the heavy curtains, he gazed placidly up at the youth he had tormented into misery. "I have high expectations of you."

"He Yu, get back here! We're starting!" the director yelled from outside.

He Yu lingered for a moment, glaring menacingly at Xie Qingcheng. "Just you wait."

"Go on, then," Xie Qingcheng said, utterly unbothered.

He Yu walked back out with a dark expression on his face.

The rehearsal resumed.

This time, it was even worse. Previously, He Yu seemed as though he was carsick; now, he looked extremely, severely, life-threateningly seasick. The more that male student clung to him and tried to drag him deeper into the act, the more vehemently He Yu resisted. It was literally like shoving an ox's head underwater when it refused to drink.

He rehearsed that scene with the other student several more times, but He Yu's performance was truly too disastrous. Every line of dialogue, every gesture and movement of his portrayal was littered with over a dozen mistakes. Not a single take came out smoothly.

Once again, the cool director shouted, "Cut!" Then, she rolled up the script and roundly scolded He Yu. "Good god, man! Are you a robot? Can you please relax your arms and legs a little?! And stop acting as though you're about to be violently assaulted, okay? You love him! You love him a lot! He's your first love, and you're only fifteen—you're very innocent, very brash and impetuous. You think that you have a beautiful future ahead of you. Your heart is filled with courage, and you're ready to take on the whole of society. Do you understand this feeling? Dage! This is the fifth time! Can you please put some heart into it?!"

Thanks to He Yu's public persona as a young man with a great temperament—without a hint of his antisocial personality—everyone thought of him as a model student, and the director wasn't afraid to harangue him like this. But He Yu didn't really have the mental energy to hold a grudge against his xuejie. His co-actor's fervent enthusiasm and sincere eyes were driving him to the brink of insanity.

When his xuejie shouted "cut," he simply allowed her to berate him as she pleased while he pressed a hand to his throbbing temples and walked around in circles trying to calm himself.

As he was doing so, he caught sight of the main culprit, Xie Qingcheng, leaning against the wall with his long legs leisurely crossed. He Yu had to stop himself from lunging at the man and throttling him to death in his rage. Xie Qingcheng shot him a cold smile, then lowered his head and took out his phone—he was about to give He Yu a taste of his own medicine. Three seconds later, He Yu's phone vibrated in his pocket.

"...Sorry, director, I just got a message. Let me check it before we start."

"Hurry up! Such a diva when your acting is so crappy!"

He Yu opened the message Xie Qingcheng sent to him in full view of the crowd.

1 unread message from Godfather.

"Godfather" was the nickname He Yu had given Xie Qingcheng on his phone. He felt that Xie Qingcheng was way too much like a feudal patriarch, to the point that he acted even more like his dad than his *actual* dad.

Xie Qingcheng's text read, *"Such dedication. I look forward to your kiss scene."*

He Yu's expression turned chilly, striking fear into the girl next to him.

"What's wrong?" she asked.

Xie Qingcheng turned his head and pursed his lips, appearing cold and calm, as if He Yu losing his mind had nothing to do with him at all. He Yu took a deep breath and fixed his almond eyes unblinkingly on Xie Qingcheng, like he wanted to pin him down and nail him to the wall with his gaze.

"...It's nothing."

Just then, the director xuejie's distinctively loud voice rang out from the other side of the room. "Huh? Really? Is that true?"

The crowd's attention turned toward her. As it turned out, the acting consultant had gone over and said something that astonished her so deeply that she couldn't help but be skeptical. But if nothing else, this xuejie respected her elders, so in the end, after a moment's hesitation, she nodded. "All right. There's no harm in trying it, so let's do as you said. It's not like his acting could get any worse."

She waved at He Yu from a distance. "Xuedi, come here for a sec!"

After some soul searching, He Yu realized that in all nineteen years he'd been alive, he'd never really been afraid of anything—but when he saw her beckoning like that, he actually found himself reluctant to approach.

Xie Qingcheng sat nonchalantly in his chair with his legs crossed. He urged He Yu on silently by mouthing, "Go on."

He Yu could only shoot Xie Qingcheng a glare that said *"You're dead! Just you wait!"* before walking toward the director like he was climbing the gallows.

No one could've foreseen the utterly unthinkable words that came so casually out of the director's vermilion lips. "He Yu, why don't you try changing your scene partner first?"

Dumbfounded, He Yu frowned. "Changing my partner?"

"That's right," the director replied with an impatient wave of her hand. She saw that the young man who was acting opposite He Yu was shocked and about to protest, but she mollified him before he could complain. "Calm down, it's just a temporary change. We don't have much time left tonight anyway."

She turned back to He Yu. "You can pick any random person here, anyone who appeals to you. I'll give you some time to talk, then I'll watch you act out a short scene and see if there's any improvement."

He Yu didn't understand at first, but as realization began to dawn, he narrowed his eyes and slowly turned his head. He ran his tongue over his teeth as he looked back, his grin spreading so wide that his canines peeked out.

"I've already made my pick, director." He looked at Xie Qingcheng, who was still watching the show in high spirits, and said with a smile, "I choose him."

"...You want the medical consultant to act this out with you?"

"Is that not okay?"

The director grimaced and said to He Yu in a low voice, "You'd better choose someone else. He's not from our school, and he's such a famous professor, it'll be hard to convince him."

"I don't feel anything toward these other people. He's the only one here I find somewhat appealing." He Yu said softly, "Xuejie, please let me try it with him."

Although this cool director was fierce, she was still very much a straight woman at heart. It was very difficult for her to remain unmoved when being coaxed so gently by a handsome young man.

"A-all right then... I'll go talk to him..."

"No need. I know him, so I can go talk to him myself." He Yu smiled, already making his way over to Xie Qingcheng.

Xie Qingcheng had already vaguely overheard their conversation and was watching He Yu walk toward him with a subtle expression. He Yu was very courteous in front of others; he took Xie Qingcheng's hand in a gentlemanly way and led him to the deserted area behind the curtain. The moment the red curtain fell, however, the gentleman's expression changed—from gentle and refined to degenerate and depraved.

Surrounded by the fluttering red curtains, He Yu leaned forward and murmured softly against Xie Qingcheng's neck. "Professor Xie, did you know that there's a thing in this world called karmic retribution?"

34

So We Went Ahead and Acted Out the Scene

As He Yu and Xie Qingcheng talked things over backstage, the cool director realized that they probably wouldn't be able to wrap up on time tonight. She tried calling the head director of this film anthology, Jiang Liping-laoshi, in hopes that she could give the facility managers a heads-up and extend the hours of operation for this auditorium. The call went through, and the director waited for Jiang Liping to pick up.

Inside one of the university's hotel suites, Jiang Liping's phone, which was lying on the bed, started buzzing.

But the phone's vibration was hardly worth noting, given the far more intense movements that were happening on the bed. The woman didn't pick up the call, preoccupied as she was with entwining her limbs with those of a man, a sensuous, intoxicated expression on her face.

It was a long time before their movements finally came to a stop.

"If it weren't for that call you got rushing me, I could have gone for even longer," said the well-muscled man to the woman in his bed as he lit a cigarette.

Jiang Liping leaned lazily against him, her eyes silkily coquettish. "You've already wrecked me plenty, what more do you want?"

Flattered, the man chuckled, looking exceptionally pleased. "How am I compared to your other men?"

"Aiyo, way to kill the mood," Jiang Liping pouted. "All the other men come and go, but you're the one and only husband for me. I'm waiting for you to propose."

The man felt like he was walking on air. He embraced her and said, "They can't satisfy you. I'm the only one who's up to the task. In that case, let's indulge in our secret affair a while longer while my wife's on her business trip in the United States."

Jiang Liping giggled, her soft, full-figured body quivering. "You've finally cheered up. Look at how distracted you've been recently!"

"Hey, that was because of..." At this point, the man shivered and stopped talking.

Jiang Liping feigned ignorance, smiling as she nestled against him. "Laogong,[4] how dare you get distracted while I'm here. Why don't we play for a while longer—how would you like it? I'll give you anything you want."

She successfully enticed him. The man swallowed hard, ready to roll around in the sheets with her again. "...You really...make me forget my worries... Come on, baby...come play with me..."

Smiling, Jiang Liping went to join him.

In the auditorium, the director hung up once again. "It's not going through," she sighed to the xuemei beside her, scratching her head in distress. "So we have to hurry up. The uncle in charge of the auditorium is super nosy, ridiculously strict, and really hard to talk to. Tell He Yu to get moving."

The xuemei replied, "He Yu's trying to persuade Professor Xie right now."

"Persuasion"? Hardly—the two of them were clearly in the middle of an argument.

---

4 *A pet name for one's husband.*

Behind the curtain, He Yu was assessing Xie Qingcheng's expression with a subtle smile. Never in his wildest dreams could Xie Qingcheng have imagined that He Yu would go to such lengths—and dragging him into it too? Hadn't that time in the hotel room disgusted He Yu enough?

Xie Qingcheng said coldly, "You want me to rehearse with you?"

"Is that not okay?"

"You're out of your mind." Xie Qingcheng made to leave.

"You asked for it." He Yu pinned him in place and stared at him intensely, as if he wanted to tear out Xie Qingcheng's bones and grind them all to dust. "You'd better not think of escaping now that it's come to this. You're the one who wanted to torment me, so if there's punishment, you'll be enduring it right along with me."

"You're the one who started it by sabotaging my computer," Xie Qingcheng said.

"That pop-up site was an accident. I've explained this to you many times already. You're going through a midlife crisis at worst, but surely you haven't gone senile yet, have you?"

This was the type of beast Xie Qingcheng hated the most—acting all prim and proper, gentle and refined in front of others, not showing the slightest hint of it when he was upset in public, so that everyone thought of him as an exemplary youth. But the moment he had Xie Qingcheng backed into a corner, the mask came off and he'd spew round after round of bullshit. He never uttered any vulgarities, but his verbal abuse was three times as cutting than if he had.

Xie Qingcheng replied coldly, "You're the one acting like a fucking adolescent with an intellectual disability." He tried to shake off the hand He Yu had clamped around his left wrist. "I don't have the energy to mess around with you. I'm not an actor. Go and find some little girl to act with you."

"How awkward would it be with a girl?" He Yu said. "Shouldn't a gay story be acted out by people of the same sex?"

"Then scram and find yourself a little boy."

"What are you saying, Ge? None of them can compare to you." He Yu had really been driven to the limit by Xie Qingcheng's dirty tactics. He'd abandoned every shred of his facade in front of Xie Qingcheng. The way he said "ge," angry and scornful, made him sound exactly like a beast in human clothing.

"You really are..." Xie Qingcheng sighed heavily, evaluating this brat he'd raised for seven years through completely new eyes, "too sick in the head. Completely sick. How did 600 Wanping Road[5] let you out?"

He Yu pointed at him, his gaze drifting down. There was a touch of roguishness on his lips, unnoticeable at this angle to anyone but Xie Qingcheng. "Look, you got so mad the Huzhou twang came out."

Xie Qingcheng was speechless.

"You know, your voice is actually pretty soft, and when you speak in Huzhou dialect, it gets even softer. It doesn't sound like cursing at all."

"Doing this scene with me—doesn't it make you want to throw up?" Xie Qingcheng asked, ashen faced.

Unexpectedly, this asshole smiled gently. Then, his expression immediately darkened. "Ge, even if I throw up, it'll be into your mouth. I won't waste a single drop of my vomit."

"...Fuck you!"

He Yu turned the other cheek to Xie Qingcheng's vitriol, his smile never slipping from his face. Even more incredible, he remembered to remind Xie Qingcheng, "It's your sister's film. Don't you want me

5 *600 Wanping Road is the address for the Shanghai Mental Health Center.*

to put on a good performance? I've already sacrificed myself; there's nothing wrong with you sharing in my bad luck."

"Since it's Xie Xue's film, don't *you* want to perform well?" Xie Qingcheng countered.

"Oh, I'm not so sure about that." He Yu drew away slightly and gazed down at him, the degree of sincerity in his voice difficult to parse. "It's not as if I like her. We're just ordinary friends, so if I really got upset, do you honestly think I'd still think of her? When the time came, she'd be the one in trouble, not me."

Xie Qingcheng glared at him.

Peach-blossom eyes met almond eyes as an undercurrent of violence surged between them. He Yu still had Xie Qingcheng's left wrist clamped tightly in his hold, the two of them locked in a standstill. He could feel Xie Qingcheng's pulse where it throbbed under his fingertips; its rhythm vibrated through his bones, through the places where their skin touched, through his grayish-blue veins, and accurately and unerringly reached the very center of He Yu's nervous system.

"...Fine." Clenching his jaw, Xie Qingcheng threw caution to the wind. "Fine. All right. I'll do it." As he spoke, he nodded in a way that made it clear how long he would be holding this grudge. "I'll fucking do it, all right? Are you satisfied?"

A hint of a smile unfurled across He Yu's face as he stared at Xie Qingcheng. It was a gentle smile, but for some inexplicable reason, it made one's hair stand on end. He Yu let go of Xie Qingcheng's slender wrist and reached up to help him straighten out the white lab coat and inner dress shirt that he'd pulled out of place.

Xie Qingcheng allowed He Yu to adjust his collar, his eyes chilly. "But let's be clear. This doesn't even count as an official rehearsal. That student director of yours is aware of this too, that this is just for you to get a sense of the scene, so it can't possibly be for real. It must be an angled shot."

He Yu said softly into his ear, "Sounds good. Holding you will be sickening enough. You think I'd want to kiss you for real?" With that, He Yu dropped his hands to pat Xie Qingcheng on the shoulder. His smile disappeared in an instant, replaced by a dark expression as he said, "Xie Qingcheng, after this mutual torment is over, we'll be even. Let's call a truce, because otherwise, I really will throw up."

Xie Qingcheng thought, *Does stealing my lines get him an extra chicken drumstick for dinner or something?*

The two of them pushed aside the curtains and walked out. They both looked very calm, as if the intense conversation had never occurred.

The rehearsal resumed.

"How much do you love me? What would you give up for me?" Xie Qingcheng fired off one indifferent word after another with a stony, oppressive aura. He didn't seem to be speaking words of love at all—rather, he was the spitting image of a household patriarch conducting an interrogation from the imperial preceptor's chair.

It wouldn't have seemed out of place if he'd finished his speech with "If you don't explain yourself, I'll break your legs."

"For fuck's sake. I can't..." The director facepalmed and was about to yell "cut" when the acting consultant stopped her.

"Wait a little longer."

"His scene partner is atrocious. There's no way..."

The acting consultant, a veteran actor, smiled and said, "There's no need to rush. Let's keep watching."

Meanwhile, He Yu was already responding to Xie Qingcheng's line. "I love you a lot."

Startled, the director turned back once more.

Huh? It didn't seem as horrible as she'd imagined?

It could hardly be considered a tour de force, but at least this time, He Yu's performance was watchable.

He Yu said, "I love you a lot. I can give up anything if you just ask."

Xie Qingcheng continued to recite his lines dispassionately. "Then look into my eyes."

He Yu really started to look directly into his eyes.

That heated gaze was almost tangible as it slid from his brows to his nose to his lips, leaving a slight itch in its wake before it fell from his lips to his neck.

"Ge, I'm looking into your eyes..."

Through all this, Xie Qingcheng never cooperated in terms of his body language. So after staring at him for a while, He Yu suddenly lowered his head and pressed closer to Xie Qingcheng's neck, where his skin was like a thin sheet of ice, and his carotid artery lay just beneath. The natural self-preservation instinct aroused a sense of danger in Xie Qingcheng, causing his whole body to immediately tense up. He nearly abandoned the performance and pushed He Yu away, his gaze swiveling elsewhere.

He Yu's lips stopped mere centimenters above the artery in his neck.

"You told me to look into your eyes, but why won't you look at me seriously?" He Yu began to improvise, his warm breath carrying this question, as quiet as a sigh, into Xie Qingcheng's ear, boring straight through the pores of his skin and snaking through his arteries to slam against his heart.

Xie Qingcheng's scalp went numb, the words "are you insane?" caught between his teeth as he swung his gaze around to glare at He Yu in disbelief.

However, this was the wrong decision.

In all honesty, He Yu's delivery was quite good, even better than the acting consultant had expected. Originally, the old consultant had wanted to have He Yu change scene partners because he realized the great disparity between He Yu and his original scene partner's levels of immersion in their roles. His original scene partner was an openly gay man to begin with, and he was clearly interested in He Yu. However, because He Yu was unused to that kind of attention, he didn't even want to come into contact with the gay man.

Under these circumstances, not only was it impossible for his partner's immersion to draw him in, but it would stir up strong resistance from He Yu and prevent him from entering the right mindset for his role. Just as a drunk person and a sober person couldn't converse on the same wavelength, what He Yu needed was someone who was at roughly the same level of sobriety to help guide him.

And while Xie Qingcheng didn't know how to act, it was obvious that the effect he had on He Yu was stellar.

He Yu wasn't guarded against him at all. Both of them were well aware of each other's sexual orientation. They were just two straight men, so regardless of whether they kissed or hugged, what feelings could possibly be involved? With this understanding in place, He Yu performed extremely naturally, so when Xie Qingcheng looked back at him, he met a pair of eyes welling with passionate emotion.

He Yu tilted his head as he inhabited the role of that fifteen-year-old boy who couldn't control his secret love and desire. His breathing quickened and his gaze filled with urgency as his lips moved from Xie Qingcheng's neck to his mouth.

He left a little bit of distance between them, but every trace of air from their breaths tangled together, like the strands of saliva left clinging to the lips after a passionate kiss. Immersed in his character, the teenage boy watched the man before him, his breaths hot and quick like they were about to solidify in midair and sink viciously and deeply into his flesh and soul.

Xie Qingcheng's entire body stiffened.

Memories of that night in the hotel in Hangshi resurfaced in his mind. When He Yu was drunk, he'd looked down at Xie Qingcheng with a gaze just as scorching. That heat and desire unique to young men was ruthlessly weighing him down.

Emotions and experiences one wasn't familiar with would always be somewhat discomfiting, and these eyes that were boring into him at such a close proximity and with such reckless intensity were unfamiliar to Xie Qingcheng in the extreme.

Later on, Xie Qingcheng would numbly think that it was perfectly normal for him to feel so shocked, to become so incredibly tense that his face paled and his entire being went on high alert, right?

Why was everyone around them laughing?!

"Okay, cut!"

The director was more than satisfied with this take and promptly called things to a halt. A gloomy-looking Xie Qingcheng immediately pushed away this much-younger schoolboy. The gentle look in He Yu's eyes also vanished in an instant. He stared pensively at Xie Qingcheng's lips for a long while, thinking about god knows what.

Then he looked Xie Qingcheng up and down a few times, a hint of a smile on his face.

"...Do...you always perform more passionately when you're hugging a chunk of ice?" the director asked He Yu with her cheek propped up in one hand. She had been sitting with her eyes glued to this process the entire time.

He Yu lowered his lashes. "I might've gotten the knack for it."

The knack was: he firmly believed that the more sincere his performance, the more he would disgust Xie Qingcheng. And looking at

Xie Qingcheng's ashen face now, it was obvious that he had achieved his goal.

The director was overjoyed. She checked her watch; it seemed there was still enough time to finish filming. "Great! In that case, let's hurry up and do the actual take right now. Come on—"

She beckoned He Yu's acting partner over. "Xiao-Zhao, get over here. Let's try to get this done in one take! Everyone, double your efforts. Before the auditorium closes tonight..."

Bang!

Before she could finish speaking, someone threw open the auditorium doors.

Everyone whipped around in surprise to see the auditorium manager calling out to them, huffing and puffing. "We're closing, we're closing! Hurry up and finish your business!"

The director was pissed. "Hey, our time isn't up yet! Look, there's still forty minutes left. How is it—"

Before the manager could say anything, a chorus of flat, mechanical voices suddenly rang out through the room.

"Drop...drop...drop the hanky, set it lightly behind your friend's back, no one let him know..."

Everyone started in shock. This voice was simultaneously coming out from everyone's phones!

"Holy fuck! What's wrong with my phone?!"

"A video popped up!"

"Mine too. I can't close it! What's going on?!"

Xie Qingcheng whipped out his phone and unlocked it—it was still usable, as the apps were starting up as normal. But a pop-up window that he couldn't close had appeared in the upper left corner of the screen. Before he could examine it more carefully, a squadron of police officers in uniform marched into the auditorium.

The leader of the squadron said gravely, "There's been an incident at the school, and there has already been one case of homicide. We will be enforcing a curfew tonight, so hurry up and get back to your dorms."

The auditorium fell deathly silent for a moment, then everyone erupted into panicked screams.

"Aaaaaaaaah!"

35

AH, ANOTHER MURDER CASE

XIE QINGCHENG AND HE YU were the last to leave the auditorium.

By the time they got outside, the crowd of students was being herded toward the dormitories by the teachers and police. An announcement was blaring from the school's public address system. "Students, please remain calm and do not wander off on your own. If you are in a remote area, contact your teachers, roommates, and classmates immediately. Please return to your dorms in an orderly fashion..."

But the volume of the announcement couldn't drown out the racket that the students were making.

Everyone outside had their eyes glued to either their own cell phones or the school's landmark—the Huzhou University School of Communications's Radio and Television Tower. This tall building had been constructed by the school specifically for its broadcasting students. Faithfully modeled after a real television station, it was surrounded by lights that could illuminate the entire tower.

However, at that very moment the control system had been taken over by hackers who had turned the tower's exterior a glaring red. It looked like a sword covered in blood that had been violently thrust into the ground. The boldface text projected onto it could probably be seen clearly from several kilometers away:

W,

Z,

L,

The "Drop the Hanky" Game of Death begins now.

In addition to the broadcast tower, the hackers' software had intercepted the signals of all the smartphones at Huzhou University. Everyone could still use their phones, but the little pop-up screen that had appeared couldn't be closed. In the darkness of night, thousands of these little windows transformed the Huzhou University campus into a fluorescent river of stars. It was just a shame that each of these stars was twinkling with a horrifyingly bizarre image.

Xie Qingcheng looked down at his phone again to find that the words in that video were the same as the ones on the tower.

They both read: *W, Z, L, the "Drop the Hanky" Game of Death begins now.*

In the video, though, below each letter was a group of extremely peculiar-looking electronic dolls. The little dolls sat in a circle, and there was a grinning, swaying girl doll standing outside the circle with a scarlet handkerchief in her hand, just like the "Drop the Hanky" game[6] that children played. Below the W, the doll had already dropped the handkerchief behind one of the boy dolls in the circle. The little boy doll ran as the girl doll chased him with a smile plastered on her face.

All of a sudden, the girl doll caught up to the boy doll, cheerfully grabbed his head—and with a bright smile, twisted it off!

---

6 A children's game similar to "duck, duck, goose" wherein all the players but one sit in a circle facing inward. One player runs around the circle and drops a handkerchief behind one of the seated players. That player must chase and try to catch the one who dropped the handkerchief before the latter reaches the vacated spot.

A few seconds later, all the phones began to play a compressed sound file of a children's song in unison. "Drop, drop, drop the hanky, set it lightly behind your friend's back, no one let him know..."

The speakers of countless phones turned this nursery rhyme into a hair-raising chorus that echoed throughout the entire campus.

The students became even more horrified and alarmed as they huddled together. Some even refused to return to their dorms, thinking that it was safer for everyone to stay together outside. Some of the more fainthearted students had already started sobbing. Phones rang incessantly all over the place, overlapping with the song—these calls were all from the students' parents. In the age of digital communication, news of what had happened at the School of Communications had quickly made it onto various social media platforms and attracted a great deal of attention, causing a huge ruckus.

"Hello, Mom? I'm fine...but I'm so scared..."

"Wahhhh, Daddy! I'm with my classmates! Mm! I won't run off anywhere. Waahhhhh..."

Amid this chaos, Xie Qingcheng, too, immediately called Xie Xue. Upon learning that she was at home making wontons with Auntie Li, he let out a sigh of relief. He explained the situation to her in simple terms, told her to mind her safety and stay at home, and made her promise to check in with him once an hour. Then, he hung up without wasting more words with her.

After he ended the call, Xie Qingcheng noticed He Yu watching him calmly. When their eyes met, He Yu shifted his gaze away. Only then did Xie Qingcheng realize that no one had expressed any concern for He Yu.

Practically everyone had received messages from their family or friends, but He Yu's phone had remained silent the whole time, like a pool of stagnant water, as still as the young man's expression itself.

Xie Qingcheng was just about to say something when the "drop the hanky" song ended and a huge photograph suddenly flashed across everyone's phones. The moment this picture appeared, Xie Qingcheng and He Yu heard a police officer next to them curse under his breath.

Immediately thereafter, the furious voice of that police officer's captain rang out from his walkie-talkie. "It's the fucking photo that the police just took as evidence at the crime scene! How the hell did they get their hands on it?!"

That caught everyone's attention.

The photograph in question was completely uncensored, and its contents were bizarre and extremely shocking. It showed the body of a man who had been strangled to death on a large, messy bed. The corpse's tongue hung out of his mouth, and he was completely naked save for a pair of red heels strapped to his feet. This room, with its king-sized bed, was a familiar sight for the students—wasn't this the hotel operated by the School of Communications?

At the start of each school year, many parents who were accompanying their kids back to campus for registration chose to stay at this hotel. The environment was quite good, and anyone with a School of Communications student ID could get a discount. After welcoming the surge of parents at the beginning of the year, the establishment was sustained by the modest but steady patronage of students and their lovers.

This time, most of the surprised gasps of "damn" that rose and fell throughout the crowd came from the male students. This was because the female students were a bit timider, and many of them were already tearfully covering their faces and looking away from this morbid picture. The boys tended to be more tolerant of these sorts of upsetting images, so many of them also recognized that this was the place where they'd often roll around in the sheets with their girlfriends. Fucking hell, that den of pleasure had now become the scene of a murder! How would they ever rent a room there again—just seeing a similar bed would cause them to wilt.

Young Master He had never been to a plebeian hotel like this one, nor did he have a girlfriend with whom to rent a room for the night. Thus, he knitted his brows, oblivious as to why there would be sexual frustration mixed in with the alarm in those cries of "damn" from the young men around him. However, he had noticed another detail in the image. Disregarding the most recent quarrel he'd had with Xie Qingcheng, he turned around to look directly into Xie Qingcheng's eyes—and saw the same suspicion mirrored in them that he felt himself.

Cheng Kang Psychiatric Hospital.

The modus operandi of this case was subtly reminiscent of the previous murder at that hospital.

First, there was the clothing—although both victims were undoubtedly male, they had been dressed in feminine attire post-mortem. Liang Jicheng had been fully dressed in women's clothes, while this corpse was wearing red heels.

Second, there was the music. Neither He Yu nor Xie Qingcheng could forget the song that Jiang Lanpei had quietly hummed in the office while she was dismembering the body. At the time, when they thought Xie Xue had been murdered, they had overheard the soft, eerily distant singing of that disturbed woman from the next room. "Drop, drop, drop the hanky, set it lightly behind your friend's back, no one let him know..."

Third, the letters "WZL" perfectly matched the ones in the mysterious message they had seen in the cave on Neverland Island.

Fearful whispers swept through the crowd as more and more students realized the similarities between this homicide case and the way Jiang Lanpei had murdered her victim.

"...Jiang Lanpei..."

"Yeah, she was singing that 'drop the hanky' song when she killed him. I read it in the papers..."

"Aren't those red heels similar to the shoes Jiang Lanpei was wearing in that photograph published in the newspapers?"

"My god... I've heard that shoes represent evil energy.[7] They can also symbolize sending someone off to their death..."

One student, who had likely become so scared that they lost control of their faculties, shrieked, "It's really Jiang Lanpei! Jiang Lanpei's vengeful ghost is out for blood!"

Their shout sent the crowd erupting into a frenzy.

He Yu had mentioned it to Xie Qingcheng before: because of what Jiang Lanpei had experienced and the way she met her end, rumors had begun to circulate amongst the students at some point after her tragic death. Some claimed that if you wrote down the name of the scumbag who was troubling you along with a cause of death and signed it "Jiang Lanpei," the woman's vengeful ghost would come and claim his life.

This photo now undoubtedly corroborated this campus ghost story. Combined with the fact that the photo was now appearing on a countless number of phones, the students couldn't help feeling extremely disturbed.

The police and teachers in charge of looking after the evacuated students watched as the scene before them became increasingly

---

7 *In Chinese, the word "shoes" is pronounced the same way as "evil."*

disorderly. They raised their loudspeakers and put their backs into yelling, "Quiet down! All students! Stop crowding here and follow your teachers back to your dorms! We will make sure that you are all safe!"

The students were driven forward like a flock of ducks, but their eyes remained fixed on the photograph of the murder victim.

Because they were very sheltered in their everyday lives, the students had a very low tolerance for grisly images like this. Still, they found themselves incapable of tearing their eyes away. They were horrified and scared, but the more scared they were, the more they wanted to look—and the more they looked, the more worked up they became.

Safely evacuating people during an emergency was a difficult task to begin with, but to make it even more challenging, the image on everyone's phones changed once more.

The image of the murder victim disappeared, and the screen reverted to the "WZL the 'Drop the Hanky' Game of Death has begun" message.

But there was a small difference now.

Behind the "W," the name of the victim, Wang Jiankang, had been typed out. The little electronic dolls playing drop the hanky next to his name had gone dark. All the smiling children playing the game had frozen in place. And the video had stopped on the frame in which the little boy's head was twisted off.

And under "W, Wang Jiankang," the electronic children beneath the letter Z who had previously been still and unmoving now began to spin rapidly. The little electronic girl grinned as she ran around the circle holding a red handkerchief. She lingered behind her "friends," preparing to drop the hanky at any moment...

The second round of the murder game had begun.

Xie Qingcheng and He Yu met each other's eyes. The same memory crossed both their minds: that sentence, "WZL will be murdered soon," that they saw in the guestbook on Neverland Island. They had both assumed that WZL were the initials of a single person's name. They never suspected that it was actually the first letter of the names of three different people...

W, Wang Jiankang, was dead.

Who could Z be, then?

Just then, He Yu's phone rang.

He froze in surprise. After seeing the name of the caller, he paused for a second before answering somewhat awkwardly. "...Dad."

He Jiwei had just left the airport when he saw the news about the homicide case at the School of Communications and the strange video, sent to him by his secretary. "What's going on at your school? What's campus security doing? How could they allow this kind of thing to happen?"

He Yu didn't respond.

"Where are you right now?" He Jiwei asked.

"Near the entrance of the school auditorium."

"I'll have Chief Li send someone over to pick you up."

"There's no need." He Yu glanced around. People were packed together like sardines in a can. And besides, Xie Qingcheng was standing right there beside him. If a police car were to come and take him away right now, even if he didn't say anything about it, Xie Qingcheng would probably look at He Yu with even more disdain in the future. "Don't worry about it. A police car wouldn't be able to drive in here anyway. I'll head back to my dorm in a little while."

"But what if something happens—" At this point, He Jiwei overheard the chaotic sounds in the background on He Yu's end.

He stopped and sighed. "Do you have any close acquaintances with you right now?"

He Yu glanced at Xie Qingcheng. He didn't know if the man could be counted as a close acquaintance of his, or if things between the two of them were still what they'd agreed upon before—the simple, straightforward doctor-patient relationship that they'd once had.

"Hello? He Yu, are you there?"

He Yu was just about to say something when he heard the voice of a boy on the other end. "Daddy, slow down! I left something on the plane. I have to go and tell the flight crew."

Upon hearing this, He Yu's expression cooled significantly. "It's fine, Dad. There's someone I know here," he said, glancing at Xie Qingcheng. "I'm with Doctor Xie."

"Xie Qingcheng?"

"Mm..."

"What are you doing with him? Is he treating you?"

To tell the truth, He Yu wasn't sure either.

Ever since that time at the hotel, Xie Qingcheng had kept on nitpicking him without ever seeming to make a serious effort to address He Yu's mental state. But somehow, He Yu's condition seemed to have improved a great deal, as his attention was no longer completely focused on what had happened with Xie Xue.

He hadn't realized it until now because he didn't have much faith in Xie Qingcheng these days. He always felt that the man was giving him a hard time on purpose so he could indulge in schadenfreude. But at this moment, it dawned on him that perhaps this was part of the treatment that Xie Qingcheng had been providing him with.

Aside from physiological symptoms, Psychological Ebola also had a significant impact on the patient's mental state. Xie Qingcheng did not ascribe to the school of thought that relied purely on medication for treatment. Rather, he placed more emphasis on guiding and establishing stability in a patient's inner world. It wouldn't be wrong to say that he tended toward idealism.

This was also why Xie Qingcheng wasn't suited for short-term consultations and was better at being a long-term caregiver. A therapist like him usually wouldn't repeatedly emphasize, "You're ill, so let's have a chat. You can talk to me if there's anything on your mind." When conducting a psychological intervention, he preferred to use methods that were the truest to life and thus the least likely to be discovered. He always wanted the patient to feel that they were a normal person.

Sometimes, when it came to psychotherapy, it didn't matter how specialized or superficially charming the doctor's words were when they interacted with patients.

Rather, what really mattered was the degree of comfort the patient obtained, and how their psychological condition changed for the better.

His recent squabbling with Xie Qingcheng had He Yu racking his brain to come up with solutions to the stumbling blocks the man had placed in his way—and in doing so, he had managed to move quite a ways out from under the shadow cast by his failed first crush.

Grappling with this realization, he grew slightly distracted as he raised his eyes to look at Xie Qingcheng.

"Why have you gone quiet again?" asked He Jiwei. "What's wrong now?"

"Nothing." He Yu cleared his throat softly and shifted his line of sight away from Xie Qingcheng. "Yes, he's treating me."

"That Xie Qingcheng... In the past, we wanted to keep him, but he didn't want to stay and he refused our invitation. Now, he insists on volunteering."

He Yu could hardly tell his father that he was the one who had gnawed on Doctor Xie back at the hotel in the midst of a flare-up, provoking the good doctor to the point that he couldn't bear to stand by and watch anymore, and that was why he was looking after He Yu in passing. "He...he's just treating me every once in a while," said He Yu awkwardly. "They're not regular appointments."

He Jiwei paused for a moment. "Very well. In that case, you should stay with him. Don't go back to your dorm; there's nothing safe about a bunch of little kids crowded together. Follow your Doctor Xie and return with him to his dorm."

"...Dad, that's kind of inappropriate."

"How is it inappropriate? He's been taking care of you since you were little. He wouldn't mind helping out with such a small thing."

"He's not my doctor anymore."

"Don't get things mixed up—people's goodwill exists apart from employment, does it not? Why else would he continue to treat you from time to time? Plus, his time with our family was perfectly pleasant, so why treat things as so cut and dried? If you're too embarrassed to ask, then pass him the phone, I'll talk to him."

He Yu's younger brother's voice came from the other end of the call once more. "Dad, why are you walking so fast? Who is it? He Yu?"

"...I understand." As soon as He Yu heard that voice, he didn't want to listen anymore. "I'm hanging up now." After ending the call, He Yu looked over at Xie Qingcheng again and coughed softly. "Uh—"

Xie Qingcheng said, "Your dad wants you to go back with me."

"...So you heard."

Xie Qingcheng made a sound of assent. He and He Yu walked ahead with the crowd. The School of Communications campus had been sealed off by now, so Xie Qingcheng had no way of returning to Huzhou Medical School, but he could go back to Xie Xue's dorm. He had just spoken to Xie Xue about it, and he knew the code for her electronic door lock.

With considerable difficulty, the two of them followed the jam-packed tide of people back to the dorm.

Xie Qingcheng opened the door. "Come in."

With the living room light turned on, the domestic atmosphere of the apartment washed away the ominous pressure that was everywhere outside. Even though the terror attack was still ongoing, an environment like this made it feel more like they were witnessing a fire from across the river or watching a movie about cops fighting criminals—it wasn't quite so suffocating anymore.

And because this was Xie Xue's house, the first thing that greeted them when they walked inside was a tea table covered in junk food and teddy bears. There were even two empty containers of cup noodles that had yet to be tossed.

He Yu and Xie Qingcheng regarded the mess in silence.

It really was very difficult to feel scared.

Xie Qingcheng shut the door and loosened the first button of his shirt. Then, with a gloomy expression, he began to clean up after Xie Xue.

He Yu looked at the living room, where there was barely any space for him to stand. He had been to Xie Xue's place before, but she'd always tidied up before inviting him over. He never could have imagined that the room might have looked like this before it had been cleaned up—it was practically comparable to a recycling center. For a moment, he actually found this revelation even more shocking than the photo of Wang Jiankang's murder scene; it was too hard to reconcile this squalid room with Xie Xue's usual fresh, clean appearance.

He leaned against the doorway for a long while with his hands folded behind his back before cautiously venturing a question. "...Is she usually like this?"

"She's always been like this." Xie Qingcheng was well used to acting like her dad. With an unfazed expression, he picked up a teddy bear that Xie Xue had tossed onto the ground, patted it clean, and placed it back on top of the cabinet.

He Yu was speechless.

"Go boil some water and make two cups of tea," Xie Qingcheng told him.

"...Okay."

As He Yu made the tea, he noticed that Xie Xue had left two sets of teaware in the sink. The leaves still in the filter were black tea, which Xie Xue wasn't very fond of. Something flashed faintly through his mind, but before he could give it much thought, he heard Xie Qingcheng call out from the living room, "Get the Tibetan tea on the third shelf of the tea cabinet—I'll have that."

He Yu assented, and instead of pondering what he'd found in the sink, he focused his attention on looking for the Tibetan tea that Executive Xie wanted in Xie Xue's cabinet, which was stuffed full of snacks and beverages.

The room was tidied up very quickly. Xie Qingcheng knew what he was doing; his stern, distinguished, aloof appearance, which made it seem as if he were entirely disconnected from the mundanities of the human world, was just one aspect of his persona. It was only natural for a man who had raised his little sister, eight years his junior, through thick and thin since he himself was still a teenager.

By the time He Yu finished steeping the tea and walked out holding the tray, Xie Qingcheng was bending down to pick up the last pile of books that his sister had tossed on the carpet.

His figure was bewitching when he leaned over, with his long, straight legs and narrow waist. His clothes stretched taut when he reached down, and the lines of his slender-but-strong waist could be easily seen through his shirt.

Seeing that He Yu had returned, Xie Qingcheng straightened up and put the books back onto the shelf before turning to look at him. He raised his chin slightly, indicating that little Secretary He ought to put his Tibetan tea onto the now-sparkling-clean tea table.

"I brewed the 'cold fragrance of snowy fields' for you," Secretary He said. "That's the one you wanted, right?"

"Mm."

Once Executive Xie had finished putting everything away and washed his hands, he sat down on the sofa and loosened his collar.

Despite the walls that separated them from the commotion, they could still hear the raucous crowd outside, and the blare of sirens. In fact, if Xie Qingcheng were to turn his face slightly to the side, he would even be able to see that bloodred tower, glowing like a sword of judgment through the living room window.

Meanwhile, on his phone, the little girl dropping the hanky was still running in circles behind the letter Z.

"Hackers?" Xie Qingcheng asked.

He Yu nodded. "Definitely. They've targeted all the mobile electronic devices in this area in addition to the radio and television tower."

Perhaps because he felt annoyed that both their phones were simultaneously playing this video, and perhaps because he had a competitive streak as a hacker himself, he opened his phone and started to type in some command codes.

"...Interesting," he said softly after a few moments. "They're using the latest equipment from the United States; I've encountered it once before. This equipment has a wide transmission range, but there's a bug: it's actually pretty easy to break through its control."

He stared unwaveringly at the cipher-breaking code on the screen, trying to penetrate his opponent's defense systems.

Sure enough, He Yu's phone fell silent a few minutes later.

Now that his phone was no longer subject to the opponent's signal transmission, he carelessly tossed it aside.

"It's that simple?"

"I must admit that my skill isn't at the bottom of the barrel," He Yu, who ranked among the top five hackers on the dark web, said modestly. "They shouldn't have messed with me."

"Then can you block their transmission to this entire area?"

He Yu smiled slightly. "Not without the proper equipment. Besides, this case is under police jurisdiction. I could easily end up being the target of their investigation if I get involved. And I won't be protecting your phone either. Let's keep it to watch the video."

He had a point, so Xie Qingcheng acquiesced.

He Yu sat down facing Xie Qingcheng and asked, "Speaking of, do you know Wang Jiankang?"

Xie Qingcheng was a professor at Huzhou Medical School, and He Yu assumed that Wang Jiankang was probably a staff member at Huzhou University. He was only asking casually, so it came as a surprise to him when Xie Qingcheng took a sip of his tea, closed his eyes, leaned back against the sofa, and said, "I do."

36

I Took Xie Qingcheng's Phone

Wang Jiankang, who was in his early forties, had been the head of the Department for International Academic Exchanges at Huzhou University. Due to work reasons, he had a very broad network and often went out with non-university people for business dinners. Xie Qingcheng had met him a handful of times and found him very irritating. Subsequently, he went out of his way to avoid Wang Jiankang, so at most, he could only say that he "knew" him and not that he was familiar with him.

"I don't believe in the supernatural. His death very likely has something to do with Cheng Kang Psychiatric Hospital." Xie Qingcheng took another sip of tea and said mildly, "Chances are, it's linked to the matter of Jiang Lanpei as well."

He Yu turned to get a glimpse of the broadcast tower. "The Cheng Kang incident has created quite the disturbance. This probably isn't as simple as just one psychiatric hospital."

Xie Qingcheng didn't need He Yu to point this out.

The perpetrators had the ability to take over the university's broadcasting tower, unlawfully force all devices within the transmission range to play the same video, and even steal photos from the police's investigation while the case was under such high security. At this rate, the chief of Huzhou City's Bureau of Public Safety was likely going to require an emergency trip to the hospital's department of cardiology.

To pull something like this off, with such clear provocation? The sheer hubris of the person standing behind the scenes was obvious.

Furthermore, this matter involved Huzhou University, where Xie Xue was currently working... As Xie Qingcheng thought this over, his head began to hurt. Without thinking, he pulled out a pack of cigarettes, but after glancing at He Yu and realizing that he'd probably take issue with it again, he ended up stepping onto the balcony.

He Yu turned around when he heard the soft click of a lighter behind him, and he saw the faint flare of the flame against the dark of night.

Xie Qingcheng held the lighter to the cigarette, and the soft glow highlighted the defined contours of his face and the length of his lashes, gilding him in a gentle veneer of deep crimson. Then he put away the lighter, and all that remained was the cigarette's flickering glow.

Just like a firefly.

Xie Qingcheng smoked the entire cigarette. Then he coughed softly as he returned from the balcony and closed the sliding glass door behind him.

"I'm gonna make a late-night snack." He still felt rather agitated and figured it would be difficult to fall asleep tonight, so they might as well eat something as they stayed up to see what happened. He asked He Yu, "Do you want anything?"

"Caviar and sea urchin sashimi."

"Fuck off."

"...Anything's fine."

With that, Xie Qingcheng went to the kitchen.

He was very deft and neat when he cooked, as if he were performing surgery—everything was in its right place, clean and tidy. As the sound of the range hood came on, He Yu looked down at his cell phone.

His WeChat messages had exploded.

They were mostly from his classmates' group chats, all of which were about the events that had transpired tonight. There probably wasn't a single person at Huzhou University who would get a wink of sleep tonight. Even if they stayed obediently with their friends and classmates inside the dorms, everyone's eyes were glued to the videos on their phones.

"Just who is Z anyway?"

"Z must stand for the target's surname. Thank goodness I'm named Xu—I'll be fine."

"Waahhhh, fucking hell, save me! My surname is Zhang!"

"It's okay, mine is Zhao. I've never disliked my name so much before. I won't be able to sleep either."

There were even some dumbasses who had spontaneously created group chats for classmates whose surnames began with Z and L, saying that they could huddle together for warmth and comfort each other.

Someone else pointed out, "If 'drop the hanky' starts playing again, that will definitely mean that the target has been murdered. My entire dorm is watching that 'drop the hanky' video, it's so scary..."

The incident had also reached the top of the news feed. However, when He Yu tried to open the article, the browser only showed that the content had already been deleted by the original poster—the internet police were probably working overtime to remove the relevant messages. He Yu could understand why—the situation had spun out of control, and there were no answers to be had. How would the next step ultimately unfold? What were the underlying stakes? Who was involved? Nothing was clear. The authorities couldn't allow such news to spread so quickly, as it could very easily result in the unchecked dissemination of rumors and large-scale panic.

He Yu had a family chat group, but no one ever really talked in there. He had good reason to suspect that his parents and younger brother had their own chat group with only the three of them. Either way, a lunatic like him would always be an outsider excluded from their family. But with an incident like this taking place at Huzhou University, Lü Zhishu had nevertheless sent a message to the chat group: *"Your dad told me what's going on. Let us know when you get home with Doctor Xie."*

He Yu: *"We're at the dorm."*

He Jiwei: *"Send a picture."*

He Yu sighed. They thought he might be lying and were just asking so they could keep tabs on him.

He got up and pulled open the door to the kitchen. "Xie Qingcheng, my dad wants me to take a picture of you."

Xie Qingcheng frowned. "I'll just call him later."

He Yu was hoping he'd say that, as he didn't want to respond to this "loving family" chat group anymore either. He tossed his phone aside and walked up to Xie Qingcheng, who was currently making noodles; it smelled quite good.

"What're you doing coming in here?"

"Watching you cook. I wanna learn a bit."

So Xie Qingcheng didn't chase him out. He was just about to make two fried eggs, but it was only after he cracked the eggs into the frying pan with one hand that he realized, distracted as he was, he'd forgotten to put on an apron.

Though he knew how to cook, he hated smelling like grease and smoke—but he had to keep an eye on the eggs, so he tilted his head slightly and said to He Yu, "Do me a favor. Bring me the apron and help me put it on."

He Yu was beyond words. He really had become Xie Qingcheng's little secretary.

"What're you looking at? Don't just stand there—hurry up."

There was nothing He Yu could do but go and fetch the apron from behind the door. He could tell it wasn't Xie Xue's at a glance—it was a very clean and simple apron, probably one that Xie Xue kept around for Xie Qingcheng.

"How do you tie this thing?"

"...You've really never done a day of work in your life."

"It's not that I don't know how to tie it—I've worn one before—but I've never tied it for someone else."

"Figure it out yourself."

He Yu worked it out after a moment. This wasn't a difficult task, so he walked up to Xie Qingcheng and wrapped the apron around him.

While tying it, He Yu once again noticed how narrow Xie Qingcheng's waist was. It had only been a detached observation before, but this time, he was winding the apron strings around his waist and even tying a knot behind his back.

He Yu was a bit taller than Xie Qingcheng, so with Xie Qingcheng standing in front of the stove and He Yu standing behind him, He Yu was able to gaze down at Xie Qingcheng as he carefully tied the apron strings. When He Yu looked back up, his eyes fell on Xie Qingcheng's bent neck.

It was pale, nearly translucent porcelain in color.

There was a tiny crimson mole on the back of his neck, off to the side.

He Yu had never looked at Xie Qingcheng's neck from this angle before. When he was younger, he hadn't been as tall as Xie Qingcheng,

so he couldn't see it, and after they met again, he never had the opportunity to carefully examine the nape of Xie Qingcheng's neck. Thus, only now did he discover that Xie Qingcheng's neck was quite beautiful. Instinctively, he said, "Xie Qingcheng, there's a mole on the side of your neck."

After a pause, he added, "It's red."

His voice was very close, and his face was all but pressed up against Xie Qingcheng's neck.

Xie Qingcheng's masculine instincts made him feel a bit threatened, so he whipped his head around without warning.

Dumb straight guys were really fucking dumb.

Under these circumstances, he'd turned back solely because of his male sense of territoriality. He wanted to confirm his safety and create some distance.

But this idiot straight guy hadn't considered, given the proximity of He Yu's voice—not to mention his hands, which were at his waist helping him tie his apron—just how little distance there was between them right now. He Yu's mouth brushed against the side of Xie Qingcheng's ear, and because neither of them reacted in time, his warm lips even touched Xie Qingcheng's cheek.

The contact was as light as a dragonfly skimming over water, yet as awkward as a raging prairie fire.

What a predicament.

Silence engulfed the room.

The side of the ear was an extremely sensitive spot for most people, and Xie Qingcheng was no exception. The contact was brief, but for just a moment, he felt that low, hot breath unique to boys and the pressure and sense of aggression from the intensely hormonal young man behind him. Xie Qingcheng coldly pushed at He Yu's chest, shoving him away.

Both their faces darkened. They stared at each other, but neither knew what to say.

I'm sorry?

But Xie Qingcheng had turned his head of his own accord. There was no chance that He Yu would apologize, and even less of a chance that Xie Qingcheng would do the same.

What are you doing?

...It was so obvious it didn't even merit a question. This was just a tragic coincidence caused by a straight man's idiocy.

They regarded each other awkwardly for a while until, suddenly, a strange smell came from the frying pan.

He Yu snapped back to his senses. "It's burning, it's burning!"

Xie Qingcheng immediately turned back around, and sure enough, the eggs had already turned black on one side...

Since he first started frying eggs at the age of eight, Xie Qingcheng had never once burnt one. It really was his unlucky day.

Suppressing his anger, Xie Qingcheng moved the frying pan aside before turning to He Yu. "What are you doing standing in here? Get out."

After he finished speaking, he took out a moist kitchen towelette and, with a chilly expression, wiped the side of his ear and his cheek where He Yu's lips had touched him.

He Yu was speechless.

An accidental brush of the lips like this was different from the scene he had acted out earlier as an intentional prank.

He Yu also felt a bit uneasy, so he bowed his head and left without another word. Returning to the living room, he felt discomfort settle in his heart—the look in Xie Qingcheng's eyes, his obvious distaste and scorn, had been much too cold.

He Yu didn't like this feeling at all.

Xie Qingcheng had held him in check ever since he was young. When He Yu met Xie Qingcheng again as a university student, he had sought to slowly remedy the psychological shadows Xie Qingcheng had cast since his childhood, going so far as to take charge on multiple occasions as the instigator of their interactions.

But because of that look in Xie Qingcheng's eyes just now, He Yu found himself instantaneously plunged back into his memories. Xie Qingcheng was still Xie Qingcheng; he would still use that dagger-like gaze to coolly and scathingly look down on He Yu's entire being.

In reality, Xie Qingcheng still occupied a position of absolute dominance.

Just as He Yu was grappling with these thoughts, a phone suddenly rang.

Thoroughly distracted, and assuming that it was He Jiwei calling back after running out of patience, He Yu picked up the call without thinking.

"Hello?"

"Hello? Xie-ge, I just got back to my phone after finishing my assignment and saw that something happened near your school. Ge, hang tight for a bit. I'm coming over right now. I'm pretty worried about you..."

He Yu held the phone a little further away from himself—he abruptly realized that he had accidentally grabbed the wrong phone and picked up Xie Qingcheng's call.

The caller ID showed that it was someone named "Chen Man." Based on his voice, he sounded like a flustered and impatient young man. And with the word "ge" spilling out every time he opened his mouth, his manner of speech was easygoing and intimate.

He Yu and Chen Man had met before—the two of them had eaten dinner with Xie Qingcheng in the dining hall and chatted for quite a while. But unfortunately, neither of them had introduced themselves by name back then. A decent amount of time had passed since, too, and voices always sounded slightly distorted over the phone. Thus, neither of them managed to identify the other through the call.

For some reason, He Yu felt rather uncomfortable. He glanced at Xie Qingcheng, who was still in the kitchen, cleaning the pan to fry two more eggs. Then he got up and walked out onto the balcony.

"Ge, why aren't you saying anything? You..."

He Yu pulled the balcony door shut and asked with utmost politeness, "May I ask who's speaking?"

"Huh? You're not Xie-ge?" The other man sounded dumbfounded. "Who are you?"

"I'm Doctor Xie's friend."

"Oh. Then can you get my ge to pick up the phone?"

He Yu smiled, but his voice grew colder as he said, "I don't believe Xie Qingcheng has a younger brother. What kind of relative are you? I've never heard him mention you before."

Chen Man paused. He wasn't stupid—he could tell that the other person was nitpicking on purpose. Officer Chen was a policeman, after all. He was always the one interrogating others; he had never encountered someone with the gall to come up to him and begin grilling him straight away instead.

Not to mention, upon listening more closely, it sounded like the other person was a young man around his own age. Staying with Xie Qingcheng at this hour after something like this had just happened—who could this young boy be? Chen Man couldn't think of anyone right now, having forgotten the person he'd gotten along with so well over the course of their shared meal.

He became guarded and suspicious toward He Yu. "And who are you? Which friend? Xie-ge doesn't have very many friends—I'm pretty sure I know all of them."

He Yu smiled as he looked out at the scarlet broadcasting tower, its light making his pupils seem rather distant. There was no need for him to introduce himself, but still he said, "I'm He Yu."

"He's never mentioned you to me before."

He Yu's expression remained unchanged. He gazed at the tower as if he wanted to say something, but he didn't know what to say. He suddenly realized that his and Xie Qingcheng's social circles didn't overlap very much.

This Chen guy...

"He Yu, what's going on?" The sliding door behind him was abruptly pulled open by Xie Qingcheng.

"...A call came for you. I picked it up by accident."

"Who is it?" Xie Qingcheng asked.

"Chen Man."

The moment Xie Qingcheng heard the name, he went over and took the phone from He Yu. Then he turned around and went back inside the apartment to take the call.

He Yu watched him in silence, rooted in place.

Xie Qingcheng was an indifferent person, not inclined to express interest or concern toward other people. Other than Xie Xue, there was pretty much no one who could get his undivided attention. But this Chen Man seemed to be an exception.

Inexplicably, He Yu began to feel even more unwell.

37

His Parents Were Killed in the Crash

"YOUR FRIEND?" He Yu asked without preamble once Xie Qingcheng had hung up the phone and returned to the room.

Xie Qingcheng hadn't planned on offering He Yu much of an explanation. Given the stereotype that important people were afflicted with short memories, he expected He Yu to have already forgotten about Chen Man, someone with whom he had only shared a single meal by happenstance. So he simply replied, "More or less, yeah. He said he just got off work and wanted to come over. I told him no."

Having dismissed Chen Man, Xie Qingcheng brought the noodles he'd finished cooking out of the kitchen. As Xie Qingcheng busied himself, Young Master He stood off to the side watching as if he were some big shot. He had no intention of stepping forward to help; he only wanted to find out more about Chen Man.

"Why would he be so eager to see you?" he pressed.

"I already said—he's my friend."

"He's pretty young, isn't he? How old is he?"

"Around your age."

"Professor Xie has so many friendships that transcend age," He Yu said. "Isn't your generation gap a problem?"

Xie Qingcheng felt that He Yu was being ridiculous, so he set his chopsticks down with a clatter and said coldly, "Do you think you can just interrogate people as you please? You're so nosy. What does my social circle have to do with you?"

He Yu stopped speaking.

It was true...it wasn't really his business. Now that he realized what he'd been doing, it occurred to him that he was actually acting kind of unhinged—why should he worry about these sorts of things?

Xie Qingcheng pushed a bowl of noodles topped with an over-easy egg in front of He Yu. "Eat your food. I'm going to call your dad."

Meanwhile, in one of Huzhou University's teaching buildings, Zhang Yong was huddled in the pitch-dark corner of an office, with the door securely closed.

Large beads of sweat rolled down his forehead. He wiped at them with a handkerchief, but the fabric was already drenched to the point where liquid could be wrung out of it.

His pig-like mung-bean eyes were fixed on the metal door, the only entrance to this room. He had been staring at it for a very long time. Ever since the photograph of Wang Jiankang's corpse had been revealed, he knew that he would be the next target.

After all, he too had taken part in designing those victims of biological experimentation who had been dragged to Cheng Kang Psychiatric Hospital against their will. He had also taken his share from those women who had lost their mental faculties and become part of the unspoken transactions of power and sex when those men were cutting important deals.

The psychiatric hospital had some truly beautiful patients too, some of whom had even been Huzhou University students who'd been conned into receiving treatment there. Those women were well-behaved and obedient, arousing the desire to violate them in many men, and they made for safe options: hardly anyone paid attention to their psychological states or took their words seriously. Some of these women were tormented to the point of insanity, even becoming amnesiacs who completely forgot the things those men did to them.

If they became pregnant, that was no big deal either—those men had worked with Liang Jicheng for many years, and Liang Jicheng understood very well how such things should be dealt with. He knew how to seek out discreet researchers to clean up the evidence of the crime.

However...

However, *he* wasn't the one who had wanted to do those depraved things in the first place! It was clearly that old senior of his who had dragged Zhang Yong into it, enticing him with immense benefits and a wellspring of carnal pleasures. That senior made him handle the affairs, saying that they were all brothers in the same boat; if anything were to happen, they would bear the responsibility together.

After Cheng Kang Psychiatric Hospital had burned to the ground, that man had even comforted them, saying that everything had been cleaned up properly. He had assured them that at most the investigation would stop at Liang Jicheng's level. And as for the rest—dead men could tell no tales, so they didn't need to worry.

But Wang Jiankang had met a terrible, sudden end just like that.

Zhang Yong's own surname and that of another one of his brothers had also been displayed in that murder video, followed by the terrifying insinuation of that "drop the hanky" game. When Zhang Yong first caught sight of the broadcasting tower, he had just come out of a teaching building. He was immediately frightened out of his wits; as he frantically ran off, he called that senior of his in a panic.

The call went through. Zhang Yong heard pleasant, relaxing music in the background, and the indistinct voice of a foreign masseuse asking how much pressure she should use.

Their lives were about to be brought to a grisly end, and this guy was still at the spa.

"Hello... Hello?" Zhang Yong's eyes were practically bugging out of his head from hatred and fear. Although he lowered his voice, it was impossible for him to suppress his fury, much less control his terror. *"Hello?!"*

"Oh." The man on the other end chuckled. "Director Zhang. It's late. Is something the matter?"

Zhang Yong was so irate that every blood vessel in his brain was about to burst. With his voice warped with rage, he said, "Who are you trying to fool?! Wang Jiankang is dead! He's dead! You said Cheng Kang was cleaned up already and told us not to worry, so what's happening right now?! Tell me!"

"Mm... That feels good. A little harder near my shoulder," the man said in English to the masseuse. Then he spoke once more to Zhang Yong in an exasperatingly slow voice. "My friend, Cheng Kang *has* already been cleaned up. But the dogs are still sniffing around over there and won't let people off the hook. They insist on scenting the trail of blood and following it to our front door. So what do you think we should do?"

"Don't you care?!" Zhang Yong cried. "You have to come up with something! You're the one who benefited the most from this. You..."

The other man cut him off with a laugh. "Director Zhang, most things in this world aren't fair. You're an adult; shouldn't you understand that?"

Zhang Yong was drenched in sweat. Staring at his phone, he realized that this person wouldn't lift a finger to help him; he might even end up harming him. A situation like this was merely the inevitable outcome of trying to convince a tiger to sacrifice its own skin.

Zhang Yong gazed up at that bloodred television tower as if he had just awoken from a dream. He tossed his cell phone into a thicket of trees so that no one could use it to track him, then sprinted frantically back into the teaching building.

Now he was shivering in one of its offices.

Huzhou University had so many buildings—there were probably thousands of offices and classrooms in total.

He had even taken off his GPS smartwatch, so he felt that he should be safe hiding in this room. If he made it through the night, he decided, he would turn himself in to the authorities. He would stop indulging in wishful thinking—if he turned himself in, he might be able to receive a reduced sentence. That would be far preferable to the end that Wang Jiankang had met—stripped naked and strangled to death...

The memory caused Zhang Yong to shudder again. He thickly swallowed a mouthful of saliva, imagining that he could almost see Jiang Lanpei's silhouette swaying before him, a ghostly woman in a red dress and red shoes who had come to take him away...

"Pah!" Trembling, in a small voice, he tried to encourage himself. "Pah, pah, pah! What are you thinking! It can't be a ghost! There's no such thing as ghosts!"

But as if to refute him, the sound of a woman's quiet laughter suddenly rang out in this locked room. "Hee hee..."

Zhang Yong jumped to his feet, his features twisted in fright. "Who's there? Who?!"

But silence fell again, as if that soft laughter had been a figment of his imagination.

Zhang Yong's flabby, sweaty back was pressed up against the icy wall. He'd chosen this office on purpose, as it had no windows, just a single door. The room was tiny; it didn't even have a cabinet for someone to hide in. Where did that sound come from? Zhang Yong was completely soaked in sweat, like a fish freshly hauled out of the water, and his heart was about to thump right out of his mouth.

And then, just like in a murder game that demanded a ceremonial segment, that music started up again.

"Drop...drop...drop the hanky...set it lightly behind your friend's back, no one let him know..."

But Zhang Yong didn't have a phone on him!

Where was this tinny electronic music coming from? Where was the phone? He comforted himself with his last shred of hope—did someone leave their phone behind in this office?

Zhang Yong struggled to stand as he sought out the source of the sound. Slowly, he moved his eyes, which were bulging like a bullfrog's, up toward the ceiling...and looked overhead...

"Aaaaaaaaah!"

His scream was so loud it could be heard throughout the entire teaching building.

The song was coming from the air-conditioning access panel!

The vent had opened at some point. A dark-haired woman in a red dress was sitting in the crawl space and looking down at him indifferently. She smiled faintly.

Zhong Yong had heart disease to begin with; at this moment, his face immediately blanched, turning as pale as a ghost, and his lips rapidly tinted blue. His Buddhist amulet bounced against his portly chest as it rose and fell in violent heaves.

Suddenly, his breath caught. Clutching his sternum, he backed up two steps and collapsed to the ground with a thud.

The ceiling of the teaching building had a series of horizontal rafters with a large, hollow space above. The students had gotten used to hearing cats and mice scampering about up there. As for the air conditioner, it was an old-fashioned model with a removable outer case that covered the maintenance access panel. Zhang Yong hadn't realized that the crawl space up there was large enough to comfortably fit a person.

The woman jumped down from the access panel, a cold, gleaming dagger in her hand.

"You... It's you...!"

Despite being terrified out of his wits, Zhang Yong still managed to recognize the woman's face. It was indescribably delicate and beautiful. But right now, in his eyes, this was the face of a malevolent spirit that had crawled out of hell!

Jiang Liping!

It was Jiang Liping!

"Since you've seen my face, you won't live past today." Jiang Liping approached him with a smile. "How would you like to die? A knife? A gun? Either would be very quick and easy..."

"Y-you're with them?! Y-you're not just a slut, you also...you also work for them!"

"That's right, I'm with them." Jiang Liping smiled sweetly. "Why else would I willingly spend all my time hiding among greasy old sleazebags like you?"

Zhang Yong backed away, step by step... Clutching his chest, he stumbled backward and caught a glimpse of the room's metal door behind him in his peripheral vision. Then—

Bang!

He had no idea where he found the energy—perhaps it stemmed from his bone-deep desire to live—but somehow, he broke into a mad sprint like a wild animal, violently crashing through the door and tearing his way out of the building.

Jiang Liping's eyes dimmed.

Zhang Yong was running away?

Even so, it didn't matter.

This area was already surrounded by perilous traps at every turn; he had merely chosen a different manner of death.

Jiang Liping knew that there was no need for her to pursue this man who had already gone half-mad—and she couldn't go after him anyway, given the police presence outside. Why else would she have chosen to sneak in via the ceiling crawl space?

She pressed a custom microphone to her scarlet lips and spoke softly into it. "Laoban, Zhang Yong escaped from Classroom 4406. He left in the direction of door 3. I'm leaving through door 6. Send some of your people to come pick me up."

Even though he was practically pissing himself in terror, Zhang Yong managed to escape from the teaching building. Drawn by the sounds of his screaming and flailing, the police rapidly approached his position in their patrol cars.

Zhang Yong never could have dreamed that there would come a day when police sirens, which were once his worst nightmare, would end up sounding like divine salvation. Sweat was dripping down his face as he shouted himself hoarse. "Help! Help! I surrender! I have information to give! Save me... There's a murderer inside that building...!"

He gasped for breath as he ran, his amulet swinging against his chest. Even now, he hadn't discovered the faint electronic glow flashing from the tiny hole in the talisman...

Knowing he had sinned, he prayed to the gods with guilt in his heart, but what did his prayers bring?

Unfortunately, only demons and monsters.

The conspirators' plan had been set in motion long ago. The moment you knelt to seek help from the gods, there would already be a pair of eyes watching you, observing your weakness and hesitation.

Zhang Yong was the organization's rotting meat, bound to be cut away sooner or later.

"Save me... Save... Ahhhhh, help!"

His screams brought the band of policemen on duty running over to him at once, armed to the teeth. Zhang Yong's eyes gleamed intensely as he used all his strength to run toward the police. He was like a drowning person trapped in a tempest, swimming desperately for the shore...

He didn't want to die, he didn't want to die...

He was almost there...

Almost...

He could already see the nervous-but-resolute face of the nearest policeman. Weeping, he stretched his hand out...

"Save me, I'll talk, I'll tell you everything, I—"

Bang!

A deafening, hair-raising noise abruptly cut off his outpouring of secrets.

It was followed by a moment of deathly stillness.

The instant Zhang Yong ran through the intersection, moments before he could reach the police, one of the dining hall's refrigerated trucks parked next to the junction suddenly roared to life. It surged forward, crashing into Zhang Yong just as he was about to surrender himself!

Everyone couldn't help but stop in their tracks to stare, wide-eyed, as Zhang Yong flew through the air and bounced off the wall with a thump.

With an audible crack, his skull split open, and blood splattered everywhere. Even before his flabby body smashed into the ground, Zhang Yong had already breathed his last. The corpse was briefly illuminated by the truck's headlights before the vehicle rolled over the body, promptly flattening half of what was once Zhang Yong beyond recognition...

After a few moments of horrified silence, a sharp-eyed police officer suddenly called out, "Captain Zheng!" His voice was tight from the tremendous shock he had just received. "Quick, look! There's no one in the driver's seat of that truck! There was no one driving it! The truck moved on its own! How did it happen?!"

The police officer overseeing this unexpected case was Zheng Jingfeng, a veteran criminal investigator. He was standing close to the intersection and happened to get a crystal-clear view of the scene. As he watched, the old investigator suddenly remembered something: a case from nineteen years ago that seemed to be replaying itself in front of him. As those wretched images from the past flashed before his eyes, Zheng Jingfeng's expression suddenly changed.

He yelled at the top of his lungs, "Get down! Everybody, get down!"

The sound of a colossal explosion rang out as flames suddenly erupted from that driverless refrigerated truck. Within seconds, the entire front of the truck was engulfed in a furious inferno...

Sputtering and coughing, Zheng Jingfeng pulled himself up from the ground. He gasped for breath as he looked toward the flaming steel machine. The driverless vehicle, its cabin that spontaneously caught fire after hitting someone, and the body on the ground that had been partially crushed... In the light of the flames, the expression on the old criminal investigator's face turned extremely ugly...

It was as if he had been transported back to that day nineteen years ago...

The scene before his eyes now was almost exactly the same as that day. The only difference was that the people who had lain beneath the wheels of the vehicle back then had been two of his close colleagues, a husband-and-wife duo.

Xie Ping and Zhou Muying.

"Drop, drop, drop the hanky, set it lightly behind your friend's back, no one let him know..."

The second mark was dead.

Once again, from countless mobile devices, the gently sinister nursery rhyme reverberated through the air over Huzhou University.

The entire campus resembled a giant's roiling belly; after a few beats of silence, it began churning as an untold number of teachers and students cried out in alarm like an earth-shattering, deafening soundwave rumbling across the university.

Countless heads bowed as everyone stared down at their cell phone screens in fright. The little electronic figures standing behind the letter Z stilled as the girl caught the boy. The boy collapsed to the ground, a bright red handkerchief lying behind him as flames erupted over his body.

A few seconds later, the murder video changed once more. This time, what appeared was another photograph, a close-up shot taken from above using a telephoto lens. This one showed tongues of flame swallowing the front of a refrigerated truck. Zhang Yong's corpse lay before the fiery beast, half of his body already crushed into gore...

"Someone else has been murdered!"

"I know him! Zhang Yong! He's the director of the Office for International Academic Exchanges!"

"So Z was Zhang Yong..."

This image was reflected in the eyes of thousands through the screens of various devices. Among them was a pair of incisive peach-blossom eyes, staring at this scene in wide-eyed disbelief.

Xie Qingcheng was frozen from head to toe. The blood in his veins seemed to instantaneously turn into ice.

He never could have possibly imagined that today, on this very day, during this video serial murder case, he would see this exact same scene: a car spontaneously crashing into a person and then exploding into flames...

It was as though an invisible hand had suddenly grabbed him by the neck and yanked him into a murky darkness. The image of Zhang Yong's body in the video overlapped with the nightmare he could never escape.

The nightmare that had persisted for nineteen years...

And the answer that he had fruitlessly sought for so long, before he had finally given up...

As an icy darkness flooded through him, Xie Qingcheng's cup slipped from his cold fingers and crashed to the floor, shattering to pieces.

"Xie Qingcheng, what's wrong?" He Yu had sensed that something was off about the person beside him. Xie Qingcheng's reaction to this photo was completely different from the first one.

When Wang Jiankang had been murdered, Xie Qingcheng had reacted like a normal person. He'd looked at the photo, analyzed it, complied with police orders, and returned to his dorm. He had done what was needed and drawn his boundaries clearly. But after seeing Zhang Yong's photograph, Xie Qingcheng paid He Yu no attention at all; he didn't even offer a single word of analysis. Instead, after thinking for a moment, all he did was pick up his phone and dial a number, his face pale. Then, without another word, he walked into Xie Xue's bedroom and closed the door right in He Yu's face.

He Yu only just managed to catch him saying to the person on the line, "Captain Zheng, it's me..."

38

Xie Qingcheng, I've Never Forgotten You

THE PHOTOGRAPH of Zhang Yong's corpse had disappeared already. The only thing left now was the last bloodred letter.

L.

The last round of the "Drop the Hanky" Game of Death had officially begun.

Inside the bedroom, Xie Qingcheng took a forceful drag on his cigarette. He had one hand braced against the wall and the other's fingertips pressed to his temple. His peach-blossom eyes looked unblinkingly at the smudge of bloody light on the broadcasting tower in the distance as he said to the person on the line, "Give me the list of suspects you've compiled for L."

Captain Zheng said some solemn and sincere-sounding words in reply.

"I'm not going to make small talk with you," said Xie Qingcheng, forcing down his emotions. "Give me the list of names."

There was silence on the other end.

"Not too long ago, I dropped off a guestbook that I found at Huzhou University at the police station," Xie Qingcheng continued. "Someone had written inside its pages that 'WZL' would soon be murdered. The message was signed 'Jiang Lanpei.' I thought it might be useful to the police, so I brought it over. You don't need to hide it from me—that book didn't show up there for no reason, especially when it contained a message that matched the videos from today's murder case."

"Xiao-Xie..."

"That was a message left by your informant, wasn't it?"

Xie Qingcheng went straight for the jugular; the other man was unable to utter even a single word of denial.

Through gritted teeth, Xie Qingcheng said, "So, all of you were well aware that WZL were in danger of being murdered, but perhaps there were some major gaps in the informant's knowledge. He could only write what he knew in the book as a warning for you to decode. If we do the math, you all must have pondered over this message about WZL for a very long time already—long enough to narrow down a list of targets. Zheng Jingfeng, don't you dare tell me that you don't have it."

Captain Zheng let out a long sigh. "I can't hide anything from you, Xiao-Xie. Listen—I understand how you must be feeling. If anyone else were in your place, they wouldn't be able to bear it either. However..."

During this pause, the lit end of Xie Qingcheng's cigarette singed the sides of his fingers, making him shudder slightly.

"However, we must maintain confidentiality..."

Xie Qingcheng suddenly snapped, revealing an uncharacteristic degree of agitation. "Confidentiality? What confidentiality? You couldn't find anything when my mom and dad died. In the end, you concluded it was just a car crash! How much time did I spend speaking with all of you back then? How much have I already sacrificed to search for an answer?! You guys knew everything, but you still couldn't find a shred of evidence! After so many years... I have a little sister, so I gave up in the end—I could only manage so much...

But now these people are stirring up trouble right before my eyes, and you still want to talk to me about confidentiality?"

"Xie Qingcheng, ultimately, you're not a police officer. You need to calm down..."

"I'm the son of two fucking victims!"

Zheng Jingfeng said nothing.

"I might be able to find someone today who can tell me who killed my parents." Xie Qingcheng's eyes were red as he pressed his forehead to the ice-cold window frame. "So tell me, how am I supposed to calm down?"

There was still only silence on the other end.

"How am I supposed to trust you guys, Zheng Jingfeng? It's been nineteen years, yet you still haven't given me an answer. Right now, you can't even stop the hackers behind this video from getting into your systems. You don't need to tell me—I already know that their malice will rise to meet the challenge. What are the chances that they'll escape unscathed again this time?

"Zheng Jingfeng, Officer Zheng, do you know what it feels like to be kept in the dark for nineteen years, never to receive an ounce of truth?! I've been enduring and waiting all this time."

"...I know. But..."

"I understand what these past nineteen years have been like for all of you, but can you all understand what this single day has been like for me?"

"...I understand, I understand," Zheng Jingfeng mumbled as if he didn't know what to say.

Xie Qingcheng paused. Blood seemed to seep from every word he spoke. "Captain Zheng. If you truly understand, then give me the list of names for L." After another pause, he added, "Otherwise, I'll think of a way to find it myself."

After several beats of silence, Zheng Jingfeng said at last, "Ah, Xiao-Xie, heed your Uncle Zheng's advice..."

He spoke some solemn and earnest words of conciliation, but this was the last straw for Xie Qingcheng. A torrent of fury washed over him. He kicked over the chair beside him.

"Go fuck yourself! What use is that? Stop giving me this bullshit!"

He threw his phone onto the table and pressed his forehead to the wall. He was so upset that he ended up knocking it hard enough for a reddish-purple bruise to begin forming. Not a single person in the world—not even Xie Xue—had ever seen him like this before. His chest heaved violently as his eyes became completely bloodshot.

He stilled for a moment, then looked over at the broadcasting tower once more.

The livestream that was playing on thousands of phones across campus was also projected onto the side of the building. Beneath the L, the hanky-dropping game was slowly underway.

Xie Qingcheng forced himself to calm down. With trembling hands, he picked up his phone again. Once he'd regulated his breathing, he dialed Chen Man's number.

Beep...beep...

"Hey, Xie-ge."

"Chen Man." Xie Qingcheng's voice was hoarse. "I need a favor. Can you see if you can help me?"

Chen Man paused. "Ge, I'll do anything you ask of me. But..." A note of pain strained his words. "But I know what you're trying to do right now."

Xie Qingcheng had reached his limit. He fumbled for a cigarette and held it between his teeth, but it refused to light.

Irritated, he tossed the lighter away and bit down on the cigarette filter. "You know?"

"I know. Every public security worker in Huzhou is monitoring this incident. Every signal tower in Huzhou University was hacked and forced to play this snuff video. We've already intercepted the hacker, but we received an anonymous threat that if we stopped the video, multiple locations throughout Huzhou would be bombed. We can't verify if the threat is real, but we can't afford to make the gamble." Chen Man's voice sounded exhausted. "Xie-ge, I know what you want to do."

Xie Qingcheng said nothing.

"I've seen the same things you have. I know you want to find L, prevent him from getting killed, and ask him about your parents' murderer and the organization they belong to." Chen Man was starting to sound slightly choked up. "I also know... I also know that my dage was trying to find out the truth for your dad, for his shifu, so he...he..."

Chen Man's audible sniffling came from the other end of the call.

Xie Qingcheng's throat bobbed, and bitterness flooded into his mouth.

Chen Man wasn't crying in front of him, just through the phone, but it still felt as though Chen Man's tears were spilling right onto his heart.

"So you can't do this favor for me?" Xie Qingcheng asked quietly.

"I can't... Those are the rules... I-I only have the lowest rank; I can't access such high-clearance information... And I...I'm a police officer... I..."

Xie Qingcheng didn't speak any further. He could curse out Zheng Jingfeng over this case, even though Zheng Jingfeng was his elder. But when it came to Chen Man, it was out of the question.

He just said an infinitely tired "All right, then."

"Xie-ge, I—"

Xie Qingcheng had already hung up the phone.

He lay on the bed as time ticked past, minute by minute. His entire body was ice-cold, from his fingertips to his heart...

"Dad! Mom!"

"Don't go over there! Xie Qingcheng! Don't!"

On that stormy night nineteen years ago, when he finally realized that the two icy-cold bodies collapsed in that pool of blood were his parents, he'd lost it and tried to sprint toward them. His father's colleagues had held him back, with several of them rushing forward to stop him.

"Who's the murderer? Who's the murderer? Who's the driver?!"

No one answered.

"Let go of me... Let me get a better look. Maybe there's been a mistake, maybe you got the wrong people...?!"

All the cops were crying, but the hands around him refused to let go.

"Xiao-Xie, don't be like this."

"The driver fled, but we'll investigate... We'll definitely get to the bottom of this and give you an explanation..."

But what explanation had they given him?

Only later did he find out that no one had fled. When the security footage was retrieved, it showed that the truck was unmanned. It seemed to have been controlled remotely, commanded to charge straight at his parents and then self-destruct. It had quickly gone up in flames, eliminating any evidence that might have been inside the driver's cabin.

Spotlessly clean.

So clean that even after nineteen years, the case remained uncracked.

Xie Qingcheng lay on the bed, feeling colder and colder. His hand was shaking too much to light his cigarette. With difficulty, he unlocked his phone and opened a document to stare at the images inside over and over.

The bedroom door opened with a click.

By now, Xie Qingcheng had already turned off his phone screen and closed his eyes. His phone began to ring, calls coming one after another—his parents' old co-workers, Xie Xue, Chen Man. But he didn't answer any of them. Instead he just lay there, letting the persistent ringtone painfully pierce his eardrums.

Suddenly, the ringing cut off. Then came the sound of the phone being powered down.

Xie Qingcheng was lying with his arm covering his eyes and forehead. Only now did he open his eyes slightly to gaze numbly at the young man who had turned off his phone.

"I heard everything," He Yu said.

Xie Qingcheng only stared at him.

"You never told me your parents passed away like that."

Xie Qingcheng tilted his head. He hadn't cried in the end; his eyes were just extremely bloodshot. He wanted to get up and leave—He Yu couldn't possibly understand these things. Xie Qingcheng certainly didn't want to talk to him about them.

He sat up and raised his cigarette with a still-trembling hand. He tried several times to light it, but he had no strength in his hands, and the cigarette wouldn't catch the lighter's flame.

His lighter was plucked from his fingers. With a crisp click, He Yu lit the Zippo and held the flame up to the cigarette between Xie Qingcheng's lips.

Xie Qingcheng wordlessly accepted his help. As he finally took a drag from the lit cigarette, the tremors shuddering through his entire body slowly settled somewhat.

He Yu sat down next to Xie Qingcheng and watched quietly as he finished his cigarette.

Xie Qingcheng was actually quite impressive, He Yu thought. Even in the face of an ordeal like this, he only forfeited some of his composure; he never lost control or suffered a mental breakdown.

He Yu rarely saw his helpless side. The Xie Qingcheng he was used to was an indomitable figure, but he seemed so weak right now. The frailty he was exhibiting, having gone through everyone he knew but failing to find anyone who would or could help him, gave He Yu an urge that he had never felt before—the urge to offer him his hand.

He Yu suddenly found Xie Qingcheng, in his despairing-yet-silent state, slightly familiar. He stared at him for a long while... before he finally remembered.

It was just like when his illness had flared up when he was eight, nine, or ten years old...after Xie Qingcheng became his personal physician. Whenever his pain was at its worst, He Yu had been just as helpless and silent, unwilling to say anything to anyone.

How had Xie Qingcheng treated him back then?

It was so long ago.

He Yu felt surprised—why did he still remember this incident?

On that day, the villa had been as still as a deserted grave, so silent one could have heard a pin drop. He Yu had been sitting on his own on the stone steps next to some blooming hydrangeas. Without shedding a tear or making a fuss, he took out a sharp silver knife and calmly sliced open his skin as if it were a leather bag with nothing connecting it to his own nervous system.

When He Yu's disease flared, he loved the smell of blood—he even craved it. Although he didn't have the right to hurt anyone else, nothing was off limits when it came to his own body. As he coolly watched the blood trickle down his hand, he felt like moss was twining over his heart, sadism spreading from his inner core out to his limbs...

Suddenly, a calm voice called out from the endless field of summer hydrangeas. "Hey, little devil."

He Yu was startled, but he immediately stowed away the knife without batting an eye. With his hand behind his back, he arranged his still-boyish face into an expression of pure innocence, piling on a child's natural naivete. He looked up to see that a young Xie Qingcheng wearing a long, white coat had walked out from the flowers.

Xie Qingcheng raised his brows as he looked down at He Yu. "What are you hiding?"

"...Nothing."

He Yu never bared his heart to anyone. He was hoping that Xie Qingcheng would just leave. With that sharp blade tucked up his sleeve, pressing against his skin, it took a great deal of effort for him to restrain the urge to use it against someone else.

But Xie Qingcheng grabbed He Yu's wrist and forced him to hold out his hand. The bloodstained knife clattered to the ground. Xie Qingcheng spied the wound on his wrist that was still dripping blood.

He Yu's whole body tensed as he waited for Xie Qingcheng to scold him.

But after a long while, the doctor only asked him a single question. "...Doesn't it hurt?"

He Yu was bewildered. His parents knew that he was sick, but they treated his illness as a source of shame, especially his mother.

"You can't hurt anyone else, so you need to learn how to regulate yourself," she would admonish him. "I can understand your physical discomfort, but how can a kid your age feel so much psychological suffering? It's because you're not strong enough."

The young He Yu would simply listen to her calmly, just as he did with every other lesson he received. He lived according to his parents' demands, molding himself into those endless prizes, trophies, and compliments. He had been smashed into pieces, each broken fragment of his flesh placed under the microscope for someone to examine.

He couldn't make any mistakes.

Every time he had a flare-up, he would carefully cover up his pain and conceal it within his thickly calloused heart.

He needed to be outstanding; he wasn't even allowed to yell when it hurt. Even if he did, it would be pointless; no one would truly pay any attention to him. Gradually, he lost his ability to express pain. From then on, it all ceased to matter.

He was just like a terrifying, evil dragon in a fairytale who had never ventured beyond his lonely island: he tormented his own heart and gnawed at his own limbs, channeling that aberrant illness that only ever disappointed people into scars he couldn't show to anyone.

As long as he didn't harm anyone else, then surely he had done nothing wrong by being ill, right?

Every sickly-sweet stain of blood was a brand that he left on his own body. Only in the name of trying to be a normal person did he choose to confine himself with fetters of his own making. The sole offering he ever made to this fiendish illness was his own blood. He had long since become used to this.

However, this personal physician wanted to free him from the metal shackles he had slipped onto his own hands; he wanted to step into his cold, lightless dragon's lair; he wanted to touch the scars on his body, of all sizes and shapes, and ask him, *Hey, little devil, doesn't it hurt?*

A fledgling dragon's low roar rumbled through his heart, feeble yet furious. But in the moment when this man reached out to try to touch his wound, he dragged his bloody, injured body away in panic, his spiny dragon tail thumping anxiously against the ground.

He wasn't used to being questioned. And even less accustomed to being cared for.

It doesn't hurt.

It doesn't hurt. Stop looking at me like that! I won't hurt anyone else, so don't bother with me, don't question me, don't get close to me. Leave me alone...

But his hand had been caught. The young doctor peeled his sleeve back to reveal the forearm he had been hiding from view.

The icy blade fell to the ground.

What the doctor saw was that, in order to curb the urge to hurt others during a flare-up of his illness, this young, childish boy had cut gash after gash into himself. Warm blood was still dribbling from the crisscrossing wounds.

It seemed like the fledgling dragon had been so spooked that he dropped the gentle, clever human mask he wore, exposing the ugly, scar-covered, unspeakably pathetic little dragon snout beneath. He thumped his spiked dragon tail and bared his sharp fangs as he howled, bringing all his defenses to bear to chase this trespasser out of his lair, "None of your business. Don't touch me."

The young doctor ignored his objections. He picked up the child and hoisted him over one of his shoulders. "Don't fidget."

He Yu began to struggle. He hated the smell of disinfectant that clung to Xie Qingcheng and the faint scent of medicine wafting from his sleeves. He also lost all ability to conceal his own violent urges. The soft hiss from between his clenched teeth was a threat, but also a warning. "Let me go, or I might hurt you..."

"How are you going to hurt me?" the doctor asked indifferently. "Do you have a plan in mind?"

When they reached the villa's specially prepared sickroom, the doctor tossed the young He Yu onto the soft children's sofa and slammed the door shut. Then Xie Qingcheng took a disposable mask from the drawer and put it on. When he turned back around, all He Yu could see were his deep, coldly perceptive eyes.

That was the first time He Yu had been regarded as more than a "model child." Under such an intense gaze, it was as though he had suddenly become a clumsy infant whose mistakes and laughable fumbles could all be overlooked. It was as though he could even reach out and ask for candy, and there wouldn't be anything wrong with that.

So he froze. He even forgot to run away.

Xie Qingcheng washed and disinfected his hands at the sink. "Give me your arm," he said. "I'll bandage it for you."

"...I'm fine. I don't mind." He Yu turned his head and gripped his bleeding arm, refusing to trust this man.

Xie Qingcheng raised an eyebrow. "You've gotten used to the scent of blood and violence, so you don't even care about hurting yourself anymore, is that right?"

He Yu said quietly, "Yes. It can't be changed, so I don't want to waste your time treating me."

"I'm getting paid," Xie Qingcheng replied indifferently.

He Yu stared at him.

"Little devil, do you think hurting yourself is right? That becoming bloodthirsty and twisted inside is the kind of thing that should just be ignored? Why don't you value yourself? If you grow too used to the smell of blood, you'll lose touch with all your human emotions. As time goes by, you'll only become more and more desensitized and mentally unwell and live your whole life like a stalk of grass or a slab of rock. Wouldn't you regret that? Doesn't it hurt?"

It was as if this conversation had happened only yesterday.

Even though Xie Qingcheng had later abandoned him, and their relationship had faded away, He Yu would always remember that day.

It was the first time that someone had ever offered him a hand and then asked him, *Doesn't it hurt?*

Why don't you value yourself...

He Yu watched as this man finished his cigarette with his head bowed.

"Xie Qingcheng, you want to know who the police believe L is, right?" He Yu asked without preamble.

Xie Qingcheng didn't immediately react.

"Don't be upset. Maybe I can help you."

Xie Qingcheng's head snapped up, his peach-blossom eyes wide as he looked at He Yu.

"Don't forget," He Yu said, "I'm also a hacker."

Xie Qingcheng stared at him.

"They're using the most advanced equipment. I actually looked into this kind of equipment as soon as it came out, just out of habit. I was able to intercept their attack on my phone just now, so I have a general idea of the software they're using. I might be able to beat the technicians these people have hired."

He Yu wasn't joking. His expression was completely serious, almost grave—as if he were facing the unassailable mountain that had always towered so high above him and saying, *I'm grown up now; I'm no longer that helpless boy who sat among the endless summer hydrangeas all those years ago.*

Xie Qingcheng was momentarily stunned. His mind was empty, his emotions twisted into a messy knot.

Some time later, he heard himself ask, "Why...would you help me?"

He Yu was silent at first. Then, suddenly, he held his hand out to Xie Qingcheng. Just the way that years ago, Xie Qingcheng had the courage to offer his hand to the child who had been suffering a flare-up of his illness, drowning in depression, and cutting himself to relieve his bloodthirsty need for violence.

"Because once you did the same for me."

Silence.

"I've never liked you, Xie Qingcheng. But..."

It was as though the fragrance of the hydrangea fields had drifted over from that flourishing summer, as the person standing offered his hand to the person sitting—

"Doctor Xie...I've never ever forgotten you either."

39

Nor Had She Ever Forgotten Her Grudge

There was a laptop in Xie Xue's bedroom, and she was one of those eccentrics rarely seen in the modern world who didn't set a password on her device.

He Yu opened the laptop. His fingers flew across the keys, his almond eyes fixed on the screen. Line after line of code flashed in his dark gaze. A few minutes later, He Yu pressed the enter key with a long, slender finger. A passage of decrypted text popped up, reflected in his retinas.

"Looks like L isn't even a list of suspects anymore," He Yu said quietly as he stared at the text in the dialog box. "As it turns out, the police already knew exactly who WZL was referring to."

Xie Qingcheng was striving to remain calm, but perhaps because he'd just been in the throes of such intense emotions, he was covered in sweat. His back tensed, and he stood straight as an arrow beside He Yu before bending down to look at the code on the laptop screen.

He Yu had intercepted three pieces of internal communications. The messages were partially coded, but since the two of them already understood some of what was going on, it was actually quite easy to guess their meaning.

"Wang Jiankang and Zhang Yong have been murdered."

"There's a mole, change the channel."

"Find the location of Lu Yuzhu's last signal. Hurry up."

Never mind Xie Qingcheng, even He Yu was dumbfounded. The last person was...Lu Yuzhu?

Lu Yuzhu was the most honest and straightforward person one could pick out of a crowd. She was a frank, chatty auntie in her forties who helped out in the school infirmary. He Yu and Xie Qingcheng had both gone to the university's infirmary before for one reason or another, and they had even spoken a few words with her.

How could it be her...?

At that very moment, next to one of Huzhou University's teaching buildings and close to where Zhang Yong had been murdered, Superintendent Zheng sat stiffly in the command vehicle. His panther-like eyes were thoroughly bloodshot, and all the policemen behind him were deathly silent.

They'd heard Zheng Jingfeng being berated over the phone by a man. The older officers knew who that man was, and even if the younger ones didn't, they could still get the gist of the conversation.

However, what had really rendered them mute were the two homicide cases that they had failed to prevent.

The flames were still raging; a group of police were in the middle of photographing, preserving, and collecting evidence from the crime scene.

Zheng Jingfeng opened the lid of his thermos and took a sip, forcing himself to calm down. "Are we still in contact with the informant who provided the intelligence report?"

His protege shook his head. "The informant hasn't shown themself since the guestbook was discovered and brought into the precinct. They said they were already in danger by then, and WZL was the last piece of information they could give us."

Zheng Jingfeng leaned back in his chair and pinched the bridge of his nose. He heaved a deep sigh. Huzhou University's WZL were going to be murdered—this was what their informant had warned them about. While *Jiang Lan Pei* was the signal they had agreed upon.

But this mysterious organization was impenetrable. There were times when the higher-ups didn't even communicate with each other, and when they did, it was often through code. The informant didn't know what "WZL" meant when they relayed this message to the police either. They could only pass on this bit of classified information to their contact as is.

Zheng Jingfeng spent a long time using all sorts of investigative techniques and linking together all kinds of clues to finally crack the code: WZL wasn't one person but rather three different individuals. This mysterious organization had used an intentionally misleading code.

As for the three people identified, they were Wang Jiankang, Zhang Yong, and Lu Yuzhu. All three were connected to the case and would be dealt with as part of the "cleanup" soon.

After cracking the code, the police had to protect the informant while simultaneously communicating with and protecting the three targets from the shadows. This was, in fact, a very difficult task. They couldn't tell the targets the truth, as that would alert the organization. They could only monitor them day and night, poised to act at the slightest sign of movement.

But even though the police were watching them around the clock, it was impossible to be on the targets' heels every single second. Besides, the informant only knew the approximate time they would be murdered, not exactly when the killings were slated to occur.

Wang Jiankang was a lecher who loved messing around behind his wife's back. Because of this hobby of his, he was already used to taking certain countersurveillance measures when engaging in his dalliances. He had been murdered in the school's hotel. On his way there, he'd gone to a dormitory building and swapped cars with a colleague. There had been a meeting at the university that day, so the teaching and administrative staff were all wearing the same uniform. After Wang Jiankang changed cars, the plainclothes policeman accidentally mistook his colleague for him. As a result, a little over an hour went by with no one watching him.

And an hour later, Wang Jiankang was throttled to death in the hotel. The murderer had subsequently put a pair of high heels on his corpse.

Zhang Yong was a cautious and cowardly person. Although he was greedy for money, he was afraid of repercussions. He might've also sensed that the organization's higher-ups didn't trust him anymore. The police had wanted to use him to get closer to the masterminds and promised to ensure his safety if he told them everything he knew.

But Zhang Yong was also wary, prone to overthinking, and suspicious toward anyone and everyone. When approached by a plainclothes officer, this singular moron immediately became convinced that the plainclothes officer was an impostor sent by the organization to test his loyalty.

Because he was dead set on protecting himself, he refused to say anything. In addition, to demonstrate his dedication, he even told his superior in the organization about what had happened that day.

After that, it became exceptionally difficult and dangerous to tail Zhang Yong. As the saying went, the mantis hunted the cicada unaware of the much-more-dangerous goldfinch behind it. While the police tracked Zhang Yong, members of the mysterious organization were likewise watching the police from better-hidden positions.

Therefore, the police's knowledge of Zhang Yong's whereabouts inevitably became less precise, in terms of both location and time. He had called the police several hours before he was run over, but after seeing the photo of Wang Jiankang's murder, he got worried that his phone's GPS would not only help the police find him but might also allow the organization to track his movements, so he threw his phone away.

Before he saw Jiang Liping, he'd still hoped that he might be lucky enough to escape disaster. As he hid in that deserted office, he'd thought that since there were no electronic devices on him that would allow him to be tracked, he might be safe.

But Zhang Yong hadn't anticipated that the organization had already planted a tracking device in the Buddhist amulet he wore around his neck...

The last living target was Lu Yuzhu.

Lu Yuzhu was the most intractable of the three.

Unlike the aforementioned greasy, lecherous men who murdered for money, she wasn't involved out of self-interest. Rather, due to her personal misfortunes, she held a deep grudge against law enforcement and society.

Lu Yuzhu's path into crime was highly unusual. Years ago, she had been the first female graduate student from her county. After finishing her studies, she returned home to give back to the place where she had grown up, becoming the secretary of her hometown's county party committee, then ascending to the highest political office of the county at a young age.

However, a few years later, an intern reporter came to the county from the provincial capital, hoping to make a blazing start to their career and brimming with simple ideas about justice. They had resolved to conduct a secret investigation of corrupt and illegal behavior in these villages, wishing wholeheartedly to break a viral news story.

Lu Yuzhu had a rather carefree personality to begin with. And since the county was a fairly remote locale, the anti-corruption workers found themselves inevitably at odds with the customs of the locals. While Lu Yuzhu's judgment was impeccable when it came to important decisions, there were times when she let a few small details slip. For instance, one of her relatives had accepted some monetary gifts from a government project. These gifts were small, more like a customary expression of goodwill among the villagers. At most, the present could have bought them a pig.

But that journalist brandished their pen and resolutely added a string of zeros to that sum of money.

How preposterous—how could such a little county have such a hugely corrupt official? Surely they ought to be suspended from their duties and thoroughly investigated?

If this story had been fact-checked in the first place, it would have been immediately apparent that this immoral journalist who brought eighteen generations of their ancestors to shame had written an outright lie. But Lu Yuzhu was unbelievably unlucky—the re-election for the county party committee secretary was coming up, and her opponent in the deadlocked race just so happened to have a relative who was best friends with the government worker heading this case.

The small village was remote, and its dealings were oftentimes shadier than what went on in big cities. After being framed several times, Lu Yuzhu ultimately found herself convicted on charges of accepting bribes.

Back then, she was still very young—her child had only been two years old, just barely able to mumble the word "Mom," when she was placed behind bars. By the time she got out, her husband had already found a new lover. Her daughter—looking fearfully at this unfamiliar, emotional woman before her from her stepmother's arms—no longer remembered her mother.

In the end, Lu Yuzhu lost all hope. She could only turn her back on her home and leave their little county.

The journalist thought that they had been disseminating justice by sensationalizing their report. The shady deals made in the lower-level departments of the county seat unbeknownst to the higher-ups, her husband's weakness and betrayal... All these events fell onto this woman as her burden to bear. A few sentences, a few sums of money, and the position of county party committee secretary were all it took to ruin the life of an ordinary person.

Because of her criminal record, it was impossible for Lu Yuzhu to find any good jobs after her release. She worked as a dishwasher, nursing assistant, housekeeper...but never for long. Once her employers learned of her past, they all ended up dismissing her, whether directly or discreetly.

When the hardest times hit, Lu Yuzhu turned to the world's oldest profession.

Among the various people who engaged her services, she saw individuals from many different occupations, including those who certainly shouldn't have been showing up somewhere like that.

In time, one of her clients noticed that she was very nimble and clever and didn't speak like an uneducated person, so out of curiosity, he asked her about her past. Lu Yuzhu initially hadn't planned on saying much, but everyone had their moments of weakness. That day, unable to restrain herself, she ended up telling her life story to this client under the dim lights of the private room. By the time she reached the end of her tale, she was sobbing too hard to speak.

The client thought for a while as he smoked a cigarette. Then he wrote down an address and told her that if she wanted to, she could go there and ask for his friend. That friend of his would arrange a stable and respectable job for her.

That was how Lu Yuzhu became a nursing assistant at Huzhou University's infirmary.

She had been working there for many years when, about two or three years ago, upper-level officials from the public security authorities came to investigate old miscarriages of justice. After looking into Lu Yuzhu's corruption and bribery case, they expunged her criminal record, detained and disciplined the journalist, and arrested the government employees who had been involved in the matter.

The young public prosecutor personally paid a visit to Lu Yuzhu to apologize and hand over her monetary compensation. A newly appointed staff member from the operations division of their county's public security authority was right behind him.

Lu Yuzhu had just finished retrieving medicine for a few students. Upon seeing the visitors, she smiled and said quite calmly, "The past is in the past. Keep the money for yourselves. I don't want it."

The prosecutor asked her why.

She looked at them coolly and said, "Do you think this money is enough to buy back somebody's life?"

Silence fell.

"My life has already been ruined, so what use is this to me? Can you let me go back to when I was twenty-five? Can you give me back my child, my husband, and my family?"

Neither the prosecutor nor the other staff member could answer Lu Yuzhu.

"Please leave."

But still, the prosecutor tried to convince her to accept the compensation.

"In that case," said Lu Yuzhu, "you should take this money and start a foundation or something to educate the media and ask them to be a little more cautious, a little fairer and more reserved, before they start writing about a person or issue. They're like locusts passing through a field—all too happy to brandish their pens and rake in the attention and money, but what do they leave behind for the people involved?"

She smiled—the erstwhile swiftest and most capable young female secretary in the county now had deep crow's feet.

"The answer is a lifetime of turmoil and suffering."

Someone like Lu Yuzhu would never rely on the police for help. If anything, she was innately predisposed to keep her distance from them—and on top of that, she supported and obeyed the organization unconditionally. So the question was, why would the organization want to "clean up" someone like her?

"Lu Yuzhu doesn't have any electronic communication devices on her person, but it's also possible that she's been using someone else's cell phone. We can't pin down her location." The police officer in charge of gathering intelligence was typing on a keyboard while relaying the situation to Superintendent Zheng. "Currently, there are 15,580 mobile phones receiving and transmitting signals in this area. It would be useless to locate every single one of their positions."

Another officer finished her phone call and approached the command vehicle. With a very solemn expression, she said to Superintendent Zheng, "Captain Zheng, we can't track her. Lu Yuzhu's ability to evade detection is the best we've encountered in the past few years. There's no doubt that she's been trained and was given a jamming device. Based on what we're seeing, only the very best fugitives could give her a run for her money."

Zheng Jingfeng said nothing in reply. His panther-like eyes were still staring fixedly at the spinning electronic children playing "drop the hanky" on the broadcasting tower.

That gaudy letter L looked like a curved hook that had been stained with blood.

L...

The old criminal investigator had been wondering this whole time, had they decoded the message incorrectly when it came to L? Perhaps it didn't stand for Lu Yuzhu. Why exactly would the superiors of such a devoted woman feel the need to murder her?

Out of these three people, she was the only one he felt uncertain about. Given the motives behind these murders, it didn't make any sense at all to kill Lu Yuzhu too.

However, no other targets had appeared.

Still, up until now, Zheng Jingfeng kept thinking... Could this letter L have some hidden meaning that they hadn't yet uncovered?

LET'S STOP THEM TOGETHER

MEANWHILE, He Yu and Xie Qingcheng were still sitting in the faculty dormitory of Huzhou University.

"Lu Yuzhu's life history is all right here." He Yu swiftly brought up all the relevant case files and perused them on the screen with Xie Qingcheng.

After reading the last line of information on her, He Yu promptly drew a straightforward conclusion. "There's no point in killing this person. She's theirs through and through."

"Then why does she need to be 'cleaned up'?" asked Xie Qingcheng.

"Cleaned up..." He Yu pondered this term, sinking into thought.

It took a thief to catch a thief.

Unlike Zheng Jingfeng, He Yu was a hacker; as such, he had a better understanding of different ways to relay information and tended to pay more attention to that kind of thing. Logically speaking, he could understand their opponent on a higher level. Years of hiding his mental illness and imitating the lifestyle of an ordinary person had polished his mind until it was warped, alert, and sharp.

He thought for a while, looking out at the broadcasting tower beyond the window that resembled a sword of blood piercing into the sky. After muttering to himself for a few moments, something related to the expression "clean up" occurred to him.

He jumped to his feet, gazing at the building behind the Huzhou University Broadcasting Tower, and a terrifying interplay of light and shadow flickered in his eyes.

L.

That's right... Throughout this entire incident, there'd been something that looked important to the scheme but was completely irrelevant and redundant: the broadcasting tower.

What purpose had it served over the course of the entire murder broadcast? On closer examination, it didn't seem to have a specific function of its own. For the time being, its role was to track the progress of the murders in real time, which was a function that wholly overlapped with that of the cell phones.

So why did they deliberately transform the broadcasting tower into something akin to an executioner's sword? Could it simply be for the sake of provocation? Interfering with the signal for the entire city was already arrogant enough—why go this extra step?

He Yu's expression turned grave. Taking control of the broadcasting tower might not have been for the purpose of displaying the murders' progress at all, but rather...

Somewhere near the tower...was the source of a signal that they needed to control with exquisite precision!

The hackers simply took control of the tower because they didn't want to be disturbed by the building's signal. And in the process, they also created a performance by giving the murders a sense of ritualistic ceremony. Their true goal was actually to stabilize the signal coverage in the surrounding area.

L... L...

Of the buildings near the broadcasting tower, which ones were worthy of notice?

The secondary dining hall... The indoor gymnasium... And also, the building that He Yu's gaze had already locked upon firmly—the library.

The Bowen Archives Building—one of the campus libraries.

Jiang Lanpei had been locked in Cheng Kang Psychiatric Hospital for nearly twenty years. Now that the Cheng Kang case and Huzhou University broadcasting tower homicide case were inextricably intertwined, the organization wanted to clean up...

Did L only refer to the "Lu" in Lu Yuzhu?

Their targets for "cleanup," were they only people?

A darkness spanning more than a decade was sure to involve numerous paper trails. Ordinary people rarely needed to be held in check by contracts, but such an organization couldn't possibly establish agreements through talk alone. And in the past, using digital copies would have been virtually impossible.

Then, if there were indeed case files, whether they were records of the people involved or what they'd done, how many volumes would have been collected over the course of ten or twenty years?

The most important files would be kept close at hand, but what about the bits and pieces that weren't so important? Would the perpetrators have taken them out and stored them in the domain of their allies, like "contracts" used to keep the members in check? To keep their co-conspirators in the shadows under control?

Wang Jiankang and Zhang Yong had both been administrative higher-ups at the university. As collaborators of the mysterious organization, they probably received portions of the records—but where would they have stored them? Those records could have been massively expansive—unsuited to being stored in a bank vault. And they wouldn't have wanted their own families to find out, so...

In the entire university, where were the most files and records stored, and where could they be kept where people would be least likely to search?

The answer was the seemingly silent and unobtrusive archival building currently hidden beneath the bloody glow of the broadcasting tower.

Every famous centuries-old university had a building filled with huge volumes of files like this. Even though digital files existed now, Huzhou University in particular still kept the age-old tradition of documenting every graduate's grades, theses, and exams on paper. Within Huzhou University's case file building, one could trace the original copies of student dissertation defenses back to more than a century ago. There were so many archival envelopes on the premises that ten whole days wouldn't be enough to organize them all.

L, Library, Lu Yuzhu.

If she wasn't the person getting "cleaned up," then she was...

He Yu turned around. "If you trust me, then come with me to the case file building," he said to Xie Qingcheng. "But my judgment might not be correct. It takes twenty minutes to get there, and we have to avoid being discovered by the police, so it might take longer than that. And if my guess is wrong, we might lose the chance to find someone who might know something about your parents' deaths. Think it over and decide what you want to do."

Xie Qingcheng had grown used to calmly bossing people around, delegating and planning for others. But at that moment, facing the truth behind his parents' deaths—unsolved for nineteen years—his thoughts were a tangled mess.

As a result, even though Xie Qingcheng faintly felt that there was something inappropriate about this, he didn't know how to sort out the chess pieces before him. Nor had he ever imagined that the only person who could show him a path forward right now would be He Yu.

That it would be this little devil.

With his thoughts in turmoil, Xie Qingcheng picked up the box of cigarettes from the table and gave He Yu a meaningful look.

It was a look that Xie Qingcheng had never given He Yu before. In the past, he always seemed to He Yu as if he was looking down on him. Even when He Yu grew taller than him, the aura emanating from his peach-blossom eyes was still one of someone looking at a youth from whom he demanded absolute obedience.

But now, Xie Qingcheng was looking at him straight on.

"I trust you," he said.

He Yu's heart shuddered.

Xie Qingcheng paused. Gazing at He Yu, he said with deliberate emphasis, "Thank you."

A few seconds passed before He Yu finally returned to his senses. "It's nothing." He suppressed that inexplicable tremor in his heart and said again, "It's nothing." He grabbed his phone as a thought suddenly occurred to him. "Oh right, Ge, wait a minute."

He Yu turned away and quickly used his phone to connect the computer to the internet and casually log onto the dark web. He looked up a program, paid for it using a MasterCard, and then downloaded it onto his phone.

"This is the mirroring software from the equipment the hackers are using," he said. "It's only a copy of the most basic part, but it should be enough in case we need to use it."

As Xie Qingcheng looked at him, once again the niggling feeling welled up that this was inappropriate. If he were in his normal state of mind, he would have realized at once why he felt that way. But at the moment, his thoughts were like half-dried glue, impossible to wade through.

Thus, by the time He Yu finished setting up the software, shoved his phone in his pocket, looked at him, and said, "Let's go," Xie Qingcheng only hesitated a moment before agreeing.

He hurried after He Yu in the direction of the archives.

Within the archives, Lu Yuzhu's face was relaxed as she walked Jiang Liping to the elevator and handed her an external hard drive.

"I've gathered the most important materials here. Executive Duan knows the password."

Jiang Liping took the hard drive and pressed it between her hands with her head bowed. After a moment, she said to Lu Yuzhu, "Lu-jie, why don't you..."

"I won't be leaving with you," Lu Yuzhu said. "Someone needs to see this through to the end. By stirring up this big of a fuss, the boss is painting a warning in blood for all the collaborators that everyone hiding in the shadows should keep their mouths shut. He's telling them they need to know the consequences of betraying him—that if he chooses to act, even under the noses of the police, they won't be able to save themselves. But there's no doubt that those hunting dogs, especially their leader, will stop at nothing to get to the bottom of this case. Otherwise, they would lose their positions of authority."

She smiled. "I know all too well how deranged those people can become when their badges are on the line."

"You're sure," Jiang Liping said.

"I'm sure," Lu Yuzhu confirmed. "I've been the domestic ring-leader behind this entire case. I must convince the police that Jiang Lanpei had ties to foreign powers, and that those foreign powers had me carry out this plot to avenge her.

"Now, I've left behind everything that the police can use as standard procedural evidence. At the end of their investigation, the only evidence they'll find will prove that this was an international crime. A few months ago, after a ten-year standoff, the boss of that overseas machinery manufacturer finally fell under Executive Duan's control. Executive Duan will wait to pile all the evidence onto them before having them killed outside the country. That fallen giant should be perfect to take the rap for the Cheng Kang case and the murdered police officers from nineteen years ago on behalf of our organization. At any rate, dead men tell no tales.

"As long as the domestic investigators can use me to show that the case is closed, most of those hounds will be dispatched elsewhere. They won't waste effort on pursuing the people who remain at large. Some remaining officers might be dissatisfied, but it'll be difficult for isolated individuals to pull anything off without more support."

With that, Lu Yuzhu looked down to check the time. Then she said to Jiang Liping, "Liping, you should get on your way. It would be impossible for you to avoid being implicated for what happened to Wang Jiankang and Zhang Yong. If you fall into their hands, it'll all be over for you. When is Executive Duan sending people to come get you?"

Jiang Liping gazed at Lu Yuzhu's face as if she wanted to say something, but in the end, she didn't manage it. After a moment of silence, she replied, "His people are already here. I'll be able to leave at once."

"Then hurry and get out of here. Zheng Jingfeng is no idiot; once he catches wind of this, he might follow the trail here."

"Lu-jie..."

"Go." Lu Yuzhu put her arms around Jiang Liping. The two of them were both undercover criminals from the organization hiding at

Huzhou University, and in some senses they were like sisters who had overcome many difficult trials together. "You must be careful—there are police informants in the organization. If our plan hadn't been leaked in advance, it would have gone even more smoothly this time."

"I know," replied Jiang Liping.

"That informant still hasn't revealed themselves... They've harmed us for so long from the shadows. After you catch them, make sure the boss tears them to pieces..." As she gritted her teeth, Lu Yuzhu's eyes shone with a fanatical brilliance. "This is my only wish before I die. I'll be watching from hell."

Jiang Liping closed her eyes, hugging Lu Yuzhu back tightly without a word. Then she turned around and entered the elevator.

The elevator doors closed between the two women, a dividing line between the darkness and the light. Behind the doors, the elevator ascended.

Lu Yuzhu turned around and headed deeper into the library's basement levels.

There, an assortment of live wires and explosive devices had already been buried. She had also killed the archives' two staff members. Even if the informant leaked this information to the police, Zheng Jingfeng had still lost to her in the end—he'd failed to locate her before she finished her plan.

They were always so useless—it was the same ten years ago, and they hadn't changed since then.

They were always too late.

Justice that arrived too late was meaningless. Once, in the past, they had taught her this lesson using her life. Now, in the present, she intended to use this life of hers to teach them a lesson in turn.

Lu Yuzhu walked to the center of the basement and carefully inspected everything again. The organization had given her the most advanced equipment. Although she had no experience with explosives, she understood the necessary procedures. As long as she put everything together according to their instructions and pressed a button on the explosive device, their people would be able to control it remotely and detonate the entire installation in less than five minutes.

Lu Yuzhu walked into the middle of that crisscrossing web of wires. She stood quietly and calmly looked over her surroundings. As soon as the explosives went off, the entire archival library and all its files, whether they were from two decades or more than a century ago, would go up in flames. And with that, the person who had once rescued her from a life of hustling received the "cleanliness" he so desired.

"Duan-ge," she said softly—speaking aloud the words that she usually only dared to murmur in her heart, an incredibly audacious manner of address. "I've come to clean things up for you."

With a quiet laugh, she pressed the button on the device.

"Duan-laoban." In a suite in a Huzhou hotel, a technician with a cigar in his mouth was staring at the laptop screen in front of him with a very ugly expression on his face. "Someone's intercepted the remote-control system for the detonator."

A man stood before the floor-to-ceiling windows looking down at Huzhou University's Radio and Television Tower. "It's been intercepted by the police?" he asked coolly. "I spent so much money hiring you, yet you can't even beat the police at your own game. You sure accepted the payment with ease."

"It's not the police." The technician wiped at the sweat on his forehead. He was so anxious that his eyeballs were bulging out like a bullfrog's behind his high-prescription Coke-bottle glasses. "The intrusion port they used isn't one that we're familiar with."

The man's interest seemed slightly piqued. "And that is?"

"I can't figure it out right now, but looking at their technique, I feel...I feel that this person is..."

"Is?"

The technician swallowed. "Edward."

His words were followed by several seconds of silence. Then a woman's voice floated out from inside the room.

Up until now, that woman hadn't spoken a word as she lay back in a recliner scrolling through Weibo and looking at the discussion topics about Huzhou University's broadcasting tower. Even though such content was quickly blocked and deleted, the messages still kept pouring in. Refreshing the page from time to time was enough to hold her attention.

But upon hearing the name "Edward," the woman's hand stilled.

"Are you sure?" she asked the technician.

"I-I can't be sure, but considering that he broke into my system in such a short amount of time, and looking at the method he used, I can't think of anyone else among the well-known hackers right now, I..."

Duan-laoban smiled faintly. "Well, if it's him, that makes things easier. Let's first see if it's actually him."

He nodded to the secretary next to him. "Give He Yu a call."

The dial tone droned several times.

"Duan-laoban, he didn't pick up."

The man glanced at the woman out of the corner of his unfathomable eyes. "I really must congratulate you, Executive Lü. You have such a wonderful son."

The woman rose from the chair, her ample figure wrapped in a luxurious custom-made silk dress. As she walked over to the floor-to-ceiling window, the nighttime city lights illuminated her face—the kindly-looking, ingratiating face of a businesswoman.

Astonishingly, this woman was none other than Lü Zhishu!

Lü Zhishu looked rather embarrassed as she drained the wine in her cup. However, she forced out a few peals of laughter. "Executive Duan, I must also congratulate you," she said to the man. "If it wasn't him, it would be very difficult to resolve this issue today, wouldn't it? If it is him, at least it will be easy to deal with. My son isn't the type to get involved with something like this of his own accord. There must be someone else with him."

As she spoke, she looked down at her phone.

The last message sent to her family group chat was from He Yu. *Doctor Xie and I have returned to the dorm.*

Lü Zhishu handed her phone to the man with a complicated expression in her eyes. "Please try not to hurt him. Think of a way to make him stop as quickly as possible."

The man glanced at the screen.

"Your dearest son and Xie Qingcheng are together again."

"They seem to be getting along quite well." Lü Zhishu was all too eager to distance her family from this development and place the onus entirely on Xie Qingcheng. "I know my son—he doesn't like Xie Qingcheng's personality, but psychologically, he's always treated him as a role model to imitate and surpass. I suppose Xie Qingcheng wanted to look into this today, so He Yu threw himself into the endeavor, hoping to show off in front of his idol."

"Idol?" The man browsed the conversation history. After a while, he said to Lü Zhishu, "In that case, why don't we pull up some old videos? It's about time we destroy the kid's...what do they call it again? His bias."

Walking over to the computer, Duan-laoban continued to give orders. "I want everything that's publicly available on the internet and all our internal files. I'll tell you which particular videos to look for."

With a full plan in mind, the man smiled coldly. As long as He Yu was doing this for Xie Qingcheng, everything would work out. Actually, it couldn't possibly be any easier to make He Yu stop. He just needed to see those glimpses of Xie Qingcheng's past.

Surely then this son of Lü Zhishu would no longer make such an effort to extend a helping hand to his Doctor Xie.

41

Because the Truth Was Never Meaningless

FIVE MINUTES, Lu Yuzhu thought. In just five minutes, everything would be over.

The detonator's clicking countdown echoed through the basement. It sounded like the pendulum clock she'd kept in her old house in the county seat all those years ago. Back when her life had been peaceful, that clock used to resound with a *tick, tock, tick, tock* as its pendulum swung from side to side.

Back then, she had thought that she would be able to live out her entire life smoothly and serenely.

All of a sudden—just as that upstart young journalist had once smashed her life to pieces—the countdown to her demise unexpectedly stopped.

In that very same moment, Lu Yuzhu heard a muffled rumble from the elevator car behind her.

She twisted around abruptly to see the elevator doors opening slowly. Inside stood a tall, well-built man with broad shoulders and long legs, his beautiful peach-blossom eyes sparking with a piercing flame.

Xie Qingcheng walked out of the silvery-gray elevator car, his gaze burrowing its way straight into her chest.

He Yu's guess had been spot-on. Lu Yuzhu was indeed here. Before he had entered the archives, the mirrored copy of the program he had downloaded on his phone had notified him of a powerful signal. When He Yu scanned for connections, he found that there was even a link to a detonator.

Multiple detonators.

The only stroke of luck amid this misfortune was that these detonators could be controlled by He Yu's copy of the software, so he managed to break through the opponents' firewall to enter the program and stop the countdown.

He Yu and Xie Qingcheng hadn't notified the police before they charged in; there wasn't enough time. Besides, they'd already confirmed that there was a mole among the police, so notifying them might only complicate matters.

The situation was as clear as day—Lu Yuzhu intended to use a suicide attack to help her benefactor thoroughly "clean up" the files that served as evidence of their crimes.

"I know there are only five minutes on the countdown. But it's stopped now." Xie Qingcheng stared at the woman. "Can we talk?"

"The countdown stopped...? How could the countdown..."

"That's all thanks to your boss's fondness for high technology." A satin-smooth voice came from behind Xie Qingcheng. That was when Lu Yuzhu realized that there was another person standing inside the elevator.

Xie Qingcheng's presence had been too arresting. When he walked out of those elevator doors as they slowly slid open, he seemed utterly indomitable, treading on her heart with every step. She hadn't even noticed the young man hidden in the shadows of the spacious elevator.

This young man wore a simple black turtleneck and appeared relaxed and composed. When he stepped out of the elevator, he was even playing around on his phone with a careless air. With his outfit and appearance, he wouldn't have looked at all out of place in a bookstore or a social club, rather than these archives.

The young man smiled at her. "Lu-laoshi, technology truly is a great thing."

But he didn't speak to her all that much—the technician on the opposing side was frantically trying to break through to the program he had just hijacked. He Yu only said a gentle, familiar hello, then leaned back against the wall to continue this silent coding battle. His expression hardened as he focused on his task, and he stopped paying any more attention to Xie Qingcheng and Lu Yuzhu's conversation.

Lu Yuzhu was a woman who had experienced many great upheavals in her life. After a moment of shock, she regained her composure. She looked them up and down, and her tensed muscles relaxed slightly. "You're not the police."

"We're not."

"The dogs have yet to follow the scent here, but you've arrived first." Lu Yuzhu narrowed her eyes. "Just who are you?"

Xie Qingcheng didn't intend to beat around the bush with her, so he cut straight to the chase. "Nineteen years ago, my parents died in a car accident. A driverless vehicle crashed into them, and after they were hit, the engine spontaneously caught fire, destroying all useful evidence. The method was exactly the same as the one your people used to murder Zhang Yong just now."

"So, were your parents traitors who deserved to be cleansed, or two police dogs?" Lu Yuzhu asked.

"They were police officers," Xie Qingcheng replied.

"Then that's a well-deserved death—not unjust at all. Surely they were honored as martyrs after their deaths?" Lu Yuzhu's face twisted into a mocking smile.

"They weren't."

Lu Yuzhu's smile froze.

"They didn't die on an assignment, and there was no direct evidence to show that they had been murdered. All their colleagues knew that it wasn't a coincidence, that it wasn't an ordinary car crash, but as long as there was no evidence to prove otherwise, it could only be deemed a mere accident."

Lu Yuzhu's eyes dimmed slightly, as if she were remembering her own past.

"I've seen your records. I know what you've been through," said Xie Qingcheng. He paused before continuing, "I know what it feels like to not receive a fair answer for so many years. Lu Yuzhu, not all police officers are utterly evil."

Lu Yuzhu didn't respond right away.

"My parents died in the line of duty when I was thirteen years old. From what I remember, they'd never done anything unconscionable. Instead, they were cruelly murdered because they were relentlessly pursuing the truth for people like you, trying to right wrongs.

"Lu Yuzhu, I know that you hate the reporter who framed you back then and everyone related to the investigation. You left your hometown and suffered so much, so to you, the verdict from three years ago came much too late—it's impossible to change the past, after all.

"But do you know just how many nameless, unknown reporters, police officers, and prosecutors fought tooth and nail, with some even sacrificing their lives, to bring justice to you and to others like you who were also falsely accused? Why do they offer their blood, their youth, their lives for matters of the past that have already been settled...for matters that may not be forgiven even if the verdict is overturned?

"Because although a belated truth cannot change the past..." Xie Qingcheng's voice trembled slightly, as though he wasn't only speaking to Lu Yuzhu but also struggling with the part of himself that had spent nearly two decades worn to the bone. "It can at least steer the future onto the right path. It allows those who have been wronged to raise their heads again, those lifeless, nameless martyrs to rest in peace, the victims to shrug the heavy shackles from their shoulders, and those outside the law to understand the meaning of justice."

Xie Qingcheng's voice was calm, and his emotions were restrained as he spoke, but his red-rimmed eyes revealed his already-broken and crumbling heart. "It can't heal the wounds of the past, Lu Yuzhu. But it's not meaningless. The truth is never meaningless.

"When the prosecutor found you and everyone bowed to apologize to you, didn't you feel...a kind of joy when the anger that had been bottled up for ten years vanished? Even though it was accompanied by boundless anguish, in that one moment, you could finally breathe."

The light in Lu Yuzhu's eyes flickered slightly.

"Your wait ended, Lu Yuzhu. I've waited for almost twenty years, yet there's no end in sight."

Lu Yuzhu looked at him, still silent.

"You can't see the people who've spilled blood and sacrificed themselves to refute your false accusations," Xie Qingcheng continued. "You don't even know their names, but for the dead and the living, they're always seeking the truth, pursuing justice for blunders they didn't commit... Do you think that's meaningless?

"For more than ten years, even as your husband betrayed you and your child forgot you, even when you yourself had forgotten what the Lu Yuzhu who had once been the secretary of Qingli County's party committee was like, these people you've never even met refused to put down your case file. Do you think they did all that just to get you an apology? At the very least, my parents didn't. As police officers, they worked to support their family, treating it as just a career. But even though that's what they would've said, in the end, they died for their careers. They didn't leave behind much money, and they didn't get to see their children grow up. When they died, I was only thirteen.

"Lu Yuzhu, you're a mother too. Can you imagine what my mother was thinking the moment she died?"

Lu Yuzhu had been listening in silence, but at these words, she suddenly shivered. It felt as though a pair of tear-filled eyes, eyes belonging to a woman who had been forced to leave her children just as she had, was gazing silently down at her from above.

"I saw it myself. Half of her body was crushed to pulp. By your people."

Lu Yuzhu couldn't say anything.

"What did she do wrong, Lu Yuzhu? She didn't say many extraordinary things throughout her life, but I still remember the one sentence she spoke with gravitas. She said that even when they are exhausted, every ordinary person longs for the truth; the people in this world must believe in something bright to strive for survival. She hoped that the police badge on her shoulder shone brightly, that it was something that the helpless could trust. But your comrades, your organization, and your people killed her. Her epaulettes were ground to pieces."

Lu Yuzhu's fingertips trembled faintly.

"The people you should hate are not the police but rather the criminals who framed and slandered you," Xie Qingcheng said. "Come back, Lu Yuzhu. Some things shouldn't have happened this way."

Lu Yuzhu looked like a wandering ghost with more than a decade of her complicated life twisting and tearing through her body. Finally, she raised her head and said to Xie Qingcheng in an unexpectedly raspy voice, "I regret it."

Now, it was Xie Qingcheng's turn to be stunned.

"I regret it..." she murmured. "Did you know...that when the prosecutor found me, this was the sentence that he repeated the most."

Lu Yuzhu said softly, "At the time, I wondered what he was actually trying to say with those words. He meant 'you lived miserably, but it has nothing to do with me.'"

She looked at Xie Qingcheng with a complicated expression.

After a few seconds, she continued, "But right now, I'm telling you that I regret it. I do feel it now, so I'm thinking that maybe... maybe he didn't mean 'it has nothing to do with me.' Maybe he truly felt distraught on my behalf. But—"

Lu Yuzhu changed the topic. Under the cold gray basement light, she said slowly, "There are some things that you can't come back from. Maybe our people had no choice but to involve the innocent. And maybe it was wrong, maybe it was a sin, but in my most desperate and unbearable moment, it was our people who saved me and gave me a place to belong."

Xie Qingcheng remained silent.

"Without them, I might have already killed myself during this long, slow search for the truth. It was too painful; I wouldn't have been able to wait until the truth came to light. I can't say that you're wrong," Lu Yuzhu said gently to Xie Qingcheng. "And I know that I'm wrong. But I belong completely to the darkness now. The light is unfamiliar to me. Right or wrong, he gave me my life. I won't betray him, even if I die."

"You don't think that he saved you just to use you?" asked Xie Qingcheng. "That he saved you for this day, so he'd have someone who would keep their mouth shut even if their life was on the line? There's a five-minute countdown on the detonator and it can be remotely controlled, so why didn't they take you with them? They want you to die in the explosion along with the things they want to destroy."

Lu Yuzhu smiled. "You're giving him too little credit."

Xie Qingcheng stared at her.

"He said that he'd take me away, that he didn't intend to leave me behind. But I was the one who wanted to stay. This case has kicked up too big of a fuss, and it's given a clear enough warning to the others; he always needed to have a few people in the country to give the police a way to close the case," Lu Yuzhu said. "If I wanted to stay alive, I could very well escape after pressing the button; he even gave me time to change my mind.

"But I don't want to," she concluded. "I don't want to fall into the hands of the police, and I don't want to return to the place where I was locked up for so long. I'm not willing to be interrogated in any way, and I don't want to cooperate. Death doesn't frighten me at all. It's only living that causes me endless despair."

As she spoke, Lu Yuzhu slowly retreated into the depths of the basement, out of the light and into the darkness.

She didn't want to step forward. She *couldn't* step forward anymore.

She reached a hand behind her—at the small of her back, she was carrying a handgun.

She had never fired a gun before. This was the last thing the organization had given to her, in the unlikely situation that it would come in handy. She wasn't sure if she could aim it accurately, but at least it was worth a try...

Her gaze fell on that young man in black who hadn't said a word from beginning to end, who was still tapping away on his phone screen at top speed.

It was true. She could no longer remember the Lu Yuzhu who had once been Qingli County's party secretary.

Her heart lurched as she soundlessly gritted her teeth and disengaged the gun's safety with a trembling hand...

Ding. The notification of an incoming message sounded suddenly.

He Yu paused in the middle of his coding battle.

He had set up a firewall to block any incoming messages, but this one had been sent by the other technician after breaking through his barrier. During their ongoing confrontation, his opponent had managed to send him an anonymous message.

It contained a video.

The message's text said, *Edward, I've identified both of you. Take a look at this first, then think about whether you really want to go to such lengths for him.*

42

TELL ME, WHAT IS THE TRUTH?

WHAT WAS this video?

It seemed to have something to do with Xie Qingcheng.

He Yu glanced impassively at the code rapidly scrolling past his phone screen. His opponent would need some time to catch up to him, but it wouldn't take long. It was very possible this video had been sent to him to disrupt his concentration.

Closing the chat window, he set the matter aside. He didn't want to get distracted.

However, a moment later, a second message jumped out like a lingering spirit that refused to move on.

Edward, I know that you suffer from a rare psychological disorder. While you were attacking our firewall, we also looked into your files.

He Yu's fingers stilled.

Though his condition was a secret, his personal hospital and physician had copies of his medical records. The organization's hacking skills were advanced enough that, with certain clues, it wouldn't be impossible for them to determine his true identity and obtain important records within a short amount of time.

Immediately thereafter, his opponent sent a third message.

That Xie Qingcheng is lying to you and using you—aren't you curious about why he suddenly stopped being a doctor?

A fourth message.

Stop throwing your life away for him. Why don't you take a look at this video?

The video pop-up appeared again, chasing him relentlessly like a venomous serpent.

He Yu's willpower wasn't that weak, so he still didn't click on it. But the fangs of that venomous serpent had indeed sunken into his flesh, causing him to hesitate for a split second.

If his opponent wanted to quickly tear through his mental barriers, they needed to be very cunning with the entry point of their attack. And the information that the other hacker was sending him had indeed been a thorn in his side for a very long time.

Why did Xie Qingcheng have to go?

He had insisted so stubbornly on leaving. Even after He Yu had set aside his pride and asked him pathetically to stay, all Xie Qingcheng would say was *Your father is the one paying me. You can't afford to employ me.*

He Yu would never forget the way he felt back then.

In all his life, he had only ever been close to two people. One was Xie Qingcheng, and the other was Xie Xue. But that day, that evening, they both became illusions that may as well have never existed at all.

He Yu had tried so hard to live—to live like a normal person, constantly refusing to submit to his inner demons. He had tried for a whole seven years.

At that moment, he had genuinely been crumbling apart inside.

But when all was said and done, he had never truly resented Xie Qingcheng. He Yu was used to loneliness, and also to understanding all sorts of people. Some time later, he did come to understand Xie Qingcheng's choice.

After all, what they had was nothing more than a simple doctor-patient relationship, a job that paid for Xie Qingcheng. Since they were neither family nor friends, it was completely within Xie Qingcheng's rights to leave at any time. And before he left, Xie Qingcheng had neither tricked him nor lied to him; he had explained his reasons very clearly.

There was no reason for He Yu to resent him.

It was true that He Yu couldn't get over Xie Qingcheng's sudden departure. But later on, He Yu had thought to himself that at least this person had come to him and given him clear-cut articles of faith so that he had the courage to properly live on. At least this person had once told him that patients with mental illnesses needed to rebuild their bridges to society and shouldn't be isolated, that he wasn't an abnormality within society.

He Yu thought he ought to understand and forgive Xie Qingcheng for that alone.

Xie Qingcheng always had a way of winning people over and gaining their understanding.

Just like his conversation with Lu Yuzhu just now—He Yu had caught a few snatches of it. Xie Qingcheng had always been a good speaker, and after so many years, he could still convince people with logic and appeal to their hearts.

When the thought crossed his mind, He Yu glanced at Lu Yuzhu's expression. He could clearly see that she had been affected. Even if she had sunken too deep into the muck, even if this brief conversation ultimately couldn't hold up against more than a decade of suffering, she was still truly moved.

Xie Qingcheng was trying to convince Lu Yuzhu to learn the truth behind his parents' deaths. So then how had Xie Qingcheng acted toward He Yu?

Had he really been entirely honest, without hiding anything?

He Yu didn't click on the video. But his gaze did wander somewhat. He looked at Xie Qingcheng facing off against Lu Yuzhu.

It was precisely during this moment of inattention that his opponent's commands unexpectedly caught up. By the time He Yu realized what had happened, they had already broken through his defensive firewall!

Beep—beep—beep—

The countdown to detonation resumed, ticking away even faster than before. The enemy technician had sped up the five-minute timer—there was now only one minute and a dozen or so seconds before the bomb would go off!

He Yu snapped abruptly back to attention and cursed under his breath. This really wasn't the time to be thinking about such things.

He immediately refocused his attention and typed a command to forcibly shut out the distraction of the video. Sweat beaded on his smooth forehead as his almond eyes stared fixedly at the screen. His fingers moved fast enough to leave afterimages, their movements blurring together.

Meanwhile, as Lu Yuzhu watched He Yu, she grew certain that it had to be him.

This young man had to be the one using his cell phone to interfere with the organization's signal. In that case, the most important person here wasn't Xie Qingcheng but rather this young man.

She walked toward him, calm and collected. Though her eyes were locked on Xie Qingcheng, as though she were still confronting him, she was really following He Yu in her peripheral vision.

As she slowly moved closer and closer, she unlocked the safety on the handgun. There were eleven bullets inside.

He Yu rapidly typed out a string of commands and hit confirm.

There was a flash of red light.

Intercepted!

The frantic countdown was halted once again.

He Yu let out a sigh of relief and looked up. Just as he was about to give Xie Qingcheng an "okay" sign, his eyelids suddenly twitched. A sixth sense made him feel a prickling sensation at the back of his neck, and he whipped his head around—

At that very same moment, Lu Yuzhu pulled the pistol out from behind her back, pointed it at He Yu, and pulled the trigger!

A bullet burst out of the barrel with an earsplitting *bang*. The recoil from the gun made Lu Yuzhu's arm go numb, and she staggered back several steps. Her shot had gone wide and hit a cabinet full of archival materials. The entire front of the cabinet caved in from the impact, a spiderweb of cracks lacing through the glass display window before it shattered violently.

"He Yu!"

Xie Qingcheng paled and immediately rushed toward Lu Yuzhu, tackling her and pinning her to the floor. Even so, Lu Yuzhu didn't let go of the gun. She struggled and screamed at Xie Qingcheng as they tussled. And although Xie Qingcheng was in danger of being shot at any moment, since his chest was so close to the gun's muzzle, he didn't let go either.

"Move aside!" Lu Yuzhu yelled, her hair disheveled, eyes bulging from anger. She pointed the black muzzle straight at Xie Qingcheng's chest, but for some reason, she didn't shoot. "Or else I'll kill you too!"

"You can take my life, Lu Yuzhu, but you can't attack him. You can't attack a child." Xie Qingcheng spoke softly to Lu Yuzhu amid the chaos, his teeth gritted.

Unfortunately, He Yu couldn't hear his words over the sounds of Lu Yuzhu's shouts. She let out an inhuman howl of fury.

Her heart had been released from its inhibitions; that first shot had killed any remaining hesitation and compassion. Whatever reason and warmth she had once possessed now began to fade quickly.

Gradually, she lost sight of the tear-filled eyes of the mother in the sky. After all, she was a woman who had been abandoned by her child.

She had been abandoned...

Scenes from the past flashed before her eyes.

The support from the county's residents, the happiness when she took office—

"Lu Yuzhu is amazing! She's the first female graduate student in our county! She graduated from a top university and came back to be the county secretary—the first woman secretary at that! So impressive! Make sure you do great things for our county!"

"Secretary Lu, thank you for helping repair the roads in our village and building Hope Elementary School. After stalling for so many years, they just weren't willing to do it."

"Secretary Lu, thank you. If it wasn't for you, my mother would have forced me to get married... I-I still want to study... Thank you for helping me, and for allowing me to continue my studies... Thank you, really, thank you..."

"Secretary Lu, why don't you accept our thank-you gifts? So many secretaries have come and gone, but none of them were like you, taking us villagers seriously and helping us with so much..."

"Thank you."

Thank you...

Suddenly, like thunder from a clear sky, she plummeted from high up in the clouds into the abyss.

"Lu Yuzhu, someone reported you. Someone reported you for embezzlement and bribery. Please come with us to the police station."

"Yuzhu..."

"Ma...ma... Mama..."

There seemed to be a blubbering child at the bottom of the abyss, bawling indistinctly. That child reached out to her and stared at her with tears in her eyes.

"Ma...ma..." she cried incessantly.

When she returned years later, the girl who had once reached out to her now stood timidly behind another woman, afraid to approach her.

"W-who are you...?"

Who are you?

Who am I? Lu Yuzhu wondered.

In a filthy hotel dishwashing room, amid piles of dirty tablecloths and tableware—

"Lu Yuzhu, faster. Aren't you from the countryside? It's just a little bit of work; how are you so slow?"

"You know, she was a graduate student."

"Eh? A graduate student doing dishes?"

"I think she studied something pretty trendy, computer information security... How weird. What happened to her?"

"Lu Yuzhu, human resources reviewed your file again. You're an ex-convict! You can't hide such a thing when applying for a job. You should leave. I'll settle your salary for this month, but you don't have to come to work tomorrow."

In the musky massage room, between the inappropriately familiar men's faces—

"This little beauty actually seems kinda embarrassed."

"Putting on airs? Whore! Aren't you just selling yourself? Saying so much nonsense even though I've already given you money! The fact that I've taken a liking to you is already a sign of respect! Yet you dare to bite me!"

A slap to the face! Then another.

Loud, silent, corporeal, intangible, from the darkness, from every direction—slap after slap struck her across the face.

Kneeling, she cried as she clawed at the ground until her hands were covered in blood, as though she wanted to dig up a bit of light and truth to show them.

Yes, she had done something wrong.

She had done something wrong—she had accepted money...but it was only enough money to buy a pig, an unwritten rule in the village, and she didn't even accept it personally. She didn't even know...

Why did she have to be reduced to this, her family torn asunder, all alone with nowhere to go!

Why...

She couldn't defend herself even if she had a hundred mouths. Everything was blotted out by a judgment she couldn't escape.

She hoped to find someone she could trust, who could bring her hope. She waited and waited, until her heart had shriveled, but all that arrived was one disappointment after another.

"My surname is Duan. Your name is Lu Yuzhu, right? You have a graduate degree."

Suddenly, there was a spark.

It was the flare of a customer's lighter.

The man was just here to relieve his boredom, to see something new, playing around with some good-for-nothing friends. He had no intention of actually slaking his desires and no interest in the women in these cheap establishments. He found her interesting, so amid those specks of light, he slowly exhaled a breath of smoke from his cigarette.

"You studied so much." He tossed the lighter onto the tea table and looked at her. "Why are you doing this kind of work?"

Lu Yuzhu didn't respond.

Maybe it was because the man's gaze was too calm, without any trace of disdain. She could even say that it was focused and earnest, genuinely interested in understanding her.

At that moment, a heavy blow suddenly struck the crumbling walls of Lu Yuzhu's heart. She endured it for a few seconds, or perhaps a dozen, but in the end, she couldn't bear it anymore. Falling to her knees, she covered her face and began sobbing bitterly, right in front of that customer...

It was as though her sobbing and despair from days past materialized once again as Lu Yuzhu snarled at Xie Qingcheng, "Don't try to stop me from protecting him!"

It was truly frightening what a person could do when they were cornered. Who knew where she found the strength, but she managed to push back against Xie Qingcheng holding her arm down and turn toward He Yu, who was standing off to the side.

He Yu hadn't run. On the contrary, when he realized that Xie Qingcheng was in danger, he came forward to help his companion. In the past, Lu Yuzhu probably would have admired a young man like this. But now, she didn't hesitate. She strained to lift her wrist, twisting her hand... With great effort, she gripped the gun and aimed it at He Yu—and pulled the trigger!

An ear-splitting *bang* rang out!

Her first shot missed. Lu Yuzhu's eyes were already red with bloodlust, her expression shattered. The veins on her forehead popped violently as she bared her teeth, looking less like a human than a captive beast. Xie Qingcheng shoved her back to the ground, yet she refused to let go of the gun, spraying bullets in He Yu's direction as if she had gone mad.

Bang-bang-bang-bang-bang!

Ignoring his own safety, Xie Qingcheng still refused to let go despite being so close to the onslaught. But when Lu Yuzhu exploded with the strength of someone making their last stand, it was impossible for Xie Qingcheng to wrest away her gun so quickly under such chaotic circumstances.

Lu Yuzhu didn't waste a single bullet on Xie Qingcheng. She kept firing at He Yu, the man who was preventing her from blowing up the archives.

Bang-bang-bang!

Suddenly, there was a dull thud.

Xie Qingcheng's eyes went wide as he whipped around, his pupils contracting. "He Yu!"

In the end, the young man was still wounded. Because he refused to leave, because he still hadn't abandoned Xie Qingcheng and fled, he had been hit.

Clutching his shoulder, He Yu leaned heavily against the wall. He was wearing all black, so the blood pouring from his wound wasn't very obvious at first. As the fresh, red blood seeped into the black material of his clothes, it didn't look so bright under the dim lights.

But when he placed a hand over the gunshot wound, pressing his cold, pale fingers to it, his hand came away dyed by gush after gush of blood. Crimson oozed over his pallid skin, creating an immediately ghastly sight.

It was as though Xie Qingcheng's vision itself had been dyed scarlet.

Seeing that she had struck him, Lu Yuzhu panted heavily from where she was still pressed against the ground by Xie Qingcheng. Looking at the blood pouring from He Yu's injury, she suddenly tossed her head back and began to laugh. That ear-piercing laugh was mournful and terrifying. Tears began to flow down her cheeks and into her disheveled hair.

"Ha ha ha ha... Ha ha ha ha ha..."

Her grip loosened, and the gun fell to the ground.

Xie Qingcheng jumped to his feet and immediately ran toward He Yu. He Yu tried to pick up his phone again with his injured arm; he wanted to finish keying in his last command. He made two attempts, but his hands were shaking too hard, so the phone, its screen already covered in blood, slipped from his grip and clattered to the ground.

"He Yu, you..."

"...I'm fine. We have to go, Xie Qingcheng."

He Yu's eyes were fierce and cold as he stared at Lu Yuzhu's face. His complexion was deathly pale, sweat dripping from his forehead. His words, however, were addressed to Xie Qingcheng.

"You won't be able to get anything out of her. She's in too deep." He paused. "I know you'll regret missing your chance with this witness, but if we don't leave now, it'll be too late."

As if to confirm his words, the other technician quickly broke through his firewall and regained control of the detonator now that He Yu could no longer keep up with the coding battle.

He Yu furrowed his brow. He wasn't all that afraid of injury, and to him, blood was an exceedingly unremarkable thing. What worried him was that his injured hand could no longer grip anything.

They'd lost control of the situation.

"Let's go."

276... 275... 274...

The countdown flew by, speeding up once again. Supporting He Yu, Xie Qingcheng turned to look at the woman collapsed amid a web of detonation wires through his bloodshot peach-blossom eyes.

Lu Yuzhu was like a moth caught in a spider's web. She occasionally trembled with laughter, but tears streamed down her face. She raised her arm and covered her eyes. The top half of her face was tearful, yet the bottom half was still twisted in maniacal laughter.

Xie Qingcheng squeezed his eyes shut. The moment he turned around, he felt as if he was moving in slow motion, as if he was looking away from the ice-cold bodies of his parents from nineteen years ago.

But there was still one last bullet in Lu Yuzhu's handgun!

As she sobbed and laughed and lost her mind, she heard them as they made to leave. She instinctively picked up the gun she had just discarded and pointed it at them...

"Get down!" shouted He Yu.

Xie Qingcheng's full attention was on He Yu's injuries, and his back was fully turned to Lu Yuzhu. So He Yu was the one who noticed Lu Yuzhu's movement this time around.

Bang!

Who knew what He Yu was thinking. Perhaps he wasn't thinking at all, and it was just the instinct of an evil dragon protecting his hoard. He immediately shoved Xie Qingcheng down—and that caused the final bullet to strike his already-injured arm, just slightly above the first gunshot wound.

He Yu's body spasmed in pain and went limp in Xie Qingcheng's arms, blood splattering all over as Xie Qingcheng looked on.

Xie Qingcheng's scalp prickled. He was a doctor, but at that moment, he was completely incapable of handling this outpour of blood...

"Why did you...!"

He Yu didn't make a sound. His dark eyes were fearful as he gazed at his wound, as if he was also thinking, *Why did I do this?*

Indeed...

Why...?

The timer was still frantically ticking away, so Xie Qingcheng couldn't afford to waste any more time. Propping He Yu upright, he grabbed the injured boy and sprinted down the corridor...

He Yu's hot blood trickled from his shoulder. As Xie Qingcheng kept running, he stopped thinking about what had happened in the past and how he had forfeited this last living witness.

Holding He Yu tightly as he ran toward the exit, he said to him, "Everything's going to be fine. I'm getting you out of here."

"...Don't worry... I'm not afraid of these things, Xie Qingcheng." He Yu's voice floated up quietly. They made it through the hallway into the main hall, their unsteady footfalls echoing behind them.

He Yu was still very calm.

"I'm not afraid of death or blood, and I don't care about pain either—remember?"

Xie Qingcheng didn't know what to say.

"It was probably because I don't fear death enough that I did that just now." The color began to drain from He Yu's lips. "It's fine."

But Xie Qingcheng cared; he *ached*. He wrapped his arms tighter around He Yu. Because He Yu had lost so much blood so quickly, his face was already alarmingly pale.

He was such a young kid—only nineteen years old. A normal kid would still be asking their parents for allowance money, cheerfully playing games, nonchalantly reading books, feeling youthful strength course through them without worries, looking forward to a future of boundless prospects.

But what about He Yu?

He knew very well that there was only darkness before his eyes; ahead of him, there were only the three long-deceased psychological Ebola patients leering at him, telling him that his entire life would be a long night without a dawn, a dead end with no way out.

But still, he gritted his teeth and struggled to crawl toward that future which might still hold some semblance of hope.

Childhood, innocence, laughter, carelessness... None of it had anything to do with He Yu.

He was only nineteen... No matter how impressive or capable, in the end, he was still a child.

At that moment, Xie Qingcheng finally woke from the muddled chaos that the desire to avenge his parents had plunged him into. He finally realized why he'd had the feeling before that something was inappropriate: he shouldn't have dragged He Yu into this.

Why did he do such a thing?

Who was He Yu to him?

This boy had already worked hard enough. Xie Qingcheng had only given He Yu the most basic kind of concern as his personal physician. How was that enough for this boy to put his life on the line and jump with him into a living hell?

Xie Qingcheng's hand, which was covering He Yu's wound, trembled slightly.

He had never felt much sorrow for He Yu before—at most, he'd felt a sense of responsibility, care, and pity. But at that moment, the young man's warm blood seemed to trickle along his skin, down his spine, to pierce his heart and stab deep into the marrow of his bones.

That was right... They were merely a doctor and a patient with a relationship of employment that couldn't be any more clear-cut. For Xie Qingcheng, because of a personal debt and the unique characteristics of psychological Ebola, he was supposed to pay special attention to He Yu.

However, the same couldn't be said for He Yu. He Yu didn't owe him anything. When he looked at Xie Qingcheng, he shouldn't have had any emotions apart from those accorded to a doctor.

Yet He Yu had still accompanied him to the library.

Just because Xie Qingcheng had said, *I want to know the truth behind my parents' deaths.*

He desperately wanted to find the perpetrator. But that had nothing at all to do with He Yu...

As Xie Qingcheng ran outside with He Yu in tow, keeping firm pressure on He Yu's injured shoulder, he said hoarsely, "I'll bring you to the hospital right away. Don't talk too much."

He Yu was very quiet.

Then, after a long moment of silence, the young man let out a soft laugh. "I'm fine, really. However, I wanted to ask you something, Doctor Xie." His breath puffed out right by Xie Qingcheng's ear. It was scorching hot, yet it seemed to carry a slight chill. "I really want to know—back then, why did you suddenly stop being a doctor? Was it really as simple as your contract coming to an end?"

Xie Qingcheng was silent.

"Why was it that no matter how I tried to keep you, you still rejected me?"

Xie Qingcheng still didn't answer.

"It's been seven years, Xie Qingcheng. My dad told me that outside of employment, there's goodwill between people. Today... Today, I really want to ask you." He Yu was still bleeding, but he didn't bother looking down. Instead, in the terrifyingly endless night, his black eyes only gazed unblinkingly at Xie Qingcheng.

The look in his eyes was the same as the one from all those years ago, when that boy suddenly became childish in his helplessness, so childish that he tried to use his allowance to convince Xie Qingcheng to stay. No matter how high that boy's pain tolerance was or how numb his mind was, after suffering these two gunshot wounds, he would still be hurt.

He Yu's voice was very soft. Perhaps it was because they had run too fast, but it even sounded a bit hoarse. "Xie Qingcheng... Back then, did you really not feel an ounce of extra compassion for me?"

43

Who Would've Thought That the Truth Would Be like This?

Xie Qingcheng stood silently with his back to the light. In the darkness of the night, He Yu couldn't decipher his expression; he only felt the hand supporting him tremble slightly.

He Yu asked another question. "Xie Qingcheng, why did you have to leave?" Even in his current state, he could still remain calm. It was as though the more terrifying and critical the situation was, the less concerned he became.

Xie Qingcheng didn't answer him.

"You lied to me, didn't you? The reason you left wasn't just because your contract was up, right?"

The look in that child's eyes.

The look in this young man's eyes.

Both were calm, childish, stubborn, but they also seemed...indifferent. They gazed at him unflinchingly, digging deeper and deeper but still unable to find the answer they sought.

Xie Qingcheng abruptly felt that he couldn't face that persistent stare. He closed his eyes. "Let me get you out of here first."

There wasn't much time left, so he redoubled his efforts and continued running toward the exit of the archives with He Yu in tow. When at last they ran out of the silent, unlit building into the noisy hubbub outside of whirling police lights and wailing sirens, it felt for a moment as if they had been dropped into a kaleidoscope.

Zheng Jingfeng had also uncovered the true meaning behind the letter L at this point. With the location deduced, the red and blue flashing police lights descended on the target like the tide coming in from every direction at once.

When Xie Qingcheng brought the still-bleeding He Yu down the steps, half supporting, half carrying him, Zheng Jingfeng pulled his car door open with a *bang* and stepped out of the vehicle.

This time, the criminal investigation unit's captain's expression was frosty. Concern and anger shone from his panther-like eyes, the two contradictory emotions flitting over his face like a shadow play, their steely blades flashing brilliantly as they glanced off each other. "Xie Qingcheng..."

"The archives are about to explode," said Xie Qingcheng as soon as he neared Zheng Jingfeng. "Don't let anyone else go in."

Zheng Jingfeng looked like he very much wanted to grab the two of them by their necks and slap handcuffs on their wrists—but then he met Xie Qingcheng's eyes... They resembled Zhou Muying's eyes so much that he found himself looking away at the last moment, unable to maintain eye contact.

There was blood on Xie Qingcheng's face. Zheng Jingfeng didn't know whose blood it was, but it made him feel incomparably guilty.

It was a fact that he couldn't allow Xie Qingcheng to get too close to the case—Xie Qingcheng wasn't a police officer, and he didn't have the qualifications to be too deeply involved. Even if everything happening now was related to the unsolved case of his parents' deaths from nineteen years ago, the only thing he could tell Xie Qingcheng was: *This is classified, you must hand the matter over to us.*

However, an individual was bound to be more flexible than an organization; the more regulated the organization, the more this held true. That was to say nothing of how there was likely a dirty cop amongst the police, or how these criminals seemed to be part of an international crime syndicate with an excellent grasp of cutting-edge technology. Although Xie Qingcheng had entrusted this case to them for nineteen years, they still couldn't give him a satisfactory answer. Even when it came to this riddle involving the archives, all kinds of obstacles ensured that the police were still slower to get here than Xie Qingcheng.

Zheng Jingfeng didn't have time to express his shock or ask any more questions. "Fall back immediately," he said into his two-way radio. "The archives are going to explode. Everyone, fall back!"

He then ushered Xie Qingcheng and He Yu into the police car and closed the door with a *thunk*. Everyone else in the car stared at Xie Qingcheng with a very strange look in their eyes.

As Xie Qingcheng glanced at the broadcasting tower not too far in the distance, it seemed to have already returned to its usual, brightly lit appearance. That scarlet "drop the hanky" game of death video had disappeared, and in its place, a person's silhouette flickered across the tower. It might have been an advertisement; Xie Qingcheng didn't get a good look at it before the police car's engine rumbled to life.

By now, the main roads of the campus were nearly deserted. The police car sped off lightning fast with its flashing red and blue lights for a few hundred meters, before—

Bang!

A shuddering sound like muffled thunder came from behind them. Followed closely by—

Ka-booom!

An earth-shattering noise, accompanied by the shrieks of all the people who had witnessed this spectacle. Sure enough, the archives had exploded. Like a landslide, shards of brick and tile buried the past in an instant.

Leaning back in the car, Xie Qingcheng would have only needed to look through the car's rear windows to see the roiling flames leaping into the air from the direction of the archives like a swirling tempest sweeping up crime and punishment in its wake. Grinding them into dust, shattering them into ruined fragments that could never be reassembled.

But Xie Qingcheng never looked back. Instead, he closed his eyes.

The clues had all disintegrated... He couldn't look back.

It was a long time before the deafening explosions subsided.

Inside the car, it was very quiet, as everyone's attention was focused on the scene of the crime. After the car came to a stop, the police officers got out one by one. There was the rustling wind blowing outside, the crackling fire in the distance, and also...

"Are you dissatisfied with something?"

It was a man's voice. It was quite loud, as it came simultaneously from several of the cell phones in the car.

"If you're dissatisfied with anything, you should take it up with the hospital."

Xie Qingcheng paused and opened his eyes—was he so shaken that he was hearing things? And his own voice, at that?

"Don't argue with me here."

No, he wasn't just hearing things. His eyes flew wide open as realization dawned. It was *that* video! The hackers had never stopped their video hijacking!

The moment Xie Qingcheng recognized the video that was being projected onto the broadcasting tower—as well as all the phones in the vicinity of Huzhou University—he immediately understood why those police officers had eyed him with such odd expressions. The video must have already been playing for a while—by the time He Yu and Xie Qingcheng had made it out of the building, the broadcasting tower had already been taken over by this scene.

Xie Qingcheng's phone was still powered off, but when he turned it back on, it was immediately hijacked by the hackers' signal, and he received the video synced to the one that was playing out on the tower.

It showed him, from quite a few years ago.

He was wearing the uniform of Huzhou First Hospital: a pure white coat with the hospital's pale-blue crest stitched onto it and a laminated name tag and two pens clipped to his chest. His surroundings were chaotic—he was encircled by the hospital's patients, who watched as he stood before the door of his unit facing a disheveled, unkempt woman.

Xie Qingcheng knew immediately what this was, and when it had happened. But...

His expression shifting subtly, he looked at He Yu.

He Yu was frowning, not yet fully cognizant of what was going on. However, he had already realized that this video was the same one that hacker had wanted him to open before—the video he was supposed to watch to see "if it was worth it."

His shoulder was still bleeding. The doctor from the police unit who was administering first aid said to him, "I'm going to help you clean the wound and stop the bleeding, but it will hurt—try to bear it."

He Yu said indifferently, "Thank you."

Pain, blood, even death—to him, they meant little. He was entirely focused on the tower and its ever-changing illumination.

The scene was still playing out.

The unkempt woman in the video was howling, "Why do you need me to show relevant ID? Why do you need the security guards to question me? Do you think it's easy for me to come see the doctor? It's so hard to register with your hospital's specialists! Scalpers have snatched up all the spots! I need to pay five hundred yuan just to get an appointment! Why does it have to be like this?[8] Apparently poor people don't just deserve to die, we also deserve to be shafted by you doctors and discriminated against, is that right? Do you think I *want* to be filthy and reeking like this? As soon as I closed my stand at four in the morning, I came to wait in line outside the hospital for you to open. Do you think I have time to be all squeaky clean and neat like you? I'm really not a bad person!"

But that young Xie Qingcheng in the video stood with his hands in the pockets of his white coat, looking coldly at the sobbing woman who was hugging her knees in front of him. He said indifferently, "You come and sit in front of my consulting room even though you're not my patient—how do I know what you're planning to do after what happened with Yi Beihai?"

"I just want to see a doctor!" the woman cried.

His face devoid of expression, Xie Qingcheng said, "You want to be treated, but I want to be safe. I'll have to trouble you not to sit in front of my consulting room. Go where you're supposed to go, whether that's internal medicine or neurosurgery. My unit isn't related to the registration number you have."

---

8 *Patients are assigned a number at registration that determines the order they're seen by the doctor; scalpers will sometimes buy up these numbers to sell them off.*

"But all the other waiting rooms are full, and I'm not allowed to sit on the floor. It was so hard for me to find this spot. I just want to rest for a bit. I've been standing all day..."

"Save your breath for the security guards. I'm just a doctor who's taking a paycheck. I don't want to run the risk of dying in the line of duty."

The patients standing around couldn't help but feel a surge of fury in their hearts. They originally had no intention of getting into a disagreement with a doctor and were doing their best to restrain their anger. But when the woman burst into tears at Xie Qingcheng's harsh, aggressively overbearing manner of speaking, someone roared at him, "What are you doing! Do you not have a mother? Surely you're not going to condemn every patient because of one bad apple? Yi Beihai was an outlier! Someone as selfish as you can't compare to Mr. Qin Ciyan at all! Do you think you deserve to be a doctor?"

Xie Qingcheng looked up, revealing a pair of peach-blossom eyes that were incisive to the point of being cruel. "I'm a doctor regardless of your opinion. I don't think dying for the sake of a patient is worth it, and to be murdered by a lunatic would be such a waste it'd be laughable. Medicine is merely a profession—you shouldn't romanticize it with selfless sacrifice and guilt-trip me like this."

He enunciated his words clearly: "The life of a doctor will always be more valuable than the life of a lunatic who can't even control himself. Do you understand?"

For a moment, everyone fell silent.

The video footage became a bit chaotic after that. In the rage of the mob, someone shoved the person who was doing the filming, causing the video to shake and become blurry. All that could be heard was the furious cursing of the patients.

As the video got to that point, notifications from various group chats and direct messages started flooding the countless phones that were broadcasting the clip.

All the phones in the car that weren't set to silent, including Xie Qingcheng's own, started buzzing incessantly.

It seemed like the video had been swiftly spread to every corner of the internet.

He Yu sat in the police car, allowing the medic to tend to the gunshot wounds on his shoulder. He'd had his forehead pressed against the window the whole time, quietly watching the video splashed across the broadcasting tower.

It was the video that his hacker opponent had sent to him, the one he'd chosen not to play.

Xie Qingcheng could feel his heart sinking.

So, this was it.

In order to mess with He Yu, their opponents had chosen to reveal this video.

Xie Qingcheng wished he could say something to He Yu, but he didn't know what he should say—or if there was even anything he could try to explain. He stopped watching the video; he knew very well what he'd said and done back then.

The sins he couldn't explain and the secrets he had to keep that were hidden within that video—at that very moment, they had all been spilled into the open for everyone to see.

He didn't care. He had known when he did those things and said those words that he'd be crucified for it after the fact, that he'd face a lifetime of criticism, that everything had a price. He'd already been prepared to keep that secret for a lifetime, and he knew very well the kind of future he'd face if the video got out.

But when his gaze landed on the still, quiet youth beside him...

He Yu's shoulder was still bleeding with no sign of stopping. The doctor had treated it with a tourniquet, but the sickly scent of blood still suffused this half-sealed police command car. Inexplicably, Xie Qingcheng thought back to a few hours ago, to the first time he looked at this youth as an equal. He Yu had extended his hand to him. At that time, no one was willing to help him; even Chen Man had chosen to follow the rules.

But He Yu had said, "I can help you."

That outstretched hand was fine-boned, broad, clean, and beautiful; even the nails were neatly trimmed. It was clear it belonged to a pampered young master who took good care of himself.

Free of blood, free of injury.

There were only faint scars on his wrists, but those had already healed.

"Why...would you help me?"

"Because you did the same for me once."

"I've never, ever forgotten."

The glaring crimson stung Xie Qingcheng's eyes.

Just as the images from that uninterruptable video cut their way into He Yu's field of vision, the scene projected on the broadcast tower changed again. It was now showing a conference room at the hospital.

It seemed as if Xie Qingcheng had just given an outstanding academic talk, and the administration was in the middle of acknowledging his professional achievement. But his colleagues clapping in the audience weren't enthusiastic about the situation at all. It looked like this video was taken soon after his contentious encounter with that patient.

The director thanked him. Xie Qingcheng stood up, and his gaze swept calmly over every single person below the stage. He didn't speak any words of gratitude. What he said was, "This will be the last time I give a talk at this hospital. I've decided to resign."

No one spoke. A few brainless medical interns were still clapping robotically, but before they could get more than a couple of claps in, they came back to their senses. Their eyes widened in shock as they stared blankly at Xie Qingcheng, their mouths hanging open. Everyone else in the audience wore the same stunned expression.

Xie Qingcheng was the youngest and most promising doctor at their facility. He was so formidable that he scarcely seemed human. Prior to his tenure, Huzhou First Hospital had never had an assistant director as young as him. Even if he'd recently made some improper remarks, it wasn't anything so extreme that people wouldn't get over it eventually. After all, what doctor didn't get into a few conflicts with patients over the course of their career?

But Xie Qingcheng said he was going to resign.

The director's expression instantly stiffened. With a dry chuckle, he said, "Doctor Xie, why don't you sit down for now? We can discuss work matters after the conference is over."

The head of medical affairs also forced a smile and took over the microphone. "Doctor Xie, you've probably been feeling upset lately. None of us can accept what happened to Professor Qin, and your unit was close to his, so you must have been close colleagues. You even witnessed Professor Qin's sacrifice firsthand, so we can understand how you feel..."

"I didn't know Qin Ciyan very well," Xie Qingcheng said, cutting her off. "Nor am I feeling upset because of Professor Qin. I just don't want to be the next Qin Ciyan."

A few of Qin Ciyan's students in the audience couldn't bear it anymore. "Xie Qingcheng, watch your mouth! What do you mean you don't want to be the next Qin Ciyan! My teacher devoted his entire life to medicine, how dare you—"

"But I don't."

Silence fell.

"Medicine is just a career to me. I will complete all my responsibilities with due care, but I don't think it's normal to give one's life in this line of work. Nor do I understand why so many of you here today feel so strongly about it to the point of finding it glorious, to the point where you would ignore your own safety to treat patients without following the proper procedures. Professor Qin is worthy of respect, but what happened to him in the end was his own fault. Why did he elect to perform surgery on an unstable man's mother when the paperwork hadn't been properly filed?"

Qin Ciyan's students shot to their feet. "Xie Qingcheng, you—!"

"Forgive me, but I don't understand at all."

The conference had become a scene of chaos; the grief and fury felt by the younger doctors couldn't be suppressed anymore.

"How dare you sneer like this!"

"What do you mean it was his own fault? You think that Professor Qin's to blame for his own death?"

"Xie Qingcheng, have you forgotten how you spoke of mentally ill patients in the past? You were the one who wholeheartedly supported letting them live in society, saying we should accept them and treat them as if they are ordinary people! How come that's changed? You got scared the moment there was an incident, didn't you? You saw with your own eyes how Professor Qin lost his life in the line of duty that day, and now you're afraid!"

"You watched as he was thrown into a pool of blood, saw the red splattered all over his office, and you got scared, didn't you? You're afraid that it will happen to you one day! All the patients you interact with are mentally ill; you're in far more danger than him! If you're afraid, just say it! No one will make fun of you! But stop cheapening Professor Qin's sacrifice!"

"Yes, I am afraid," Xie Qingcheng replied coolly.

The young doctor gnashed their teeth. "And yet you have the guts to talk about not discriminating against the mentally ill—"

"Tell me, how do you talk to cancer patients? Do you tell them, 'Oh, my condolences. You're about to die soon'?" There wasn't the slightest hint of expression on Xie Qingcheng's face; his features were colder than hoarfrost. "I'm sure you don't. The truth is one thing, and the words we say are another. As a doctor in mental health, I need to give my patients hope and encouragement. I need to let them feel as if they're being treated like normal people. But ask yourself, everyone. Do any of you truly feel no apprehension at all toward mentally ill patients who are identified as dangerous? Which one of you would willingly interact with them alone and go so far as to hand your life over to such patients without the slightest reservations? Could any of you do it?"

"So...everything you said was nothing more than superficial platitudes... You're just... You're just a despicable fake putting on hypocritical airs!"

Xie Qingcheng didn't argue with the people who had lost their tempers; just as always, he was extremely calm, so calm he almost seemed callous, so callous he almost seemed cold-blooded. "Qin Ciyan might have been a saint. But I'm nothing more than an ordinary person. When I come to work and put on these clothes, I'm a doctor who's treating his patients. When I leave work and take these clothes off, I have a family—I have a wife and a little sister to take care of. I haven't reached Qin Ciyan's level of enlightenment."

No one spoke.

"If you want to become Qin Ciyan, then go ahead," Xie Qingcheng said, removing the medal which he'd just received and putting it back into its velvet-lined brocade box. His gaze was extremely sober and exceedingly calm. "I just want to be an ordinary person."

At this point, the video suddenly flashed and abruptly flickered and faded to nothing.

Now that the countdown on the WZL death game had concluded, the police couldn't allow the perpetrators to continue their outrageous behavior. They had gained the ability to reclaim control over the information transmission channels a little while before—but they didn't dare to act rashly on the chance that it would precipitate a terror attack on Huzhou's innocent citizens. So they could only let their opponents do as they wished.

But now, there was no way the police could allow the video to continue playing. With an order from the top, the "bloody sword" broadcasting tower that had bustled with activity for the whole night seemed to wake up from its demonic possession at last as its central power supply was cut off.

A *bang* rang out with the massive power outage.

Like curtains lowering over a stage at the end of a play, the entire broadcasting tower went dark as all its light vanished in an instant. Like a giant beast that had been tranquilized in the middle of the school's campus after spending the night going berserk, it had returned to being utterly, deathly still, without any signs of life.

Behind the broadcasting tower, the conflagration was still raging, its soaring flames dyeing the night sky over the archives crimson. Police officers surrounded the area around that centuries-old building blazing away; someone had dialed the 119 emergency dispatch line.

Every corner of the campus was in an uproar; no one was sleeping tonight.

But inside the car, it was deathly silent.

The video was gone.

The scene was over.

But He Yu's eyes, which had been fixed on the broadcasting tower this whole time, were still gazing at that completely darkened building—he hadn't moved a muscle, extraordinarily serene to the point of being a little frightening.

"The vast majority of mental illnesses are normal people's responses to abnormal circumstances..."

"Social inequality, abnormal environments; the main culprits dealing the greatest damage to their *psyches, very ironically, nearly all originate from their families, from their workplaces, from society—they originate from* us."

"He Yu, sooner or later, you'll have to depend on yourself to walk out of the shadows in your heart."

"You need to rebuild the bridges that link you with other people and society."

"I wish you an early recovery."

"Hey, little devil."

"Doesn't it hurt...?"

Silence.

At this moment, the words that Xie Qingcheng had said back then—the words that pried open the shackles in He Yu's heart, the encouragement that convinced He Yu to grudgingly view Xie Qingcheng as different from the others, the comfort that Xie Qingcheng once gave He Yu when he had been going through his most difficult times—they all seemed to float up like a cloud of dust, rendered indescribably ridiculous and cold.

He Yu looked at the tower.

His eyes were just as terrifyingly black as that unlit building.

Counting the days, it couldn't have been more than a month after this video was filmed that Xie Qingcheng resigned from his post as his personal physician and then disappeared without a trace. It was as though Xie Qingcheng had been escaping from the lair of a predatory beast, or perhaps fleeing from someone with a contagious disease.

As the medic cleaned the wound in He Yu's arm, it suddenly seemed to throb with agonizing pain. Otherwise, why would he feel cold all over? And why would he have gone so pale?

"He Yu."

He Yu didn't answer.

"I meant..."

He Yu heard Xie Qingcheng's voice from beside him. Patiently, he waited for Xie Qingcheng to finish his sentence.

One second passed, then another.

But Xie Qingcheng did not continue.

He really had said all those things. No matter what the reason was, no matter his goal or the secrets hidden within his words, they had all come out of his own mouth. In the wake of Qin Ciyan's murder, it was true that He Yu was the one Xie Qingcheng had sacrificed.

The truth was that he didn't have any excuses to explain himself to this young man.

He Yu suddenly felt ridiculous—he disliked doctors to begin with, and he had disliked Xie Qingcheng in particular from the start. How had this man earned his trust and persuaded him to open the gates of his heart to him? Hadn't it been precisely because of this so-called "equal treatment"—because Xie Qingcheng had viewed him as someone who was a part of regular society, supporting him as he walked out of his dark dragon's lair and ventured into the boundless sunlight outside?

But after Qin Ciyan's murder and before leaving his post, what had Xie Qingcheng said when He Yu wasn't around, in places he didn't even know of?

He Yu slowly closed his eyes. He felt like someone had backhanded him viciously across the cheek. That slap had traveled through many long, heavy years before coming to land on his face, so it should have lost its momentum. He Yu didn't think that he could possibly feel any emotional disturbance from this slap.

But he still felt a faint, stinging pain in his flesh.

"All right. I've bandaged your wounds for the time being," said the police medic who'd been overseeing He Yu's treatment. "I'll have someone to take you to the hospital. You still need to get this looked at as soon as possible. Come with me to the other car."

There was no response from He Yu.

"Hello?" the medic prompted.

He Yu opened his eyes. He was too calm—so calm he seemed a bit terrifying.

Phone calls were furiously pouring in one after another on Xie Qingcheng's phone, whether out of care, concern, or a desire for confirmation...the callers had various motives.

Xie Qingcheng didn't pick up. He just stared at He Yu's profile.

In a gentle, refined tone, He Yu said to the police medic, "Thank you for going to such trouble."

Then, with one long-legged stride, he got out of the car. He took a few steps forward. It wasn't until this moment, when he was about to leave, that he was finally willing to stop and turn his head slightly to the side. The flashing red and blue police beacons illuminated his unblemished face with a steadily flickering border of light.

He smiled softly, firelight flaring through his dark eyes. "Doctor Xie. Who would've thought that the truth would be like this?"

Xie Qingcheng didn't say a word.

"It must have been such a sacrifice on your part to pretend for so many years. You've really worked hard."

It's truly too ironic, He Yu thought.

All these years, the one thing he feared the most was being treated like he was different from the rest. It was Xie Qingcheng who had walked into his lonely lair and bestowed upon him a beautiful set of convictions, giving him a layer of armor to carry through life for the first time and allowing him to believe that someday he could find a bridge he could cross to the rest of society.

He had believed in Xie Qingcheng so firmly. No matter how much He Yu disliked him, no matter how clearly Xie Qingcheng drew the lines between them, no matter how callously Xie Qingcheng had left back then—He Yu still understood his reasons, and he'd clung to those words of encouragement like a fool. Wearing the armor Xie Qingcheng had given him, he'd soldiered on with this stubborn attachment for so long.

But, as it turned out, the inside of that armor was lined with thorns.

He Yu had thought that it could fend off the mockery flung at him from the outside world, but in the moment when he least expected it, hundreds of thorns and thousands of blades had been released from the inside, piercing through him from head to toe.

The articles of faith that Xie Qingcheng had given him were false. Even he had lied to him.

"Xie Qingcheng, if you really were so scared of me, you could have told me directly right from the beginning. You didn't need to put on an act, and you especially didn't need to tell me so many great principles against your own beliefs. At least that wouldn't have been so..."

He Yu trailed off, leaving his sentence unfinished.

His silhouette looked terribly lonely, but his voice was still exceedingly calm—just the way Xie Qingcheng had once hoped for him, just like Xie Qingcheng had once taught him to strive for. The epitome of calm.

In the end, He Yu only chuckled. The blood he'd lost was still on Xie Qingcheng's hands, but his mocking laughter had already floated into the wind.

Then, he turned around completely and followed the police officers toward the other car without so much as a backward glance.

Once

It was as if that thirteen-year-old boy had once again appeared before his eyes—gazing at him, obstinate and helpless, as he silently restrained his feelings with all his might.

The day Xie Qingcheng left the He family, he felt he saw something precious in that youth's eyes, something that didn't just belong to a patient. But his heart was too hardened, and he wasn't very sensitive to certain emotions in the first place. Besides, he had been caught up in so many other things at the time and hadn't been inclined to consider a child's feelings very carefully. Thus, he had instinctively doubted that those eyes contained emotions that transcended a doctor-patient relationship.

He'd had to leave.

He Yu was indeed someone he had sacrificed—someone he had abandoned.

Amidst the chaotic aftermath of Qin Ciyan's murder, He Yu was the child that Xie Qingcheng had steeled his heart to leave behind...

Once, when that child had been dragged into a whirlpool by the undertow of his illness, he had looked at Xie Qingcheng with that same unwavering gaze. The look in He Yu's eyes was like that of a fledgling dragon who had held out its little claw to humans and trusted them only to end up being deceived. Its wings were broken, its spine torn out, and its talons snapped. Injured, it lay on the rock in a daze, its little wings and claws caked with blood. But it was a dragon; in order not to lose face, it didn't dare to wail too loudly.

He Yu was a prideful person, so he had said with as much self-control as he could muster, "Xie Qingcheng, in these past few years, I've gone through many doctors. They had me take medicine, gave me shots, and looked at me with an expression that said that I was a singular, unique patient. You were the only one who was different. You were the only one who treated me like someone who should integrate into society. You told me that taking medicine and getting shots weren't the most important things, and that the most crucial step was to make connections with others and build up a strong sense of self—that's the only way I can keep holding on. Xie Qingcheng, we're not very close, but I still..."

Xie Qingcheng had said nothing when He Yu trailed off.

"I...I thought you saw me as a normal person with feelings, not just as a patient."

Despite his prideful heart, He Yu had still been forced to say something so childish in the end.

"I have a lot of allowance, I can—"

I can hire you.

I can keep you here.

Could you please not leave?

Could you please stay with me?

At that time, Xie Qingcheng had thought that He Yu's intense unwillingness to let him go was perhaps wholly due to Xie Xue. Perhaps even He Yu himself had thought the same.

But in reality, it wasn't.

When Xie Qingcheng closed his eyes and thought back to that period of time, he remembered how he would sling a much younger He Yu over his shoulder when he refused to receive his shots or take his medicine, how He Yu's scrambling hands would obediently relax, how he could almost feel the weight of the boy calmly going limp against his shoulder.

"Doctor Xie."

"Xie Qingcheng."

That voice had transformed from soft and immature to raspy as He Yu entered adolescence. Even later, it held a sorrow that was forcibly covered up with stubbornness and indifference: "Xie Qingcheng, you might not be mentally ill, but you're even more heartless than me."

You're heartless...

My illness hasn't gotten better yet. It's still severe, so why did you abandon me...?

Bang! That earsplitting gunshot, the blood that spurted out and spilled over his palm, that young man's coldly penetrating almond eyes in the darkness.

Doctor Xie, who would've thought that the truth would be like this...? To pretend for so many years... You've really worked hard.

When an abandoned, injured fledgling dragon gazed at the human who had trodden its innocence and enthusiasm underfoot, would it have an expression like this?

The warm weight on Xie Qingcheng's shoulders seemed to fade away. He closed his eyes. The only heat that remained now was in the place where He Yu's blood had splashed onto his palm.

Suddenly, someone spoke up from behind him. "You must be very tired."

The weight on Xie Qingcheng's shoulders returned as a hand pressed against that exact same spot.

He opened his eyes. He was in the police station. The person pressing a hand against his shoulder was Zheng Jingfeng. Amidst the chaos and hubbub, Xie Qingcheng had been lost in his memories of his past with He Yu.

It was already very late now. Xie Qingcheng was sitting in an interrogation room across from a young policeman who had already spent more than an hour recording his testimony. After greeting Zheng Jingfeng, the junior officer tidied up his files and left.

Xie Qingcheng wasn't Zheng Jingfeng's relative, but Zheng Jingfeng had been especially close to his parents, so he had recused himself from the investigation and only entered the interrogation room now.

"Want a smoke?" Zheng Jingfeng tentatively struck up a conversation with Xie Qingcheng.

"Yes, please," Xie Qingcheng replied wearily.

Zheng Jingfeng passed him a cigarette and sat down opposite him. After lighting the cigarette, Xie Qingcheng bit down on the filter and slid the lighter back across the table.

As he took a drag, he slowly raised his exhausted eyes. Zheng Jingfeng met them. Even though he knew the man before him quite well, Zheng Jingfeng still found himself slightly unsettled by Xie Qingcheng's gaze at that moment. It was too unyielding, too sharp. Like a dagger or a boulder. Like the eyes of his deceased mother and father.

Or perhaps it was even more unnerving. Because when Zheng Jingfeng looked at Xie Qingcheng now, after everything that happened tonight, those eyes didn't hold much vulnerability at all. He only looked tired.

The hand that Zheng Jingfeng was using to light his cigarette trembled involuntarily.

"Why aren't you saying anything?" Xie Qingcheng's voice was slightly raspy, which at least made him seem a little more like a normal person. "You didn't come in just to sit there."

"Because I don't feel like saying what I ought to say. You knew the risks, yet you still insisted on doing what you did." Zheng Jingfeng heaved a sigh. "Plus, whether you believe it or not, I was thinking about how to comfort you the whole time before I came in. But now that I'm here, I've realized that it's not really necessary." Lao-Zheng looked at Xie Qingcheng's practically expressionless face.

Xie Qingcheng dragged the ashtray toward himself. Then, he plucked the cigarette from his chapped lips and tapped off the ash. "Indeed, it's not necessary."

"But, you know, looking at you right now, there are a few things I can't help thinking about."

"Like what?"

Zheng Jingfeng sighed deeply. "I'm reminded of when you were little..."

Xie Qingcheng said nothing.

"When I first met you, you were still in elementary school. Your mom had caught a cold that day, so you decided to come to the cafeteria all on your own to get her food." Zheng Jingfeng's steely eyes misted over with softness at his reminiscence. "Your mom loved egg drop soup with tomato. You weren't very tall back then, so you couldn't reach the ladle when you stood next to that big pot of soup. When I saw you, I went over to help... When you looked up to thank me, there was no need for an introduction—I knew right away, the moment I saw your eyes, that you were Zhou Muying and Xie Ping's kid. After that, you'd often come to the bureau to do your homework. When you were tired, you'd drape your mom or dad's jacket over your shoulders and take a nap at the table while you waited for them to finish their work. I've met a lot of the kids from our unit, but you were the quietest and most mature of them all."

Zheng Jingfeng exhaled a ring of smoke and tilted his head back, following it with his eyes.

"Later on, I couldn't help but be curious. I asked your dad, 'How did you teach your kid to be so well-behaved?' He laughed and said to me that no one told you what to do. That was just your personality. I didn't believe him, I just thought Lao-Xie was showing off, so I ran over to ask you—I don't know if you still remember, but back then, I asked you how you were so impressive... You showed me your prize from a martial arts competition that you had just won that day," the old captain said. "And then you told me...

"You wanted to be a police officer."

At the same time, Xie Qingcheng said, "I wanted to be a police officer."

The two of them fell into silence.

After a while, Zheng Jingfeng said, "At that age, most children only have vague ideas when you ask them about their dreams for the future. But not you—as soon as I saw the light in your eyes, I knew that you were serious. You were probably sure about it since you were little, so you always lived more solemnly than other kids your age because of that concrete goal."

Xie Qingcheng finished smoking his cigarette and lit another one.

Zheng Jingfeng said, "You shouldn't smoke so much."

"It's fine. You can continue."

Zheng Jingfeng sighed. "But no matter how calm and cool-headed you were back then, you still seemed like a normal person. When I look at you now, really—I'm worried about you. An ordinary person wouldn't be able to bottle up their emotions so tightly. It'd drive them crazy. Xiao-Xie, there's really no need for you to be so tense."

"I don't feel tense, nor do I feel tired," Xie Qingcheng said. "You don't have to come up with weaknesses for me. I'm already very used to my current state. Weakness is for women; it's not a problem I have."

That annoyed Zheng Jingfeng so much his head began to hurt. He pointed at him. "That's such a sexist way of thinking. You really ought to fix that. It's a good thing the female colleagues in our unit aren't here—if they were, no matter how handsome you are, they'd all roll their eyes at you, and I daresay you'd deserve it. More power to them! What kind of outdated nonsense are you spouting?!"

These kinds of things didn't matter to Xie Qingcheng. He fiddled with the cigarette's filter paper. "Enough small talk, Captain Zheng. Let's get to the more important matters at hand."

"What exactly are you saying isn't important?" Zheng Jingfeng glared at him. "Let me ask you this: Is your life unimportant? Are those outrageous videos that were projected onto the broadcasting tower unimportant? You haven't checked your phone—they're having a real field day online. You sure are something, Xie Qingcheng, to have pissed off that criminal organization so badly that they went out of their way to stream your video free of charge. You tell me, does that count as important? Also, you and your little friend were both inside the archives when it was about to explode—yes, *I* believe that things happened the way you two described, but do you really expect the people further up the chain of command to accept it? Do you really think things work that way? You'll need to be questioned, and so will your little friend. Does *that* count as important? And another thing, you—"

"How are his injuries?" Xie Qingcheng interrupted Captain Zheng's torrential tirade.

Lao-Zheng started in surprise. Since he'd entered the room, this was the first question Xie Qingcheng had asked that sounded slightly human.

Xie Qingcheng felt guilty about He Yu.

He very rarely entertained feelings of guilt over anyone, much less someone significantly younger than him. To put it harshly, there were times when Xie Qingcheng looked at these youngsters and felt as though they didn't seem all that much like living, breathing creatures.

That wasn't to say that he didn't treat them like human beings. Rather, he simply didn't attach much importance to how they felt about him.

He Yu was no exception.

Even though Xie Qingcheng had interacted with him for so many years—from when He Yu was seven until he turned fourteen, Xie Qingcheng had been the He family's personal physician—he had never placed He Yu on the same level as himself, nor had he ever considered him someone he could speak to casually or treat as an equal.

He had always told He Yu what to do, and apart from unilaterally giving instructions, he had never sought to obtain anything from He Yu. More importantly, he'd never thought that there was anything he could possibly get from such a youth.

Now Xie Qingcheng had realized for the first time that He Yu had already grown up; that he possessed emotions and personal desires that he couldn't disregard.

He thought back to the glacial expression that had filled He Yu's eyes before he left. Then, he looked down at the dried blood on his body once more. For the first time, he clearly felt toward He Yu the stirrings of emotions that exceeded the limits of what he would ordinarily feel for a patient.

He asked again, "Captain Zheng, how is he doing?"

"Your little friend must have taken the wrong medicine today." Zheng Jingfeng shook his head. "He's not even related to you, and he followed you into the archives anyway? And you—how could you allow him to join in on your nonsense and do something so dangerous?"

Xie Qingcheng lowered his eyes in silence.

At the time, his mind really had been muddled, his sense of awareness obliterated and his whole being torn asunder by nineteen years of agony. When he and He Yu had gone to the archives, his only thought had been that perhaps he would be able to finally get some kind of answer about the organization that had killed his parents. He had utterly failed to consider the reality that his actions were far too risky.

It was only when Lu Yuzhu pulled out a gun that he'd abruptly come to his senses. But by then, it was already too late.

"You should be glad that Lu Yuzhu didn't know how to use a gun, or the two of you would have died right there inside that building. And even if *you* lived, if he died, how could you possibly face his parents?" Zheng Jingfeng raked his fingers through his hair, deeply vexed. "Speaking of which, he's He Jiwei's son! You've got some fucking nerve, using He Jiwei's son for your own purposes. His parents called our higher-ups, asking what in the world was going on. Thank god he only got shot in the arm and didn't manage to break anything. Otherwise, I'd—I'd—" He jabbed his finger at Xie Qingcheng sharply several times. "I'd like to see how you'd deal with the consequences!"

Xie Qingcheng closed his eyes. He Jiwei had called him a number of times, but he hadn't figured out what he could possibly say to the man, so he hadn't answered. Later on, He Jiwei sent him a message asking, *"Why did He Yu do something like this with you?"*

Xie Qingcheng didn't know either.

Perhaps it was because He Yu really had thought highly of his philosophy once. Perhaps seven years of companionship had led

He Yu to think that their relationship amounted to more than the flimsy connection between a doctor and his patient.

But now that those videos had been played...

The original answer no longer mattered.

As he left, He Yu's gaze had been cold. As cold as the first time they'd met, or perhaps even icier, as if he were looking at a fraud. After careful thought, Xie Qingcheng realized that no matter how much He Yu said he disliked him, he had never shown him that sort of expression before. He had never shown anyone that kind of expression before.

Even during the flare-ups of his illness when he was mad and bloodthirsty, vicious and merciless, he had vented all of it onto himself; all the harm he enacted was self-directed. Xie Qingcheng was the first person he had torn into with that frightful gaze.

"Ah, all right, all right. Your little friend isn't in any serious danger now, so don't overthink it." Zheng Jingfeng had misunderstood Xie Qingcheng's silence. He folded his hands on the table and softened his voice a bit. "Just like you, he'll need to undergo all the necessary procedures and investigations. We'll explain everything to his parents, but as for whether you should follow up and offer them your own apologies, you can figure it out yourself."

"Mm." Xie Qingcheng felt agitated; he had already finished his second cigarette.

He reached for a third, but Zheng Jingfeng put a hand over the box.

"Are you trying to destroy your lungs, or what? You smoke and you smoke and you smoke—who smokes like that, huh? I thought you couldn't stand other people smoking when you were younger. What happened to you?"

"I'm irritated."

"Even if you're irritated, you can't smoke like this."

Xie Qingcheng said nothing.

"I know that you're fucking irritated today. My head hurts like hell too. My grandson's in the hospital with a 39-degree fever and I haven't even had time to call him back yet." Zheng Jingfeng rapped his knuckles against the table. "So, deal with it! Wait till I finish talking!"

Xie Qingcheng sighed. "Fine, talk."

"I was listening to your testimony in the surveillance room just now, and I believe everything you said. But I'm telling you..." Here Zheng Jingfeng's gaze became a bit evasive, and for some reason, his forceful voice began to soften. "Don't get your hopes up. My guess is that Lu Yuzhu's death was planned for a long time, and she was the person the organization set up to take the fall. They even left behind a trail of clues that directly implicates her in tonight's murders—all the necessary documentation will line up accordingly, fulfilling the conditions to close the case. This whole thing got too big, and you know that the bigger the incident, the more it demands a quick explanation. The policemen on the ground aren't idiots—they know there are massive gaps in the details, but some of the higher-ups can't handle too much pressure, and they might not look too deeply into whether everything stands up under close scrutiny. They may even be eager to wrap things up immediately."

Barred from smoking, Xie Qingcheng fiddled with the lighter instead, flicking the switch again and again. "And they have protection amongst the higher-ups, don't they?" he said, lifting his blade-like gaze to pierce the man across from him.

"We don't know who it is or how broad their reach is, but seeing as they dared to do something like this, there's no doubt that they have someone backing them," Zheng Jingfeng replied. Then, before

Xie Qingcheng could say a word, he added, "Don't ask me, fuck if I know."

"True, I shouldn't ask you." Xie Qingcheng leaned back in his chair. This was the police department—what could Zheng Jingfeng possibly say? And if he knew who the "protection" was, would he really just be sitting here like this?

"Actually, the objectives of their operation tonight are also very clear," said Zheng Jingfeng. "First, to clean up any traces left in the archives. Second, the reason they made such a racket was because they discovered the existence of people like Zhang Yong—people with weak personalities and shaky ties to the organization who might turn to the authorities. Tonight's broadcasting tower death game was a warning for all Zhang Yongs, letting them know that even if they're tailed and protected by the authorities, the organization can still kill them right under the police's noses. They're putting all their collaborators and underlings in their place."

He went on, "Third, they wanted to wrap up the Cheng Kang incident. They sent Lu Yuzhu out on a suicide mission, and they might send other scapegoats out in the future. They're taking advantage of those among us who'd rather minimize the impact of the case and rush to close it as quickly as possible. Even if there are police officers who want to investigate this further in the future, they would be acting alone, with their own meager abilities... And I'm not discounting the possibility that there's a huge mole in the force."

Zheng Jingfeng's eyes fell on Xie Qingcheng. "But what I don't understand is the last part."

Xie Qingcheng already knew what Zheng Jingfeng was talking about, but he still asked, "What do you mean?"

"Why would they play those videos of you at the end?"

It was likely because they had discovered that the people attempting to stop Lu Yuzhu were Xie Qingcheng and He Yu. All they would have had to do to come to this conclusion was steal a portion of the school's security footage. But the fact that they had used this method to stop He Yu from helping Xie Qingcheng meant this organization already knew that He Yu was mentally ill—and that Xie Qingcheng had once been his personal physician.

This information wasn't widely known. Zheng Jingfeng didn't know about it; not even Xie Xue did. In all the years that Xie Qingcheng had been employed by the He family, he had always told others that the work he did was related to a project for He Jiwei's pharmaceutical company. With that in mind, Xie Qingcheng had even suspected He Jiwei for a split second, but it was really a rather absurd idea. He Jiwei was He Yu's father, and he had once helped Xie Qingcheng a great deal—he wouldn't do such a thing.

Besides, he realized, the secret of He Yu's mental illness wasn't ironclad. The He family had plenty of servants who all knew a thing or two; with so many people in their home, something was bound to slip out. That made it extremely difficult to use this fact to narrow down the suspects to a certain group of people—to say nothing of how these criminal masterminds had a hacker who had the ability to go through various online databases as if they were unguarded and treat confidential data like freebies open for the taking.

Zheng Jingfeng scratched his head in irritation as he saw Xie Qingcheng spacing out. "I'm asking you a question, Xiao-Xie."

"I'm not sure." Even now, Xie Qingcheng did not tell Zheng Jingfeng about He Yu's condition. "They probably realized that I was trying to stop Lu Yuzhu and wanted to teach me a lesson."

Zheng Jingfeng stared at him in mild disbelief. Likewise, Xie Qingcheng gazed back at Lao-Zheng without blinking.

At last, Zheng Jingfeng sighed. "That's just great. In that case, they've achieved their goal." He pushed his own phone toward Xie Qingcheng. "Take a look for yourself."

The internet had already exploded with discussion. For one thing, Xie Qingcheng's words were absolutely callous and improper and poked at many people's sore spots, and they'd even involved the esteemed Professor Qin Ciyan.

For another, this criminal organization had gone to the trouble of broadcasting an old video of Xie Qingcheng after completing their "drop the hanky" death game. Although the video had circulated through the internet at one point, not many people had watched it—after all these years, it hadn't even reached a couple hundred views. It was very unlikely that the organization played it just because they thought Xie Qingcheng was handsome. No one could possibly know that this video had been selected specifically to drive a wedge between Xie Qingcheng and He Yu, the hacker who had been with him at the time, so everyone had begun to speculate whether Xie Qingcheng was somehow linked to the mastermind of this terrorist attack.

All sorts of opinions had popped up very quickly. Xie Qingcheng, a plain, ordinary former doctor and current Huzhou Medical School professor, had actually become a trending topic.

"Like what you see?" Zheng Jingfeng felt both helpless and aggrieved that Xie Qingcheng wouldn't listen to his advice. With his emotions in a jumble, Zheng Jingfeng's words sounded a little like a scolding a father would give his child.

At this moment, one of Zheng Jingfeng's subordinates called for him from outside, so he got up, patted Xie Qingcheng's shoulder, and sighed. "How impressive. Even the celebrities aren't as handsome as you. It's just that you have such an unpleasant mouth. Did you take the wrong medicine that day? I can't believe you'd say something like that. What was up with you?"

"Nothing."

"What do you mean, 'nothing'? Was that even you? How could I not fucking know you? If you don't explain everything as soon as possible, just wait and see what happens. The public's opinion has already—"

"Do you think you know me very well, Officer Zheng?" Xie Qingcheng stared at him. "Those were all my true feelings."

"True feelings, my ass. I've known you and your parents for forty years if you add both generations together. How could I not know you..." Zheng Jingfeng's tone softened once more when he met Xie Qingcheng's eyes. "Forget it. If you don't want to talk about it, then just forget it! I won't force you, and in any case, no one can stop you from doing whatever you want, even if you end up beaten to a bloody pulp. I give up, okay?"

Xie Qingcheng remained silent.

"Take care and rest up. Once you've recovered, go see that little friend of yours." It was quite evident that this was something Zheng Jingfeng only chose to tell him at the last minute. "For some reason, he's been burning up with a high fever, even though the wound was treated in time so it wouldn't get infected."

Xie Qingcheng looked up, his hands imperceptibly balling into fists. An unexplainable high fever was one of He Yu's symptoms when his psychological Ebola flared up. Then he...

"But I don't know if he'd want to see you. He seemed to be in a pretty bad mood—he didn't say much beyond answering the necessary questions." Zheng Jingfeng sighed. "He's already gone to the hospital. You can contact him yourself later."

45

He Didn't Care Whether He Lived or Died

Sure enough, He Yu refused to see Xie Qingcheng.

It was as though he was determined to evaporate completely from Xie Qingcheng's life—every message Xie Qingcheng sent him was like a pebble dropped into a bottomless sea. Xie Qingcheng had gone to the hospital, but He Yu was unaccustomed to the hubbub of public hospitals and had been quickly transferred to a private clinic. There, Xie Qingcheng found himself barred at the door.

The next few days were also extremely chaotic for Xie Qingcheng.

Xie Xue, Chen Man, the old neighbors who were worried about him, his colleagues, his supervisor... All sorts of people sought him out to ask him just what had happened that night and why his face would be projected onto a broadcasting tower by a criminal organization. On top of all that, he was also summoned to the police department from time to time for further questioning and to complete the necessary procedures.

He knew that the internet was having a field day over this incident, but it had surprisingly little effect on him, as he had absolutely no time whatsoever to sit down and check social media.

Naturally, Xie Xue gave him a lengthy phone call, sobbing the whole time. She asked him where he was so she could come find him, only for him to reject the idea point-blank by refusing to tell her his exact location.

Fortunately, Xie Xue had never seen pictures of their parents' murder scene. In order to protect her, Xie Qingcheng hadn't described their parents' deaths to her in concrete detail; he didn't want her to become like him, ensnared by endless despair. Xie Qingcheng wished for her to know as little as possible.

Chen Man also came to see him.

Chen Man was different from Xie Xue in that he knew all the facts of the situation. He was the first to drop by when Xie Qingcheng was still undergoing his first round of interrogation. He didn't belong to Zheng Jingfeng's department, so he'd had to take time off to rush over. The moment he stepped through the door, he immediately pulled Xie Qingcheng into a hug. He was an impulsive person, but it took him an unexpectedly long time to force out a few muffled words.

"Ge, are you trying to scare me to death?"

Xie Qingcheng noted the dark stubble covering his jaw; it seemed that these past few days, this kid hadn't even bothered to groom himself properly. Sighing, he patted Chen Man on the back.

Later on, as the investigation drew to a close, Chen Man once again came to give Xie Qingcheng a ride home.

That day, Xie Xue had originally planned on coming along as well, but due to the continuous stress she had been under she was feeling rather ill; Xie Qingcheng had her take sick leave and return to Moyu Alley where she could rest under the care of Auntie Li. He returned to the Huzhou Medical's faculty dormitory with Chen Man.

The university's faculty housing was assigned based on seniority, and Xie Qingcheng's living accommodations were more spacious than Xie Xue's. Of course, Xie Xue's dorm was filled with a mess of random junk, whereas Xie Qingcheng's bachelor apartment was essentially just four bare walls, utterly cold and cheerless.

"Ge, you should rest and lie down for a while. I'll go make you something to eat."

Chen Man stepped into the kitchen. He'd been to Xie Qingcheng's dorm a few times and was familiar with the place.

As the range hood whirred to life, Xie Qingcheng lay down on the sofa in exhaustion. Dimly, he felt that this scenario seemed a bit familiar. It was only later that he remembered: the day he had an allergic reaction to mango and got a fever, He Yu had come over and busied himself in the kitchen just like this.

Xie Qingcheng opened the address book on his phone, swiping past his pile of unread messages until he finally reached He Yu's name. Their chat history was still frozen on the messages he had sent He Yu inquiring after his condition.

He Yu still hadn't responded.

After a moment's contemplation, Xie Qingcheng dug up He Yu's phone number from his address book and called him once again. As expected, the line went dead after a few rings.

Xie Qingcheng sighed softly. He didn't even know how to coax women, much less a sulky young man. Not to mention, this was a young man who wasn't just angry right now, but also hurt and despairing. Not knowing what to do, he pressed a hand against his forehead for a long, long while. Then he wearily set his phone aside and turned to enter the bathroom.

After he'd washed up and come back out dressed in a bathrobe, Chen Man was in the living room setting the table.

"Ge, do you want..." Chen Man looked up as he spoke, and his words came to an abrupt stop. He saw Xie Qingcheng wearing a snow-white bathrobe, leaning lethargically against the window frame as he lit the cigarette held between his lips.

Xie Qingcheng's hair was still dripping wet, but he couldn't be bothered to dry it. Shimmering droplets of water pregnant with some unspeakable, hidden desire rolled down his neck, slowly melting into the shadow beneath the collar of his bathrobe.

Xie Qingcheng was in a rather poor frame of mind, so he didn't pay much attention to his appearance. He took a drag of his cigarette and coughed quietly as he turned to look at Chen Man. "What were you about to say?"

"Oh, I-I said..." Chen Man's face had turned red, but unfortunately, between his own terrible mental state and the room's dim lighting, Xie Qingcheng didn't notice.

"I said, do you want any vinegar? I cooked some dumplings."

Xie Qingcheng said absentmindedly, "Anything is fine."

Chen Man bolted back into the kitchen, turning so quickly he nearly tripped over a power strip.

Meanwhile, Xie Qingcheng carried on leaning against the window and finished his cigarette. Then, after a moment's consideration, he sent He Yu yet another message.

"About the matter at the archives, I still want to say thank you."

Flakes of cigarette ash floated through the air, carried off by the wind like sea jellies gently drifting through water. Xie Qingcheng gazed silently at his screen for a while, then added, *"I'm the one who didn't think things through. I'm sorry."*

He knew that what He Yu wanted to hear might not necessarily be these two sentences. He Yu had been deeply hurt by the things that he had said in that video. But Xie Qingcheng didn't know how he should go about explaining himself. He couldn't explain even if he wanted to.

"Ge, the dumplings are ready. Come and eat."

Turning off his phone screen, Xie Qingcheng walked over to the dining table.

The dumplings Chen Man cooked had been wrapped and delivered by Auntie Li. Thin skins encased a healthy dollop of spring bamboo shoots and pork blended in aspic jelly. Chen Man had scooped the dumplings out and dished the soup into a separate bowl so that the food would cool faster. Exhausted and starving, Xie Qingcheng inhaled some thirty dumplings in a single breath.

It was only now that Chen Man said quietly, "Xie-ge, you need to stop doing things like this. Do you remember how you counseled me back when my brother passed? You told me that no matter how sad I was, there was no way I could change the past. That if I wanted to live on, I would have to pull myself back together again sooner or later."

Xie Qingcheng didn't respond.

"You talked to me about what happened to your mom and dad then, too... I was just a kid back then and I was slow on the uptake, so I asked you why you didn't keep pursuing the trail. You said that getting an answer was very important, but there were times when a person couldn't remain bogged down in the mud for the sake of an answer. You desperately wanted to know the true reason your parents died, the identity of the killer who orchestrated their murders... But if you were to risk it all for that endeavor, it would've been impossible for you to continue supporting your family. You still had a sister, and..."

"Xie Xue has grown up," Xie Qingcheng said. "If this were ten years ago, I would resist the urge to demand the truth, because the cost of obtaining it might be something I couldn't afford to pay. But Xie Xue is an adult now, and I don't have a wife or child to raise. I've been selfish for nineteen years, but now that I finally have no attachments to worry about anymore, there was no way I could turn a blind eye when the clues to my parents' murder were right there."

Chen Man very rarely raised his voice in front of Xie Qingcheng, but when he heard this, he could no longer hold back. "Ge, what the hell are you talking about? You're saying that if you died now, it wouldn't even matter, right? Because you successfully brought up your sister and saw us become independent, we'd just be able to accept it if you died, right?! Xie-ge, you... How could you say that?" His voice shook. "How could you think that?"

Xie Qingcheng gave no response.

Chen Man suddenly felt sincerely frightened by this man. Xie Qingcheng could make a plan that took into account the safety of everyone around him, but he wouldn't factor in his own life at all. When he considered whether he could afford to die, his decision didn't hinge on whether he wanted to live, but rather, if the people he was taking care of would be able to survive independently if he died.

In the face of enormous danger, he was even self-destructive.

"You're only... You're only living for other people? You think that as long as you've made proper arrangements for everyone, then your own death doesn't even matter, right?"

Xie Qingcheng sighed and pulled out a cigarette. "That's not what I meant—"

"You're not allowed to smoke anymore."

Chen Man shot to his feet and pinned Xie Qingcheng's hand down, snatching the cigarette, lighter, and box away with an ashen face. Then, he tossed them into the trash right in front of Xie Qingcheng.

Xie Qingcheng didn't get up from his chair. A long time later, he said, "Chen Man, I don't think my life doesn't matter."

"Then what *did* you mean?"

"I didn't mean anything, but one has to have priorities in life. Raising Xie Xue was once the most important thing to me; that always had to come before seeking the truth. But now I've completed that task, and I have no attachments holding me back. So seeking the truth is now of utmost importance."

Chen Man's eyes were red. "But your life is also very important. To me, it's more important than the truth."

Xie Qingcheng replied, "You're a police officer."

"But I'm also Chen Man."

For a long time, no one in the room spoke; there was only the continuous tick-tocking of the clock on the wall.

In the end, it was Xie Qingcheng who couldn't bear seeing Chen Man like this. He sighed and changed the subject. "Sit down. Eat with me."

Chen Man said nothing.

"Stop fussing, come sit." In Xie Qingcheng's eyes, he was already making a concession by saying this.

Though Chen Man was reluctant to concede, the pressure from Xie Qingcheng's aura was too strong; he never had the power to resist it for long. He staunchly held his ground for a few more seconds, but in the end, all he could do was slowly sit down under Xie Qingcheng's pointed stare and pick up his chopsticks again...even as tears dripped into his soup throughout the rest of the meal.

In a villa somewhere in the city, a woman's voice rang out.

"What?! You're saying He Yu has the blood toxin?" Lü Zhishu gaped in astonishment at the person before her, only managing to digest the information after great effort. "Executive Duan, surely you're joking..."

Duan-laoban flipped a page of his newspaper. "Executive Lü ought to be very happy to have a son like that."

Lü Zhishu dragged the red nails of her stubby fingers through her hair, her eyes filled with shock. She muttered to herself for a while before she looked up and said to the man in front of her, "As...as Number Four, the organization has always considered him defective goods. These past few years, I've raised him just like an ordinary patient; I never thought that he would have a disease-linked ability, nor...nor have any of you found him valuable as a potential research subject..."

Duan-laoban smiled. "Then it's clear that it's only natural for humans to make mistakes."

She didn't reply.

"During the investigation into the patients escaping from Cheng Kang Psychiatric Hospital, it was discovered that both He Yu and Xie Qingcheng went back into the burning building," he said. "After they reentered, a lot of patients were rescued at an unusually fast rate. They told the police it was because some of the doors didn't have padlocks and were only bolted from the outside—that explanation might be able to convince the police, but it's not enough to convince either one of us."

Duan-laoban took a sip of his strongly brewed pu'er tea and said languidly to Lü Zhishu, "However, Executive Lü need not worry—since He Yu is your son, he's one of ours."

Lü Zhishu's eyes lost focus as she shook her head. "No, with his personality, I'm afraid he wouldn't..."

"A person's heart is made of flesh, and blood is thicker than water. Even if he doesn't yet, he'll be standing on our side sooner or later.

What kind of son would disobey his mother?" Duan-laoban gave her a smile that didn't reach his eyes.

Lü Zhishu said nothing. The aged pu'er tea was sweet and rich on the tongue. Duan-laoban took another sip.

Lü Zhishu said, "Executive Duan, when it comes to this matter, I can't guarantee you anything. If he really does have blood toxin, he's never mentioned it to us before..."

Executive Duan laughed out loud.

"Executive Lü, could that just be because you're too biased? Even I know that you and your Lao-He don't spend much time with your elder son at all. Of course he's going to be distant from you two. But after what happened with the broadcasting tower, I think he might not be such an indifferent person after all—that Doctor Xie fellow you hired for him merely accompanied him for a brief period and showed him a bit of respect, yet that was enough for him to go to such lengths for him."

At the mention of this, Lü Zhishu became unexpectedly indignant. "If that bullet had hit him somewhere vital, then..."

"Don't you have He Li too? Surely He Li is more important to you?" Amused, Duan-laoban examined Lü Zhishu's face—it resembled a milkshake that had been poorly mixed, covered in bright splotches of color. "In the future, you and Lao-He should remember to save some parental devotion for your eldest. He Li is a normal kid. I know you like him. But now that He Yu has blood toxin, it would be ideal if he listened to us unconditionally. It would save us a lot of trouble if we didn't have to force him." Duan-laoban poured himself some more of the red liquid from the teapot and said mildly, "You can take your time with this, Executive Lü. Rome wasn't built in a day. Give him some more attention bit by bit, and in time he'll forgive the way you neglected him before. There's no rush."

This time, he poured some tea for Lü Zhishu as well and gestured to the teacup. "This pu'er tea Xiao-Shen brought back from Yunnan is really quite good. Executive Lü should try it."

Seeing that Lü Zhishu was frozen in place, the look in Executive Duan's eyes sharpened slightly. "Oh, you—you've been very clever all along. That's why you've been able to deceive your Lao-He for so many years. Your acting skills are no worse than those of the little idols Executive Huang keeps around. But when it comes to acting, it's possible to get too emotionally invested or flub your lines. Executive Lü, do you understand what I mean?"

Lü Zhishu swayed unsteadily where she stood, as though his words had stabbed her in the foot.

Executive Duan smiled. "We've been collaborators for a long time now. I understand you even better than your Lao-He. When it comes to those matters from your past, Executive Lü, as long as you're cooperative enough, I'll always help you keep He Jiwei in the dark—no need to worry. Take a seat."

He pushed the teacup closer to Lü Zhishu. "Try it. Don't you love tea?"

At last, Lü Zhishu sat down slowly on the couch across from him. She tentatively touched the rim of the cup with her fingers, which had gone cold with fright. Only after she adjusted to the warmth did she lift the cup and take a sip.

She swallowed the tea, the tannins bitter on her tongue.

Lü Zhishu forced a smile. "It's very good."

Executive Duan looked at the uncertain expression on her face and said mildly, "Executive Lü, just give it your best effort—it takes a very long time to win somebody over. But there's no need to feel too much pressure. Your esteemed son is only nineteen. The disease differentiation of psychological Ebola becomes more pronounced with time, so let him slowly train his abilities by himself for now; don't lay your cards out on the table until later. I trust that by that time, he'll willingly become one of our members."

"Then...what are your plans for training him, exactly?"

"Let's wait and see," Executive Duan said in a relaxed voice, like he was playing an extremely interesting game. "We'll take it step by step. He was an unexpected surprise to begin with, so I'm thinking that we might not need to plan too far in advance with him yet. Besides, he must have been deeply hurt by that Doctor Xie of his recently. When young people receive a shock, they should be allowed to adjust to it themselves—we'll let him be for now."

With that, he leaned forward to brew more tea.

"We have a lot to do too. The murder videos this time should have intimidated the rats that needed intimidating. We need to keep a close eye on Cheng Kang and Huzhou University and wrap things up cleanly. We've tossed a bone to the dogs, so we have to watch them gnaw on it until they're done. Since we've already led them to that scapegoat overseas, we need to ensure that they don't come sniffing around here."

After he finished speaking, Executive Duan poured some more tea for himself with an air of self-satisfaction. "Be nicer to He Yu, but remember that it needs to seem natural. If He Jiwei finds out that something is amiss, the one who'll suffer losses will always be you."

Lü Zhishu looked at the image of her flabby, formless face reflected in the cup of tea. After a long while, she murmured, "All right. I understand."

46

He Had Been Deceiving Me All Along

He Yu had indeed gone insane.

Many days had passed since that night of horrors; he had, in fact, been discharged from the hospital some time ago, but he hadn't told anyone, and he didn't return to his house either.

Everyone seemed disgusting and fake to him now. He had an apartment in one of the newer districts of downtown Huzhou, one he hadn't visited very often even after getting the keys. For now, he had chosen to live there by himself. He'd been deeply stricken when he saw those videos of Xie Qingcheng, but after returning to his senses, he refused to accept that Xie Qingcheng was a coward who was afraid of mentally ill patients.

At the hospital, once he'd calmed down a little, he wondered if he was the one who'd misunderstood—if the criminal organization had taken Xie Qingcheng's past videos out of context because they had another motive. Xie Qingcheng was not that kind of person.

He Yu went home with that thought in mind, clinging to the last of his hope—he wanted to verify the facts for himself and didn't want anyone to disturb him. But what he didn't expect was for the things he dug up to be far crueler; the video he had seen was just the tip of the iceberg.

The truth was too terrifying. The more he investigated, the sicker he became.

The medicine intended to control his symptoms lay on the table, untouched after he had taken a few pills—because it had absolutely no effect. The results of his personal investigation destroyed his sense of self even further; some pills were no longer enough to control his downward spiral. It felt as if lichen had grown over his heart, as if all his senses had gone numb. He wanted to kill. He wanted to drink blood. Morality and legality suddenly felt utterly irrelevant.

During a flare-up of psychological Ebola, his very life seemed unimportant; he wasn't afraid of death, so why would he fear society's rules?

He Yu sat in a black armchair. His phone had rung countless times, all calls and texts from Xie Qingcheng, but he didn't pick up or read any of them. He just stared at the white wall in front of him. It was about five meters high, so wide and tall it seemed like the massive screen in a movie theater. And right now, it was covered with densely packed projections of text messages.

This was everything from the past few years that he'd been able to recover from the cloud using illicit technology. Xie Qingcheng's private messages—messages about He Yu.

He Yu was an elite hacker. He'd always been extremely talented in this field, but having the capability didn't mean he would actually do certain things—just as there were many people in the world capable of committing murder, but few actually became killers. There was a clear boundary in He Yu's heart, one he'd never crossed in the past. But it was only when he opened those dusty doors and stepped inside that he saw the kind of spectacle that lay within.

What he saw made his blood run cold. Even though too much time had passed and the recovered messages were incomplete, what he'd gathered was more than enough to shake him to his core.

Beginning with the earliest recovered content, he saw his father offering a high salary to Xie Qingcheng to treat He Yu. Xie Qingcheng had been rather reluctant at the beginning, saying that although Case #3 had already died, they had extremely violent tendencies before their death. Even though he was sympathetic to He Yu's plight, he seriously had no wish to waste his time on a long-term engagement with a psychological Ebola patient.

Xie Qingcheng: Treating a patient like this won't go anywhere, nor is it very meaningful. I want to use this time on more worthwhile tasks.

He Jiwei: He Yu is different. He's still too young. He definitely won't go the same way Case #3 did. I know you don't find psychological Ebola uninteresting, Dr. Xie. On account of our past friendship, please at least come over for a chat and meet my son.

Xie Qingcheng: Executive He, I have more important things to do. And I can't endorse the companionship treatment method that other doctors have suggested to you. Maintaining a long-term relationship with a doctor will result in the patient becoming reliant on them; when the time comes, forcibly ending the treatment will be like quitting a drug and will be more likely to trigger negative emotional backlash instead.

He Jiwei: But I have no other choice. Trying this is my last option. Dr. Xie, could you please at least meet with him once, for my sake?

Getting Xie Qingcheng to come had been so difficult, requiring countless pleas and appeals.

And as for the day he left?

The day he resigned, He Jiwei had sent him a message.

He Jiwei: Dr. Xie, you've still decided to quit.

Xie Qingcheng: Yes.

He Jiwei: If nothing else, there's still human connection aside from the contract. You've always been very good to He Yu. Sometimes, you'd even argue with me on his behalf...

Xie Qingcheng: I would do the same for anyone. Because it is part of what I was paid to do.

He Jiwei: But He Yu has already developed a reliance upon you. You must know this.

Xie Qingcheng: I told Executive He at the very beginning that a long-term companionship style of treatment would have this kind of effect on the patient. To be honest, this was all within our expectations.

He Jiwei: To him, you're different, Doctor Xie...

Xie Qingcheng: But to me, he's the same as any other patient. There's no difference whatsoever.

The conversation didn't end here.

He Jiwei: Xie Qingcheng, if you're so dead set on leaving, I can't stop you. But we originally agreed on ten years for the contract; since it's ending early, there are some remunerations I promised you that I won't be able to honor entirely.

Xie Qingcheng: That's fine, I don't mind.

Once it got to that point, He Jiwei had more or less realized that anything he said to Xie Qingcheng would be useless.

After a long moment of silence, he switched his tone.

He Jiwei: Then think about how you're going to tell him. You're leaving so suddenly. At the very least, you have to come up with some way for him to accept it as quickly as possible.

In contrast, Xie Qingcheng's response was surprisingly direct.

Xie Qingcheng: If Executive He has no objections, I plan to tell him that the contract was originally set for seven years. This will make him feel better. But I will also need your cooperation.

He Jiwei: Xie Qingcheng, is this matter really nonnegotiable? Did the Qin Ciyan matter shake you up so badly that you need to do things so finally?

Xie Qingcheng: Executive He, this isn't a matter of finality. This is just a job.

Xie Qingcheng: I couldn't possibly feel anything more, and I never have.

Xie Qingcheng: I must resign.

He Jiwei: You can't wait till the end of the contract?

Xie Qingcheng: I can't.

He Jiwei: Xie Qingcheng, your heart is truly colder than I had imagined.

Xie Qingcheng: For him, this is the kindest lie.

The city lights twinkled from beyond the window, and the massive billboards flashed at irregular intervals, spilling into He Yu's living room like crystalline ripples, scouring away the countless messages projected onto the wall as if washing away the makeup that Xie Qingcheng had put on. It felt as though He Yu had finally seen Xie Qingcheng's true face today.

The patience, equality, and acceptance with which he had treated him were all fake. It was a mechanical repetition, a performance of civility, all empty theory—carried out to appease and deceive him. Even the contract period he cited at their parting wasn't true.

Back then, He Yu had even believed it—believed that Xie Qingcheng was determined to leave because his time was up.

As it turned out, this was the actual truth...

Ten years. Xie Qingcheng should have accompanied him up until he graduated senior high. But after the Qin Ciyan incident, Xie Qingcheng didn't hesitate. He would happily forgo extra wages if it meant he could leave He Yu. How terrified had he been?

He conspired with He Jiwei to lie to He Yu, but he could still speak of great principles with such calm conviction, telling him that this was how normal relationships came to an end.

All of the rationality belonged to Xie Qingcheng, while He Yu seemed like an immature, unreasonable clown.

So stupid...

It was all a lie!

A lie!

Those words that Xie Qingcheng had once said to encourage him, the ones that had maintained his sense of self as he struggled through the agony of a flare-up, were indeed no more than the empty platitudes a psychiatrist told their patient.

Just like a surgeon would tell a late-stage cancer patient, "You still have hope if you hold on." But the doctor already knew that there was no hope.

Like police would persuade a youth on the verge of suicide by saying, "You're not ugly. Why would you think that way? Everyone is special. There will always be someone who likes you. Come down, give me your hand." But could the police really not see the young man's hideous face and flabby body?

Those were just the emptiest of consolations.

Xie Qingcheng's views on treatment and the principles that guided He Yu to integrate into society had once given He Yu ten years' worth of support; even though Xie Qingcheng chose to leave in the end, He Yu hadn't felt any hatred toward him.

He strove to understand the principles of which Xie Qingcheng spoke, he tried to understand the end of a relationship between two normal people that Xie Qingcheng described.

In the end, he'd made peace with Xie Qingcheng's choice and with himself. But he hadn't expected that none of Xie Qingcheng's words were sincere, that they were just a doctor's method of treatment, some pretty words. Even the contract period Xie Qingcheng had told him about was an invention.

He Yu found himself thinking of the time he and Xie Qingcheng bumped into a gay couple at the dining hall; at the time, both of them had been very uncomfortable and rose in unison to change seats. He'd felt a little surprised and asked Xie Qingcheng, *Aren't you a doctor? How come you can't bear to see them either?*

Xie Qingcheng had told him back then that a doctor's medical philosophies were entirely separate from their personal opinions. As a doctor, he did believe that homosexuals didn't have any mental problems, but as Xie Qingcheng the individual, he personally couldn't accept that kind of relationship at all.

Now He Yu understood very clearly.

As a doctor, Xie Qingcheng was willing to guide him toward society, to treat him like a normal person. But as Xie Qingcheng, he hadn't developed any sort of connection with He Yu. Not only did Xie Qingcheng leave He Yu of his own volition—He Yu couldn't help but recall that Xie Qingcheng had once had Xie Xue keep her distance from him as well.

Xie Qingcheng had been frightened—he'd run, he'd rather not earn more money if it meant that he and his family could get further away from He Yu...

He Yu leaned back into the armchair, staring at it all with his chin in his hand. Slowly, he began to smile. His lips were razor thin; from the side, their upward curve seemed somewhat sinister.

"Are all you doctors really so insincere?" he murmured softly to that lonely white wall. The wound on his shoulder was still covered in bandages. Blood seeped out, followed by a dull throb of pain that spread from the wound like snake venom to his fingertips and heart.

"What a great disguise you wear...Xie Qingcheng."

At that moment, He Yu suddenly felt that everything he'd done in the past was ridiculous, like a joke—what was the point of "controlling one's inner heart?" What "shackles of illness" could be thrown off?

In the past few years, what exactly had he been striving for, insisting on, and believing in?

He slowly closed his eyes. Along with the throbbing of the gunshot wound in his shoulder, the scars on his wrists also seemed to sting faintly. He wondered how Xie Qingcheng had managed to go so far with his falsehoods, covering his eyes with both hands and having him follow along so ignorantly and stupidly for so long.

Xie Qingcheng said to him that being sick was nothing to fear.

Xie Qingcheng told him that he could say "it hurts" when he was in pain, that he could ask for sweets, that no one would laugh at him.

With every word, Xie Qingcheng had knocked down the sturdy fortress around his heart. He Yu had once thought that what Xie Qingcheng had extended to him was a pair of warm outstretched hands, but in the end, it was no more than an ice-cold knife.

He Yu protected himself very well, but Xie Qingcheng's knife had stabbed hard into the depths of his heart.

It was too tragic.

He Yu had lived nineteen years wearing a flawless mask. He never said anything genuine to others, nor did he receive much sincerity in others' words. In those nineteen years of pain and sickness, Xie Qingcheng was actually the only one to ever ask him, "Doesn't that hurt?"

Doesn't that hurt...

He Yu slowly stood up from the armchair, lifting a hand and pressing it over his heart.

He looked at the earth-shatteringly cold messages in front of him, as if he were standing in the bone-piercing gale of a winter blizzard. He lowered his head, bent down, and slowly began to laugh...

It was so funny. It seemed as though he'd truly, actually, genuinely experienced how terrifying pain could be.

Was this what it meant to hurt? This deception, all of his futile struggles, all of his idiocy and loneliness...

If this was what it was like, he'd rather have gone on living numbly forever. What was wrong with being a stalk of grass? Why did his heart have to be ravaged by lies?

He read onward, page after page, file after file, message after message, poring over everything line by line, every word like a knife to his heart. He'd always thought his heart was thickly calloused, but in this moment, it hurt so much it felt as if his own flesh didn't even belong to him anymore...didn't belong to him...

He Yu reached up to touch his forehead. His fingertips were ice-cold and all his limbs felt numb. He'd learned enough. He suddenly rose, violently sweeping everything off of the tea table in front of him. Shattered fragments crashed across the floor.

Panting, he went to find the projector remote, picked it up, and tried to close this Pandora's box. But...

At that very moment, amidst this exploding star of messages, he saw a text belonging to Xie Xue.

It had been sent six years ago. On his birthday.

Xie Xue: Gege, Auntie Li's sick. I've gone with her to get an IV. When will you be back from your work trip? These hospital procedures are so confusing, my head hurts. I wish you were here...

When He Yu first saw this message, all he felt was a gentle tug in his mind, like a moth that had yet to realize it had landed in a spider's web. But after a few seconds ticked by, he suddenly looked up, staring at that message in disbelief. The moth in the spider's web began to struggle, flapping furiously, iridescent dust falling from its wings, its fluttering movements stirring an earthquake in his memories.

Six years ago?

On his birthday?

That day...

That day, hadn't Xie Xue been with him?

47

It Hurt Too Much

SIX YEARS AGO, in the cold and quiet He residence, there was no laughter and no companionship.

Although the household staff had prepared a cake for him on He Jiwei and Lü Zhishu's orders, He Yu didn't eat it. It was his birthday, yet his parents weren't present and were instead in Yanzhou with his little brother. They'd said they had to meet with an important client that day and would have to wait until after the discussions ended to see whether they could fly back in time. He Yu didn't have many friends either, since he was mostly cordial and distant with his classmates. It would have been awkward to invite any of them to his birthday party.

That day, Xie Qingcheng wasn't in Huzhou either; he was on a work trip as Xie Xue's message had stated, attending a conference.

Not even the heavens were cooperating that day; the rain poured down as the wind blew wildly. He Yu stood in the living room watching the floor-to-ceiling European-style windows become an eerily fluctuating ink painting, framing the torrential deluge outside.

A bell tolled once—twice—three times—

The large clock in the residence sounded every hour, accurately announcing the time on its clock face.

From afternoon, to evening, to nightfall.

"Young Master...don't wait any longer. Executive He and Executive Lü said they won't be able to get back today..." Unable to bear it any longer, the housekeeper cautiously stepped forward and draped a jacket over He Yu's shoulders. "You should go to bed."

"It's okay. It's not like today's a formal holiday or anything." When He Yu turned his head, he was unexpectedly still smiling. "Go do what you have to do. I'm going to watch the rain for a while longer, but I'll rest soon."

The housekeeper sighed softly and left.

Was it really okay? Did it really not matter?

Of course not. He was just waiting.

He thought that there must at least be one person in the world who would remember him, who would miss him, who would brave the wind and rain to keep him company in the dark. He wasn't such a bad person that he deserved to be punished with loneliness like this, right?

He waited.

And waited...

"He Yu! He Yu!"

After an indeterminate length of time—it seemed like it was right before the clock bell struck midnight—he heard someone knocking on the door, and a girl's faint voice that sounded so indistinctly through the wind and rain that it seemed like an illusion.

He Yu's eyes widened slightly, and he hastily rushed over to open the door.

Standing outside, panting slightly, was Xie Xue—the only girl he was close to. The only playmate who had stayed with him for so many years. She was wearing a raincoat, and her rain-drenched face looked ice-cold. But when she looked up at him, her gaze was warm.

Sniffling slightly, she took off her raincoat with a smile, revealing the birthday cake that she had carefully hidden underneath.

"I made it in time, right?"

"Why did you come..."

"I didn't want you to spend your birthday alone. How sad would that be?" Xie Xue wiped away the water that was dripping from her hair and said, "I made your favorite chocolate cake for you. Gosh, I nearly drowned out there. It's such a big storm, what the hell..."

In that moment, He Yu's resentment seemed to dissipate as the void in his heart was filled. He grabbed Xie Xue's freezing hand and pulled her inside. He felt like his voice was a little raspy as he said, "I also didn't think I should be alone..."

"How's that possible? How could you be alone? You still have me. I'll always stay with you."

He Yu said nothing.

"Happy thirteenth birthday, He Yu." The girl smiled brightly, becoming the most brilliant ray of sunshine in the shadowy home.

It was so long ago, He Yu couldn't quite remember what had happened afterward. He only remembered that when he went to the refrigerator, looking for a piece of that unfinished chocolate cake, it was already gone.

Of course, the untouched desserts that the nanny baked for him had disappeared along with that piece of cake.

Seeing his dejected face, the nanny quickly explained before he could get mad, "Those things aren't fresh anymore—it's not good for you to eat them, so they were tossed... If you want, we can make them again tonight."

But even if they were to make it again, it still wouldn't be the cake that Xie Xue had brought for him on that rainy night.

He Yu had said, "It's fine, forget it."

Now, He Yu looked at the projection before him, his spirits plummeting into a pool of ice. He clearly remembered Xie Xue coming to his house on that day.

That day he'd...he'd...had someone with him; someone had remembered him...

But the contents in the projected images in front of him couldn't possibly be fake. He had gathered the information himself from the backups on cloud storage.

Xie Xue: Gege, Auntie Li's sick. I've gone with her to get an IV. When will you be back from your work trip? These hospital procedures are so confusing, my head hurts, I wish you were here...

How could this be?

How could this be?!

He pulled out his computer and his fingers flew over the keyboard, his expression twisted and his eyes nearly insane, as if he was about to dig up a grave of information, pry open the coffin, and exhume the corpse, seeking a truth that had been buried for ages.

He rapidly retrieved the messages from those dates.

Xie Xue's, Xie Qingcheng's, He Jiwei's, Lü Zhishu's.

The truth was like an incorruptible corpse, and from within the cloud's database, it gave him a coldly eerie sneer.

Lies...

Lies...

Lies!

Because too much time had passed, most of the chat logs could no longer be retrieved, but the messages that he successfully restored were enough to prove that, on that night, on the night when he had needed Xie Xue the most, she...hadn't come at all.

He Yu even saw the message she had sent to Xie Qingcheng the next day.

Xie Xue: Ge, He Yu asked me if I could go to his house to play and spend his birthday with him, but Auntie Li was so sick yesterday and I was so busy that I forgot to respond to him. I feel so embarrassed. Can you apologize to him for me? I don't have the guts to explain it to him...

Xie Qingcheng: There's no need for you to get so close to him.

He Yu kept searching.

The timeline inched forward...

And became even more shocking.

He found a certain chat log.

It was a conversation between Xie Qingcheng and He Jiwei.

He Jiwei: He Yu seems to create a sort of delusion when he's at his most helpless, and the object of his delusion is your little sister. I've recently discovered by accident that some of the things he told me didn't happen at all. Doctor Xie, this kind of situation...

Xie Qingcheng: It's very normal for him. I've known about this behavior of his since the beginning.

He Jiwei: How could this be...

Xie Qingcheng: He Yu needs a friend who's around his age, but he isn't willing to open his heart to any of his peers. His way of thinking is unique and precocious, so most children his age don't quite understand him. Because of his long-term isolation, he needs an outlet to vent his emotions, and at such a time, his closest peer can very easily become his own reflection.

He Jiwei: His own reflection?

Xie Qingcheng: Yes. Some children with autism or other psychological conditions will imagine a friend as they're growing up, and with that friend, they can hand over their heart without reservation. That friend may not exist at all, or they might only exist in part. The patients make them up to fulfill the intense longing in their own hearts.

Xie Qingcheng sent another explanatory message to He Jiwei.

Xie Qingcheng: Actually, it's not just children with mental illnesses. Normal children will also develop some delusions when they're lonely. For example, if they're an outcast in class and have no friends, they'll make up a friend for themself and believe that they're the only person who can see and communicate with that friend. This is a child's instinctual psychological defense mechanism.

Xie Qingcheng: But people who aren't mentally ill are able to distinguish imagination from reality and realize that these are illusions. They know that they're born from the comfort they so desire. But for a child like He Yu, it's hard for him to recognize this—especially because his delusion is only partially imagined.

He Jiwei: By only partially imagined, you mean...?

Xie Qingcheng: Xie Xue does exist—she's my sister, and she's his closest friend who is indeed very nice to him. But I know my sister very well. She's always very enthusiastic around people, and although He Yu is a good friend of hers, they aren't particularly close yet. There are certain things that she wouldn't do for him.

Xie Qingcheng: However, with respect to He Yu, his mind needs to be supported. The things that he hoped Xie Xue would do but she didn't were filled in by his imagination. He only has one friend, and he doesn't want to be disappointed by his only friend. And so, his subconscious mind will try to convince him repeatedly that such things really did happen in the past, that Xie Xue really did do all of those things.

He Jiwei: But this is so mystifying that it's hard for me to believe.

Xie Qingcheng: It's not mystifying at all. The human brain is a very complex, precise instrument; such a phenomenon can occur if there's an error in a person's memory and the error is continuously reiterated.

Xie Qingcheng: It's just like how some people confuse dreams with reality, or the so-called Mandela effect.

He Jiwei: The Mandela effect?

Xie Qingcheng: It's not a strictly academic concept, but it's useful as an explanation. Executive He, you can understand it as when entire communities of people share discrepancies in their memories. If you search the internet, you can find many examples of it. For example, does Mickey Mouse wear overalls?

This time, it took He Jiwei some time to respond, as if he had been shocked stupid by Xie Qingcheng asking such a cute question during such a serious conversation.

He Jiwei: I think so.

Xie Qingcheng: He doesn't. But many people believe that he's always worn overalls—this is the Mandela effect. It's an erroneous memory that has been repeatedly affirmed by the human brain, resulting in this kind of impression.

Xie Qingcheng: Executive He, you can think of Mickey Mouse as being equivalent to my sister—she exists, but she's actually never worn overalls. However, He Yu used his own imagination to fill in the two nonexistent overall straps, resolutely believing this to be the truest reality of the matter.

He Jiwei: Then, is this considered a delusional disorder?

Xie Qingcheng: It can't be called that. To He Yu, this is a way for him to protect, comfort, and redeem himself.

A long time passed between this message and his next.

Xie Qingcheng: Executive He, with all due respect, you and Executive Lü don't spend enough time with him. Even children with healthy mindsets can hardly endure such neglect, never mind the fact that he's mentally ill.

Xie Qingcheng: He can't get any care and love, but he's stubborn about showing vulnerability. Perhaps stubborn isn't the right word, but he knows that it's useless to cry or beg because nothing will give him the reaction that he wants, so he's already used to internalizing everything and defending himself. The Xie Xue he imagined was actually his own reflection the entire time; it was his own heart that comforted him, borrowing Xie Xue's image to tell him what he wanted to hear.

Reading these old messages, He Yu thought about the wishes that were buried deep within his heart...

For example, *I'll always stay with you.*

For example, the words that he never got to hear face-to-face: "Happy Birthday."

Didn't he long for someone to gift those words to him?

But he never got to hear them...

Xie Qingcheng: Since nobody told him, and since he's someone with a strong sense of self-respect, he would never say such things to himself. Therefore, his brain relied partially on his imagination to fulfill his wish while maintaining his dignity at the same time. This is a kind of psychological self-defense mechanism that people have, so there's no need for you to worry too much.

He Jiwei: You've known about this all along?

Xie Qingcheng: I've observed it for a while now. I can't tell him about this, since the shock would be too much. But I always tell Xie Xue to stay a bit further away from him. Xie Xue shouldn't be the person on whom he develops an emotional dependence. Neither of us should be, Executive He. Sooner or later, we'll have to leave.

Xie Qingcheng: I'm a doctor, not He Yu's relative. I can't possibly waste an entire lifetime on a single medical case, and Xie Xue even less. I can only give him guidance, not the type of love he lacks and wants to have. My sister is the same.

He Yu didn't continue reading the following messages; they were no longer important. Knowing this was already enough.

More than enough.

Xie Qingcheng had been deceiving him all along, and Xie Xue wasn't real either. Of the two of them, one was the person who'd once given him the strongest encouragement with his articles of faith, allowing him to believe that there would come a day when he could return to regular society, while the other was the person who'd given him the warmest companionship, who would always rush to his side in the nick of time when he was at his most hopelessly desperate.

Just like how on the night of that torrential downpour, she'd knocked on his door while shouting his name, taken off her raincoat, and presented him with the chocolate cake that he wanted.

He never could have imagined that perhaps that the cake, and that Xie Xue...never existed at all.

Meanwhile, Xie Qingcheng had witnessed his pitiful, lowly self-comfort; the man had seen it all and knew it very well.

No one had ever loved him.

It was his own idiocy! He was too foolish, too stupid, too desperate in his yearning to walk amongst the warmth of the crowd. In order to become a normal person, in order to tuck his hideously ghoulish face away, he'd forged a faintly glimmering glow from within his own bloody skull.

Xie Qingcheng had seen it, but he had said, *"I can't possibly waste an entire lifetime on a single medical case, and Xie Xue even less. I can only give him guidance, and not the type of love he lacks and wants to have. My sister is the same."*

But if someone possessed love in the first place, why would he lie even to himself? What kind of liar would trick the entire world yet end up deceiving himself the most? Only the poorest, most destitute of liars.

The things he had were too few, and the tears he'd shed were too many. Even "Happy Birthday" was something he could only obtain through his own imagination. If he didn't lie to himself, what could he rely upon to continue living with a smile?

So, even in front of himself, he would wear a smiling mask tightly bolted to his face, which he was loath to take off. He would lie even to himself.

Xie Qingcheng was right. He did have self-respect. He didn't want to be seen as a patient, a madman. He knew that, given the He family's status, many people were waiting to see him come crashing down, to watch him make a fool of himself, to look at his corpse and rejoice in his blood. Thus, he strove even harder to prove himself; he didn't want to receive anyone's pity by showing them his scars.

He Yu stood in the empty living room for a very long time.

He stood there so long that time seemed to become slightly hazy. His gaze was light yet sharp, repeatedly sweeping over the ice-cold tide of messages before him. In the end, that sharp look seemed to have been eroded by the tide, becoming scattered and unfocused.

He slowly closed his eyes.

His mask had grown into his flesh, but Xie Qingcheng had cruelly torn it away. He reached up and touched his own face silently.

It hurt.

It hurt so much...

It hurt so badly it made his heart and entire body shudder.

It felt as though he'd lost everything overnight.

Xie Qingcheng's articles of faith were fake, Xie Xue's closeness was fake; the consolation he had given himself was fake, and in the end, even his self-respect, even the hard shell he used to protect himself, that mask, had been smashed to pieces. Only now did he suddenly realize that—as it turned out, his laughable, clownish face had already been exposed to Xie Qingcheng for many years.

So what exactly was he persevering for? And why did he have to be so stupid?! Risking his life to accompany that person for just a word of acknowledgment in return, or to repay the wisp of hope that Xie Qingcheng had once given him...

He'd disregarded his own life to gain favor with a liar for an all-encompassing lie!

He Yu started to laugh softly. He doubled over and leaned against the wall, laughter growing louder and louder, madder and madder, like a vengeful ghost stirring in its grave. The wraiths of sickness in his heart glided out in their hooded cloaks; he put his hand to his forehead as his laughter turned deranged—it seemed furious and hateful, sorrowful yet crazed, as tears fell incessantly down his cheeks...

It really hurt too much.

He saw Xie Qingcheng reach out to him with an open hand, but what lay in his palm was an ice-cold scalpel. This was the actual truth.

He saw Xie Xue pass him a piece of chocolate with a smile, but he blinked his eyes, and she was only gazing at him from afar.

This was the actual truth...

And then he saw... He saw himself standing before the floor-to-ceiling window. A storm was raging outside. The antique grandfather clock in the old residence rang twelve times—it was midnight, and he was surrounded by endless darkness.

But no one knocked on the door.

No one had ever knocked on the door.

He waited from darkness until dawn. The storm had ceased, and the long night had brightened, but he never managed to get a single, sincere wish of "Happy Birthday."

This was the actual truth.

Then, he saw himself strapped to a bed, gagged, as needles pierced his skin. He struggled and wailed like a dying beast, but he couldn't call out anyone's name.

He was a solitary island.

There were no bridges.

This was the actual fucking truth! The truth!

A child who was denied love. In order to resist the demons in the depths of his mind, to keep striving to live on, he lied to anyone and everyone—even himself—for so many years...

He Yu leaned against the wall. He'd already vengefully ripped away the bandages from his shoulder, allowing his wound to tear open. His blood was everywhere. Only the scent of it could please him and ground him and make him feel that he was actually alive! He had a body. The blood he shed was warm. He was a living, breathing person. He was alive... He was alive...

He buried his hands in his hair, knuckles whitening, veins protruding. He was like a blinded dragon with its claws torn out. Having lost the treasures he cherished and the lair he relied on for refuge, he'd been forced out into the sunlight, beneath the clear sky, with each one of his ugly scabs on display for everyone to see and ridicule as they pleased.

He'd finally woken up from his dream.

He'd been struggling for almost twenty years, but he was still insane.

No one had ever loved him, no one had ever cared for him.

He had nothing but a clumsy lie.

He'd never actually managed to earn anything.

48

MADNESS

IT HURT too much.

The lie about the contract, the truth about Xie Xue, the deception Xie Qingcheng had created, the way he fled without so much as a backward glance...

It was as if He Yu had lived the past nineteen years in a dream. He'd thought that he had disguised himself very well and tricked everyone, but in reality, *he* was the wretched lunatic who had been deceived.

He Yu clutched his head and howled grievously, like a trapped, blood-soaked beast that had fallen into a snare. The voice that came out of his throat was so hoarse and wrecked that it didn't even sound human. In his eyes, vacant confusion was mixed with frantic madness. He sat in his corner, curled up, hugging himself as though he was afraid of the cold.

What articles of faith?

All lies!

What warmth?

An illusion!

He was a madman; a delusional invalid; an ugly, laughable, absurd, comical idiot who had exposed his scars to everyone without even realizing it!

He seemed extremely pitiful, like a fetus that was about to die within its mother's body—isolated from the outside world, his umbilical cord cut, unable to breathe, sinking into an endlessly oppressive suffocation. He could only cry out from underwater, but no one ashore could hear him.

He could only hold tightly onto himself. The only warmth he could feel came from him alone... It had all been his own sad attempts to comfort himself.

He Yu clawed at his hair, then froze in place for a stretch of time. His eyes grew redder and redder as his sense of self grew dimmer and dimmer. Finally, he stopped wailing and sat up calmly, his body unfurling as he tilted his head back to look at the ceiling.

Then, he stood up.

His eyes were drawn to the display cabinet—reflected inside was his unbearably wretched silhouette.

So frighteningly unfamiliar.

The suppressed darkness and violence in his bones abruptly burst out as he grabbed a metal ornament from the side and smashed it into the cabinet with a loud bang. It was as if he had gone insane!

The evil dragon had been unleashed from its shackles. The devil inside him emerged from the cave and soared into the sky, summoning a vengeful rainstorm as it roared and bellowed. He Yu was completely swallowed by madness, howling as he smashed practically everything in the house, ripping open his wound even further in the process. The sickly stench of blood filled the air, but he didn't care at all.

He tore down the curtains and smashed the television, laying waste to every single thing within reach.

Surely, some offerings ought to be made to commemorate the death of his inner self.

He didn't know how long this crazed venting went on for, but regardless of how good the soundproofing was in his building, his neighbor downstairs couldn't take it any longer and ran up to knock on his door. He Yu abruptly opened it. His hand, holding a length of steel pipe that he had wrenched from the window, was still dripping blood. The room behind him was in shambles.

He Yu stared at the neighbor with a pair of bloodshot eyes. "Can I help you?"

The neighbor was so terrified he nearly pissed himself as his legs gave out, but He Yu grabbed him by the collar and pulled him upright. A heavy metallic stench flooded the neighbor's nose as He Yu's blood stained his luxurious silk nightgown.

He Yu asked menacingly again, "Can I help you?"

"No, no, no!" The neighbor hadn't expected to be faced with such a bloody and violent spectacle. The pale young man with the handsome face standing inside the apartment had an aura so evil he seemed like one of those crazy vengeful spirits on TV. The neighbor didn't dare say anything more. With his jowls trembling and thighs quaking, he clasped his hands together in a placating manner. "Ge, da-ge! Do whatever you like, whatever makes you happy, whatever makes you happy."

He Yu shoved him away and closed the door with a bang.

Stumbling, the neighbor practically crawled his way back into the elevator. Even before reaching his own door, he had already begun wailing in a trembling voice, "Wifey—wifey, save me..."

He Yu's rampage had been interrupted by this person's arrival.

Panting, he turned his head and looked around. How did this place look at all like a home? It was clearly the site of a chaotic battle.

After surveying the room with his bloodshot eyes, He Yu concluded that there was indeed nothing left for him to smash. He tossed the steel pipe aside, stepped over the ruins, and walked into the bathroom.

He looked at his ashen face in the cracked mirror. His reflection was fractured, just like the many different faces he showed to society.

He Yu stilled and allowed his breathing to return to a steady pace as his lips slowly stopped trembling...

His grief and madness had passed. Now the only thing he had left was serenity—a terrifying serenity. He had finished violently venting his feelings, and his entire lair was destroyed. What should he do next?

He still had to go outside. By now he had reached a point where he didn't even care whether he was normal or not—he wanted to reveal this abnormal appearance of his, to unfurl his craggy wings and fly out of his dark cave to roar at those so-called normal people.

The young man in the mirror slowly looked up. A hand dripping with blood stroked his cheek, then slowly clawed at it. A faint smile appeared at the corners of his mouth—it seemed gentlemanly and refined, but was, in reality, more unfeeling than it had ever been.

Meanwhile, far off in Huzhou Medical's faculty dorm, Xie Qingcheng's eyelid twitched a few times as a vague sense of unease settled over him.

He and Chen Man had finished eating dinner, and once he'd helped clean up the table, Chen Man prepared to head home.

Before leaving, Chen Man said, "Ge, I'll drop by again tomorrow night. Um..."

"Hm?"

"Don't go online for the next few days," he said softly. "It's not worth it."

Xie Qingcheng knew he was talking about the internet's reaction to the videos that had been displayed on the broadcasting tower, but Chen Man was overthinking it. Xie Qingcheng wasn't the kind of person who paid much attention to online news in the first place, especially when his real life was already such a mess.

But he assented. After seeing Chen Man off, he went downstairs to buy another pack of cigarettes. He called Xie Xue as he smoked.

Xie Xue's condition wasn't much better, but she was a bit more comfortable since Auntie Li was staying with her. As the siblings talked, Xie Qingcheng suddenly received another call. He said a few more words to Xie Xue, then hung up.

The call was from Zheng Jingfeng.

"Hello, Lao-Zheng."

"Xiao-Xie, a member of our unit just saw the kid who was with you at the archives."

Xie Qingcheng's chest tightened. "He's been discharged from the hospital?"

Zheng Jingfeng grunted in affirmation, but this was obviously not what he wanted to talk about. "Yeah. Oh, right, how old is that kid? Eighteen? Nineteen? I've forgotten..."

Xie Qingcheng paused for a moment before replying, "Why do you ask?"

"Do you think I want to? Weren't you the one who told me to let you know if anything happened?"

Xie Qingcheng's knuckles turned white. "What happened to him?"

"It's not really a big deal. Ah, I've realized that there really is a gap between the bourgeoisie and us proles. Fuck, at eighteen or nineteen, I was still spending all my time in training. Anyway, my guess is that even though that little friend of yours was discharged from the hospital, he's still in a lousy mood—he drove a fancy car to the Skynight Club... Oh, look, there are even messages about it in our work group chat. Apparently, he drove the sports car like a rocket, and they only finally managed to pull him over in front of the club. He cooperated, but his attitude was so fucking vile. When he got out of the car, he slammed the door and told them to just tow his car and fuck off to save him the trouble of finding a driver."

Xie Qingcheng had no response to that.

"And you're familiar with the Skynight Club, right? It's not a decent place at all—you can't say it's illegal, since it conducts its business properly and doesn't cross the line, but everyone knows how shady things can get at nighttime entertainment establishments..."

Xie Qingcheng took a deep breath, and He Yu's gentle, thoughtful visage seemed to appear before him once more. Regardless of whether that appearance of his was feigned, it still transformed into the cold, blood-stained face that had turned to look back at him in front of the broadcasting tower.

"I see." Xie Qingcheng pressed a hand to his forehead as he leaned against the window. "Thank you, Lao-Zheng."

"All right, then. You should listen to me more in the future and stop obsessing over your parents' case. You need to let your heart breathe. I can't bear seeing you like this."

"Okay."

After hanging up, Xie Qingcheng put on his jacket and headed over to the Skynight Club.

He thought of a younger He Yu standing in front of the sofa, unwilling to sacrifice his self-respect but also reluctant to see him leave; the sorrowful, stubborn boy who had forced himself to act as though nothing was wrong as he looked at Xie Qingcheng.

"Xie Qingcheng, I have a lot of allowance. I can..."

I can hire you.

I don't want to sink into this maelstrom. Please save me...save me, okay...?

He never saw the words He Yu couldn't say, the cries for help he couldn't utter. He Yu's own self-respect allowed him to preserve the last shred of dignity he had in front of Xie Qingcheng, but he missed his last chance to ask for help.

That year, Xie Qingcheng left He Yu. But when they met again, He Yu didn't seem to resent him all that much. And in Xie Qingcheng's time of greatest need, it was this child who had gone with him into the perilous lair of a beast—and nearly paid for it with his life.

When He Yu reached his hand out to Xie Qingcheng, he said that someone had once done the same thing for him. But Xie Qingcheng had done that because of his position, because of his job, because he had been performing his duties as expected of his station.

So then, why did this child do it?

Xie Qingcheng closed his eyes.

Zheng Jingfeng's words echoed in his ears. He said that He Yu had gone to patronize the Skynight Club, that He Yu had a vile attitude...

Xie Qingcheng knew that He Yu had never acted like that in the past.

For the sake of acknowledgment, for the sake of others' gazes, for the sake of reintegrating into society, and for the sake of stubbornly resisting his illness, He Yu never yielded to his desires; he never drank from Mephistopheles's poisoned wine. He refused to sink into depravity, refused to admit defeat; he lived by working ten times, a hundred times, harder than ordinary people, striving for perfection in everything that he did. He was too afraid of disappointing others.

As a patient, he tried to rely on his own efforts so that others wouldn't give up on him, so that they wouldn't equate him with the deceased cases of #1, #2, and #3.

He had been doing his utmost to cry for help the entire time.

That was why he was so afraid of making mistakes, afraid that he wasn't outstanding enough, afraid that others would be disappointed in him.

But in the end, he had still been abandoned.

"Xie Qingcheng, you might not be mentally ill, but you're even more heartless than me."

The words contained a restrained mockery, but that mockery had carried a heartfelt plea. And although Xie Qingcheng had heard those words, he'd failed to hear the boy's hidden imploring as he wept tears of blood.

Xie Qingcheng knew.

In all of that, he had truly let He Yu down.

That child used to trust him so much. Even though he'd never been particularly kind to him, always dealing with him in a strictly businesslike manner, it was already an instance of sincere and equal treatment that was difficult to come by for He Yu.

He Yu hadn't been wrong when he'd cursed at him. Xie Qingcheng was the heartless one, the one who had gotten everything wrong and failed to do anything right.

The club manager of the Skynight Club was a clever old man. His suit was crisply ironed, his face was overdone, and his personality was as slick as a rat that had scuttled out of a puddle of grease.

"Aiyo, Young Master He," he groveled. "A rare guest, a rare guest..."

He'd overheard everything that had happened just now between He Yu and the traffic officers. Although He Yu didn't come to Skynight very often, he was still considered part of the clientele. In the past, when he needed to network on behalf of his family, he'd brought clients here to relax. He usually only ever stayed for a brief while. He would chat for a spell with the people he brought over in that gentle, refined way of his, stoking the atmosphere, then he would head downstairs and sign the check, telling the manager to put the balance on his card before leaving.

But today, things were different.

The manager's eyes gleamed as he noted that Young Master He had come alone today. The entire city had heard about what had happened at Huzhou University by now. Given He Yu's leading role in that fiasco, the manager thought it completely normal that he would feel unsettled or behave erratically. He supposed that getting shot had made this young man reconsider his life and that he must have come to the conclusion that his days should be filled with more excitement. Thus, after finally seeing the light, he had come here to search for the true meaning of life, just like the other young masters of his generation.

To the manager, He Yu was a walking black Amex. He rushed forward and welcomed him with a smile. Even if Young Master He said that he wanted the manager's mom to come sit and talk with him, the manager likely wouldn't have hesitated to make a fucking long-distance phone call and buy her a ticket for the earliest flight in.

"Young Master He, which floor will it be for you tonight? I'll arrange the best service for you right away..."

He Yu had only done the bare minimum to patch up the gunshot wound on his arm before heading out. He was still wearing a simple, long-sleeved black turtleneck shirt with a pair of jeans. He'd even put on a baseball cap that gave him a student-like aura. But from beneath the shadow cast by the brim of his cap, one could see that his almond eyes were enshrouded by an uncommon darkness.

When He Yu lifted his head, the extravagant, dazzling lights of the Skynight Club shone in his overcast eyes.

"The top floor," he said.

This level consisted of a number of large private rooms. The waitstaff of these rooms were exceedingly secretive and had been personally trained by the owner, each one cleverer than the next. It was a place that was perfect for discussing all manners of business.

Of course, the price was likewise sky-high.

The eldest scion of the He family was really something else, the manager thought; he hadn't even bothered to dress up properly and yet he was demanding access to the top floor. He was lucky that he ran into the manager himself today. If he'd been dealing with one of his slow-witted underlings instead, with this incredibly casual student getup he was wearing, Young Master He likely would have found himself denied entry.

The manager thanked his lucky stars that he had been able to avoid such a scene of carnage. Given He Yu's unusual appearance and attitude today, this young man might actually end up tearing the place up if he was angered.

"Lead the way," He Yu said mildly as he stuck his hands into the pockets of his jeans.

The manager hastily bowed and said with a smile, "Yes, yes, come this way, Young Master He."

49

Descent

MONEY-SQUANDERING establishments like this, with their stink of perfume, were usually off-putting to He Yu. But now, this was the only place where he could experience a hint of the carnal warmth of the human world.

"Young Master He."

"Hello, Young Master He."

The hostess was reverential as she opened the door to the private room; she welcomed him with her head lowered, not even daring to raise her eyes.

The Skynight Club was a den of decadence where bodies writhed in luxurious debauchery. It was operated as a fully aboveboard entertainment venue, but all the hosts it employed were not only fit and beautiful, but they were also excellent conversationalists; even the revelers on the dance floor at the ground level were gorgeous. Many of these handsome men and beautiful women were willing to be taken out by clients on their own time, and when it came to a private relationship between individuals, well, that was just ordinary pleasure sought between couples in the middle of the night—just a fortuitous encounter, right? Simple romance. It was no one's business to interfere.

With the lure of such temptations, there was always a stream of luxury vehicles lining up outside the Skynight Club's front doors, and countless pairs of pale, milky legs would climb into their car seats and snuggle up to those VIPs with a smile as they rode off into the night.

He Yu had come here tonight with the malevolent intent to lash out. Falling into the muck had ignited a self-destructive kind of thrill in him.

It was the same mindset as that of a student who had put all his efforts and savings into his studies but failed to achieve respectable test results. No matter how hard he had strived, when the motivation to keep pushing onward finally dried out, when he failed the entrance exam once again, he would inevitably abandon himself to despair.

He Yu had finally figured it out. Why should he have to suffer so much just to hear pretty lies?

In a place like the Skynight Club, people would trip over themselves to cozy up to him; he could hear all kinds of pleasant talk and gentle coaxing all night long without a repeated word from any of them. He didn't need to lie to himself at all; as long as he opened his wallet, there were plenty of people who were happy to deceive him.

They wouldn't run off halfway through like Xie Qingcheng, and they definitely wouldn't scorn his lack of allowance during their escape.

"Young Master He, these are the brightest hostesses that I have on staff. They'll be in charge of serving your private room, so if there's anything you need, please don't hesitate to let them know."

He Yu didn't bother getting up from the sofa. He watched with an apathetic expression as the manager on duty, having received his permission, brought in two lines of hostesses. These were the top-end staff at the entertainment venue, each of them a different flavor of beauty. They filed in with smiles on their faces and stood behind the manager as he introduced them one by one. After that, the manager astutely took his leave, closing the door smoothly behind him.

"Young Master He, is there a game you would like to play today?"

Although this customer had a rather unfriendly look on his face, these well-trained hostesses nevertheless maintained their sweet smiles as they tentatively sounded him out.

After a moment of silence, He Yu smiled. "Let's break out some drinks. I feel bad, making all of you stand here so awkwardly."

The heavy, gilded drinks menu was passed into his hands. It was fucking first-degree robbery; bottles costing less than ten thousand yuan were a rare sight, but there were plenty of wines with price tags of a hundred or two hundred thousand yuan.

Leaning indolently back against the sofa, He Yu checked off everything on the front page without batting an eye. Then, his eyes fell on a signature liquor named Plum Fragrance 59.

He'd been here with clients countless times and knew exactly what kind of signature liquor this was. The string of zeros listed on the drink's price tag, as well as the three flaming heart symbols beside it, made certain that the customer knew what kind of *experience* this drink would provide. When He Yu had picked up the check on his previous visits, he'd see "Plum Fragrance 59" listed on almost every bill.

"You might think that it smells very sophisticated at first," a half-drunk scoundrel who'd recommended it to He Yu had said as he laughed into his ear, "but...it's also very cheap and depraved. You know what I mean, Young Master He?"

He Yu checked off Plum Fragrance 59 and carelessly passed the order list over to the young woman closest to him.

The hostesses glanced at each other as excitement and delight filled their eyes. When they walked into the room, they'd thought that He Yu would be a tough customer. However, they were finding that he was actually handsome and pleasant—and generous, at that. They didn't even have to coax him into ordering the most expensive champagne tower on the menu.

"Young Master He, do you play dice?"

He Yu smiled and said mildly, "I do. I'm just afraid you won't be able to keep up with me."

The girl who had asked the question flirtatiously chided him, "Well, if I can't keep up with you, Young Master He ought to be a gentleman and let me win."

"That's right..."

Soft, warm bodies pressed closer into his sides, against his arms and legs, as He Yu looked at them with calm indifference. Indeed, given his current status, what kind of fawning ingratiation couldn't he afford, as long as he didn't seek sincerity?

Bottles were opened and the champagne tower was built. The girls giggled ecstatically as they grew increasingly fearless in the glimmering liquid light.

"Young Master He, why are you here all alone today? Where are your friends?"

"Young Master He, can you tell us about what happened at Huzhou University? The rumors are wild, and I want to hear your side of the story..."

Amidst the gentle banter, He Yu's cell phone suddenly began to ring. He glanced at it, and his expression subtly shifted. It was Xie Qingcheng.

"Who is it?"

"It's nothing," replied He Yu. After a beat of silence, he propped his chin on his hand and casually swiped a finger over his screen to reject the call. He turned back to the girl before him, who had been in the middle of cracking a joke. "Go on."

Seeing He Yu's interest in her joke, the girl poured even more enthusiasm into her speech.

A few seconds later, Xie Qingcheng called again.

The phone rang nonstop, clamoring for him to pick up. A particularly audacious girl hid a smile behind her hand as she asked, "Is it Young Master He's girlfriend?"

"You're joking." He Yu rejected Xie Qingcheng's call again.

This time the silence lasted longer, but a little over a minute later, the phone began to ring for a third time. He Yu was about to reject it, but his finger froze as it landed on the screen.

This time, the call wasn't from Xie Qingcheng but Xie Xue.

After a brief hesitation, he answered his phone.

"He Yu." Xie Xue called out from the other end of the line.

"Mm."

"He Yu...I-I wanted to ask you...about that day on campus. What exactly happened to my brother when he was with you?" There was a tearful note to Xie Xue's voice, causing the fake smile that He Yu was wearing for all these strangers to fade slightly. "Why did those old recordings of his suddenly get streamed on the murder video channel? I was afraid to look at first...but today, I did a thorough search online and found so many people cursing him. Did you know...there were even people who posted our address online, and someone came to vandalize our front door... I really... I'm really so upset right now... and I'm too scared to call my brother too. Even if I called him, he wouldn't say anything, he'd just scold me for searching up all these things even though he told me not to. I..."

Xie Xue couldn't bear it any longer and burst into tears. All that remained on the line was the sound of her sobbing.

The hostesses of this money-burning establishment had no idea what was happening. They kept smiling as they poured He Yu's wine.

He Yu stroked a hand through a woman's long hair with a twisted tenderness, but as he listened to Xie Xue's tearful lament, the light in his eyes dimmed, the sounds of her despair passing through the speaker and soaking directly into his heart.

"I don't know what to do anymore..."

For a moment, He Yu thought of Wei Dongheng. Even though he was the one Xie Xue had a crush on, when something happened, she chose to go to He Yu instead. He felt slightly comforted for a moment, but then he remembered that Wei Dongheng had taken a leave of absence to visit his father in the military due to the death of an older family member, so he was at a heavily fortified army base with hardly any signal. Besides, He Yu thought, it was just a secret crush—Wei Dongheng might not even know what major Xie Xue taught, so of course she wouldn't seek him out.

"He Yu..." Xie Xue sobbed spasmodically, her voice like an injured kitten. "What should I do...? I wanted to help my brother out, so I-I started a livestream to explain, but..." She whimpered. "I wanted to have a proper conversation, but no one was willing to calmly listen to me tell the whole story... They started to curse at me halfway through, or just didn't listen at all... They even said that I was a fraud, that I wasn't his little sister, that I'm...I'm..."

She sucked in a breath but didn't continue. She sobbed for a while before saying helplessly, "They thought I was trying to use the murders to go viral, so they reported my video... Some people even said that my parents were the real culprits behind the scenes... He Yu, you know they've been gone for years. The dead should be respected. I thought we could leave the deceased out of it...but th-they...they asked me to show my parents' cremation certificate...!"

Xie Xue wept bitterly, unable to continue speaking.

He Yu's knuckles had gone slightly pale.

He was too used to treating Xie Xue well, so upon hearing her cries, his first instinct was to comfort her, to help her solve her problem. But just as he was about to speak, he recalled her messages to Xie Qingcheng.

That human warmth slowly retreated from his disease-ridden, decaying heart. He fell silent.

A voice inside him sighed and tried to coax him. Although Xie Xue wasn't as good to him as he'd imagined, when all was said and done, she hadn't known anything. At the very least, she was the person he was closest to and the one who treated him with the most tenderness. That was enough.

But another voice stabbed into his flesh. There was no need for him to be benevolent or caring anymore. In fact, he should stop being so stupid.

"Can I ask you something, Xie Xue?" He Yu finally said.

"Mm... Go...go ahead..." Xie Xue sniffled.

He Yu, seated in the luxurious private room, said to the girl who was curled up in her rundown and shabby little house, "When the hackers played those videos on all the mobile devices around Huzhou University that day, you saw them too."

"I did..."

"Your brother is a doctor in a field related to psychiatry. It's understandable that he would be attacked if he says things like that. The internet fosters a more emotionally volatile environment in the first place; when nobody has to put a face to the words they're saying or reading, they act much more aggressively. I don't think it's at all strange that he's getting cursed at."

"But it's just a few words he said... All these years, he's always been diligent and responsible when it comes to his work. He's never done things carelessly, you know this..."

"I know," He Yu interrupted her. He'd almost never interrupted Xie Xue before. "But I also know other things about your brother, like how he told you to stay away from me."

Xie Xue seemed to be at a loss for how to respond, as if she didn't know the reason for the turnaround in his attitude.

He Yu, however, was so calm it was disturbing.

"Xie Xue, there's only one thing I want to ask you right now. Hearing your brother warn you about me all these years—have you ever suspected that I might be mentally ill?"

"I—" Xie Xue froze at the unexpected question.

Had she?

Had she ever?

In the countless days that had passed, had she ever felt just a sliver of hesitation toward He Yu because of Xie Qingcheng's words? Had she ever suspected, deep in her heart, that the reason why Xie Qingcheng had lived in the He family's residence for so long and admonished her constantly was because He Yu was also a patient? Did she really have no suspicions at all?

"I..." Xie Xue wasn't any good at lying. She paused, hesitating for a long while as she held her phone dazedly. "But...but how would you... Even if you were, then... No, no. You're so outstanding, you definitely wouldn't..."

He Yu's eyelashes quivered, casting wispy shadows over his face. He smiled softly and said, "You're right, I'm not."

One of the hostesses lit a cigarette and tried to pass it to He Yu. He took it, glanced at it, and then returned it to her with a smile and a polite shake of his head. He seemed calm on the surface, but there was a deranged darkness in his eyes.

"Then, He Yu, can you—"

"No," He Yu said gently. "Xie Xue, I'm sorry. I can't."

He was still smiling as he spoke, but the dull pain in his heart was boring through his chest with a force powerful enough to splinter the sky. His cold fingertips played with the woman's hair.

"I have some business to take care of tonight, so I can't step away. Why don't you find someone else to keep you company?" He Yu's lips parted. "We weren't all that close to begin with, isn't that so?"

The girl at the other end of the line was dumbfounded. She'd never seen this side of He Yu before. She'd never heard him speak in a voice so gentle and refined yet devoid of the slightest hint of emotion.

Or perhaps the emotions entwined within were simply too deep, too profound. So profound that they'd crushed that youth—the He Yu that she knew, the He Yu that he himself knew—until he was mangled beyond recognition.

He Yu didn't wait for Xie Xue to reply. He hung up, smiling.

He'd been completely right. Xie Qingcheng's presence had rendered all his past efforts completely futile; he and Xie Xue could never have gotten together.

No. Perhaps, from Xie Qingcheng's perspective, it wasn't just Xie Xue that He Yu shouldn't be having an intimate relationship with, but anyone at all.

Seeing that he'd hung up, the girl clinging to his side, who was the prettiest in the room, pouted. "Young Master He, what do you want to play next?" Her fingertips stroked his thigh indecently.

He Yu put down his phone and stared disdainfully at her. In a mild tone, he said, "Take your hands off me. I don't like it when people touch me without permission. Sit properly, and don't pull any of your tricks. Otherwise, I'll need to ask you to leave."

His erratic behavior gave the girl a fright. The room fell silent. Everyone else sat up straighter, unsure of what to do.

He Yu ignored them as he drank on his own. He even uncorked that bottle of Plum Fragrance 59.

"Young Master He," the leader of the group tried to remind him, "this liquor..."

"I know what this is."

He was very aware. He'd only uncorked the bottle—if or when he would drink it depended on how he ended up feeling.

The atmosphere had become strained, and the girls didn't dare to make a sound. They stood there frozen like that until their feet started aching in their eight-inch heels.

Then, a clamor came from outside the room.

"Sir, you can't go in there..."

"Sir—*sir*—"

All of a sudden, the door to the private room was rudely thrown open.

He Yu looked askance at the intruder.

The man who appeared before He Yu's icy-cold eyes, wearing a white button-down shirt and slim-fit dress pants, was none other than Xie Qingcheng. He hadn't picked up any of Xie Qingcheng's calls, so Xie Qingcheng had come barging in himself.

The manager on duty by the door turned pale with fright. "Y-you useless waste of space! How could you let someone up here?"

The complexion of the bouncer who was trailing Xie Qingcheng had likewise turned waxy, but before he could say anything, He Yu spoke up lazily from his spot on the sofa. "Forget it." His voice carried the hint of a sneer, cold enough to cut through bone. "He's quite formidable. It's to be expected that you couldn't stop him. Since he's already here, you might as well just let him in."

He Yu was speaking to the two employees, but his eyes remained unblinkingly fixed on Xie Qingcheng.

Xie Qingcheng had rushed here, so he was panting through parted lips, his breathing a bit uneven. Several strands had escaped from his usually neat hair and spilled over his keenly penetrating eyes, which sparked with flames like dots of crimson ink fallen into water.

He Yu stared into those eyes for a while before speaking with surprising composure. "Doctor Xie, please come in."

"Ah...this..." The bouncer who had been trying to stop Xie Qingcheng still hadn't caught up with this sudden change in circumstances.

The manager, however, had a keen eye and was quick to react. How could he not recognize Xie Qingcheng? He'd been all over the internet for the past few days—he had suffered a shock at Huzhou University alongside He Yu. There was definitely some kind of unusual dispute between these two VIPs, and outsiders had better stay as far away as possible to avoid getting swept up in the impending hurricane.

He shot the patrolling guard a meaningful look, and the two of them quickly retreated from the scene, closing the door that Xie Qingcheng had thrown open as they left.

Inside the room, the two men looked at each other, neither of them speaking a word. But the instant their eyes met, both of them knew what was going through the other's mind.

It had only been a handful of days since their last meeting, but at this moment, their perspectives had already been turned on their heads—their positions had been reversed, and everything had changed.

50

I Was No Longer Who I Was Before

"How did you know I was here?"

He Yu poured a glass of red wine for himself. After pouring another for Xie Qingcheng, he gestured to the woman beside him to pass the drink over.

Xie Qingcheng didn't take it.

He Yu interlaced his fingers and looked at him calmly. After a moment, he said, "Doctor Xie, if you really want to have a proper conversation with me, it would be best if you finish this glass of wine."

Suppressing a myriad of complicated emotions, Xie Qingcheng looked down at him from where he stood and tried his hardest to keep his cool. "He Yu, it's time for you to go."

"Don't say that—people might think we have some sort of special relationship." He Yu smiled. The alluring woman beside him lit another cigarette; surprisingly, he accepted it this time. As he stared unblinkingly at Xie Qingcheng with his almond eyes, his lips parted to take the cigarette. He took a slow, deep drag, then gracefully and unhurriedly breathed it out, dispersing a cloud of gray smoke.

He Yu was a social smoker. When he was networking, he would sometimes accept a cigarette with a shallow smile to blend in. But he didn't enjoy smoking, and he never touched them in private.

Before now, Xie Qingcheng had no idea that He Yu, as someone who abhorred smoking, could hold a cigarette in this effortless, even well-practiced manner.

"Give Doctor Xie a cigarette too."

The woman lit another cigarette as directed and held it before Xie Qingcheng.

Xie Qingcheng didn't take it. "I don't smoke."

He Yu laughed, pressing the hand holding his cigarette against his forehead. "My god... Doctor Xie, you are really a complete hypocrite, aren't you. How did I never realize?"

"There are many things you don't know," said Xie Qingcheng. "If you leave with me now, you can ask me whatever you want. As long as I can answer, I'll tell you everything."

He Yu, who was lazily reclining against the sofa, sat up at Xie Qingcheng's words. Straightening up, he propped his elbow on the back of the sofa, then nodded with a sigh.

"That's right. There are many things I don't know." He raised his puppy-like almond eyes—though right now, the look in those eyes was eerily cold, more reminiscent of a wolf.

"For example..." Xie Qingcheng prompted.

"For example, the reason why you suddenly refused to keep working at the hospital back then, or why you suddenly began avoiding me as if I were some vicious snake or scorpion..."

He Yu paused. He didn't plan to mention Xie Xue or the contract to Xie Qingcheng yet. He'd already said enough. What was the point of adding more and further highlighting his own idiocy?

"Xie Qingcheng—" He Yu's pupils drifted upward as he glanced coldly at that man, pausing between every word he ground out. "I didn't know about any of this back then."

Xie Qingcheng closed his eyes. "Is that why you abandoned yourself to this den of iniquity?"

The girls of this den of iniquity lapsed into silence.

He Yu's smile widened, menacingly revealing the canines that he usually kept hidden. With this subtle change, his normally gentle features became rather sinister.

"First of all, Doctor Xie, this is an above-board establishment which doesn't deal in sex, gambling, or drugs. The girls who work here are beautiful and attentive in their service, but that should be of no consequence to you. If I spend a hundred thousand yuan on a bottle of wine, I'd hardly expect to be served by a bunch of hideous trolls. Secondly, Xie Qingcheng, may I ask why you always hold yourself in such high regard?"

Xie Qingcheng was silent.

"Just who do you think you are? Don't tell me you think that no matter where I go or what I do, it's all because of you?" He Yu's smile disappeared, leaving behind only storm clouds in its wake. "Professor Xie, I know that older people like to put on airs. Plus, you're quite a successful professor, so there are always plenty of students chasing after you and fawning over you. You feel like you're on top of the world, right? It makes sense that you'd get used to being treated like a big shot wherever you go. I get why a middle-aged person like you might have that kind of problem. But just so we're clear, I only do things when I feel like it."

He Yu tapped away his cigarette ash and leaned back, resting his other arm against the back of the sofa. "It has absolutely nothing to do with you."

Only then did Xie Qingcheng notice He Yu's bloodshot eyes and his sickly, discolored lips. He Yu was in an even worse state now than during the severe flare-ups he'd had in the past. Xie Qingcheng's heart lurched.

He Yu often had a high fever during his flare-ups, and Xie Qingcheng knew his symptoms better than anyone. He subconsciously reached for He Yu's forehead to check his temperature.

He Yu's hand snapped around Xie Qingcheng's wrist. He didn't appear to be exerting himself, but despite his lack of expression, his fingers tightened with a force that brooked no refusal.

"Mm. If you have something to say, then say it properly. There's no need to get physical," he said, gazing at Xie Qingcheng. "I don't think we've ever been so close that you can touch me however you like."

Xie Qingcheng's arm slackened, and the light in his eyes gradually dimmed.

The two of them stayed deadlocked for a spell before He Yu loosened his hold and Xie Qingcheng lowered his hand.

"He Yu," Xie Qingcheng said eventually. He turned away to avoid He Yu's dark, icy gaze. "Regardless of whether you believe it or not, the things that I said back then... They weren't about you. I wasn't talking about you."

"What things?" He Yu feigned confusion, dipping his head in thought. Then he grinned. "Oh—'I don't think dying for the sake of a patient is worth it, and to be murdered by a lunatic would be such a waste it'd be laughable.' Well said. You have a point. Why would you need to explain any further?"

He looked around and continued mildly, "Don't tell me there's a lunatic among us? Shouldn't those people be shut away, locked up in cages and restrained, treated with electroshock therapy, and force-fed medicine? If it comes to it, it's best to cut open their skulls and slice through their nerves. How can we possibly allow them the freedom to breathe fresh air whenever they please? Don't you agree?"

Xie Qingcheng didn't respond. The private room was filled with too many onlookers, and He Yu's status as a mentally ill patient was a secret that few were privy to. He fell silent for a moment before he raised his peach-blossom eyes and asked, "Can you send these people out?"

"Why?"

"There are some things that I'd like to say to you in private."

He Yu smiled. "I don't think that's necessary. I think we can skip the lecture, Doctor Xie. You have so many students waiting for you to expound on universal truths to them—there's no need to waste your energy on me. It's not like I'm anything special to you, and the same can be said for what you are to me. This is fine. I'd rather not complicate our relationship any further. If that's all, then you can go."

Given Xie Qingcheng's temper, in the past, he definitely would have given He Yu an earful and then forced him to obey his commands. But standing before He Yu now, knowing he was the one at fault, Xie Qingcheng only said, "What can I do to make you go home? Your parents wouldn't want to see you like this."

It would have been better if he hadn't mentioned He Jiwei and Lü Zhishu, because the moment he brought them up, He Yu's mood immediately darkened. He stared at Xie Qingcheng. After everything they'd said, they'd still ended up looping back to his parents.

He thought back to the messages Xie Qingcheng had sent to He Jiwei. Those had been much more genuine than anything he said to He Yu. Perhaps in Xie Qingcheng's mind, only He Jiwei was a person who could stand on equal footing with him.

The day Xie Qingcheng quit his job, He Yu had abandoned his dignity and pathetically tried to use his allowance to keep this man from leaving. It was because he'd believed that if Xie Qingcheng left,

Xie Xue would disappear too, and he would once again fall into that inescapably terrifying loneliness.

Back then, he had said to Xie Qingcheng, *I have a lot of allowance. I can...*

But Xie Qingcheng had interrupted him, launched into a slew of bombastic, pretentious-sounding rhetoric, and told him that first and foremost, his employer was He Jiwei. He said that He Yu couldn't possibly afford to hire him, and that he might as well save his insignificant pocket money and spend it on cakes to make himself happy.

He Yu should have known right then and there that to Xie Qingcheng, he was only ever He Jiwei's son. If not for his father, Xie Qingcheng might not pay him any attention.

He Yu's already grim mood crept even closer to madness at this thought, but his expression remained apathetic.

He carefully examined Xie Qingcheng as he slowly finished the wine in his glass, thinking of He Jiwei, thinking of the broadcasting tower, thinking of Xie Xue, thinking of the sincerity that he had never once received... He hated Xie Qingcheng so much. He wanted to tear him to shreds.

As He Yu poured himself another glass of wine, he realized that the cup in front of Xie Qingcheng was untouched. He grew even angrier, sneering, "Doctor Xie really has no sense of etiquette. What kind of person comes to apologize by bringing up someone's parents to subdue them, and without even deigning to share a drink with them? Are you planning on saving the wine in your glass to raise fish with?"

He grabbed another empty cup, picked an open bottle at random, and filled the glass to the brim.

"Take a seat. Since you're here, you might as well sit down and drink with me for a while. We can talk afterward. Doctor Xie, you don't smoke. Could it be that you also don't drink?"

Xie Qingcheng knew he wouldn't be regaining the dominant position in their relationship today. So he did as He Yu said, wasted no more words, and sat down on the sofa across from him.

"If I drink, will you leave?"

"Is Doctor Xie willing to risk his life to accompany a degenerate like me?"

The private room was deathly silent. As if affected by the tension between the two men, everyone else barely dared to breathe. Amidst this nerve-racking silence, Xie Qingcheng reached over and into that invisible bloody maelstrom. He picked up the wine glass from the low marble table and plunked it down in front of him. Through the swirling liquid, beneath the hazy lights, Xie Qingcheng's features looked as cold and hard as sedimentary rock at the base of an icy pool.

He raised the glass of dry red wine and drained it in a single gulp. Then, he picked up the other glass of liquor that He Yu had poured for him and likewise tossed it back without blinking.

The strong alcohol burned a path down his throat.

He Yu finally smiled. "Excellent. Xie-ge can really hold his drink."

He tilted his head, eyes still fixed on Xie Qingcheng, and said to the young woman beside him, "Pour him another glass."

The lead hostess was silent, but her face blanched. She gathered her courage and leaned down to whisper a few words into He Yu's ear.

He Yu started in surprise, his gaze sweeping over to the bottle of liquor that he had just poured for Xie Qingcheng.

Plum Fragrance 59...?

H-he had accidentally given Xie Qingcheng a glass of aphrodisiac liquor!

He Yu had been planning on using this liquor to help himself let loose, since he was in a bad mood today. But he had accidentally made Xie Qingcheng drink it instead. His eyes shot up to

Xie Qingcheng's face, only to meet the man's cold, stern gaze. The liquor's effect had yet to kick in. Xie Qingcheng still had no idea that he had been drugged.

But He Yu knew that Xie Qingcheng wouldn't remain sober for long.

"You might think that it smells very sophisticated at first, but...it's also very cheap and depraved..." The words that He Yu's half-drunk friend had said into his ear resurfaced in his mind.

How could he have made such a stupid mistake? Why hadn't he taken a good look at the bottle when he poured the drink?!

His heart began to pound. Cold sweat dripped down his back. But in the several dozen seconds of silence that followed, He Yu's mood went from shocked to calm, then from calm to crazed. The mistake had already been made, so did that mean he *had* to rush Xie Qingcheng to the hospital? He could never.

Besides, there was no point in taking Xie Qingcheng to the hospital. The aphrodisiac only provoked desire. It wasn't poison.

He Yu stared fixedly and silently at Xie Qingcheng, dressed impeccably in his neat attire, his appearance stern and self-restrained and his face exceedingly dignified. This unintended accident sparked an idea in He Yu's crazed mind that roared into a flame.

Perhaps...fate had willed this?

This was retribution. This was Xie Qingcheng's retribution! He was reaping what he sowed. Even fate couldn't stand his hypocrisy any longer, so it brought him this coincidence.

Xie Qingcheng was only human, and all humans had desires. When they were consumed by a desire that they couldn't satisfy, they would fall into a wretched state, begging on their knees for gratification.

He Yu stared at Xie Qingcheng in silence. His curiosity was ignited. How magnificent a sight would that be, if Xie Qingcheng were to burn in the flames of this liquor and kneel before him, unable to even talk properly as he drowned in desire and completely lost control of himself?

Xie Qingcheng set down his empty glass. "Is this enough?"

He Yu didn't answer. That idea of seeing Xie Qingcheng succumb to desire was still circling his head, tempting him. But because giving him the first cup of Plum Fragrance 59 had been unintentional, He Yu was still a bit hesitant to proceed.

Xie Qingcheng said, "If this isn't enough, I'll keep drinking with you. I can drink until you're satisfied and willing to leave. As long as you don't lose yourself tonight, as long as you don't make a mess of yourself here."

Startled, He Yu looked up. "Why?"

Xie Qingcheng told him with deliberate emphasis, "Because this was my mistake. And since it was my mistake, you shouldn't be the one paying the price."

In his muddled state, He Yu's heart stuttered violently, just like it had all those years ago when Xie Qingcheng had told him for the first time that the mentally ill ought to be given equal treatment. But then rage overtook him. He was irate with himself. Why, after it had already come to this, would he still be moved by a few paltry words from this person?

This vehement rage only encouraged He Yu's cruelty. His hesitation vanished, and he finally decided to carry out the malicious plot brewing deep within his mind.

He slowly leaned back and splayed back against the sofa. He sighed softly. "Xie-ge... Look, you're trying to placate me again."

This sudden change in address seemed to give Xie Qingcheng some hope. He gazed at He Yu, who had propped a hand against his cheek and was still sighing.

"But, for some reason, I'm still willing to let you placate me," He Yu said.

"He Yu..."

"Xie-ge, tell me, is everything that you're saying to me this time the honest truth?"

Xie Qingcheng looked into his eyes. For some reason, he felt a faint discomfort in his heart. He said, "It is."

He Yu watched him quietly for a long time before his face broke into the expression he used to wear, like that of a fledgling dragon. "You're not lying to me?"

"I'm not lying to you."

"Then let's make a pinky promise."

He Yu slowly leaned forward and offered his finger. He had made a very childish request, as if he had also drunk too much. But the moment Xie Qingcheng extended his own finger, He Yu suddenly opened his hand, reached forward...and coldly caressed Xie Qingcheng's handsome face.

He looked at Xie Qingcheng in amusement, the fledgling dragon's innocence transforming into the sinister gloom of an evil dragon right in front of Xie Qingcheng's eyes.

"How naive of you, Xie Qingcheng. Were you really going to make a pinky promise with me? It's such a pity that this time—I was the one who was lying to you. How could I possibly trust you again so easily? You hurt me so deeply."

The hint of light in Xie Qingcheng's eyes dimmed once again. In the prolonged silence, the youth watched the fire fading from the man's eyes.

"How about this," He Yu said after some thought.

He sat back up, calmly picked up that bottle of Plum Fragrance 59, and signaled for a pretty, clever woman to bring over an empty glass.

He personally filled it more than half-full and placed it on Xie Qingcheng's side of the table.

The lead hostess's face paled in fright. She'd assumed that since He Yu knew about this strong liquor, he wouldn't give this man any more. That one glass would be difficult enough to handle—but here He Yu was, pouring Xie Qingcheng yet another nearly full glass.

"The sight of you like this moves me a little," He Yu said mildly. "I can give you another chance. But you have to show me your sincerity."

The first glass had been a mistake. But he was going to coax Xie Qingcheng into downing this second glass of his own volition.

"I don't have many requests. Just drink a few more rounds with me, and when I'm satisfied, I'll leave with you. I won't force you, but if you've truly begun to care about me, you'll be willing to grant me this much." He Yu looked up. "What do you think?"

Xie Qingcheng looked at him in silence. Then, a moment later, he raised the glass that He Yu had poured for him once again.

"As long as you'll go, I'll drink."

He Yu watched as Xie Qingcheng tilted his head back, his throat bobbing as he swallowed. Amidst his own tipsiness burned a densely roiling cloud of resentment.

Drink it. Drink it all.

Once you've drunk enough of this liquor, your retribution will come.

Retribution, He Yu thought once more.

He would be able to see all of Xie Qingcheng's ugly desire, see him lose control in front of these women, painfully ensnared yet unable to satisfy his need.

That was what they called karma, what they called a complete loss of face.

The hostesses in the room barely dared to breathe. They could see that Young Master He was messing with this man on purpose.

He had generously poured the Plum Fragrance 59 into a large wine glass, and from the way things were going, he seemed to be planning on having this man drain the entire bottle.

Two women standing near the back of the room trembled in fright, tugging at the hems of each other's miniskirts. One whispered to the other, "What should we do?"

"What else can we do? Stand here and keep them company."

"I'm so worried something will happen. The last time a big shot drank a bit too much, he nearly tormented the mistress he brought with him to death. What if Young Master He makes us help him later..."

"Don't worry, don't worry, w-we can still refuse. We're only here to serve drinks. Everything else is personal business where all parties have to be willing... Even Young Master He can't force us..."

"But..."

Their voices were a bit loud. The lead hostess standing in front overheard them and turned back to give them a warning glare. Afraid to make another sound, the two girls looked down, their hearts pounding in their chests.

The third glass was downed.

A light flush appeared on Xie Qingcheng's face, and his eyes began to lose focus. But he had yet to notice anything wrong with the liquor. He only looked at the young man in front of him.

He reached up and pressed a hand to his forehead. With a drunken and slightly nasal tone, he said, "He Yu, that's enough. Stop this and come home with me."

He Yu poured Xie Qingcheng another full glass of the liquor and pushed it over. In a voice that had become soft and was no longer as icy-cold as it was when Xie Qingcheng first arrived, he enticed him, "All right, of course I'll go back with you. You're such a prestigious person. I'll listen to everything you say... Come, Xie-ge, have another glass. After this, the whole bottle will be pretty much gone, so don't waste any of it now."

Xie Qingcheng leaned back against the sofa. Those peach-blossom eyes of his were already bloodshot and a little misty under the influence of the alcohol. His face had also become rather flushed. But he was still neatly dressed, his shirt securely buttoned up, not showing the slightest inclination of breaching decorum.

He downed the fourth glass of liquor.

The bottle was almost empty, yet Xie Qingcheng was still in full control of his faculties and did not take even the slightest glances at the beautiful women surrounding him.

If someone had faked it for long enough, part of their act would become fused to their true self, wasn't that right?

He Yu fell silent. He was a little displeased, a little irritated. He thought that perhaps because Xie Qingcheng had been single for too long, he needed some egging on. He looked up, shooting a glance at the two women standing next to Xie Qingcheng.

The two quick-witted jiejies immediately realized what they needed to do. One of them picked up the glass with a smile, while the other walked around the back of the sofa and sat down coyly, leaning into Xie Qingcheng.

"Hey, handsome..."

"I heard Young Master He call you Xie-ge, so I'll call you that too, all right?" The girl's body bent in a supple arc as she looked up coquettishly and exhaled a fragrant breath into Xie Qingcheng's ear. Her manicured hand drew closer to Xie Qingcheng's broad chest, and she slid her fingertips over the rigidly fastened collar of his ascetic dress shirt. After all, men's collars were designed to be undone by others.

Xie Qingcheng was handsome and brimming with masculinity, so genuine interest bled into the girl's provocative teasing. "Xie-ge, why don't I drink another glass with you...?"

A slap rang through the room as Xie Qingcheng grabbed the woman's slender wrist in a vice grip, making her flinch.

He closed his eyes for a beat, and some lucidity returned to his gaze. He shook her off. "Get off me."

The woman was speechless.

"Get off. Stop acting so shamelessly."

The woman turned pale before flushing red. Finally, she looked awkwardly toward He Yu, unsure how Young Master He would react.

And then she saw He Yu's downright terrifying expression as he stared fixedly at the man sitting across from him. He Yu was leaning back against the sofa, one elbow extending across the back of it and his other hand holding his wine glass. His slender legs were crossed, and his eyes were icy-cold, overflowing with frost. Since his plan had failed, he had finally stopped pretending.

"You..." Xie Qingcheng's head throbbed as a terrible fever flashed through him again and again. "Are you leaving or not...?"

He Yu sighed. "You can't even utter two words of sweet talk without reverting to bossing people around. Xie-ge, you are such a heartless bastard." He paused, and a dark, dangerous smile bloomed at the corners of his mouth. "Mm. I'm willing to go with you now. But at this point, can you even leave?"

Xie Qingcheng's gaze inched up slowly. Even the rims of his eyes seemed to be burning.

He finally realized that something was wrong. The effects of Plum Fragrance 59 had begun to rush madly through his entire body. Xie Qingcheng gasped for air as his body's visibly adverse reaction to the alcohol manifested right before He Yu's eyes. Xie Qingcheng's originally pale skin flushed an unnatural shade of pink, like a spot of rouge frozen within a slab of ice. It was as though the liquor had soaked into his very bones.

"This liquor..."

"It's a little expensive," He Yu crooned. "But it's a good vintage."

"You...!"

"Doctor Xie treated me so well; of course I have to return the favor. Isn't that right?"

Xie Qingcheng jerked to his feet. He never could've imagined that He Yu would go this far. Flames of fury burned directly into his suppressed inner heart as he swept everything off the tea table, shattering the wine glasses and liquor bottles and sending shards across the floor.

He stepped over the tea table and grabbed He Yu by the lapels. "Are you fucking insane?! You... He Yu... You actually..."

"Yes?"

Xie Qingcheng's voice was shaking with fury. No matter how guilty he felt, his eyes still reddened with rage at what this lunatic had done. "You drugged me!"

51

I Wanted Him to Submit

"GE, DON'T TALK nonsense." He Yu pressed a finger to his lips before immediately curving it and dropping his hand. He smiled faintly with his eyes lowered. "It was just a few glasses of liquor. What drugs are you talking about? Besides, no one forced you to drink. You drank it all of your own volition. Why are you blaming me for your intoxication?"

Xie Qingcheng grew even more furious. "You're unbelievable... He Yu, this is absurd, how could you..."

He Yu smiled quietly, maintaining that same gentle mien as before. However, the facade only persisted for a few seconds before collapsing, as Xie Qingcheng's last sentence tipped his temper past a critical threshold. He didn't want to pretend anymore. His face changed as he struck back before anyone could react, grabbing Xie Qingcheng's hair and ruthlessly shoving him to the floor.

Bang!

The back of Xie Qingcheng's head crashed down on the edge of the marble table. Xie Qingcheng, whose body was weak from the effect of the liquor, let out a low gasp of pain as blood immediately gushed out of the wound.

"Aaah!" Some of the timider girls couldn't help but shriek out of fear that a serious fight was going to break out, like birds startling at the twang of a bow.

He Yu rose to his feet and looked down indifferently at Xie Qingcheng.

The injury was only superficial—it looked scary, but it wouldn't kill him—but the metallic scent of blood stoked He Yu's madness. His expression was glacial, but a twisted fire seemed to burn within his dark eyes.

"Listen, Xie Qingcheng. You'd better stop lecturing me." Grabbing a fistful of Xie Qingcheng's hair, He Yu yanked his head up, forcing him to look at him. Then, he slid his hand down to run his thumb ever so slowly over Xie Qingcheng's lips as he whispered, "You don't have the right to teach me a lesson, nor do you have the status or authority."

The man's lips were cold as ice, while the youth's thumb was hot enough to burn. But it wasn't hot enough to thaw that ice; no pleasant words could be dragged from Xie Qingcheng's lips.

He Yu and Xie Qingcheng stared at each other.

He Yu's temper suddenly flared, like a spark bursting into flames. He straightened up and kicked Xie Qingcheng squarely in the chest, hard enough to make the tea table skid across the floor along with him. Wine glasses shattered all over the floor with a great crash.

The girls scattered in fright, then huddled together in the corner like a flock of startled birds as they watched these two guests who had suddenly come to furious blows.

He Yu gazed at the man lying on the floor, his eyes filling with the bitter hatred he had finally unleashed. "What I really can't stand is when you lecture me with a mouth full of lies. Your legs are too weak to even stand up right now, so you should learn to kneel and prostrate yourself—and shut your mouth. *That's* how you should behave."

He lowered his almond eyes and elegantly straightened out his shirt with no expression on his face, then sat back down onto the leather sofa.

Xie Qingcheng was half-leaning against the tea table, coughing softly. He hadn't often been hit before. When he was younger, he was usually the one dishing out the beatings, and when he got older and settled down, he no longer needed to resort to violence to solve his problems. This was the first time someone had smashed his head down and kicked him to the ground. Not only that, but his opponent was just a kid, still in school.

Xie Qingcheng didn't even register the pain—when he pressed his hand to the wound at the side of his head and came away with a palm full of blood, he only felt an overwhelming rage flood through him, making the scene in front of him swim before his eyes. But what was even more terrifying was the restless arousal coursing through his body, growing fiercer by the second.

He had never experienced a feeling like this before. He barely ever reacted to desire; that was just the kind of person he'd always been. But he had drunk too much of that drugged liquor, and its cumulative effect was igniting practically all of the compounds in his body with a chemically induced fire. He forced his eyes shut, trying to suppress that terrifying tremble within him, but it was no use. Even his breathing had become abnormally heavy, and his clothes were a hot layer around him. It was like his entire body was about to be swept away by lust powerful enough to burn him up alive.

"He Yu... Fuck you..."

"You still have the energy to cuss me out? Did this shady nightclub water down the liquor or what?"

He Yu carelessly shoved the girl beside him, who was trembling from head to toe.

"You. Go help our guest up."

Even though the girl was terrified out of her mind, she had no choice but to approach Xie Qingcheng, her small face deathly pale, and lean down to help him up.

As Xie Qingcheng got a whiff of that soft, cloying sweetness, the effect of Plum Fragrance 59 seemed to intensify. Panting, he fiercely pushed the girl away.

"Get away... I told you to get away from me!"

Frightened to the point of breaking down, the girl scrambled backward with a quiet sob, as if she wanted to hide in a corner of the room.

But He Yu intercepted her.

With his eyes fixed on Xie Qingcheng, He Yu pulled the girl toward him and gestured for her to kneel beside him. He carelessly stroked her hair with one hand as she curled up by his feet, as if he was petting a cat or a dog.

"Xie Qingcheng," He Yu said. "You've been married before. How are you still so awful at showing favor to the fairer sex?"

Xie Qingcheng raised his thoroughly bloodshot eyes. The young man gazing down his nose at him from high above was alarmingly unfamiliar.

All these years, even though He Yu had been an evil dragon hidden in a rocky cave complete with horns, fangs, and a vicious tail, he could always see the subtle emotions on the faces of humans. He knew that he had to sheathe his piercing talons before he touched the cheek of a human with his sharp claws, that he mustn't incite people's terror.

But he didn't want to disguise himself any longer.

He took in all of Xie Qingcheng's resentment, but his heart was perfectly calm. He'd always been such a cruel and unfeeling person, hadn't he?

He Yu gently but insistently poured a glass of red wine for the petrified girl beside him, forcing her to choke down its contents even as she held back tears, all the while stroking a faultlessly considerate hand over her back. "Don't worry, everything's fine."

Then he said to Xie Qingcheng, "Just look at how badly you've scared her. If she's not to your liking, you should just tell me. I'll find someone else to attend to you. I'll keep swapping them out until you're satisfied."

Xie Qingcheng rested his forehead in a shaking hand without a word. The drug had already stoked the heat within him to the point of madness. His mind began to blur, making him feel as though his very blood had caught on fire. He leaned back against the tea table, gasping for breath, his eyes suffused with red as he shuddered uncontrollably from head to toe. Humans were fundamentally weak in the face of such primal desire. Even such a cool-headed and self-disciplined man had no way of staving off the fervent lust that this drug stirred up inside him.

He Yu wound his fingers through the young woman's long hair repeatedly as he gestured toward another girl. "Your turn now. Go serve him properly. Be smart about it now."

"Stay away," groaned Xie Qingcheng.

The girl paused, stuck between a rock and a hard place.

He Yu said mildly, "Just do as I say."

Steeling herself, the hostess pulled Xie Qingcheng upright and tried her best to bring him over to the sofa. But she wasn't very strong to begin with, and Xie Qingcheng was heavy; in the process, the woman inadvertently landed in Xie Qingcheng's arms.

She cried out softly, "Aiya..."

Xie Qingcheng's scalp went numb. It had indeed been ages since he last slept with anyone. He had never been enthusiastic about sex when he was with Li Ruoqiu, and after they broke up, he had basically been celibate. He rarely even took care of things by himself. With the drugged liquor fanning the flames and heating up the lust in his body to its boiling point, he found himself reacting against his will when that supple body leaned into him, even though he was so furious he wished he were dead.

As it turned out, Xie Qingcheng happened to be just this woman's type—handsome and tall with an especially masculine aura, so ascetic and self-controlled even as his body burned with lust and gave off a man's uniquely male hormones. Emboldened, she wrapped her arms around him and enthusiastically pressed closer.

Xie Qingcheng abruptly ducked away from her. He said in an extremely hoarse voice, "Get away from me..."

"Ge..."

Xie Qingcheng bellowed harshly, "Are you deaf? I told you to get away from me!"

He Yu looked on coolly from across the room. This man was really fucking good at acting and restraint, he thought. Even at this point he could still control himself, remaining solemn and composed, unwilling to even touch a woman who had thrown herself at him. He'd spent so long masquerading as a respectable person that he didn't want to remove his mask anymore, did he?

Just as there were those among the hostesses who were meek, there were also some who were more daring. One of the girls, seeing the way Xie Qingcheng never spared a single glance at her or her fellow hostesses, was suddenly struck by an idea. Hoping to win He Yu's favor with an unconventional gambit, she assumed the role of a bumbling advisor and whispered to him, "Young Master He, about this friend of yours... Could it be that he's..."

He Yu didn't catch her drift. His face cold, he asked, "He's what?"

Instead of saying it outright, the girl said, "Young Master He, we also have some very handsome male hosts here..."

It took three seconds for He Yu to figure out what she meant.

"He's not. That won't be necessary."

Xie Qingcheng was as straight as an arrow. He'd be disgusted to no end by the attention of those girly little homos.

The girl, however, had a look on her face that said, *Well, it's not like you'd necessarily know whether he's gay or not.* Given the people who patronized this establishment, what kinds of outlandish clientele and acts of absurdity hadn't these hostesses seen? Young Master He really was too young and lacking in imagination.

Of course, this disrespectful thought had to be kept to herself. Since Young Master He had vetoed her suggestion, she couldn't insist any further. But for some reason, the girl's words made He Yu think back to Neverland and the guestbook he had seen.

There had indeed been a lot of bottoms who had written in the guestbook, all of them thirsting after Xie Qingcheng, saying he was so manly, that he was the ideal top. And what about himself? He was the one who kept getting harassed by men in the past, and those blind bastards in that guestbook had even said that they wanted to top him.

He Yu got mad just thinking about it. To outsiders, he was always weaker than Xie Qingcheng. Even in this aspect, he was inferior to Xie Qingcheng.

But now, who was the one who was helpless before the other? He looked down at Xie Qingcheng's flushed skin and the silent endurance etched into his features. He actually seemed a bit fragile.

He ought to let those damn gays who called Xie Qingcheng "ge" and thought he was invincible see him now—*this* was the ideal top of their dreams? Such a lustful, wretched appearance, burning under the influence of alcohol yet still unwilling to touch those women.

Now, if *he* were the one being topped—that would be more like it!

The idea made He Yu's heart skip a beat, although he didn't know why. The very thought of Xie Qingcheng getting fucked sent a subtle thrill through his cerebral cortex, as if some nerve had been struck with a jolt of electricity.

A crash snapped He Yu out of his daze.

The girls were just as shocked. Xie Qingcheng's body was enduring such unbearable torment that he'd abruptly crushed the thick, branch-shaped glass lampstand near the tea table into pieces. He curled up on the ground in pain, the veins on his hands bulging as his body trembled.

The girls who could help relieve his torment were right next to him, yet he would rather endure it all the way through, unwilling to touch or look at them, even if he tortured himself to death.

These girls had seen their share of nasty perverts and usually spent their time rejecting and pushing them away. This was the first time they'd met such a gentleman, and even in their confusion, they felt somewhat bad for him.

Finally, the lead hostess spoke up. "Y-Young Master He, why don't we try to resolve this a different way... If you have any resentment or grudges, you can resolve it in private in the future. But let's just leave it at this for today, okay?"

She had a conscience, after all, and didn't lack guts. Besides, there was a limit to the service offered in this establishment. If they really crossed the line, there wouldn't be enough tea at the police station to go around.[9] She saw how bad Xie Qingcheng's condition was and how hard he was struggling, and even as her heart pounded in terror, she gathered her courage and lowered her head to try to talk He Yu around.

---

9 *"Drinking tea" is a euphemism for being forced to meet with the police.*

"We're just a small business; we can't cross certain lines. Otherwise, we couldn't bear the liability and continue with our work. Thank you for your understanding, but..."

He Yu didn't respond, still staring at Xie Qingcheng. He tightened his hold on his glass, the veins on the back of his hand protruding one after another.

Had this man taken his disguise to such extremes that it had become genuine?

Rather than being forced into giving a shameful performance before these women, Xie Qingcheng had turned the tables and caused He Yu to lose control of the situation. The leader, those hostesses... When they looked at Xie Qingcheng, their eyes were filled with admiration and pity.

He Yu rose to his feet and slowly walked over to Xie Qingcheng. After a few beats of silence, he said mildly, "Forget it. This is just between him and me. You can all leave."

Overwhelmed with relief, the girls' only thought was that if things continued like this, there was no imagining the kind of trouble these two nutcases would stir up tonight. With Young Master He's permission, they streamed from the room and made a hasty escape. A couple of girls even looked at Xie Qingcheng rather woefully before they left, hoping that nothing bad was going to happen to him.

Now it was only the two of them inside the private room.

He Yu gazed down at Xie Qingcheng, who was struggling in pain on the floor...

In the end, he was still the loser, wasn't he? He was still the fool, while Xie Qingcheng was still the immaculately dressed, righteous gentleman.

Was there no way for him to force the ugly side of Xie Qingcheng out and make him plead for mercy?

In the hazy lighting that brimmed with desire, He Yu swept his eyes over Xie Qingcheng's broad forehead, the stark line of his jaw, and further down, to the bob of his throat, the honest reactions of his body... He had been driven to this point, yet not a single button of his shirt had been undone.

This person's masculine willpower and pride were just that strong.

Though he trembled as he burned in the flames of desire, Xie Qingcheng was still aware of what had happened. He slowly looked up and said to the young man before him, "Are you done...messing around? If you're done, you should come back with me. He Yu, you've lost. You..."

It seemed like Xie Qingcheng had more to say, but another wave of lust swept over him and he snapped his eyes shut, bloodied fingers clenching tightly on the edge of the tea table. It was too unbearable...

Every second of every minute was torture. He had to use all his self-control to prevent himself from doing something an elder shouldn't in front of He Yu.

He had to keep himself under control.

He couldn't...

Swollen beads of sweat dripped down his flushed face, the jut of his throat bobbing continuously as he swallowed.

He Yu's eyes followed the up-and-down movements of Xie Qingcheng's Adam's apple before lifting back up to meet his gaze. Beneath those long, trembling lashes, his peach-blossom eyes brimmed with moisture. The plum liquor had melted them into twin pools of water, yet when he looked into He Yu's eyes, they were still so calm.

He Yu felt that roiling flame in his chest bare its teeth and claw through his heart. Would he really fail to penetrate deep beneath this man's armor, touch the softest parts of him, and find his true face?

No... He had to make Xie Qingcheng pay the price.

Because Xie Qingcheng was a liar.

A liar...

A liar!

His rage surged. Sneering, He Yu suddenly picked up a glass of wine. With a slight tilt of the cup, wine began to pour like a trail of blood, seeping into Xie Qingcheng's slightly gaped collar.

Xie Qingcheng was trying to provoke him, to toy with him. Well then. Wasn't Xie Qingcheng the one who kept refusing? Wasn't he the one who wanted to let those women go? In that case, He Yu would like to see just how this man planned on enduring his desire! Could he really endure it to death?!

The trail of icy-cold wine wound its way down Xie Qingcheng's scalding skin like a snake. He trembled at its touch, unable to prevent a gasp from leaving his lips. But when he met He Yu's eyes, he cut that inhalation off halfway, biting it between his teeth.

The red wine quickly soaked through the weave of Xie Qingcheng's white shirt like a flower painted onto his chest—or perhaps it was a pool of blood. Drop by drop, the entire glass of wine was spilled until the whole thing had been poured onto Xie Qingcheng's body, filling the air with the bitter and astringent scent of tannins.

Incandescently furious, He Yu grabbed Xie Qingcheng by the neck and stared down at him. "Pretend! Keep pretending! How much longer are you planning to keep this up?!"

Xie Qingcheng's body temperature was soaring, and He Yu's palm tingled from the heat.

"Give it up," said Xie Qingcheng. "I'm a man...not a beast. Don't you know...the biggest difference between humans and animals?" His lips trembled as he spoke, and his eyes were filled with extreme disappointment as he looked at He Yu. "Humans can control themselves."

These words, along with Xie Qingcheng's gaze, made He Yu feel as if he'd been ruthlessly scalded. Xie Qingcheng was lying beneath him, looking up at him, but at this moment, He Yu knew—Xie Qingcheng had reclaimed his former position. He was once again superior to He Yu.

Provoked to absolute fury, the resentful anger that had just erupted within him revived itself in an instant, surging into his heart at full force in a raging torrent. He was driven to the verge of madness, to death, and only Xie Qingcheng's misery and loss of control, only Xie Qingcheng's fresh blood and utter breakdown could save him.

But how could he force Xie Qingcheng into such a miserable state? How could he make Xie Qingcheng lose control?! Even after pouring all that liquor down his throat, those women couldn't entice him.

The thought of those women still pissed He Yu off. Other than serving wine, they couldn't do anything that crossed the line, so how could their indirect seduction possibly be enough? Moreover, they'd lost their courage the moment Xie Qingcheng yelled at them.

They were all trash.

Useless!

If He Yu wanted to achieve his goal, he could only rely on himself.

Rely on himself.

Rely on himself...

"We also have some very handsome male hosts here."

"Xie Qingcheng is a total manly man, an ideal top."

"Young Master He is an ideal bottom. I totally want to fuck him..."

The messages from the guestbook twisted together with the hostesses' words in He Yu's mind. He Yu raged to himself. Why did everyone always think that Xie Qingcheng was stronger than him? Even in this respect, they assumed that He Yu would be weaker.

But now, Xie Qingcheng was the one collapsed in front of him with no ability to fight back. He Yu could fuck him if he wanted! "Total manly man," his ass. The "ideal top?" Wouldn't he be no different from a woman once he got fucked? Then those idiots would realize, just like he had, that everything about Xie Qingcheng was an act! Xie Qingcheng would be nothing more than a "total manly man" who'd been fucked by another man...

The moment this thought popped into his head, He Yu was immediately and thoroughly disgusted by himself.

Absurd. Far too absurd. How could *that* have crossed his mind?

They were both men—*straight* men. He couldn't do such a thing. Men were all disgusting... The bodies of his own sex...

But...

But was he supposed to just accept defeat and bow down to Xie Qingcheng with a downcast look on his face? He had spent so much time and effort pouring a whole bottle of Plum Fragrance 59 down Xie Qingcheng's throat, yet he was still going to lose to Xie Qingcheng?

If he did, he would be nothing more than a dog to Xie Qingcheng for the rest of his life, unable to raise his head ever again. He was in too deep now. He didn't expect that making Xie Qingcheng drink would be so easy, but that making him lose his composure would be so hard.

He Yu strode over to him and looked at this unsalvageable farce of a situation.

Xie Qingcheng was feeling extremely unwell. It was impossible for him not to give in to his desires tonight. But he was such a tough person that he'd rather be tortured to death himself than bully those pitiful women.

He Yu looked at his dazed face, his eyes clouded with lust, his parted, panting lips.

He Yu didn't like men's bodies, of course. But he was contemplating the only path left open to him, a path that might possibly end with Xie Qingcheng showing him weakness. Gazing at Xie Qingcheng's current appearance, he realized that through this sequence of coincidences, he had found the answer to a question that had long plagued him.

What did Xie Qingcheng look like in bed?

This question had popped into his head in the past when he saw Li Ruoqiu and Xie Qingcheng's marriage bed.

He Yu had never realized this himself, but no man who was genuinely as straight as an arrow would have wondered what another man would look like lost in the throes of passion. But he had wondered. Many, many times.

He thought that Xie Qingcheng was too cold, too stiff, too abstinent, so he couldn't even imagine what he would look like intertwined with a woman.

It was only now that he finally got his answer. Now he could see Xie Qingcheng's face, up close and personal, as he was tormented by desire, as his body was burned by aphrodisiac liquor. That was when he realized that, even though he found other men's bodies repulsive... Xie Qingcheng was different, somehow, from what he assumed married men would be like. He was just too abstinent and restrained.

Sinful, yet alluring. Like a deity ensnared by a snake.

He Yu looked at this familiar-yet-unfamiliar body, at this man who had once been so imposing to him, and mulled numbly over his complicated emotions. He found that, more than anything else, he was filled to the brim with excitement at the novelty, and a sort of wild, vengeful exhilaration.

He had truly gone insane tonight. He had lost all reason. Everything in his past had been destroyed: Xie Xue was fake.

The contract period was fake. Xie Qingcheng's words were fake. Everything he thought he knew had been turned completely upside down.

In the past, He Yu might have held firm that, no matter what, men were not to be touched. Not for any reason.

But tonight...

Xie Qingcheng had destroyed eleven fucking years of his faith.

His whole world had been overturned.

What was the big deal?

What did sex matter?

He'd come here to cut loose. He was planning to do something that he never would've done before, something scandalous and shocking, to destroy the foolish He Yu that he had been before.

So, what would be more perverse than sleeping with women in a nightclub? The answer was already on the tip of his tongue.

The more He Yu thought about it, the stronger the thrill running through him became. This was the thrill of rejecting his past self, the thrill of destroying who he used to be.

He wanted to destroy himself.

And at the same time, he wanted to destroy the Xie Qingcheng who had deceived him and left him in such a miserable state.

As his eyes sought out Xie Qingcheng's face, lust-filled yet restrained, the nature of his gaze began to shift, ever so slowly...

He Yu knew that it was disgusting for a man to fuck another man, but if he was the aggressor, that would make it different from the way he had been harassed by those men in the past... He would still be the one abiding by male instinct.

But Xie Qingcheng?

As a straight man, even if Xie Qingcheng had been unable to hold back and slept with a woman, he would have only been a little bothered and embarrassed by it. But if Xie Qingcheng really did get fucked by He Yu...

Then... Putting himself in the other's shoes, to a manly man like Xie Qingcheng, wasn't that a much greater blow?

Having come to this decision, He Yu felt enlightened. He had been foolish before. He was a freak, so, moving forward, he would become a freak through and through. It made perfect sense for him to resort to the most excessive, cruel means to destroy both himself and the target of his hatred. Why in the world should he settle for the well-traveled path of female temptation?

Xie Qingcheng was already engulfed by lust anyway.

If, during the process, he could arouse Xie Qingcheng, that would be even more hilarious—the mere idea of Xie Qingcheng wanting him, Xie Qingcheng wanting him with no regard for his own dignity... If word got out, it might even kill him!

He Yu had truly gone insane. So insane he trembled with it, so insane he would stop at nothing, so insane he disregarded the very idea of consequences.

With a slap of skin against skin, He Yu grabbed the wrist of the still-dazed Xie Qingcheng.

In the dimly lit private room, Xie Qingcheng heard He Yu's low voice as the young man faced him with his back to the light, his figure tall and straight, his aura unspeakably, terrifyingly domineering.

"It's too early for you to say whether I've lost right now." He Yu leaned in, his breath gently brushing across Xie Qingcheng's carotid artery as he murmured like a snake, dangerous yet enticing. "As for you and me, Xie-ge, let's see where we stand after tonight."

To Plunge into the Abyss with Him

Xie Qingcheng had no way of knowing that, due to the destruction of He Yu's perceived reality and the obliteration of his articles of faith, he had been seized by the urge to overturn his former principles entirely from the inside out. But even so, the moment He Yu pinned him down, without even blinking, Xie Qingcheng still reached out with his unrestrained hand to grab a nearby wine bottle and smash it against the nearest surface.

He Yu's eyes darkened. "What are you doing?"

Xie Qingcheng was already on fire with scalding lust from the Plum Fragrance 59. He felt like the uncontrollable physiological reactions were breaking him down, but he was hardly the type to submit so easily.

He didn't say anything, only continued to pant for breath as he stared up at He Yu with panther-like eyes. Then, he picked up that broken wine bottle and stabbed it into his own forearm without flinching!

Blood gushed from the wound.

Xie Qingcheng squeezed his eyes shut and bit down hard on his pale lower lip. The agonizing pain just barely shocked him out of the quicksand of desire. Chest heaving, Xie Qingcheng slowly set down the bloody weapon and leaned back against the tea table.

He Yu stared at him with an ugly look on his face. He watched as Xie Qingcheng gasped for breath, taking in in the taut stretch of his dress shirt, his wine-stained collar, his bleeding arm.

As He Yu stared, he tightened his grip on Xie Qingcheng's arm. Warm droplets of blood slowly seeped through his fingers.

Silence fell over them both.

In this moment of lucidity, Xie Qingcheng strove to control his breathing as he looked at the youth in front of him through teary eyes.

After a moment's pause, he rasped, "He Yu, let me ask you... You actually *are* bothered by the things that I said in those old videos, aren't you?"

He Yu didn't say a word. He let Xie Qingcheng's blood drip like tears from his fingers, each drop splashing onto the cold tiled floor.

It wasn't just the old videos, he thought.

He'd seen nearly all the messages Xie Qingcheng had sent during those few years.

In the end, He Yu just sneered. "You've already asked me this question, and I've already told you the answer. I don't care. Who still cares about all that?"

"But you're not very good at lying. If you really didn't care, you wouldn't be acting like this today." Xie Qingcheng was still panting, sweat beading on his face. He knew that his composure wouldn't last. He had to use the brief time he'd bought himself to persuade He Yu to act more rationally, or at least with a little more lucidity.

He Yu was silent.

"Little devil... To be honest, back then..."

It took a lot out of Xie Qingcheng to talk about such things. The drug was too strong—it quickly relaunched its conquest over his blood, flowing to the very tips of his fingers. Xie Qingcheng squeezed his eyes closed, and when he opened them again, they were misted over with pain. But still, he suppressed the agony, his Adam's apple bobbing as he swallowed thickly.

"Back then...the reason I didn't want to stay on as your personal physician wasn't because I found you appalling or frightening. It wasn't because I was worried that you would become the next Yi Beihai to my Qin Ciyan. It wasn't any of those things. You were already fourteen when I left you, He Yu. I could accompany you for seven years, or even another seven, but could I accompany you for a lifetime? Staying by your side after you graduate and start work, after you get married and have children... That's not realistic. I'm only a doctor. Sooner or later, you'll have to depend on yourself to walk out of the shadows in your heart. That's what I believe, and it's why I left."

Xie Qingcheng paused, holding He Yu's silhouette in his eyes.

"He Yu... I think you probably understand this. How many people have it easy in this world? You don't need to look any further than the foyer of a hospital, the doorway of an ICU, or the entrance of a trauma center. I know that you're in pain, but at least you're alive. You shouldn't..."

But right now, He Yu didn't fully understand what Xie Qingcheng meant to say. He was burning up so fiercely that his ice-cold heart was scalding with it; he'd never experienced a rage so fiery before. He viciously grabbed a fistful of Xie Qingcheng's short hair and sharply yanked him up from the floor. "You're saying that I shouldn't *what*? What shouldn't I do?! Xie Qingcheng... Do you really have any idea how much pain I'm in? Numb and closed-off, with no control over my emotions—during a flare-up, I don't even know who I am! I'm completely hollow, it's like my insides have rusted away or been gnawed empty. Not a moment goes by where I don't think about just ending it all. I've told you this before. Over the course of those seven years, I described it to you countless times... but you still have no idea what it's like.

"Why did you agree to treat me, huh? Since you think that I should go look at a hospital, that my suffering is nothing compared to those patients', why did you agree? Did you think it was interesting? The rarest disorder on Earth, Psychological Ebola, without a single identical case in even the records of Yanzhou's oldest hospitals. How fascinating, Professor Xie. You found this clinical specimen novel enough to add a splash of color to your research portfolio, didn't you?!"

He Yu kept his voice low, but the light in his eyes trembled with fury.

"The patients you talk about—whether they're cancer patients or people with ALS, at least everyone understands the kinds of illness they have and how severe the symptoms are. They can find people who share the same suffering, huddle together for warmth, and encourage each other...but what about me? I'm just a research specimen to you people, an interesting lunatic, a beast in a cage. Is it refreshing, Xie Qingcheng? Leaving once you're done gawking and having fun? You even tried to deceive me with some ridiculous lies as a parting gift! And now you're *still* trying to tell me what I shouldn't do or what I'm allowed to do. Don't you find it cruel, Xie Qingcheng?!"

A nearly imperceptible flicker of light seemed to flash through Xie Qingcheng's eyes at this cutting interrogation, but as he lowered his lashes, that faint glimmer quickly disappeared without a trace.

"I still feel that way, He Yu," he said. "As long as you're alive and still want to save yourself, no matter how lonely or painful it is, you'll always manage to make it through. That is, unless you choose to give up on yourself even before you die. A human heart can be very strong, He Yu. You shouldn't believe in me. You should always believe in your own heart."

"Easy for you to say." He Yu stared into Xie Qingcheng's eyes. Every word was accompanied by the metallic scent of blood, as though it had been flayed from his hatred. "Easy for you to say...Xie Qingcheng. You're neither sick nor in pain. You're just wagging your tongue and criticizing me for giving up. What do you know? If you were the one suffering the torment of this disease, how much better would you do? Xie Qingcheng, *you're* the one who loves washing your hands of matters and disappearing without a trace. *You're* the one who left the He family because you couldn't cure me. *You're* the one who resigned and switched professions at the first sign of trouble."

Every word was sharpened to pierce through Xie Qingcheng's harsh dignity. "Your hypocrisy disgusts me. You've been pretending for so many years... Even now, you're still pretending!"

One could have said that He Yu had still possessed a shred of rationality before. But at this moment, he was fully consumed by fury.

He grabbed Xie Qingcheng's messy hair with no care for his grimace of pain, then dragged him up and tossed him onto the more spacious of the long sofas beside the marble table. Then, he silently turned and drew out the other yet-unopened bottle of Plum Fragrance 59 and uncorked it without the slightest expression on his face.

Xie Qingcheng's head nearly blew up from rage at the sight of that strong liquor. The heat of desire was already making him fall apart after chugging one bottle of the stuff, but here He Yu was, opening another fucking bottle!

"What the hell do you want...!" At this point, even Xie Qingcheng had a note of fear in his voice. He summoned all the strength in his limp, helpless body to try to pull himself into an upright position.

But before he managed to sit up, He Yu brought over the bottle of liquor. He didn't even bother with wine glasses, he just grabbed Xie Qingcheng by the jaw.

Xie Qingcheng, who was nearing his breaking point, went pale as a sheet at the sight of that Western-style bottle, bigger than his face. Finally giving up on having a proper conversation, he started furiously cursing. "You little bastard, you fucking lunatic, if you don't want this to end up being a murder scene you'd better get the fuck out of here—"

"That's right, I am a lunatic," said He Yu emotionlessly. "Did you only just find out? Well, it's too late." With that, He Yu tipped his head back to take a large gulp from the bottle himself. Then he pried Xie Qingcheng's teeth apart and force-fed the chokingly pungent Plum Fragrance 59 to Xie Qingcheng from his own mouth.

Xie Qingcheng struggled so hard that half the liquor ended up on the floor and most of the rest ended up on his clothes. Even though he didn't drink much of it, it was still strong enough to make him choke. Once He Yu let go of him, Xie Qingcheng slumped across the sofa and started coughing violently, as if trying to force all the oxygen from his lungs.

Liquor mixed with blood, and blood mingled with sweat.

Xie Qingcheng was trembling all over, in part due to rage, but also because of the lust that had begun its frantic, gnawing onslaught on his body again. He felt as if countless insects were biting into his bones, his body tingling and limp as he burned up all over. The sensations were terrifyingly unfamiliar. His face began to flush again, but what shone clearer than the lust was his fury. He was completely livid now. After his coughing fit, he turned and glared viciously at He Yu before he'd even steadied his breathing. He didn't bother to curb the sharpness of his tongue. "What kind of beastly behavior is this? Not even animals could manage what you're doing! He Yu, you've really gone crazy..."

"This is beastly already? Professor Xie, you're inexperienced indeed. There are far beastlier things. Why don't I give you a demonstration right now?"

He Yu tossed the glass bottle, swirling with the final dregs of liquor, onto the floor, then stood up and stepped forward. Xie Qingcheng was just about to sit up, but He Yu pinned him back against the sofa's soft cushions and clamped his wrists together. He Yu's bangs hung down as he stared at Xie Qingcheng, who'd been completely soaked through by the alcohol. There was a hint of hair-raising viciousness in his gaze.

Xie Qingcheng gasped for breath. "He Yu..."

Hearing Xie Qingcheng call his name like that, with a hint of fear seeping into his voice, He Yu felt a surge of pleasure in the pit of his belly. Scarlet light gleamed in the dark, terrifying pits of his eyes.

He kept Xie Qingcheng pinned with his own body as he cooed at him softly, sounding gentle yet deranged. "Don't be afraid, hm?" There was still a trace of Plum Fragrance 59 between his lips. He licked them and smiled, as if savoring the taste. "Do you know why I had to drink some of this too? Because I despise you, and I despise men. If it weren't for this liquor, I'm afraid I wouldn't be of much help in certain matters, nor would I be able to provide satisfactory service."

He Yu patted Xie Qingcheng on the cheek. "Xie-ge, I've always been filial and respectful to you. You came here just for me, but I didn't treat you with enough hospitality. If that gets out, what would happen to my reputation? So, if you don't like those people, then I won't force you. But aren't you uncomfortable because you got yourself too drunk?"

After a few seconds of dumbfounded shock, Xie Qingcheng's gaze finally began to show some terror as he watched He Yu yank open his collar. The tightly fastened buttons came undone, exposing the flushed skin underneath.

"In that case, I'll give you a hand."

By now, He Yu had been provoked so far that he'd lost any interest in slowly enticing Xie Qingcheng. Xie Qingcheng would not hesitate to mutilate himself to maintain lucidity, so He Yu realized that relying on drugs alone would be useless. He had fully taken leave of his senses now; all he wanted was to savagely tear apart all the disguises covering Xie Qingcheng, and the more he thought about it, the more of his reservations he lost.

Grabbing Xie Qingcheng by the neck, he said deliberately, word by word, "Today, I can personally give you relief. I'll bring you to the peak of pleasure myself."

Xie Qingcheng lost it. "He Yu! What are you trying to do?!"

"What am I trying to do? As a formerly married man, do you have to ask?" He Yu pinned down the madly struggling man underneath him. After a cup of Plum Fragrance 59, He Yu's own senses had become significantly more sensitive. Tearing Xie Qingcheng's facade apart was thrilling enough, but now that this man was twisting and turning beneath him, burning hot all over, with his clothes in disarray and stained with blood, his struggling movements actually stoked He Yu's flames even higher.

He Yu stared at him with the eyes of a predator, as if he planned to gouge holes into his flesh.

"Ge..." His breath was searing as it puffed gently over Xie Qingcheng's face and intermingled with his. "What do you *think* I want to do..."

Xie Qingcheng was straight from head to toe and apathetic to sex to begin with—and he knew that He Yu was a straight man too, and homophobic to boot. How could he have possibly let his thoughts roam in such an outrageous, insane direction?

It was only when He Yu wrenched Xie Qingcheng's wrists up over his head with one hand and began undoing the buttons of his dress shirt that realization crashed down on him like lightning. His peach-blossom eyes flew wide open, and his face blanched as he stared at He Yu in utter disbelief. For a moment, he couldn't even be sure that this was reality.

But he could see He Yu's youthful face—fearless, bloodthirsty, sickly, perverse, and crazed—the face that held a single-minded desire to devour all of Xie Qingcheng's dignity.

Xie Qingcheng knew that He Yu had really lost it. He began to struggle beneath He Yu's hands, even though struggling had long since become futile. He shouted hoarsely, "He Yu, you... You fucking... I'm fine... I don't need your help! Get lost! You'd better get fucking lost! What the hell do you want!"

On Xie Qingcheng's habitually composed face, He Yu saw terror, pallor, and ruination... These emotions burst like delicacies across He Yu's tongue, causing his desire to swell even more greedily. He restrained Xie Qingcheng, who'd slumped down onto the sofa, with fingertips that were like blades moving to slice Xie Qingcheng open bit by bit as he lay beneath him.

He Yu's handsome face twisted into a smile. "Professor Xie, Doctor Xie, Xie-ge. You must understand everything by now." His low voice blazed, scalding Xie Qingcheng's rapidly heaving chest. "I'm going to fuck you all night. You'd better remember to moan loud enough for me."

His hand slipped leisurely down, and his fingertips caressed Xie Qingcheng's trembling lips.

Xie Qingcheng squeezed his eyes shut, looking on the verge of being driven insane. However, he didn't have an ounce of strength remaining in his body. The longer this went on, the quicker his energy left him.

"If you fucking dare… You psycho…"

Heedless of his words, He Yu began to pull at Xie Qingcheng's clothes with a determined look on his face. No matter how much he shoved at him, Xie Qingcheng failed to fend him off, and in the end, he could only tighten his grip around his belt buckle. But He Yu pounced and began to kiss Xie Qingcheng across his newly bared shoulder, the nape of his neck, his collarbones…all the way down, burying his head of black hair in Xie Qingcheng's chest as he licked the man's pale nipple with his rough tongue, then sucked it viciously.

Xie Qingcheng's eyes widened, and he flailed like a fish out of water, but He Yu only pinned him down with a fresh burst of force. Under the influence of the excessive dosage of aphrodisiac liquor he'd imbibed, lust gnawed at every bit of him, and he truly did feel an instinctive yearning to entangle passionately with another body.

When someone was fully engulfed in lust, it didn't even matter all that much if their partner was of the same sex. This was bestial instinct. But Xie Qingcheng remembered that he was a human, and that he was He Yu's senior and an old friend of He Yu's father. He absolutely shouldn't—absolutely *couldn't* act like this.

A tormented look crossed his face, intense lust clashing with extreme hatred. Unable to bear it, he turned his head to the side.

He Yu was kissing his chest. Feeling the tremors running through Xie Qingcheng's body, he looked up at him and saw the loathing on his handsome face, covered by a red flush. He Yu felt a powerful thrill unlike any he'd ever experienced before—powerful enough to override the distaste he felt for men's bodies, urging him to toy with Xie Qingcheng no matter the method.

This was a Xie Qingcheng that He Yu had never seen before—a Xie Qingcheng who was paying the price for his lies and deception.

Savage desire flamed in He Yu's eyes. The pleasure of revenge could utterly subsume his disgust, just as the thrill of domination could override his instinctive rejection. He Yu started to regret that he'd come to this realization too late, that he hadn't found this method of shattering Xie Qingcheng earlier.

As they were tussling, He Yu had already completely undone Xie Qingcheng's shirt buttons, exposing the wine-stained skin beneath. Xie Qingcheng's chest was very broad, his muscles firm and powerful without being exaggerated, and the lines of his torso were sharp and clean. It was every bit the body of an adult man. He Yu was a bit put off, but he felt his blood heat up once again at the sight of Xie Qingcheng's current appearance.

Didn't Xie Qingcheng say he couldn't give him anything?

Didn't he believe that He Yu was undeserving of love?

Xie Qingcheng—the one who stood at his lofty height and never took anyone seriously; the one who'd restrained him and disciplined him; the one who had scolded, threatened, and lied to him since he was young; the one who even told He Yu that he couldn't afford to employ him when he left.

Xie Qingcheng—that stern, composed man who stood at the lectern and received the admiration of countless students; that man who seemed omniscient and omnipotent.

A full-grown, adult man.

Purely masculine, mature, formidable, and coolly detached, his aura so stalwart it was more than enough to attract any number of girls, someone who'd once been married to a woman. No one would imagine that he'd submit to anyone, no one could imagine that he too could get fucked—not an overwhelmingly manly man like him.

But now, he had thrown himself into this trap of his own volition. He was being restrained by He Yu, lying under him and trying to refrain from trembling.

The things He Yu wanted and the warmth that he craved—Xie Qingcheng could give it all to him. Xie Qingcheng could give it to him himself!

The young man swallowed thickly, burning with an unbearable heat as his blood came to a boil.

"Doctor Xie, you'd better keep this in mind. What happened tonight was because you drank too much and couldn't take it. You were so pathetic you needed my help. As for me, I'm not weak and cowardly like you. I'm willing to sacrifice myself in order to take good care of you. I don't need your thanks. I'm happy to help."

He Yu pulled Xie Qingcheng's shirt off, then took some black restraints out of the drawer beside him—this place had no shortage of implements like these—and tied Xie Qingcheng's hands tightly together.

"I still remember how you escaped from Jiang Lanpei's knots that day on the roof. Don't worry, this is a robber's knot. You won't be able to undo it."

53

To Have Him in My Grasp

"He Yu, you... Get lost... Fuck off!" shouted Xie Qingcheng.

He Yu didn't fuck off. Instead, he bent down and stared into Xie Qingcheng's eyes for a long while. Then his hand slid down further to the ice-cold metal buckle of Xie Qingcheng's belt, which clicked crisply as it was undone.

Xie Qingcheng closed his eyes, a burst of humiliation exploding inside his mind and seeping out through every bit of his body. But the stimulation he felt was still real. His body had fallen under the control of his drug-addled hormones; it no longer belonged to him. Such an extreme yearning for relief was impossible for him to repress.

Meanwhile, He Yu soaked in every single one of Xie Qingcheng's rare reactions to desire. Each one spurred him on, encouraging him to toy with him even further. Despite his aversion to men's bodies, he pressed a hand against Xie Qingcheng, then stared into his face and asked him a question, although he knew the answer perfectly well: "Xie-ge, I thought you didn't care about sex? Why is it that I can feel you pressing against me?"

He Yu bent lower.

Exhaling against Xie Qingcheng's ear, he murmured, "Not to mention, I'm a *man*."

Xie Qingcheng was so furious he wanted to die. "Let go..." he rasped. "Fucking...let go of me..."

He Yu was trying to tease Xie Qingcheng, but he truly wasn't used to seduction. He let go and bent down to suck the blood off Xie Qingcheng's lips. Xie Qingcheng forcefully twisted away, causing He Yu's lips to press against his soft, sweat-soaked earlobe instead. The searing heat made his scalp prickle.

"Why are you avoiding me?" He Yu wrenched Xie Qingcheng's face back. "It's not like we haven't kissed before." He lowered his head and brought their mouths together once again.

His bloodthirstiness was only a pathological impulse, but at the moment their lips touched, he felt a thrill more pleasurable to him than the metallic scent of blood.

Perhaps it was human nature. When you had some mental obstacle you'd yet to cross, it was like you were faced with a dark forest, the shadows so deep you couldn't see your own outstretched hand—a place you'd refuse to step into no matter what. But once you took that first step and caught a whiff of the cloying fragrance of the wildflowers within the darkness, those hesitant steps would speed up. You'd think to yourself, *So this is what this place is like. There's nothing to be afraid of.* And your previous obstacles wouldn't feel like they mattered at all.

He Yu had kissed Xie Qingcheng before. But back then, he hadn't been in a sober state of mind and couldn't remember too many details. This time, as he sank into the slick, scalding heat of their kiss, he didn't let go even when the blood was quickly licked away. He kept caressing those soft, alcohol-soaked lips with his own. Xie Qingcheng was such a cold and unyielding person, but his lips were extremely tender. The delicate flesh seemed as if it could melt in his mouth, like berries soaked in wine. He Yu felt a faint current jolt up from the base of his spine, thrilling and prickling with arousal. It was a shame this sensation didn't last for very long, though, as a sharp pain suddenly lanced through his lip.

"Xie Qingcheng, you bit me?"

He Yu stroked the corner of his mouth—it was bleeding.

Xie Qingcheng's lips were drenched with crimson. Even the rims of his eyes had gone red, and he was panting so hard he couldn't speak.

He Yu stared at him for a moment. He looked as if he was going to flare into fury, but he took a sharp turn and gave a cryptic sneer before fearlessly dipping his head to exchange another bloody kiss with Xie Qingcheng.

Xie Qingcheng was truly disoriented. He'd forgotten that He Yu craved blood and didn't fear any pain, that this would only add fuel to the fire and heighten his excitement.

In their second kiss, the metallic taste of blood filled their mouths. Young people couldn't help but be overeager with this sort of thing, filled with a potent desire, savage and uncontrollable. He Yu tried to pry open Xie Qingcheng's teeth during the kiss so he could shove his tongue into his mouth, but of course, Xie Qingcheng refused to let him in, his eyes red as he silently kept his mouth closed. His disgust rose, and after enduring for a while longer, he reached his limit and steeled himself to try to bite He Yu again.

But as soon as he parted his teeth just barely, the boy charged in without the slightest reservation, as though wholly unafraid of his sharp tongue and sharper teeth. Xie Qingcheng was shaking all over with hateful fury, but just as he was about to savage He Yu again, He Yu, as if predicting his next move, picked him up from the sofa and set him on his lap without breaking their kiss.

Xie Qingcheng's face blanched. He found himself sitting on something solid and scalding hot. He could feel the young man's sinister, impulsive, still-contained desire even through their clothes.

Xie Qingcheng, a man who'd suffered all sorts of major upheavals throughout his life, who'd stood before the most dangerous surgeries with unparalleled calm and peerless composure, felt so much dread in this moment that his scalp seemed to tighten with it. He couldn't believe what was happening to him, and in his shock, he forgot to bite He Yu.

He Yu cloyingly explored every centimeter of his mouth, both out of curiosity and the desire to humiliate him to the fullest. By the time Xie Qingcheng escaped from his fog of terror, He Yu had already retreated. But their lips were still very close together, so close the slightest movement would bring them back into contact. Silvery threads of saliva hung between their slick, reddened mouths, hanging on the verge of separation, as if they'd kiss again in the next moment and merge seamlessly back together.

"Xie Qingcheng..." Lashes fluttering, with their foreheads still pressed together, He Yu whispered in a low, hoarse rasp, "Come on, bite me. The harder you bite, the more blood will spill...and the more enjoyable it'll be for me."

He turned to press his lips against the throbbing pulse of Xie Qingcheng's neck, over a wound that he had bitten into the skin in his earlier fit of madness. The blood had yet to dry and stood out stark against Xie Qingcheng's skin like a red mole. He Yu mouthed over that vulnerable stretch of skin repeatedly, murmuring into it as intimate as a lover's whisper. "Remember, I'm a psy...cho."

He Yu grabbed Xie Qingcheng by the waist and thrust his hips upward, listening with absolute satisfaction as Xie Qingcheng cried out in extreme fury laced with hints of fear.

Xie Qingcheng panted breathlessly. On the one hand, this type of sexual contact felt very pleasurable; regardless of whether it was moral, or with someone of the same sex, being drugged with an aphrodisiac made him desperate for release. But at the same time, he could still grasp at the final wisp of his rationality. He ground out, his voice hoarse, "He Yu, let go. If you do this, I'll..."

"You'll what? Tell Xie Xue? Do you want me to break the news on your behalf? Let her know that her godlike gege is currently being pinned beneath her student, being kissed and caressed, about to get fucked all night long..."

His words struck through Xie Qingcheng's disorientation like a bolt of lightning. The last hints of color drained from his face.

"No? Then perhaps the police? It's not like I forced you into this. You were the one who drank that liquor and couldn't handle the effects. It's just intoxicated misbehavior; do you really think they'll do anything? At most, we'll end up making tabloid headlines. I have no sense of shame. I don't care. But I wonder how those students of yours will look at you when you stand at the lectern in the future, Professor Xie."

With a sneer on his lips, He Yu closely examined Xie Qingcheng's pale face.

"A man who's been fucked by a student from a neighboring university? When the time comes, I doubt I'll be the only one they see as a psycho."

Xie Qingcheng closed his eyes.

"I'm a very reasonable person. I'm giving you a choice. The phone is right here. Whether you use it is up to you."

Xie Qingcheng said nothing.

He Yu knew that he was trapped. Even a man like him was helpless sometimes. He stared at Xie Qingcheng for a while longer, as if trying to engrave the man's current appearance deep into his mind.

Xie Qingcheng had witnessed his stupidity for years without telling him a thing. Now it was He Yu's turn—he wanted his own chance to watch Xie Qingcheng lose his composure. And, as it turned out, this course of action would give him everything he wanted.

This thought made him even more excited, so he went to kiss Xie Qingcheng's lips again, indulging in that soft flesh.

Even though Xie Qingcheng didn't call anyone to save him, and even as the torment of Plum Fragrance 59 gnawed at him like a thousand ants chewing at his insides, he endured and did not react at all to He Yu's kiss. His peach-blossom eyes had frozen into ice, while his lashes seemed to have frosted over. And so, after a momentary entanglement, He Yu's initial satisfaction began to wear off.

It was like kissing an ice statue. No matter what he did, no matter how he provoked or degraded him, Xie Qingcheng remained silent.

How cold. So cold it infuriated He Yu. But it also made him feel the urgent need to shatter this rigid layer of ice, like ice-fishing in winter. He wanted to break Xie Qingcheng open, gouge him apart, and pierce him through. To reach the yielding, bountiful water underneath.

As this whim flashed through his head, He Yu's greedy ambition swelled even further. The desire to bore through the ice in search of water became terrifyingly urgent. Although Xie Qingcheng could no doubt sense it, his hands had been bound and his whole body was limp from the strong liquor he'd drunk, so he couldn't break free. All he could do was stare at He Yu viciously through bloodshot eyes.

He Yu's hands roamed beneath the loosened shirt. After finishing up some sort of exploration, he looked up to meet Xie Qingcheng's eyes. Eventually, as if provoked by Xie Qingcheng's misty yet still viciously frigid gaze, the youth's blood started to burn. Even the shirt that barely covered Xie Qingcheng's body presented too much of an obstruction to him.

If Xie Qingcheng was trying to be all neat and ascetic, then He Yu just had to turn him into a complete wreck and feast upon the sight.

He Yu looked at the man in his arms. Xie Qingcheng's shirt had long since slipped down to his elbows, his broad, sturdy chest fully exposed to the young man's eyes. It was even covered in the faint red marks He Yu had left with his lips and teeth.

He Yu gazed darkly at the man in front of him for a long time. Xie Qingcheng used to be a piece of cake he couldn't afford, someone he couldn't manage to keep. He'd even tried to make his own sister stay away from He Yu.

Very well... Very well.

Then he'd just make Xie Qingcheng reap what he sowed and repay him with his own body!

He Yu was painfully hard and swollen. He didn't want to wait anymore, and his madness surged through the last of his reservations. He picked Xie Qingcheng up, his hands digging into his waist as he carried him deeper into the inner chamber of the private room.

"He Yu! Let go! Put me down!"

The inner chamber was a lounge room, and it was decorated suggestively, with dim lighting and even rose petals scattered on the bed. He Yu scoffed out loud at the sight before tossing Xie Qingcheng directly onto the bed and pinning him down with his own tall, heavy body before Xie Qingcheng had the chance to struggle upright.

By this point, no matter how straight Xie Qingcheng was, he truly did believe that He Yu was going to follow through on his threat. The tendons of Xie Qingcheng's bound hands bulged as his nails sank into his palms, and he trembled violently.

"You..." he rasped with bloodshot eyes, "You fucker, if you dare do this to me... Just wait and see...how I'll deal with you!"

He Yu didn't waste any breath on him whatsoever. He'd also had some liquor, and Xie Qingcheng's appearance had riled him up so much that he felt like his brain was on fire. He yanked open the bedside drawer without a word. Digging through it hastily, he found a box of condoms, which he tore apart. Then, right there before Xie Qingcheng's bloodless face, he unzipped his jeans and pushed down his underwear.

When the young man's dick sprang out, even the habitually composed Xie Qingcheng felt his mind go blank. His lust-flushed face was overtaken by a terror so great that it even took the edge off his drug-induced desire.

It was too terrifying. The events that were transpiring and the youth's size—both were far too horrifying.

He Yu looked up. His eyes were so twisted they no longer resembled those of an ordinary human. He knelt beside Xie Qingcheng, and that thick, veiny cock gave off a faintly musky scent as he shoved it in Xie Qingcheng's face.

Xie Qingcheng's voice shook. "He Yu… You motherfucker…"

In the dim light, He Yu took out a condom with one hand and quickly slipped it over his hard, scalding length. He didn't care how Xie Qingcheng cursed him. He didn't plan to waste breath on Xie Qingcheng at all. His eyes were already blazing red, completely absent of rationality. All he wanted was to fuck the man in front of him.

Grabbing Xie Qingcheng by the waist and lifting his long legs, He Yu lined himself up and tried to shove his way in.

Xie Qingcheng already found sleeping with another man absolutely unacceptable, but it looked like He Yu wanted to go all the way to home base. He didn't think kissing, groping, or using hands or mouths was enough—he wanted to go inside on his first try!

Xie Qingcheng broke down completely. "Fuck off! Get the fuck off! He Yu, you're fucking insane! What's wrong with you?!"

In response, He Yu only manhandled his legs even more savagely, forcing him to wrap them around his waist. He Yu turned to press a kiss to the side of Xie Qingcheng's leg, sending another irrepressible thrill of satisfaction through Xie Qingcheng amidst his immense terror and fury.

After kissing him, He Yu tried to push into Xie Qingcheng once more.

This truly was something that only a virgin could have done—and a straight virgin at that. Frowning, He Yu took a few tries to line himself up properly, but by the time he'd painstakingly pressed the searing tip of his cock to Xie Qingcheng's entrance, he found it was so tight that he couldn't thrust in at all.

He Yu was deeply irritated, and his dick was achingly hot and hard; his hunger to be inside Xie Qingcheng was driving him insane. He stared down at Xie Qingcheng with an unnatural bloody glint in his eyes.

"Why won't it go in?" he demanded, panting as he continued trying to force it.

Xie Qingcheng was dazed and aching all over, countless impulses exploding through his mind. It was impossible for him to think straight through the extreme psychological humiliation and insane physiological stimulation.

Having run out of patience, He Yu grabbed Xie Qingcheng by the waist and dragged him closer. The youth's hot sweat assaulted Xie Qingcheng's senses, becoming an intense aphrodisiac. It dripped from He Yu's body, landing on Xie Qingcheng's sturdy chest as he bucked his hips forward, grinding and thrusting at him incessantly and roughly urging, "Let me in..."

Xie Qingcheng's eyes were already scarlet. "Like hell I'd let you... Fuck off!"

It was He Yu's first time trying to fuck somebody. Driven by emotion and lust, even his breathing had become intensely ragged.

He gave Xie Qingcheng's flushed body a dark glare. Struck by inspiration amidst his sheer discomfort at being unable to shove his way in, he reached down to probe at that small hidden opening with his fingers.

Xie Qingcheng gasped before biting furiously down on his lip at once. His face had gone white. Of course a finger could fit, but in all his years of life, no one had ever tried to enter him like this. Humiliated and in pain, he didn't find it pleasurable at all, and his erection began to flag.

But He Yu seemed to have figured out what to do. Watching Xie Qingcheng calmly, he pushed his finger into him, mimicking the rapid thrusting motions of sex until Xie Qingcheng began to frown and shake his head again and again. He Yu's eyes darkened further, and when he sensed that the opening had relaxed slightly, he impatiently added another finger.

When the second finger entered him and quickly began to thrust, Xie Qingcheng was driven even further past his limits. He'd already bitten his lower lip bloody, and his eyes were dazed and unfocused.

As a doctor, he knew what the last step of gay sex was. He understood that given He Yu's level of ability as a straight virgin, he was about to endure untold suffering tonight. In his delirium, Xie Qingcheng instinctively tried to turn and look for a lubricant. He caught sight of a bottle of lube in the bedside drawer that He Yu had yet to close.

But that type of lube was for women... Even if it had been for men, Xie Qingcheng still couldn't possibly speak up. He had his pride. No matter how much torment he was going through, no matter how destructive it was for his mental state, he still had his pride.

He only glanced at the bottle before he turned away and covered his eyes with his wounded arm to avoid the nightmarish scene before him.

He Yu had already gotten three fingers in, but Xie Qingcheng was still very dry. The condom was lubricated, but it wasn't enough for a man.

He Yu recalled the strange expression on Xie Qingcheng's face when he'd turned his head a moment ago. A wisp of lucidity returned amidst his all-consuming lust as he looked askance with his almond eyes. It was then that he saw the bottle of lube in the drawer, with words such as "For Her Pleasure" faintly visible on the packaging...

He Yu panted out a breath. He rose slightly and shoved Xie Qingcheng's face down. He didn't say a word, but his actions were those one would take with a bitch to be muzzled, commanding him to sit and behave, degrading in the extreme. He went to grab that tube of lubricant, squeezed it open, and smeared the product over his hand. He stroked it over himself, then scooped up some more and shoved it roughly into Xie Qingcheng's hole.

Xie Qingcheng gave a muffled grunt and the veins in his neck protruded as He Yu fingered him savagely.

Although this lube had a sensitizing effect on women and wasn't as effective on men, it worked more than well enough as a lubricating agent. This time, He Yu found it had become noticeably easier to fuck into Xie Qingcheng. He stared dark-eyed at how his fingers made that pale entrance twitch and gape as the lubricant squelched with each thrust. Some of the milky white fluid even seeped out along the rim.

He Yu could feel his own breath burning even hotter. His cock was so hard, he couldn't wait even a second longer. He withdrew his fingers all at once, bringing traces of sticky fluid with them. He could feel the way Xie Qingcheng's abdomen shuddered.

Adjusting the condom, he lined himself up once again with Xie Qingcheng's softened hole.

"Xie Qingcheng." He Yu, who'd been mostly engrossed in his task and working in silence, finally spoke. There was a mad glint in his eyes, along with a boundless and unfathomable lust. He nudged the tip of his cock at the entrance to Xie Qingcheng's body, pressing against it but not pushing in. With Xie Qingcheng's legs wrapped around his waist, He Yu leaned forward and grabbed him by the chin. "Do you know that I'm about to fuck you?"

"You fucking..."

"You haven't ever been fucked here, have you? Then you'd better take your time feeling it. Get a good taste of how I'll fuck you inside, just like how you used to fuck your wife."

The thick cock that had spent so long pressed intimately to that soft opening suddenly shoved in with a savage burst of force.

"Ah!" Caught off guard, Xie Qingcheng cried out with his eyes wide, trembling all over.

He Yu also gasped. A spurt of lubricant was pushed out with a squelch, splashing between their connected bodies.

Neither of them made another sound for a while. The room was filled with raging waves of desire and heat, and everything felt as if it were happening through a misty haze, like an absurd dream.

But it was all real.

Xie Xue was fake, He Yu thought, but the fact that he was fucking Xie Qingcheng was real. What was this world coming to...

Xie Qingcheng felt completely destroyed. He was a manly man to the core, but right now, he was being forcefully fucked by a boy who was still in college, and his legs were spread open like a woman's as that boy plunged in. He could even feel He Yu throbbing inside him from the burst of intense stimulation.

This sensation hurt him worse than death. But at the same time, the lustful cravings brought on by the drug made him feel a borderline perverted thrill.

Once he'd plunged inside, He Yu clenched his teeth, his own scalp beginning to prickle with heat. He had never imagined that he would get in bed with a man before, so he had never realized that fucking a man's body would feel so good. Overwhelming pleasure crashed down over him like a tsunami. As a virgin, he had no sexual experience, and Xie Qingcheng was even tighter than a woman. Hot and tight, under the effect of the aphrodisiac, that tiny entrance was eagerly sucking him in like a little mouth, enveloping him and welcoming him in. When he thrust inside, he only barely managed to stop himself from coming on the spot.

And then there was Xie Qingcheng's hoarse yet passionate cry. Though it had merely been something that slipped out when Xie Qingcheng was caught off guard, the thrill of it was enough to ruin him. He had never heard Xie Qingcheng make that sort of sound before.

He Yu took a moment to catch his breath. Then, seeking even more stimulation and response, he swallowed and leaned down to grab Xie Qingcheng's face. "Doctor Xie, you're so tight inside, hot and tight..."

As he spoke, he started to move his hips in a shallow back-and-forth motion, the kind of gentle fucking that was more of a dragging friction. He wedged his hips tightly between Xie Qingcheng's thighs, and every time he drew out only a little before pushing back into him, slow and deep.

"Ah..." Xie Qingcheng was also losing his mind.

He had never felt such arousal before. The drug made his body extremely receptive to any kind of sexual contact, and all his reactions were amplified. The shock of He Yu forcing himself on him had left him unable to catch up with the situation at first, and the light in both of his eyes was a scattered mess. Almost subconsciously, he began to cry out hoarsely in time with He Yu's movements.

But as the feeling of intrusion and tingling sensation grew stronger and stronger inside his body, Xie Qingcheng sobered up slightly. Once he realized that those frighteningly hoarse cries, thick with lust, were coming from his own throat, he bit down on his lip, refusing to let even the slightest of moans escape him.

But that handful of cries was enough for He Yu. Hearing that impassioned voice that his Doctor Xie had never let out before sent his arousal into overdrive. He grabbed Xie Qingcheng's waist and sped up his movements, plunging violently into that soft, tight embrace with all his strength.

Skin slapped against skin. The mattress shook violently as the sound of bodies colliding echoed through the sequestered lounge room.

Xie Qingcheng couldn't take He Yu's sudden change of pace, suddenly going from fucking him slowly to slamming urgently into his insides with no sense of restraint. Xie Qingcheng's handsome face shattered completely as his body was rocked by He Yu's thrusts.

After fucking him for a while and getting no response, He Yu became dissatisfied once more. Panting quietly, he looked down at Xie Qingcheng's face and tried to provoke and humiliate him further. "Aren't you the epitome of propriety? Hmm? What proper doctor would moan like this on his own patient's cock... Go on, moan again. Are you trying to seduce me with that voice? How badly do you want me to fuck you like this... You've been sucking me in this whole time... Can't you feel it?"

He Yu slammed into Xie Qingcheng even harder as he spoke, thrusting nearly balls deep inside him on a few of his thrusts.

It was too good. He Yu had never felt so good before. Wave after wave of pleasure threatened to overwhelm him. Xie Qingcheng was so hot inside, and with all the lubricant He Yu had used, he was wet, too, surrounding the condom with white froth as He Yu thrust in. The wet sounds were a continuous reminder to the two people desperately entangled with each other on the bed: they were doing it. A grown man and a teenage boy; a truly absurd relationship.

He Yu was fucking Xie Qingcheng wildly, furiously, starving for warmth.

The slap of colliding bodies, Xie Qingcheng's low gasps, He Yu's mumbled words of depravity, and the heavy creaking of the rocking bed all echoed through the room nonstop.

As He Yu lost himself in the heights of pleasure, he suddenly felt something warm and hard rub against him. He looked down, only for his eyes to darken even further.

He took a moment to gather himself. Then, with another deep thrust into Xie Qingcheng's trembling, sweat-slick body, he leaned down and breathed quietly against the messy hair of Xie Qingcheng's temples. "Look at how hard you've gotten with my cock in you."

"Motherfucker!" Xie Qingcheng's eyes were fierce, as if he were about to take a vicious bite out of He Yu, but he couldn't seem to raise his voice. His whole being was in shambles.

He Yu nipped at Xie Qingcheng's neck as he ground into him again and again, that slick cock thrusting and sliding inside him. Xie Qingcheng could even feel the aggressive raised vein along the young man's length. His legs trembled as the waves of tingling and tightening pleasure inside his body drove him to the brink of madness. He nearly began to cry out again, but he forced the sound back down his throat.

He hadn't forgotten what he had said before. Humans were different from animals because they could control themselves in the face of desire. He couldn't control his physiological reactions, but at the very least, he could control his words and voice. He could control his heart.

He Yu's gaze turned cold as ice yet slimy with unwelcome intimacy. "All these fighting words. You're saying you want me to fuck you till you come tonight, is that right?"

"Get the fuck off... Motherfucker! Nngh!"

He Yu's response was to slam into him like a beast, spraying fluids everywhere.

Xie Qingcheng couldn't bear it anymore, and the world flashed before his eyes. These thrusts were forceful, vicious, and rushed, almost desperate. They were so rough that Xie Qingcheng struggled to breathe; his eyes lost focus, and his awareness began to dissociate as he was forcefully railed. In this half-conscious state, it felt like his body didn't even belong to him.

Dark. Everything in front of him had gone dark.

But the physical sensations coming from his body remained clear and distinct. He could feel his lower body being penetrated at a frantic pace, the pleasurable thrill from the stimulation of one particular spot making him wish he could just die.

There was also He Yu's sweat dripping down from his chest, drop after drop, falling from his incessantly rocking body onto Xie Qingcheng's abdomen.

Limp and insensate with pleasure, Xie Qingcheng was breaking down completely...

Amid the haze, he heard He Yu pant an old resentment into his ear. "Didn't you say before that I didn't have the money to hire you? What about now? Never mind hiring you, I'm fucking you right now—are you satisfied?"

Then He Yu pulled out, and after swapping the condom, he thrust back inside Xie Qingcheng with violent force and began to fuck him wildly.

He Yu buried his face in the crook of Xie Qingcheng's sweat-soaked neck. As he pushed into Xie Qingcheng again, into that place as soft as the tender meat inside a clamshell, he caught a whiff of the fragrance he'd coaxed from this man's body.

In the midst of his intense arousal, He Yu didn't even realize that he had thought the word "fragrance" to describe the scent on Xie Qingcheng's body.

He had always disliked Xie Qingcheng's scent. It was like tissue paper, like ice-cold medicine, making him think of whitewashed hospital walls and the harsh smell of disinfectant.

But when it was blended with the warmth that He Yu had ravished out of him, the essence of the scent seemed to have changed. Ice turned to water, and water turned to steam. Shrouded in this warm fog, Xie Qingcheng went from that ever-indifferent, unfeeling doctor to a wretched and trembling plaything beneath his body.

The pleasure of domination and revenge made the scent of Xie Qingcheng's body seem like the fragrance of an opium poppy.

He Yu fucked Xie Qingcheng too many times that night. Without any of his usual composure and skillful ease, he really was just a brainless little rascal, thrusting into Xie Qingcheng uncontrollably again and again. Xie Qingcheng stayed nearly silent throughout the entire process. He even suppressed his panting breaths, leaving his lower lip mottled with blood from the way he kept biting himself.

The drug made his whole body burn red-hot, and whenever he was fucked in a certain spot, it felt too good—so good he got hard again, so good he came.

But mentally, he couldn't endure it.

He had straight man cancer to begin with—he suffered the paternal variant of the disease and thought very highly of himself. On top of that, he was indifferent to sex. He would simply rather die than endure the things He Yu was doing to him.

He looked past his sweat-dampened lashes at the well-built silhouette of the young man in his hazy field of vision. Perhaps it was to add to his sense of shame, but not once this entire night—even when they had gotten onto this big bed, even up to this very moment—had He Yu taken off his clothes. He had only pulled down the fly of his jeans.

The boy was dressed neatly from head to toe, while the man didn't have a single stitch of clothing on him.

Suddenly, a cell phone rang and startled He Yu.

He leaned forward to pick up his phone. He looked at the caller ID, then answered it in a hoarse rasp. "Hello?"

"You haven't gone to bed yet, have you?" The call was from He Jiwei.

"Nope," He Yu replied in a gloomy voice, thrusting forcefully into the man beneath him while taking his father's call.

"How's your injury?"

"Everything's fine."

"Your mother and I will be back in a few days. We'll be staying for a while longer before we leave again this time. Remember to come back home for dinner. Don't stay out overnight on your own."

He Yu hummed in assent.

He Jiwei paused and then asked, "It's so late. Have you gotten home yet?"

He Yu paused.

Of course, he couldn't tell He Jiwei that he hadn't gone home yet because he'd gone and bedded an old man thirteen years his senior at a club. And that the man was Xie Qingcheng, no less.

But a thrill ran through him at the thought, making his already-hard cock swell even further. He thrust into Xie Qingcheng slowly but ruthlessly, over and over, until even the toes of the man underneath him were curled taut. Xie Qingcheng's face and body were both drenched in sweat, but he still didn't make a single sound. As he fucked him, He Yu replied in a low voice, "I'm still out with a friend."

"Oh," He Jiwei said. "Well, you should get home soon, it's getting late. And don't get mixed up with any shady characters. They'll be a bad influence on you."

Unable to resist, He Yu restrained the sound of his panting and thrust in deeper. This sort of slow fucking was torture, insufficient to slake the thirst of his desire. He put the call on speakerphone and tossed his phone to the side. Then he grabbed Xie Qingcheng, carried him over to the side of the bed, and stepped off the bed himself. Still on the phone with his father, He Yu pinned Xie Qingcheng down again at the edge of the mattress and pounded into him ruthlessly, trying to force a sound out of Xie Qingcheng's mouth even as he was already on the verge of a mental breakdown.

Xie Qingcheng's body rocked with each impact as the bed shuddered in concert with a series of muffled thumping noises.

He Jiwei didn't notice, or perhaps he simply couldn't fathom that He Yu would get up to any trouble in his personal life, so he carried on speaking to He Yu as he normally would. He Yu listened absent-mindedly, grunting in perfunctory affirmation from time to time. Then he lowered his head to kiss and suck on Xie Qingcheng's thin lips, thrusting deep into him as the mattress creaked dully. The slick, wet sounds of their kiss seeped into their eardrums.

Xie Qingcheng finally reached the limits of his endurance. He opened his eyes and gave He Yu a furious glare as he hissed with overwhelming hatred, "He Yu..."

He Yu hadn't anticipated that Xie Qingcheng would actually dare utter a word. He shifted upright and shoved a hand over Xie Qingcheng's nose and mouth. The look in his eyes was ferocious, but he still maintained his concentration and held his breath.

As expected, He Jiwei paused. "Your friend?"

"Mm."

"Which one?"

"You don't know him."

With He Jiwei deterred, He Yu stared relentlessly at Xie Qingcheng's face. His expression was predatory, filled with more hateful resentment than desire. He looked Xie Qingcheng up and down, taking the measure of this man who was covered in the marks of dominance he had left all over his body. There was even a streak of cum that he had maliciously smeared on his cheek.

"All right then, Dad, if there's nothing else, I'm gonna hang up first. I'll head home soon."

"Okay."

As the phone screen went dark, He Yu's expression darkened along with it. He grabbed Xie Qingcheng's face. "You have the nerve?"

Xie Qingcheng's voice came out unbelievably hoarse from between the flash of his gritted teeth, yet his words were still cold and ruthless to the extreme. "You're the one acting like a little bitch."

In response to this humiliating rebuke, He Yu seized Xie Qingcheng's hair and dragged him to the middle of the bed. He then climbed onto the bed himself and grabbed Xie Qingcheng by the waist, forcing him onto all fours. He looped an arm around him, propping one hand against the sagging mattress and gripping Xie Qingcheng's waist with the other, squeezing hard enough to leave black and purple marks. Leaning over Xie Qingcheng's body, he fucked into him wildly in retaliation. Xie Qingcheng tried to crawl forward to get away from him, but He Yu pulled him back even more fiercely than before with a violent yank on his hair.

Xie Qingcheng felt like he was about to be smashed to pieces, like he was about to fall apart. His legs were so shaky they nearly collapsed beneath him. His vision kept flashing dark even as he felt He Yu snake a hand around his abdomen and press his lips close to the back of his ear. He Yu breathed heavily as he berated him, "Still so close-lipped, huh? If you wanna be fucked to death, just say so! I think men are disgusting, but as long as you want it, I'll make sure you're satisfied."

Xie Qingcheng was in so much pain he couldn't speak as he leaned over the obscene mess they'd made of the mattress. Even though He Yu had already loosened the restraints on his wrists, he truly had no strength left to struggle. Clawing at the bed, he could only grasp intermittently at the wrinkled bed sheets.

Suddenly, He Yu grabbed his hand, his fingers folding over his own as if he wanted to subdue him like this forever. Their fingers interlocked against the mattress. Sweat dripped from the young man's body and landed on Xie Qingcheng's back, scalding the bruised skin there like beads of hot wax.

Xie Qingcheng's toes curled in both pain and pleasure. He Yu fucked him with inhuman stamina for more than half an hour before Xie Qingcheng finally felt that he was going to come again. With only the thin rubber of the condom between them, he could feel the hard, hot length buried inside him throb dangerously, swollen and scalding. It was as if He Yu's unrelenting thrusts had made it into a branding iron, shoving deep into his abdomen like it was about to pierce through his belly.

"Ah... Ahhhh... *Aah!*"

In the end, Xie Qingcheng couldn't hold back a hoarse cry as he completely lost all sense of rationality. The drug had made his body unusually sensitive. He couldn't help himself from sucking in and clamping down on the cock that brought such a maddening, almost terrifying pleasure to his body, and no matter how much he rejected the mere idea of it, he still tightened wetly around it as he felt it pulse inside him.

In the end, He Yu viciously snapped his hips forward as he panted on top of Xie Qingcheng, driving balls deep into him as he came in spurts. As He Yu reached his climax, Xie Qingcheng came too, just like that, from being fucked from behind by a teenager...

Gasping for breath, eyes unfocused and body drenched in sweat after this ferocious pounding and release, he was finally veritably fucked unconscious.

54

The Beginning

THE THICK CURTAINS in the private room were pulled tightly shut, barring any sunlight from streaming in.

Once Xie Qingcheng finally woke up, he had no idea how much time had passed.

He felt sore everywhere, disoriented and lost, and it was a long time before the terrifying memories from last night finally slammed into his mind like a crashing car.

He was speechless.

Last night, he had been...

Xie Qingcheng's eyes were crimson. For a moment, he was sure he must have had a horrible nightmare caused by exhaustion. He even closed his eyes for a while before opening them again, weakly wishing to find himself in his dorm room at the medical school, or the old residence at Moyu Alley.

But he wasn't.

No such miracle happened.

He was still in this private lounge room reeking of sex, lying completely nude and utterly bedraggled on the huge bed with half the sheets spilling onto the floor.

He Yu had already left.

With his bloodshot eyes open, Xie Qingcheng tried to force himself to stand, only for an agonizing stab of pain emanating from his lower body to bolt through him, causing him to collapse heavily back onto the bed.

At least He Yu had used a condom, even if nothing else he'd done was humane.

When Xie Qingcheng pushed himself slightly upright on the bed, he could see several used condoms strewn over the bedding. The sight of their contents turned even the tips of his fingers red with humiliation and fury.

True, he did feel remorse toward He Yu. He did feel that he'd been too heartless before, that he'd never treated He Yu as an equal.

Prior to this outrageous incident, he'd been thinking of trying to build a new relationship with He Yu—one that had nothing to do with that of a doctor and patient, one that was simply between He Yu and himself. He'd never considered forming a long-term bond with a youth before, but when He Yu had reached out to him without hesitation, Xie Qingcheng's paternalistic heart had finally been moved.

In that moment, he'd realized that perhaps he might've really been in the wrong with the way he'd handled certain things. He Yu was just young; his emotions weren't weaker than anyone else's. Perhaps Xie Qingcheng shouldn't have chosen to leave so brusquely back then.

He'd thought that, as long as He Yu forgave him, he was willing to keep He Yu company for a long while this time around—as long as He Yu needed it, as long as he was still capable.

But He Yu had committed this beastly, abominable act that went completely beyond the confines of Xie Qingcheng's imagination.

Xie Qingcheng couldn't accept it, even on pain of death.

A straight man had actually fucked another straight man.

And the condoms on the bed bore witness to how many times he'd done it.

But what was more terrifying was that by the end of the ordeal, Xie Qingcheng had completely lost control because of the drugged wine. He'd madly remained on all fours while getting fucked so hard he started dripping. He'd even climaxed repeatedly from being filled. Eventually, even though he had nothing left to release, his body still frantically sucked He Yu's cock in, his legs sprawled apart as his hips swayed from the force of the thrusts.

Now sober, Xie Qingcheng felt so humiliated that he wanted to die, so disgusted that he wanted to throw up. He reached up and rested a hand over his eyes, hiding everything from his view. He spent a long time resisting the urge to lash out, but in the end, he couldn't stop himself from grabbing the lamp from the bedside cabinet and smashing it to pieces.

He Yu had gotten so into it by the end that he'd snapped the restraints on Xie Qingcheng's wrists. Even now, there were still red marks on Xie Qingcheng's skin.

Thank god He Yu had left. If he were still here, Xie Qingcheng couldn't guarantee that he wouldn't do something beyond the bounds of rationality.

He Yu had almost driven him crazy.

Ding.

The phone that had been thrown onto the ground along with his clothes started ringing.

Xie Qingcheng was irate, and he had no intention of picking up. But the ringing persisted as if it wouldn't stop until it had dug him out of this grave of sex. Xie Qingcheng swore furiously. He made himself grab his phone, his body aching as he reached over, and picked it up with difficulty.

It was Chen Man.

"Ge."

"What is it?"

Chen Man started with shock. "Why does your voice sound so hoarse?"

Xie Qingcheng stayed silent for a moment. Then he sighed deeply. "If you have something to say, just say it. If you don't, then I'm hanging up. I'm busy."

Chen Man hastily replied, "Something's happened at home..."

The events of last night had affected Xie Qingcheng deeply. His heart pounded as waves of weakness washed over his body. On hearing what Chen Man said, cold sweat beaded all over his back as his grip on the phone grew white-knuckled. "What happened?"

Half an hour later, Xie Qingcheng appeared in the main hall of the club in his wrinkled, wine-stained shirt.

When he first woke, he couldn't even stand up. His legs buckled when he got off the bed and an unfamiliar yet terrifying throb of dull pain accompanied his every movement. Xie Qingcheng had grabbed the corner of the bedside drawer, the veins on the back of his hand protruding.

He was filled with extreme hatred and extreme shame.

Before he left the private room, he took an arduous shower in the bathroom. He always acted with swift decisiveness and never did things sloppily, but now, it took him a long time to put on even a single article of clothing. When he tried to put on his slacks, his face went white with pain.

He took a deep breath to gather himself, acting as though nothing wild and uncontrollable had happened, then strode out of the private room, pale as a sheet. He was practically gritting his teeth as he walked, expending a significant amount of his energy to straighten his back and maintain his usual posture.

But when the staff saw him, they were still shocked.

Xie Qingcheng's skin was too pallid and as thin as paper. He looked like a ghost stepping into the dim light of dawn.

"Sir...do you...need any help?"

"No," Xie Qingcheng replied.

"In that case, please settle last night's bill, sir."

Xie Qingcheng thought he'd gone deaf.

"Sir?"

"..."

Xie Qingcheng was accustomed to acting like a true man's man, and being fucked for an entire night couldn't change that. Even if he thought He Yu was much too shameless, he'd still foot the bill because that was what a man ought to do.

Thus, he responded with an ashen face, "All right. I'll pay."

"Sir, would you like to pay by card or..."

"By card."

"Please come with me to the reception desk."

The staff member tapped away at the computer and pulled up a bill.

Out of habit, Xie Qingcheng asked, "How much is it?"

The staff handed him the bill and very respectfully said, "The total for last night's private room comes to 1.68 million yuan."

Xie Qingcheng, who was in the middle of extracting his card, paused. All faculties of speech left him. He took the bill and glanced at it. The astronomical number written on it made him wonder if there might be something wrong with his eyes too.

It really was 1.68 million.

Sky-high alcohol fees, service fees, room fees, and compensation fees for damages.

Xie Qingcheng pressed a hand against his forehead. "I need to make a call. Do you have cigarettes? And a clean shirt."

With the 1.68 million yuan bill before him, Xie Qingcheng had totally given up on caring about the price tag of these items—the cigarettes and shirt would be a drop in the bucket.

After he borrowed the bathroom and changed into the shirt that a hostess brought him, Xie Qingcheng leaned against the sink, tapped out a cigarette with trembling hands, and lit it with his lashes lowered. He took a long drag before dialing the number of the person he currently wanted to murder.

If he'd had the money, he would have rather paid for it himself. But unfortunately, he couldn't fork out the ridiculous 1.68 million that had been spent overnight.

1.68 million yuan...

It was such a shockingly auspicious number that it could give someone a heart attack.[10] He Yu had fucked him all night, but it was Xie Qingcheng who had to pay the 1.68 million yuan for the alcohol, service, and room?

What exactly did *he* order? A fucking massage service?!

That bastard had even fucking run away, just like that.

"Hello, the user you have dialed is currently unavailable. Please try again later..."

Xie Qingcheng irritably ended the call. He went to He Yu's WeChat profile, forcefully tapped out some words, and then hit send.

To his surprise, WeChat immediately sounded with a notification. He'd been about to toss his phone aside, but he paused—and his eyes widened, reflecting a bright red exclamation mark on the screen.

"The message you sent has been rejected by the recipient."

Xie Qingcheng stared at the screen in grim disbelief. Now he'd really gone blind.

10 168 is pronounced similarly to 一路发, meaning a lifetime of good fortune.

He Yu had blocked him?

"Fuck," Xie Qingcheng muttered in a low voice. He was so hoarse he sounded like he was about to start emitting smoke.

He Yu. Actually. Had. The. Nerve. To. Block. Him?!

It was a blessing that Xie Qingcheng didn't really use social media, otherwise he would have realized that He Yu's actions were remarkably similar to those of some particularly contemptible youths who deleted the other person's contact information seconds after a one-night stand.

But this didn't stop Xie Qingcheng from becoming enraged. After such a disgusting turn of events last night, shouldn't *he* be the one blocking He Yu instead? Did He Yu even have the right to block him?

Xie Qingcheng very rarely lost control of himself, but at this moment, when he threw his phone onto the sink with a *clack* and lifted his eyes, the man looking back at him from the mirror seemed as ferocious as a ravaged beast that had been driven into a corner.

"He Yu...!"

Meanwhile, Young Big Shot He had genuinely forgotten about paying the bill.

By now, his madness had already subsided slightly, and the effects of the alcohol had likewise worn off. But his mind was still in turmoil.

When he had woken up in the morning and found himself sleeping on his stomach, he could sense that something wasn't quite right. As soon as his eyes refocused, he saw Xie Qingcheng lying under him on the mattress in an utterly wretched condition. He was sprawled out on top of Xie Qingcheng, having slept the entire night with his face tucked into the crook of the man's neck. His posture was just like that of a wounded fledgling dragon that had folded its wings and curled up its tail to rest, having flown arduously across the sea and finally found a warm, humid lair. The little dragon had been so tired, thirsty, and lonely on its journey, so after drinking its fill of water at long last, it clicked its snout, settled into its new den, and slept until daybreak in perfect satisfaction.

But upon waking up, the young dragon was struck dumb. Those shattered, frantic memories from the night before rushed back like a wild snowstorm.

He must have had a nightmare or been possessed by a demon. Or perhaps that Plum Fragrance 59 that he downed wasn't liquor but a magical potion that could rid one of homophobia with just a couple of sips. Otherwise, how could he have done something so completely unhinged with such fervent passion? That was a man!

He had done those things to a *man*...

He Yu looked down at Xie Qingcheng's face and reached out a hand to turn it toward him, his fingertip brushing against Xie Qingcheng's bloody lips.

Although he was still unconscious, his lips trembled slightly as though responding to He Yu's touch. Xie Qingcheng looked like a crumpled sheet of tissue paper, stark white with a few spots of cinnabar on its surface. That handsome, chiseled face utterly lacked any trace of femininity...

He Yu scrutinized it for a long time with an indescribable feeling in his heart.

Disbelief.

Madness.

Loathing.

But such secrets of the flesh were buried deep below the surface, yet to be uncovered. He Yu looked at Xie Qingcheng like a dragon gazing down at a human sacrifice on a bed of rock. The dragon detested humans, so it should have driven him away or devoured him in a single bite. It should never have madly rampaged onto the bed with that human in tow.

Now He Yu was like a strange creature gradually leaving madness and coming back to his wits. He looked over the crimes that he had wrought, his eyes reflecting the image of the human that he had tormented to the point of devastation.

Normally, he found homosexuality incredibly disgusting. Even he himself had no idea what had happened to him. Had he really been so angry, so drunk, that he had completely lost his mind? No matter how violent or impetuous he had been, he shouldn't have used this man's body to vent his emotions that way.

His illness caused his heart to become desensitized and cold, but it felt as though he had fallen even deeper into an ice cave. He sat up on the bed and looked at the chaotic mess surrounding him, his mind filled with the irrepressible images of Xie Qingcheng with his legs tangled around his waist, falling to pieces before his eyes, full of suffering and desire.

He had really done those things.

He Yu's mind froze over as he stared numbly at Xie Qingcheng's unconscious face. The excitement of having doled out his revenge swirled around his brain even as looking back on his overindulgent descent into madness left him soaked in a chilly mire of regret. How could he have...

He felt extremely disquieted, but ultimately, another burst of resentment welled up within him. Xie Qingcheng only had himself to blame for this. Who asked that man to deceive him for seven years—and then another four after that...?

So, while on the one hand, He Yu was disgusted...on the other, a flower of malice silently unfurled in his heart. It suddenly struck him that he ought to take something as a memento of this crazed, sinful entanglement.

After all, this had been his first time. He wouldn't want to see Xie Qingcheng again; by the same token, he imagined that Xie Qingcheng would hate him to the bone for this and be just as unwilling to see him. And so, after thinking it over, he finally dug out his cell phone from the clothes that were tangled up like the cast-off molted skin of a snake, pointed the camera at the still-unconscious man, and took a few pictures of his soundly sleeping face.

At this very moment, He Yu was looking at the photos he'd taken of Xie Qingcheng's sleeping visage. The man in the pictures looked extremely weak and exhausted, with clear bite marks on the broken skin of his lips. It was obvious at a glance what he had been doing with someone else before falling asleep—as was the fact that he had been on the receiving end.

As He Yu stared, his ruthless, unfeeling mind kept replaying how destroyed Xie Qingcheng had looked beneath him the night before and the handful of hoarse moans that Xie Qingcheng hadn't managed to stifle. He thought coldly, what sexual apathy? How many times did he lose himself last night? As expected, everything about Xie Qingcheng was fake.

But for some reason, a warmth started to seep into He Yu's blood.

As he was lost in thought, his phone began to ring. An unknown landline number was calling him.

"Hello?" he answered.

A voice came from the other end of the line. It was the same voice that had sounded so pleasantly low and raspy when it cried out last night—but right now, it was as cold as hoarfrost.

"He Yu," Xie Qingcheng said, "have you no fucking sense of shame?"

Less than twenty minutes later, He Yu, who had just turned tail and run after fucking someone, drove back to the Skynight Club. The tall main doors of the club opened, and the hostess welcomed Mr. He in with her head respectfully bowed. He Yu looked just like he always did—clean-cut and minimalist, gentlemanly and courteous. A paragon of propriety.

No one would ever think he'd done something as preposterous as recklessly screwing another man.

When He Yu walked through the doors into the lobby and looked around with his almond eyes, he immediately caught sight of Xie Qingcheng standing next to the reception desk. Xie Qingcheng's face was so pale it was unsightly, but he was somehow still able to stand upright, with his slender waist and long legs ramrod straight.

Just as He Yu appeared to be a respectful and gentle client from a scholarly family, Xie Qingcheng didn't look at all like someone who had just spent an entire night being tormented by a younger man.

He had already changed into another snow-white dress shirt, and his hair had been washed and combed. He had the same domineering aura He Yu was used to seeing, as incisive and chilly as a dagger.

But while nothing seemed different on the surface, their relationship was no longer the same—it was no longer innocent.

Looking Xie Qingcheng up and down now, it was as if He Yu's gaze could cut through his prim and proper exterior to see the blood and flesh, the muscles and bones within. It was as if Xie Qingcheng wasn't wearing any clothes at all.

Meanwhile, the moment Xie Qingcheng caught sight of He Yu, his blood pressure shot up. It was only because they were in a busy lobby and he didn't want to become a household name that he managed to forcibly suppress the urge to kick and stab He Yu to death.

"Mr. He, here is your bill from last night," said the hostess, handing He Yu the receipt.

Although she was well-versed in the service etiquette of her profession, the events from last night were way too bizarre. When the young hostess had verified the items on the bill for the private room on the computer, every line that appeared shocked her to the core. Huh... It looked like they had smashed the entire private room...

Did they fight?

They must have.

But when she read further down and saw that the lubricant in the room was also on the bill, as well as the condoms, the young lady became even more shocked.

After they finished fighting, they slept together?

This was utterly unheard of!

A sense of feminine sympathy arose in her, so when she handed the bill to He Yu, her voice softened a great deal and she was brimming with compassion.

That's right, the one she sympathized with was He Yu.

He Yu looked way too pretty. Though he was tall, he seemed very slender and elegant in his clothes, and his face had an especially delicate, refined, scholarly quality to it. He looked nothing like Xie Qingcheng, who, despite being in so much discomfort he could barely hold himself upright, still managed to arrange his features into an icy-cold expression.

As a result, the young hostess misunderstood completely and had concluded that Xie Qingcheng was the one who had used all those condoms on He Yu. She thought that, with his handsome looks, Xie Qingcheng must be living off his partners, and that, after tormenting Young Master He all night long, he'd turned around and summoned the young master back here to foot the bill.

It was too shameless!

After He Yu settled the payment, the young lady bowed and courageously gave him an encouraging look. Meanwhile, it was only because of her high standards of professionalism that she was able to resist rolling her eyes at that bastard Xie Qingcheng before turning and walking off in her heels.

He Yu and Xie Qingcheng stood in silence by the large, round table in the lobby.

Fortunately, both these gentlemen had some sense of shame in the presence of others. That was the only reason they didn't start a shouting match right there in the club's lobby. The rushing sound of water from the Three Lucky Gods fountain in the lobby became the backing track of their silent stare down.

Xie Qingcheng gazed at He Yu with his bloodshot eyes. He Yu could put on airs with that face of his, but there was a glint of madness in his eyes that only Xie Qingcheng could see. That madness seemed to taunt Xie Qingcheng, as if shamelessly saying, *Yeah, I've done it and I don't plan on seeing you ever again. What are you going to do about it?*

Eventually, Xie Qingcheng stood up. To the casual onlooker, his posture seemed just as upright and straight as before, and his footsteps as brisk as the wind. But He Yu could see a slight unsteadiness in his stride.

Xie Qingcheng walked up to He Yu, his steps heavy and his gaze terrifying.

For a second, He Yu grew apprehensive and felt the urge to turn tail and run. But he immediately dismissed his kneejerk reaction as ridiculous. The only reason he was feeling that way was because Xie Qingcheng had held that sort of oppressive power over him since his childhood, leaving it practically etched into his DNA. It would still haunt him on occasion even now.

He Yu shoved the unbidden trauma from his mind and swore that he'd never let anyone—especially the person in front of him—know about the thought that had just crossed his mind. He calmed himself down and stared back at Xie Qingcheng unblinkingly. Then, after just a moment, he broke into an unexpected smile and said slowly in a soft voice, "Xie-ge, don't you hate me so much that you want to kill me right now?"

55

I Did *Not* Run Away!

"KILL YOU?" Xie Qingcheng gritted out each word through his teeth. "Aren't you the clever one. Is that why you ran away?"

He Yu hadn't expected him to say something like that. A gash immediately appeared in the easy nonchalance and grim fierceness he had only just cobbled together, and it revealed a youth's mortification underneath. The boy's smile faded in an instant and his face paled slightly.

"I didn't run away!"

"You didn't run away?"

"That wasn't running away. I just... I..."

"You just?" Xie Qingcheng narrowed his eyes, closing in on He Yu with each step.

He Yu didn't know how to respond.

"You just woke up early, pulled up your pants, and, upon seeing that the weather outside was nice and you were feeling fine and dandy, decided you might as well go for a healthy, relaxing morning jog? Because you didn't want to be disturbed by the fiasco from yesterday, you blocked my fucking phone number and WeChat, and then you thought, 'All is well with the world,' as you walked straight out of the room, so cheerful that you even forgot to take care of the fucking bill you ran up? Is that it?!"

He Yu's expression turned even uglier, as though he'd been poisoned.

"You're truly a piece of shit, He Yu. You're a piece of shit who only knows how to run away after you've done something wrong."

He Yu's face went ashen, his embarrassment and anger mixed with some indignation and even a bit of humiliation. "I said I didn't run away! I came back and paid the bill right after I got your call, didn't I?!"

Xie Qingcheng lost his temper too. "Have you no shame? You think I *wanted* you to pay the bill? Listen, if it weren't for...I'd never want to see you again for the rest of my life!"

His Fatherliness wasn't lying. If he had 1.68 million yuan on his card, then he really would have settled the bill himself and never would have bothered with calling that bastard He Yu back here to begin with. He was a man too! As if he wanted He Yu to pay for the room!

He Yu glared back at him through this torrent of verbal abuse with a stricken look on his face.

Even though they both subconsciously kept their voices down, it was impossible to conceal the hostile atmosphere crackling between them. When the young lady who had just taken care of their bill stole a glance in their direction from the reception desk across the lobby, she really couldn't help but roll her eyes at Xie Qingcheng this time.

Fucking hell. This grown-ass man spent 1.68 million yuan of the young master's money in a single night and was still giving him a hard time? Could he possibly be any more shameless?!

Their confrontation dragged on for a long while, until He Yu reined back his anger and made a pointed decision to stop talking to Xie Qingcheng about this. Steadying his breathing once again, he forced himself to calm down.

"So, what do you want to do about it now?" he said contemptuously. "Since I've already come back here, why not just ask the front desk for a knife and kill me outright?" He Yu's voice was laced with vicious sarcasm as he stared at Xie Qingcheng.

"Kill you?" Xie Qingcheng laughed bitterly. "You're too naive. I want to take a fucking knife and dissect you alive, piece by piece!"

He Yu smiled as if he had been expecting this, but his eyes still reddened and his face still paled. "All right...all right. That's fine. Whatever you say, it's all fine, Xie Qingcheng. Whether you want me to undergo death by a thousand cuts or whip my corpse to shreds, I don't care. It doesn't actually matter to me whether I die or not. Dead or alive, I'm just garbage that no one gives a shit about anyway." It was difficult to tell whether the corners of He Yu's mouth were curving out of ridicule or self-hatred. "Did you know...in the past, I believed all those lies you told me. I was such a damn idiot, trying so hard for so long. And now, my faith has crumbled overnight, all thanks to you. In fact, I wish Lu Yuzhu's aim had been a little better when she fired that gun. I wouldn't be so disgusted now if I'd just kicked the bucket right then."

His dark eyes moved slowly and landed on Xie Qingcheng. There was a note of pain suppressed within his voice when he said, "You wish the same thing, don't you? It would've been cleaner if I'd died back then—you wouldn't be in such an awful situation now either."

Xie Qingcheng jabbed a ferocious finger at He Yu with a savage, snarling force, but before he could say anything, he found his heart unexpectedly rattled at He Yu's mention of Lu Yuzhu.

He didn't know if He Yu had said it on purpose, but the matter with Lu Yuzhu in the archives was precisely why Xie Qingcheng felt he owed He Yu a debt.

A myriad of hateful emotions welled up in Xie Qingcheng's heart, but his ears seemed to echo with the sound of that gunshot. The blood that had spilled from He Yu's shoulder had been so red, searing its crimson color painfully into his retinas.

In the present moment, the crack of that gunshot transformed into a vine that wrapped around Xie Qingcheng's rage and reined it in, stopping him from ruthlessly slapping He Yu across the face.

"He Yu," Xie Qingcheng finally spat, gritting out each syllable with deliberate emphasis. Between the discomfort in his body and the torment of his mind, this pointless bickering with He Yu had left his voice incredibly hoarse—weak, yet icy. "You want to hash this out with me today, do you? Fine. All right. Then listen up. Even if I didn't do everything right, even if I didn't want to take the risk and continue being a doctor, even if I let down my teachers and was disdained, cast aside, and looked down upon by my former colleagues...I didn't deserve to be tortured like this by you. I may not have handled everything perfectly, and I may have made you resent me, but when I was treating you, I never did anything that I truly need to apologize for."

He Yu didn't respond.

"Be reasonable," Xie Qingcheng continued. "What you did—don't you find it despicable?" He took a deep breath. Battling his intense headache and dizziness, he murmured in a voice that sounded slightly wet, "Think about it."

If their earlier argument had only made He Yu feel embarrassed... then these words truly stabbed him where his scars hurt the most.

He hadn't planned on talking to Xie Qingcheng any more than absolutely necessary. Nor had he wanted to bring up the matter involving Xie Xue. But suddenly, he couldn't hold back anymore. Under the watchful gazes of numerous pairs of eyes, he pulled Xie Qingcheng into the bathroom and locked the door with a *click.*

"What do you want me to think about, huh? Xie Qingcheng, what do you want me to think about?! Do you still think that I don't know anything?" He Yu's emotions were becoming frenzied. "Let me tell you, I know everything now! I understand everything! Delusional disorder, self-preservation, nihilism—all those things I remember Xie Xue doing, they were all just figments of my imagination I was using to numb myself to the fact that they were things I could never have. I understand it all!"

Xie Qingcheng's face paled, making him look even more like a wandering soul.

"I know everything..." He Yu's eyes were unhinged. Although his voice was very soft, every word seemed to slice into Xie Qingcheng's face like a knife. "Doctor Xie, you knew everything too, but you didn't say a word. You just stood by as I made a fool of myself because you were worried that I would become too attached to her, that I wouldn't be able to accept the truth—so you stalled and didn't tell me anything, reminding her to stay away from me the whole time."

He Yu went on. "For seven years, even my old man knew that the only friend I relied on was nothing but a figment of my imagination. I was the only one who didn't know! I only dug myself deeper! Did you have fun watching this farce play out? Was it funny, Xie Qingcheng? Don't you think you were being incredibly cruel and arrogant, never once taking my feelings seriously? What exactly am I in your eyes? A partially imagined person—even if I only wanted a tiny bit of comfort, I still had to rely on a partially imagined person! There's never been anyone who truly loved or cared about me. Even on my birthday, I could only spend it by myself...and rely on a delusion to give me a birthday wish and a piece of cake."

He Yu grabbed Xie Qingcheng's neck, staring at his face. Xie Qingcheng looked pale, but his skin was burning. He Yu had tormented this man for the entire night, and although Xie Qingcheng could still endure it through sheer force of will, He Yu could tell that he had a fever the moment he touched him.

The heat lingered in He Yu's fingertips as he stared him down.

Eventually, He Yu heard Xie Qingcheng say, "Even if you gave me a second chance, I would still do the same thing. I would still have her stay away from you and choose not to tell you the truth."

Enraged, He Yu slammed Xie Qingcheng against the wall of the bathroom, the deep black tiles a striking contrast to the man's paper-white face. If it wasn't for the heat seeping into his palm, He Yu would have thought that Xie Qingcheng was carved from snow, that he would simply melt away.

Xie Qingcheng coughed lightly, but his eyes were as frosty and sharp as the first time he and He Yu met. "He Yu, I did it because I knew you wouldn't be able to bear it otherwise. This was the best way. And no matter what you believe, I don't think I was wrong."

Xie Qingcheng had originally wanted to say, *I owe you, He Yu. I owe you a debt of sincerity from the past. You chose to give me your heart—you held your heart in your hands and stood on your tiptoes to hand it to me, but I treated you as a mere patient and couldn't see the desperate longing in your eyes, the desire for someone to accompany you sincerely and wholeheartedly.*

It's true that I was too unkind.

It won't happen again.

I don't really know how to be gentle with my words, and I'll probably still be stubborn and cold, but I'm willing to become your bridge. Because when I was helpless and alone, you were the one who chose to help me. In return for the bit of encouragement I afforded you that I never once considered a kindness, you were the one who nearly gave your life away.

I might not be able to give you everything you want, but I can stop being Doctor Xie to you and become just Xie Qingcheng.

As long as you're still willing.

These were the thoughts he'd had in mind, that he'd wanted to act upon, before last night.

But now, everything had changed.

He didn't want to say any of this to He Yu anymore. The burning in his body, the pain between his legs, and the blurriness of his vision were all marks of disgrace that He Yu had left on his body. It was as though that modicum of sentiment that Xie Qingcheng had possessed had been wiped away in a single night.

Even with He Yu grasping his face, Xie Qingcheng's eyes beneath his messy fringe were still as incisively sharp as ever. He forcefully pushed He Yu away and lit a cigarette right in front of him. He took a drag in annoyance, then stubbed out the cigarette on the wall beside He Yu with a hiss.

With eyes rimmed red, Xie Qingcheng stared intently at He Yu.

"In those seven years, I did everything that I should have as a doctor. But in response, you committed an atrocity last night. Let me tell you this, He Yu—you're a fucking beast, worse than a pig or a dog."

Xie Qingcheng straightened up, moved around He Yu, and, suppressing his intense discomfort, strode to the door. However, his hand had barely touched the door handle when He Yu abruptly pinned him in place.

"Motherfucker, what more do you want?!" Caught off guard as He Yu pressed him against the bathroom door, Xie Qingcheng's peach-blossom eyes hardened. "I don't have the time or energy to waste on you right now. Something's happened at home, and I have to get back! Get the fuck off me right now!"

For a moment, He Yu truly wanted to strangle Xie Qingcheng. He'd originally assumed that Xie Qingcheng would be a little weaker, a little softer, when facing him, since he'd already been inside him, but that wasn't the case at all. Incredibly, Xie Qingcheng had become even colder than before, like a slab of sedimentary rock frozen under a sheet of ice. Every word that came out of him was frigid.

His attitude made He Yu, whose mental state was already deranged, even more irritable. The bloodthirsty, violent thoughts in his heart surged like a storm. He Yu didn't know what he wanted to do, but if he had a gun now, he might have killed Xie Qingcheng on the spot and left behind an obedient corpse. But when he grabbed Xie Qingcheng by the arm and dragged him back to press him against the door, their breaths intertwined, and upon hearing Xie Qingcheng's muffled cry of pain, He Yu froze again.

Words left him. Images from last night flashed through his eyes like a carousel lantern.

"Let go of me... Fucking... Fuck off!"

With Xie Qingcheng's feverishly burning body struggling beneath him, He Yu found that he was...actually...a little turned on...

Xie Qingcheng had yet to detect He Yu's reaction, but He Yu was shocked to his core. He straightened up in alarm, his almond eyes wide, and acted as though Xie Qingcheng was carrying some sort of aphrodisiac on him. He didn't dare to approach the man any further.

Last night had been an accident. He Yu had drunk the Plum Fragrance 59 aphrodisiac liquor too. He'd had no reason to think he'd have any untoward thoughts toward Xie Qingcheng once everything was over and done with. The sexual relations that had transpired between them had been a coincidence, a consequence of him pouring the wrong drink—it couldn't even be counted as a deliberate one-night stand. How could he still have any reaction to Xie Qingcheng?

Xie Qingcheng had no idea what was going on, but if He Yu had let go of him, that could only be a good thing. He took a gasping breath and glared at He Yu, hackles raised. Then, he straightened out the collar of his shirt that had been tugged into disarray.

This shirt was actually a bit small, as the club only had a few spare articles of simple clothing in an incomplete set of sizes. They didn't have a shirt in the right size for Xie Qingcheng's 180 cm-tall physique, so the sleeves were too short, revealing a length of snowy-pale wrist.

Xie Qingcheng rarely wore short sleeves. Even on the hottest days, he was always impeccably attired in long-sleeved button-down shirts.

In a properly fitted suit, it was usually impossible to see above a man's wrists, so He Yu very rarely caught a glimpse of this part of Xie Qingcheng. Even when the two of them were together last night, He Yu had been so turned on and caught up in his senses that his eyes had mostly been fixed on Xie Qingcheng's face, as he didn't want to miss a single moment of Xie Qingcheng's weak, desperate expressions. At the time, it was like his existence had sunk into that soft, wet warmth as he experienced a pleasure that he had never felt before. That feeling had been so thrilling that he hadn't paid much attention to the rest of Xie Qingcheng's body. Even when he folded his hand over Xie Qingcheng's toward the end, he'd been too focused to spare a single glance at Xie Qingcheng's wrist.

Only now did he remember that there was a tattoo on Xie Qingcheng's wrist, one that he had seen a long time ago. And it was at this very moment that he once again glimpsed Xie Qingcheng's fair left wrist. Just above that slender, pale wrist was a long line of delicate, ash-colored letters.

Here lies one whose name was writ in water.

He Yu stared at that tattoo. It had been so many years... If not for this chance encounter, he would have all but forgotten about the words on Xie Qingcheng's wrist.

Meanwhile, Xie Qingcheng pulled his shirt back into place. He shot He Yu a vicious glare before turning around, pushing the door open, and walking out. The bathroom door slammed shut with a *bang.*

He Yu stood inside alone, facing the spot where the two of them had just been ferociously tangled up. He was still for a long while, allowing his absurd desire and tumultuous heart to settle down.

Those words kept flashing before his eyes as Xie Qingcheng's voice, ice-cold even as it seemed to be suppressing some kind of emotion, echoed in his ears.

"In those seven years, I did everything that I should have as a doctor. But in response, you committed an atrocity last night. Let me tell you this, He Yu—you're a fucking beast, worse than a pig or a dog."

"Think about it."

"Think about it..."

Like the pages of a bygone chapter blown open by an unexpected gust of wind, the evil dragon clearly recalled something that had happened in his childhood years.

Something related to that tattoo.

56

AND I DID *NOT* COPY HIM!

BACK THEN, He Yu had still been in junior high—a time when young men and women seemed to undergo new changes every day, shooting up vigorously like green sprouts.

He Yu grew taller with each passing day, his youthful figure becoming very sturdy and upright as his voice suddenly deepened. His newly tailored uniforms were beginning to look too short after only half a semester, so he often left two buttons on his white shirt open and bought shoes several sizes up.

Aside from the physical changes, the tone of his social interactions also began to change.

There were suddenly way more tittering girls around him, girls who would immediately fall quiet when he drew closer and then burst into giggles again after he walked away.

In his desk drawer, aside from his neatly placed textbooks, sealed envelopes of varying colors began to appear. They contained sheets of paper spritzed with perfume and covered in insipid words of love that gave him goosebumps.

Even worse, sometimes he would be stopped in the stairwell of one of the school buildings by a girl whose face he couldn't even remember, one who would hand him a gift with hopeful anticipation, and he would have to smile politely, give her appropriate assurance and comfort, and try his hardest to reject her without hurting her feelings.

He invariably found this so troublesome it made his head ache.

He could admit that he put on more of a pretense than Wei Dongheng, the popular, good-looking boy several years older than him. Whenever this happened to Wei Dongheng, he'd roll his eyes while giving a rejection, the words "I'm expensive, you can't afford me" written clearly on his face. Meanwhile, He Yu needed to show utmost consideration for his reputation.

Wei Dongheng was handsome, but he had nothing else going for him. Everyone knew he was a worthless slacker. He Yu, however, was a xueba, an outstanding model student who never made the teachers worry. As such, He Yu could only repeat the same dull rejections over and over again—he even had to comfort the girls after he rejected them. His patience soon wore thin, waiting for a love letter from Xie Xue that never came while countless other girls showered him with unwanted affection.

Indeed, by the beginning of his adolescence, He Yu had already confirmed his feelings for Xie Xue. Though he appeared unaffected on the outside, he paid special attention to Xie Xue's every move with detached eyes, patiently listening to her prattle on about all her favorite male celebrities and trying to figure out common traits in the people she liked.

In the end, using an IQ that could solve math Olympiad problems in seconds, He Yu came to a conclusion that was hard for even him to accept.

Xie Xue was a brocon. The men she approved of, whether they were actors, singers, or fictional characters, always had something in common with Xie Qingcheng: they were all unbridled, or arrogant, or cold, or unyielding, just like him.

That wasn't to say that she actually wanted to date her brother, of course. It was just that although her brother was afflicted with straight man cancer and had a ton of annoying shortcomings, Xie Xue nevertheless admired him from the bottom of her heart. Back then, her taste in men had been undoubtedly influenced by Xie Qingcheng, and she felt that men like her brother were the most reliable.

The influence was so subtle that Xie Xue didn't even realize it.

"Ah, this actor is so warm. He looks like my brother when he's cooking," she would say without thinking. Or "Ah, this actor is so handsome. My brother plays basketball like this too." Or "Ah, why does this actor have such long hair... My brother says men should look like men and be more masculine..."

He Yu was quite conceited; he had always thought that he was good-looking and had decent taste. He didn't understand what was so great about an old man like Xie Qingcheng, who had already been battered by the tides of time. At first, he was unwilling to compromise and wanted to drag Xie Xue's sense of aesthetics over to his side instead.

But regardless of whether he was gentle and respectful or arrogant and depraved, if Xie Xue didn't sense anything about him that reminded her of Xie Qingcheng, she would remain completely uninterested in him.

"Don't loosen your buttons. Students should look like students," she would chide him. Or she would comment, "You should wear your cool-weather slacks. Your school's gym shorts are too casual. They don't suit you."

Later, after a bit of thought, Xie Xue actually dug out an old class photograph of her brother in high school. Perfectly earnest, she pointed at the tall boy in the corner and said, "See, you'd look better like this."

The Xie Qingcheng in the photograph was very young and very handsome, but to He Yu, he looked massively old-fashioned and stuffy. What kind of person would wear their full uniform so stiffly and clean himself up so meticulously that it looked like he had disinfected his whole body and was about to walk into the ICU? Even the age of the photograph couldn't hide the glaring whiteness of his T-shirt.

And his legs—it was truly a waste to hide such a long pair of legs under those slacks. Everyone else in the group photo was wearing summer shorts; only Xie Qingcheng was bundled up in cool-weather attire, an indifferent expression on his face as if the calmness of his heart could keep him from feeling the heat.

Was Xie Qingcheng crazy?

How could *this* be called good-looking?

But Xie Xue said, "It is! And look at the hairstyle he had, the clothes he was wearing. Aiya, even though their faces don't look alike, his steady temperament is just like Francis Ng's character in *Infernal Affairs II*, the family head da-ge from the Ni family. So handsome, so strong, so elegant, *so* much more handsome than all you schoolboys now!" She paused for a moment before clarifying to He Yu, "I'm not talking about you, of course. You're all right, but your temperament is more like that young Officer Lau. He's a villain, and he looks a bit roguish sometimes when he smiles."

Xie Xue had been really into *Infernal Affairs II* around that time. She watched that movie repeatedly, and everything that popped out of her mouth involved the characters' names. Then, she sighed, "My family's genes are just too powerful. My brother's just too handsome."

He Yu looked at the elegant, refined, and proper-looking youth in the photo and flipped the picture frame face down with an apathetic expression on his face. "How is he handsome?" As if that wasn't enough, he flipped the photo back up a moment later and took another look at it, then said coldly, "Ugly."

This time, he didn't have the chance to turn it face down again before Xie Xue snatched the photo away and began to rant. "Pah! You're just jealous of my beauty! Jealous of my brother's good looks!"

He had nothing to say to this woman. Never mind her saying that he was jealous of Xie Qingcheng's good looks, but what the hell did she mean that he was jealous of *her* beauty... Wait, no, there was absolutely no way he would be jealous of Xie Qingcheng's good looks either. He Yu was so handsome that half the girls in his school had given him chocolates or love letters by now. Why would he be jealous of a boring, outdated old man?

As if *he* cared what Xie Qingcheng looked like.

But He Yu had truly been dealt a heavy blow that day. After sending Xie Xue home, he sat at his desk playing with his phone, turning the display on and off over and over again. Flashes of shadow and light weaved through his eyes—when it brightened, he saw only the glow from the phone, but when it darkened, the screen reflected his face, which had already begun to show hints of his future handsome demeanor.

He Yu stared at his reflection for a while. Then, after rolling his eyes and muttering a curse, he unlocked his phone again and sulkily typed out "*Infernal Affairs II Francis Ng*" and pressed "Search."

On that hot and muggy afternoon, the boy sat at his desk, kicking his fair, toned, long legs in his school gym shorts underneath the table. He stared indifferently at all the stills from *Infernal Affairs II* on his phone screen, looking at that stern underworld triad boss. His face turned gloomy as he stared, as though the actor owed him a hundred million yuan. "What's so great about this prim and proper vibe… What's so great about him? Is he handsome? He's not handsome at all."

Early the next morning, when Xie Qingcheng walked out of the He residence guest room where he was staying with a yawn, he nearly ran straight into He Yu's nose.

Startled, Xie Qingcheng shot him a glare that was still heavy with morning grumpiness. "Little devil, what are you doing?"

Truthfully speaking, it was no longer fitting for Xie Qingcheng to call He Yu "little devil" by then. After He Yu hit puberty, his height shot up suddenly. Xie Qingcheng had always been accustomed to lowering his head to look at He Yu, but in the blink of an eye, he had to get used to looking straight on at this boy who was more than a decade his junior. The boy was still growing too, so perhaps it wouldn't be too long before Xie Qingcheng would need to learn how to look up at him…

This was probably why he had been rather unfriendly toward He Yu during that time.

Whenever he spoke to He Yu, Xie Qingcheng would subconsciously lower his head and look down. As a result, he would find himself looking at either He Yu's school uniform shorts and long legs or his feet in his size 9 sneakers.

But that day proved to be an exception.

That day, when Xie Qingcheng glanced over, what he saw wasn't He Yu's school uniform shorts but an ironed pair of tailored cool-weather dress pants.

Briefly dumbfounded, Xie Qingcheng shifted his line of sight upward.

Good lord. He didn't know if He Yu had gotten his medication mixed up or what, but he had changed into an exceedingly clean polo shirt that was so white it practically glowed, with the collar buttoned all the way up. He had even changed his hairstyle; his face was usually covered by his bangs, but now, he had gotten a fresh cut that exposed his brows and forehead.

He Yu's appearance looked rather familiar...but Xie Qingcheng couldn't quite put his finger on what this style reminded him of.

"You changed your style?"

He Yu curled his lip and scowled without answering. Then, after stewing in silence for a long while, he asked with a face so ashen it looked like he had inhaled poison gas, "What do you think?"

Xie Qingcheng was baffled, but he carefully looked him over from head to toe. "It's all right. Better than before."

"Hmph."

"It's just that it seems kind of familiar."

"Hmph!" He Yu rolled his eyes and walked away with a bounce in his step and an air of secrecy.

Xie Qingcheng was left standing there, still slightly out of it, stroking his chin and muttering, "What's gotten into that little devil..."

Naturally, He Yu's outfit that day was met with Xie Xue's enthusiastic approval.

"Wow!" she exclaimed. "Hey, handsome, you look amazing today! You're so cool!"

He Yu's heart swelled with delight even as he acted like her praise didn't mean anything to him. He said mildly, "I don't know about that. My hair got a bit too long, so I just told the barber to cut it however he wanted."

"You really look sooo good!"

He Yu was overjoyed, but the expression on his face only became more inscrutable and cooler. From that day on, he started to carefully study how that old man Xie Qingcheng dressed and carried himself, clicking his tongue in disdain even as he strived to emulate him.

As a result, there came a day when He Yu was watching Xie Qingcheng wash his hands with his sleeves rolled up. Suddenly, he noticed the tattoo just above Xie Qingcheng's left wrist, which was like a bracelet of tiny, slanting English words. At the time, He Yu had found it rather odd that Xie Qingcheng had a tattoo—had even *he* once been cavalier and rebellious in his youth?

It Was Just a Tattoo

"What are you looking at?" Xie Qingcheng finished washing his hands, wiped them dry with a couple of tissues, and glanced mildly at He Yu.

The young He Yu asked, "Doctor Xie, on your wrist..."

Xie Qingcheng's eyes darkened. He looked down to see that his sleeves were rolled up high enough to reveal the skin above his wrist and immediately went to pull them back down. But it was too late. He Yu was already asking, "What does it say?"

Xie Qingcheng didn't answer for a few seconds, his motions stiff as he unbuttoned his cuffs and smoothed them back out. Then he said with an indifferent expression, "Here lies one whose name was writ in water."

He Yu recognized the quote: it was the same one carved into the grave of the English poet John Keats. "Why did you get that tattooed? You like tombstones?"

Xie Qingcheng rolled his eyes, lifting his wrist to refasten the button of his sleeve properly. "I like Keats."

In those days, He Yu usually didn't talk back to Xie Qingcheng. Even though he was thinking, "Just because you like Keats doesn't mean you have to tattoo his epitaph on your arm," he didn't ask any more questions. It was clear from Xie Qingcheng's unhappy expression that he didn't feel like wasting his breath on him.

He figured, though, that Xie Xue probably liked her brother's weird taste, so she must approve of him inking an epitaph onto his own body. With that thought in mind, he went to a tattoo parlor near his school that very same night.

The owner welcomed him with a broad smile and handed him several thick volumes of reference images. He Yu lowered his head and looked through those pages full of flying gods and supernatural creatures for a while as the owner gave a steady stream of recommendations.

"The most popular one is this flying dragon tattoo. Look at these claws, it—"

"Are there any epitaphs?" He Yu interrupted.

"Huh? Epitaphs?" the owner repeated, confused.

Of course, the tattoo parlor didn't have any samples of something so bizarre, but the owner had seen shady characters from many walks of life come through his shop with all sorts of peculiar requests. As a result, after a beat of surprise, he continued his enthusiastic recommendations. "I don't have epitaphs, but if you want some cooler words, young man, 'om mani padme hum' is very popular right now."

He Yu smiled courteously. "In that case, I'll decide on one myself."

In the end, he gave three lines to the parlor owner.

Nothing of him that doth fade,

But doth suffer a sea-change,

Into something rich and strange.

"This is quite long," said the owner, "so it will hurt for quite a while. Plus, it has to be broken into several lines. Would you like to find something shorter?"

He Yu said, "It's fine, I want this one."

There were, in fact, shorter Latin epitaphs on the graves of other poets, but He Yu wanted something exactly like Xie Qingcheng's—

a long line of text wrapping around his wrist like a bracelet—so he chose this poem that had been engraved onto a tombstone.

When the owner rolled up He Yu's sleeve, he received a great shock. "Aiya, you have so many scars here! What happened here? Are people bullying you in school—a good-looking kid like you? And they all look like knife wounds?"

He Yu frowned. "Can't you tattoo over scars?"

"I can. Of course I can. I can put it here, over this really obvious one, to cover it up..."

"There's no need to cover it up. I want the tattoo slightly above my wrist." He Yu gestured at the spot, "Right here. Thank you for your trouble."

Thus, the verses were inked, burning like a brand on the youth's wrist. The flesh reddened where it had been pierced as the slanting letters of specially formulated ink sank into his skin. He Yu looked at the tattoo, feeling deeply satisfied, and left the little tattoo parlor after paying the bill.

But he hadn't anticipated that he would be allergic to the tattoo ink.

He woke up the next day feeling dizzy. Not only was the writing on his wrist so inflamed it was unreadable, but his head ached and burned from the allergic reaction.

Unfortunately, that hapless little brother of his was having a celebration later that day for starting school. He Jiwei and Lü Zhishu were both with their younger son in Yanzhou—which was all fine, except that Lü Zhishu called He Yu seven or eight times to remind him to join the video call with his brother on his computer.

"As his elder brother, and as an example to everyone, don't you think you ought to wish your little brother smooth sailing in his studies?" Lü Zhishu had nagged.

On top of having a distant relationship with his parents, He Yu was proud and withdrawn, so he wasn't willing to say anything that made him look soft or weak in front of them. Naturally, he couldn't tell Lü Zhishu that he was sick. So he pulled himself upright, grabbed his laptop, and curled up on the sofa. When the time for the video call came, he opened the webcam and put on his flawless mask of perfection, sending his congratulations to the people on the other end of the call in a manner perfectly befitting the occasion.

Suddenly, a slender hand reached past him from behind and unequivocally slammed the laptop on his knees shut, ending the video transmission. He Yu twisted around in astonishment to see Xie Qingcheng standing behind the sofa.

Xie Qingcheng, with his broad shoulders and long legs and poker face, lowered his peach-blossom eyes to look down at He Yu from above. "You should rest properly if you're sick."

"I wasn't done talking to them yet," He Yu protested.

Xie Qingcheng reached out a hand to feel He Yu's forehead. His hand was slightly cool and felt indescribably refreshing on He Yu's burning skin. Instinctively, He Yu let out a sigh, his eyes falling half-closed as he subconsciously leaned forward and pressed his head gently into Xie Qingcheng's hand. It felt so wonderful that, for a moment, he couldn't even finish the rest of what he was going to say.

"Little devil, you have a fever." Xie Qingcheng leaned over He Yu where he was sitting cross-legged on the sofa and took the thin laptop from his lap.

He Yu snapped out of his daze and stopped in the middle of rubbing his head against Xie Qingcheng's hand. "My computer..."

Xie Qingcheng had no plan to return the computer to him. "It's just a first-day-of-school celebration. You've come down with an extremely high fever. Why didn't you say anything to anyone?"

"It's fine. You don't need to worry so much about such a small thing." He Yu tried once again to reach for the laptop in Xie Qingcheng's hand.

Xie Qingcheng held up the laptop even higher. "You're my patient. If I don't worry about you, then who will?"

He Yu didn't reply to that, but he reached over the back of the sofa to grab Xie Qingcheng's arm. He glared at Xie Qingcheng and opened his mouth a few times to refute him, but he couldn't find the right words to say.

The two of them remained in their respective positions—one sitting and reaching out to grab the other's arm, and the other standing while looking back at him. An evening breeze swept over the pure-white sofa as rich light trickled in through the slightly open window, giving the scene the appearance of an oil painting.

Perhaps in that moment, this sick, lonely boy was so pathetic that he falsely perceived a hint of softness in Xie Qingcheng's ever chilly and emotionless eyes.

"He Yu," he said. "You're much too tense. There's no way you can do everything perfectly."

"Doctor Xie, you're only a doctor," He Yu argued. "You don't have to consider these sorts of things for me. Give me back my laptop. I need to finish what I was doing."

The two of them stared each other down. In the end, Xie Qingcheng lifted the laptop and tapped it gently against He Yu's forehead. "Doctor's orders."

Then Xie Qingcheng's gaze dropped downward, inadvertently sweeping over the sliver of skin peeking out from under He Yu's sleeve.

He frowned. "What's wrong with your hand?"

As if electrocuted, He Yu immediately withdrew his hand and tried to tug his sleeve back into place. But Xie Qingcheng was already a step ahead of him. He reached out to grab He Yu's arm at once and pushed his long sleeve up...

...For a moment, neither of them spoke.

At last, Xie Qingcheng asked, "You got a tattoo?"

"No."

"So that isn't tattoo ink on your wrist?" When He Yu didn't reply, Xie Qingcheng continued, "Are you looking for trouble? How old are you again? Does your school even allow this?"

He Yu didn't say a word, but his invisible dragon's tail began to thump against the ground in restless irritation.

Xie Qingcheng's gaze traveled back and forth between He Yu's wrist and his face. After a while, something seemed to occur to him. "He Yu, are you...copying me?"

This time, he had truly stomped on the little dragon's tail. A stricken expression overtook the boy's face, but he couldn't manage a single word in self-defense. He could only glare daggers at Xie Qingcheng, his face twisting up as though he'd eaten some fatally poisonous mushroom.

"Are you copying me?" Xie Qingcheng pressed.

He Yu leapt up from the sofa in an attempt to flee. "The tattoo artist designed it. Who's copying you? You're not handsome at all, you're not good-looking, and I don't like your taste either..."

But he had overestimated his physical condition. He hadn't taken more than a couple of steps before his legs went weak underneath him. It felt like he was walking on cotton. Then the world suddenly spun around him, and by the time he got his bearings, Xie Qingcheng had already picked him up around the waist just like when He Yu was little and hoisted him over his shoulder like a sack of potatoes.

The problem was that back then, He Yu had only reached Xie Qingcheng's knees. But now...

He whipped his head around, furiously flustered as he stopped feigning docility. Pinching the back of Xie Qingcheng's neck, he yelled, "Put me down! This is too embarrassing..."

"If you don't want me to suplex you, get your pointy little claws off my neck."

"Put me down first! I'm already twelve!"

"I'm still older than you, even if you reverse the digits. No matter how tall you get, you're just a little devil who's still in junior high."

"Xie Qingcheng!"

Xie Qingcheng paused for a beat. When he continued speaking, his words were as indifferent as ever, but his voice seemed to carry the faintest hint of a smile indicating that their strict doctor-patient relationship had crossed some boundary. "He Yu, I didn't know you admired me so much."

"Who are you saying admires you?!"

"You like Shelley?"

"No way! I like tombstones!"

The racket had lasted all the way to He Yu's bedroom.

Even now, as an adult, He Yu had no idea whether that faint smile in Xie Qingcheng's voice had just been his own fevered imagination, especially when so much time had passed and he could no longer remember many of the details all that well. But the one thing he could still clearly remember from that night was that after Xie Qingcheng had carried him back to his bedroom and given him a shot of antihistamine, he had gone out to the bedroom's balcony and made a very long call to Lü Zhishu.

He Yu was lying on the bed, and he couldn't hear what Xie Qingcheng was saying through the floor-to-ceiling glass doors. But he could see Xie Qingcheng lift a hand to rub repeatedly at his brow, like he was suppressing certain emotions as he spoke. By the end,

Xie Qingcheng was clearly angry, hurling harsh reproaches at Lü Zhishu with a furious expression on his face.

To be honest, there's really no need for this, He Yu thought, nestled in his blankets as he watched Xie Qingcheng struggle to communicate with his mother. *There's really no need.* What meaning was there in care that was received by asking, in pity that was given by begging?

Later on, when Xie Qingcheng pushed the balcony door open and walked back into the room, He Yu hastily flipped over on his belly and closed his eyes, pretending he was asleep to prevent himself from getting even more annoyed. He could smell that faint icy scent of disinfectant on Xie Qingcheng's body, but for some reason, perhaps because he was also wrapped in the chilly moonlight of a bright evening, it didn't smell as bad as it once did.

Xie Qingcheng thought that He Yu was already asleep, so he kept his voice quiet when he said, "Forget it."

The moonlight was clear and cold as it spilled onto He Yu's bed. But, for some reason, those words revealed a bit of unprecedented warmth.

He Yu could tell that Xie Qingcheng's voice was a bit hoarse from spending so long fruitlessly arguing with Lü Zhishu.

"Little devil... Get some rest. I'm not busy these next few days, so I can keep you company."

Right in that moment, He Yu felt as if his heart was suddenly seized with an indescribable pain. It was a sensation he'd never felt so clearly before. It was like there was a rusty knife within his chest that had grown together with his flesh, and it had been abruptly awoken by those words and started to twist inside him, struggling to be drawn out.

It hurt so much he couldn't breathe, but he had to stay quiet so that Xie Qingcheng wouldn't realize that he was still awake.

He knew Xie Qingcheng had failed to negotiate anything from his mother. He wasn't at all surprised by this result, but he suddenly realized that before Xie Qingcheng, there had never been even a single person who had strived so hard to make sure that he wouldn't be lonely.

There had never been a single person who chose him over He Li, who stood on his side and asked his parents, who were practically strangers to him, *Why?*

He Yu tilted his face into the shadows, his thick eyelashes quietly lowered. There, tucked away where Xie Qingcheng couldn't see, a tear slowly welled out and slid down his cheek, landing silently in the goose down bedding. Amidst this unfamiliar burst of pain, He Yu kept quiet, kept pretending, until finally falsehood became truth, and he gradually fell asleep for real.

The next morning, He Yu's fever broke and he woke up very early.

The sun shone in through the gauze curtains, which swayed slightly in the wind as birds chirped outside the window. His head felt so clear, as though it'd been freshly washed.

Blinking, he collected himself and flipped over to get up. That was when he saw Xie Qingcheng beside the bed, asleep with his head on his arm and several strands of hair tumbling over his brow.

It was the first time he had seen Xie Qingcheng sleeping. He was tranquil, calm, and as serene and translucent as a diaphanous spirit, like the first glow of dawn cast over the windowsill after the passing of night.

He Yu's gaze subconsciously shifted down to Xie Qingcheng's wrist. One of the buttons had loosened in his sleep, so his sleeve splayed open, exposing a section of slender wrist with clear skin and elegant bones. In the morning light, it was almost shockingly pale.

He Yu looked at the line of words on that pale wrist, which he had glimpsed but never examined closely before.

Here lies one whose name was writ in water.

He Yu left the nightclub with his emotions in a chaotic tangle. He wandered about without any set destination in mind, constantly thinking about such random things... But why did he remember those past events?

No matter what happened in the past, no matter what Xie Qingcheng had been feeling when he said, *Little devil, it's all right. I can keep you company,* it was all fake.

The extent to which Xie Qingcheng had moved him back then was equivalent to the depth of the ruthless wound he had stabbed into his heart when he left without the slightest hesitation.

To be honest, over the years, He Yu had often wondered in the middle of the night why Xie Qingcheng had to leave.

Was he not good enough?

Was it because he hadn't been able to become a normal person like Xie Qingcheng wanted?

That day when He Yu was still in ninth grade, when his fourteen-year-old self stood stiff as a pole before a departing Xie Qingcheng, he hadn't even had the courage to ask that man, *Xie Qingcheng, tell me, those words that you said to me, the warmth you showed me—did I make it all up?*

Was it my misunderstanding?

Was all that we shared just a pure, simple doctor-patient relationship?

It's been seven years.

Xie Qingcheng, even if you were just casually treating a stray dog, you have to get a bit attached in the process, right? So how could you break things off so cleanly? How could you leave just like that... How could you spout all those justifications, talking about working relationships, contracts, rules—as though you'd conveniently forgotten that you also occasionally showed me those bits of care and warmth that perhaps had no place in a doctor-patient relationship.

But having been abandoned like that, he felt too humiliated. His sense of self-respect had suffered a grievous injury, as though Xie Qingcheng had landed an excruciating, scorching slap across his face.

It hurt so much that He Yu was never willing to recall this moment later on.

And in the end, no matter how much he thought about it, it was all nothing more than his one-sided fixation. He had too little affection, so whatever he received from another, even if it was mere scraps, he treasured as his own and hoarded as if it was a priceless gem. It was laughable.

How humiliating.

He Yu's pride caused him to take all those tiny stirrings of emotion and suffocate them with his own hands, then ruthlessly slam the coffin shut and seal them away—until this very moment.

He Yu closed his eyes, the casket of memories opening as he recalled the scene when Xie Qingcheng stood on the balcony and argued with his mother without backing down, when Xie Qingcheng pushed open the door and walked inside with an air of fatigue, and when Xie Qingcheng's sigh landed next to his pillow.

Forget it.

Little devil... Get some rest. I'm not busy these next few days, so I can keep you company.

Xie Qingcheng had given him faith and companionship, but then he left so completely, so heartlessly. He could always remain calm and coolheaded, clearly weighing the pros and cons of the situation.

He willingly studied psychology, yet he left the hospital because he didn't want to become the next Qin Ciyan. He made pleasant statements about how the mentally ill should be treated equally, yet he claimed that people's lives could be sorted according to their worth—that the lives of doctors were much more valuable than those of the mentally ill.

Xie Qingcheng was too complicated, too paradoxical.

Aside from the man who had truly been tormented to the point of helplessness beneath him last night, He Yu didn't think there was a single facet of Xie Qingcheng that was real.

Everything about him was fake.

That man was like a kaleidoscope, but He Yu was too young, so he couldn't make sense of him.

After walking for a long time without any particular destination, He Yu finally returned to his senses to realize that he had inadvertently walked to Xie Qingcheng's neighborhood.

The words that Xie Qingcheng had left behind after their fight echoed through his ears once more. *"Something's happened at home, and I have to get back! Get the fuck off me right now!"*

He Yu stood near the curb, his hands shoved in his pants pockets and a dazed expression on his face as he looked at the chaotic scene at the entrance of Moyu Alley in the distance. There were even a number of police officers gathered there.

He had a vague idea of what must have happened at Xie Qingcheng's house.

It Wasn't Like He Was a God

HE YU STOOD quite a way off from the commotion, at a rather distant corner, and no one really noticed him.

This tiny alley could hardly be considered a tourist spot or a viral place of interest, but it had been completely surrounded by an impenetrable mob, with many members of the crowd holding their cell phones aloft and raising a ruckus.

Meanwhile, Xie Qingcheng had returned by taxi to Moyu Alley just moments earlier.

Because his and He Yu's shared fit of madness last night had dragged on for too long, by the time he woke up, it was no longer early. And with the argument, payment, and back-and-forth that had ensued afterward, the sky had already begun to darken by the time he made it back to Moyu Alley. On a normal day, everyone would already be at home eating dinner by now.

But that was not the case at Moyu Alley today.

When Xie Qingcheng drew closer, he found a group of civil police standing at the gates. They were preventing the throng of people holding up phones and taking photos and videos from entering the area.

Seeing that it was a one-way road, the taxi driver said, "I'll have to park here."

"Here is fine, thank you," Xie Qingcheng replied as he paid the fare.

As soon as his long legs stepped out of the taxi, blinding flashes of white light filled his vision. For a second, he thought he must be feeling so terrible that his vision was blurring—only to realize that the lights were coming from the crowd, who were frantically snapping photos and videos of him while being held back by the police officers. With such an enthusiastic spectacle, someone not in the know might even think that some celebrity had arrived.

"It's him!"

"Xie Qingcheng, could you tell us what the broadcasting tower murder case has to do with you?"

"Why would a criminal organization play videos of you? Why only you and not anyone else? Do you have some connection to Cheng Kang Psychiatric Hospital?"

"People on the internet are saying you were involved in the plan to imprison and molest mentally ill women. Aren't you going to dispel the rumors?"

"Xie Qingcheng, why would you insult Professor Qin Ciyan? He was a national hero like no other! Do you have no conscience?! How can someone like you be a doctor, a teacher?! Go put yourself behind bars!"

Xie Qingcheng had already had a rough idea of the situation before he arrived. Thanks to the Huzhou University broadcasting tower case, his home had become an unfortunate epicenter of chaos. Someone had leaked and spread Xie Qingcheng's home address online, so the little internet celebrities with their video cameras and bystanders with simple ideologies all began to show up like piranhas scenting blood, pouring into Moyu Alley in droves.

Not only had his house been defaced with paint, but his next-door neighbors had been affected too. Auntie Li had rushed outside to argue with them, but she had been recorded and the video had been subsequently spread online. The netizens said that she was Xie Qingcheng's mom, just some harpy throwing a tantrum. Xie Xue had been smeared even more absurdly. People were claiming that she was Xie Qingcheng's mistress, the "other woman." The person who uploaded that video got a ton of views for it.

Later, Xie Xue had called the police in tears. Chen Man was among the police officers who arrived on the scene, and they chased all those people out of the alley. The ones making an especially big racket were taken directly to the police station to drink tea.

After that, some of the troublemakers stopped splashing paint and disturbing the residents, but a number of them stayed camped out by the gates. They knew that Xie Qingcheng would eventually come home, and look! Wasn't he here right now?

"Get his picture!"

"Xie Qingcheng, look over here at the camera."

Look, my ass. Xie Qingcheng ignored them completely as he slammed the car door, pulled aside the police cordon, and walked in with an aura befitting a VIP. As a result, the shabby little Huzhou taxi took on a quality akin to the luxury car of a mafia boss.

"Ge! Ge!"

It was surprisingly quiet in the alleyway. Xie Xue was sitting on a little stool in front of their house, but the moment she saw Xie Qingcheng, she jumped up and launched herself at him. Her velocity combined with her 45 kg body weight nearly broke Xie Qingcheng's already painfully aching back, causing him to stumble back a few steps.

Ordinarily, her big brother could catch her with one hand and even spin her around several times with ease, but Xie Qingcheng couldn't even handle her tackle hug now. Startled, Xie Xue looked up at him with puffy red eyes. "Ge, what's wrong? Are you feeling unwell?"

"It's nothing." Xie Qingcheng coughed quietly. "I lost my footing."

Chen Man also walked over. "Xie-ge."

All their neighbors were gathered in the courtyard. The uncles and aunties were waving their palm-leaf fans, shooing away the mosquitoes and flies. They all turned to look at Xie Qingcheng when they saw him return, but no one spoke.

Dressed in a floral nightgown, Auntie Li was sitting beneath an old camphor tree, wiping her tears. She had gotten her shoes mixed up when she'd shoved her feet inside them in a hurry to shuffle out the door.

Xie Qingcheng, still holding Xie Xue, patted her on the head and back to console her, then looked around. Because of all the internet celebrities who had poured in earlier, the shabby but quietly elegant alleyway had been rendered a hideous mess. Uncle Liu's flowerpots had been smashed, Auntie Zhao's fence had been torn down, and even the doghouse for Mrs. Wang's son's husky had been flattened into a pile of wood by the crowd's stampeding feet.

The dog was still standing dumbfounded at the side, likely because it had yet to recover from what had just happened. It thought to itself, wasn't property damage supposed to be a dog's realm of expertise? How was it that these people were so much more beastly that they even managed to destroy its doghouse?

Even more unsightly was the bloodred paint that had been splashed across not only the Xie family residence but also two neighboring households. Shockingly, someone had also spray-painted the words "fuck off" in crooked letters using scarlet spray paint.

Xie Qingcheng had a sturdy, resilient psyche, so he didn't become demoralized in the face of all this destruction. In fact, he didn't even seem to be all that negatively affected—indeed, after his experiences last night, what could possibly affect him now?

He did feel very apologetic that others had been involved, though, so after a long moment of silence, he turned toward the neighbors in the courtyard and said, "I'm sorry for disturbing all of you with this mess."

The evening wind rustled through the courtyard, blowing through the loquat tree, the creeping ivy, and the pajamas of the old uncles and aunties.

After a long pause, Granny Zhang spoke. "Xiao-Xie..."

Xie Qingcheng didn't respond. He assumed Granny Zhang was talking to Xie Xue. It had been years since any of his neighbors had called him Xiao-Xie. Everyone thought he was cold and formidable, so they all referred to him as Professor Xie or Doctor Xie, and he had only been called Xiao-Xie when he was still in school. It was only when Granny Zhang walked over with faltering steps and reached out to grasp his arm with a hand that was covered in skin like old tree bark that he realized she was actually calling out to him.

"Um, Xiao-Xie, don't be scared... We've all left our phones inside. None of us have them with us right now, so no one's going to take pictures of you or hurt you here..."

Xie Qingcheng started in surprise. Only now did he see the tears of concern welling up in Granny Zhang's age-blurred eyes.

"It's all right, dear child, go get some sleep. The police are here, so those people can't get in. As for the yard, we'll clean it up... Don't think too much about it. It's all right, it's all right."

"Yeah, Xiao-Xie, it's all right."

"Those people are a bunch of monsters in human skin. Don't take those influencers to heart."

"That's right. Besides, this fence of mine has been up for a decade already. This is a perfect opportunity to get a new one."

"Xie-gege, I can get a bigger doghouse too. I bought this one when Awoo was still a puppy. It's a squeeze even when it's just sleeping."

When he was outside the alleyway just moments before, Xie Qingcheng had felt rather numb. Verbal abuse mattered very little to him; it was nothing more than dust in the wind that he didn't need to care about. He couldn't even be bothered to spare his detractors a single glance. As long as no one was injured, everything was fine.

But in this moment, looking at these old neighbors who he regularly crossed paths with, who he'd lived alongside for over twenty years, he suddenly felt something in his heart shatter. It was boiling hot but had a dull pain alongside it.

"I'm really very sorry. I've troubled you so much."

He didn't know what he ought to say, especially when he saw that the white magnolia tree in Uncle Liu's yard had also been trampled, its elegant sheltering branches toppled between spilt mud and shattered pottery.

It was as if his heart had likewise been scraped by those broken pieces of pottery. Looking at Uncle Liu's stooped figure, he said, "This is the tree that Auntie Sun planted."

Auntie Sun had been Uncle Liu's wife. She had passed away from lung cancer several years ago, but when she was still alive, she liked white magnolias the most. She had planted this tree with her own hands over twenty years ago, back when she was still a young auntie with a clear and powerful voice, and Uncle Liu was still a vigorous man with a ramrod-straight back.

A flowering tree unmoved by twenty years of wind and rain had been snapped at the waist under the trampling feet of a single evening's surging crowd.

Uncle Liu stared at the rings of the tree's trunk, spacing out. Each ring was like the shadow of a happier time, a ripple raised by her smile.

Xie Qingcheng was a man of steel, but this time, after a long stretch of silence, he couldn't seem to suppress the slight hoarseness of his voice. "I'm sorry, Uncle."

At long last, Uncle Liu finally drifted back to reality. "Aiya, it's all right, Xiao-Xie," he said. He walked over, leaning on his cane, and patted Xie Qingcheng on the back just like during his younger years, when the uncle who worked at the steelworks would pat that young man's back with large hands as sturdy as iron towers.

"It's all right, it's just a tree. Just as long as everyone's okay, just as long as everyone's okay. A tree... A tree can...be replanted..."

But as the old man said this, he couldn't help but bow his head and wipe away the tears in his eyes.

Everyone knew that even if they planted another tree, it wouldn't be the same one. The person who planted this one had already been laid to rest. Now the tree had followed in her footsteps, like the fading years of their youth.

Uncle Liu dragged a faint smile back onto his wrinkled face. "Back then, you were the one who bought this tree for Wanyun from the garden market. Your parents helped her plant it. Do you think I've gotten dementia in my old age? I still remember everything."

"That's right," someone else chimed in. "Xiao-Xie, we've lived together for almost twenty years, how could we not know what sort of person you are, and what sort of people your parents were? No matter what they're saying out there, you and Xiao-Xue still have all us neighbors. Don't worry, okay? Go inside and get some rest. Wash up, you look exhausted."

"Yeah, hurry and wash up. Your face is so gloomy. Aah, if your parents were alive to see it, they'd be dying of heartbreak..."

Xie Xue raised her head from within Xie Qingcheng's arms and looked tearfully at everyone around them. Then, unable to bear it any longer, she buried her face in her brother's chest again and started sobbing loudly.

After thanking everyone and apologizing profusely, Xie Qingcheng brought Xie Xue back inside their house. Chen Man and Auntie Li followed them in.

From the inside, the paint on the windows looked even more like streaks of blood left behind by a sinister set of claws. Xie Qingcheng had no words.

"Xie-ge, don't worry too much," Chen Man said. "These people are like a swarm of locusts; they'll be gone before you know it. They're just looking for trouble, and I've asked my colleagues to settle things with them one by one. The police will stay here at Moyu Alley for the next few days, so there won't be any more problems..."

Xie Qingcheng coughed softly. His whole body was aching and burning with fever, and he was barely hanging on through sheer force of will. The dim lighting inside the room was the only reason no one could tell he was clearly ill.

He tapped out a cigarette and was about to light it when he caught sight of Auntie Li. He put the lighter back down again without saying anything.

"Ge, what are we supposed to do now..."

"Xiao-Xie, was there some sort of misunderstanding about the matter with Professor Qin back then? You...you mentioned him a few times before and always spoke highly of him. When you said those things, you must have... You must have had a reason." Auntie Li wiped her tears. "Can you think of a way to explain this to everyone? Hmm? Then those people will stop chasing after you and giving you a hard time..."

Xie Qingcheng remained silent.

After a beat, Auntie Li urged, "Xiao-Xie, say something."

Outside, the darkness of the long night was oppressively heavy.

Inside, the people closest to him were right by his side.

Xie Qingcheng's trembling fingers fiddled unconsciously with his steel lighter, igniting it, then putting it out, then igniting it, and then putting it out again...

Finally, he tossed the lighter to the side again and closed his eyes. Although his voice was hoarse from exhaustion, it was resolute and unyielding. "There wasn't any reason."

It was Auntie Li's turn to be dumbfounded.

"No one has accused me falsely. I said it and I meant it. I truly couldn't accept the ridiculous things that Qin Ciyan did. My attitude had changed by then, and my relationship with him wasn't very good either. I said those words on a moment's impulse when I was lacking in judgment."

"But Ge—" Xie Xue spoke up.

"I'm not perfect, Xie Xue. Your brother is an ordinary person—there are times when I get scared and worried. You were still so young back then, and I saw him get murdered right in front of my eyes. There was no way I could keep on working in the healthcare system... I got scared, so I quit. That's what happened."

A lengthy silence followed.

When Xie Xue spoke again, her voice sounded like a kitten's helpless mewl. "Ge, can't you be honest, even with us?"

Xie Qingcheng spent a long time lost in thought, with specters from the past seeming to flash across his field of vision. Eventually, he closed his eyes, lowered his head, and gathered his hands together, pressing them between his brows. He said softly, "What I said is the truth. I'm sorry... I've disappointed you all."

And so that conversation ultimately concluded with a drawn-out silence. Everyone in the room listening to him knew very well that Xie Qingcheng was stubborn to a fault.

"There's thirty thousand yuan on this card," Xie Qingcheng said at last. "Auntie Li, please take it. We still need to compensate the neighbors for their damaged property, even if they said that there's no need. If not for me, they wouldn't have been drawn into this mess. I'll think of ways to take care of anything that's left. Please stay at home and don't worry about it."

"Xiao-Xie..."

Xie Qingcheng had the exact same peach-blossom eyes as his mother, Zhou Muying—and there was an identical flintiness in them as well.

Auntie Li's heart twinged again.

An orphan abandoned at a temple, Li Miaoqing had worked as an escort in a Huzhou nightclub in her youth. As she waited upon those clients and attended to their needs, everyone called her a whore who stank between the legs. Once, when Zhou Muying was on assignment during a crackdown on the sex trade, she brought her in for questioning.

Back then, Li Miaoqing didn't listen to anyone. She sat in the interrogation room with a cigarette she'd obtained from another police officer between her lips, unwilling to answer a single question.

Still, she said to Zhou Muying, "They said I'm just a whore who stinks between the legs. So what. You might've caught me, but I'm just going to turn around and keep selling myself—as if you can stop me!"

Zhou Muying replied, "Li Miaoqing, you're only seventeen. I don't want to lock you up. Once you enter that place, it'll leave a stain on you for the rest of your life. I know you don't have parents or a family. Here's my card—this is my office phone number, and this is my personal number. Call me if you ever need anything. I'm not just a police officer—I'm a woman and a mother too. I don't want to see a girl who hasn't even come of age yet go down this path. You don't need to call me Officer Zhou, you can just call me Muying. I can help you. You don't need to be afraid."

Back then, when that same pair of peach-blossom eyes looked at her from across the interrogation room, Li Miaoqing had felt like an earthquake was tearing through her body, radiating out from the epicenter of her scarred and battered heart.

Later on, she became a member of Zhou Muying's eclectic circle of friends. At that time, their relationship was very steady. Zhou Muying always looked after this young woman who had lost her way, and she even invited her over for the New Year. She never once looked down on her.

When Zhou Muying and Xie Ping fell on hard times and couldn't find a suitable place to live, Li Miaoqing asked around in Moyu Alley, where she herself was living, and found a deal on a second-hand house. That was how they became neighbors. Over the course of the next two decades of trials and tribulations, Li Miaoqing never earned a living through such sordid means again. She became a tailor and made qipao, and she sewed countless beautiful gowns for Zhou Muying.

Now Li Miaoqing was gray at the temples, and Zhou Muying was nothing more than bone beneath the Yellow Springs. The last qipao she made for her Zhou-jiejie was Zhou Muying's burial dress, cut from a gorgeous brocade. She'd deliberately sewed it in a long-sleeved style to cover Zhou Muying's severed arm.

Because Li Miaoqing knew that Zhou Muying wasn't just a police officer. She was also a woman, a mother, a wife. She liked being beautiful. And she *was* the most beautiful...with those bright, resolute eyes.

Right now, it was like those eyes had crossed time to gaze at Li Miaoqing's creased, wrinkled face through all the years that had passed.

"After everything that's already happened, this is really nothing to me," Xie Qingcheng insisted.

In the end, Li Miaoqing let out a sigh and didn't speak any further.

Xie Qingcheng helped the older woman and the younger girl to their respective rooms to rest.

Outside, it began to rain.

The hour grew later.

Xie Qingcheng put on a fall jacket and took out two umbrellas, handing one to Chen Man.

"You should go home, it's getting late."

"Ge, you're not staying here tonight?" Chen Man was a bit surprised. Given Xie Qingcheng's personality, he'd expected him to stay with Xie Xue today.

But Xie Qingcheng really couldn't hold on any longer.

He felt like his forehead was on fire and his body was made of cotton, never mind the aching pain radiating from that one unspeakable part of his body. If Chen Man had been a bit more observant, he would have realized that Xie Qingcheng had hardly sat down the entire night.

"I'm not staying. There are some things I need to take care of at school, so I'm heading back to the dormitory."

"Why don't I give you a ride..."

Xie Qingcheng pushed the door open, and a chilly gust from the autumn rain blew into the room.

"There's no need." With the black carbon fiber handle of the umbrella in hand, wrapped up in his fall windbreaker, Xie Qingcheng walked into the pitch-dark night.

He couldn't pretend for much longer. He could feel that his back was drenched in cold sweat as flashes of heat surged through him. His face was burning, and everything was spinning before his eyes as though half of his consciousness had been yanked harshly out of his body.

Chen Man said, "Then you..."

"I'm leaving. Thanks for your hard work today. You should go home soon."

By the time Xie Qingcheng walked out of the alley, it was already past two in the morning, yet there were still people braving the rain and waiting outside. Xie Qingcheng had to admire their persistence. He called a taxi from within the police cordon. When the car arrived, he folded his umbrella and ducked inside, cutting off the explosion of camera flashes and noise on the other side of the door.

The moment he entered the car, he couldn't take it any longer. Leaning back in exhaustion, he lifted a hand to cover his eyes.

The cabbie asked him, "Da-ge, where to?"

Xie Qingcheng didn't answer.

"Da-ge?" The other man called out several times before Xie Qingcheng slowly resurfaced from his fevered confusion.

He knew that he really ought to go to the hospital. But he didn't want to at all. What was he supposed to tell the doctor when he got there? He would rather use all his pride and fortitude to take that secret to his grave than breathe a word of what had happened within the confines of that small room in the club to anyone. How could he possibly explain the reason behind his fever to the doctor?

He was a doctor himself. He might as well just go home, take some anti-inflammatories, and leave it be.

So, Xie Qingcheng discarded the word "hospital," which had been at the tip of his tongue, and instead replied, "The Huzhou Medical School faculty dorm, thanks."

The cabbie sped off.

Xie Qingcheng didn't see Chen Man lingering amongst the noisy crowd. After standing there for a long time, the young police officer's brow creased with worry. Finally, he turned around and went back into Moyu Alley, only to come out again a while later.

Xie Qingcheng also didn't see He Yu sitting behind the glass display window of the 24-hour convenience store across the street, drinking a cup of coffee. Or how, after tossing his coffee, He Yu tugged down the brim of his hat and walked out of the store.

59

Just My Girlfriend

Xie Qingcheng crumpled the moment he got through the door of his dorm. Using the last of his strength, he threw himself into the bathroom, where he collapsed over the edge of the sink and threw up immediately.

All that strong wine, on top of the drugs—he'd forcibly endured it for so long, maintaining his strong persona in front of the others. He hadn't softened or bent his waist a single iota when he faced He Yu, remaining upright and poised like a javelin the entire time.

He did all that just to avoid losing his dignity in front of He Yu, although he'd already lost his body to the scoundrel. It was only now that Xie Qingcheng was alone that he finally went limp and started throwing up violently until he felt like he was about to puke out his gallbladder as well. His ears rang, and his vision seemed to be veiled with black gauze, making everything he looked at dark and blurry.

No.

He couldn't fall apart...

He had to take some medicine, and then...

Xie Qingcheng scrubbed his face at the sink and repeated this to himself. However, his consciousness faded away mercilessly, indifferent to his miserable begging.

In the end, he stumbled on a step and collapsed in front of the sink.

Just before he passed out, he blearily saw someone open the dorm door. It was Chen Man, holding the key he'd gotten from Xie Xue. He started anxiously looking around the moment he entered the room, and his eyes eventually landed on Xie Qingcheng, who was lying on the icy tile.

"Xie-ge?!"

Xie Qingcheng heard Chen Man's voice and, in his delirium, strove to stand up. He wanted to finish playing out this performance.

But it wasn't just the exhaustion in his limbs. Even his eyelids had become extremely heavy. All that remained on his retinas were flickering shadows, and all he knew was that Chen Man ended up running over and kneeling anxiously by his side as he checked his condition.

After that, Xie Qingcheng completely lost consciousness. When he woke up, a great deal of time had passed.

He was lying on an articulated sickbed beneath a white hospital blanket, and there was an IV attached to his hand. He found the flow of the drip uncomfortably fast and wanted to move, but all he could do was twitch his fingertips slightly where they lay on top of the blanket.

"Xie-ge!" Seeing that he'd woken up, Chen Man snapped to attention where he'd been standing guard at his bedside and hastily grabbed his hand, asking with audible worry, "How are you? Do you still feel unwell?"

"I'm fine. Why are you..."

"I was worried about you, so I asked Xie Xue for the key to your dorm and followed you back and found you passed out. By the time I got you to the hospital, your temperature was already at 39.8 degrees. The doctor said that the high fever was from a severe inflammatory response, and that it would've gotten very serious if you'd come any later." Chen Man's eyes were red, like a rabbit's. "Why didn't you say anything? How could you just...just..."

Xie Qingcheng's consciousness was slowly returning to his body.

He closed his eyes, taking a moment to gather himself, then slowly turned his head. His arm lay exposed over the blanket. His palms were still covered in cuts from the shattered wine bottle, and his wrists were still covered in marks from He Yu's knots.

He instinctively wanted to hide the evidence of his disgrace back under the covers.

But Chen Man had clearly already noticed. He gazed at Xie Qingcheng. "Did someone beat you up?"

Xie Qingcheng didn't know what to say.

"Did someone attack you because of those videos, because of the rumors and gossip?"

Xie Qingcheng coughed softly. "Do I look like someone who's too weak to hit back to you?"

"But—"

"I was in a bad mood and hurt myself." Xie Qingcheng's voice was low and hoarse as he spoke to Chen Man. "That's why I didn't say anything."

Chen Man looked as if he didn't believe him at all.

But Xie Qingcheng didn't want him to keep asking questions. "I'm a little hungry. Could you go get me a bowl of congee?"

Chen Man left absentmindedly, his hair a tousled mess, only to hurry back a few seconds later—he was so out of it he'd forgotten his phone.

After Chen Man left, the surroundings went very quiet. This was an area set aside for emergency patients who required IV infusions, and the beds were separated from each other by light blue curtains. Xie Qingcheng could hear the faint sounds of nearby patients sobbing quietly in pain. With his eyes open, he suddenly felt a little envious.

Ever since he was little, he almost never cried. It felt like the right to vent in that way had never belonged to him.

His throat was painfully dry, and his mouth felt like a parched desert.

He didn't know how much time had passed when the curtains opened again. Xie Qingcheng thought Chen Man had returned, so he opened his eyes.

"Doctor Xie, it's me."

Xie Qingcheng was stunned.

The newcomer was a director of Huzhou First Hospital's emergency department. He had a very steady temperament and observed events with meticulous care. Regarding the Qin Ciyan event, he'd always held a different perspective from other people, and he didn't have any hard feelings toward Xie Qingcheng.

"We did some examinations when you were brought in," the director said, peering at him over his surgical mask. "Doctor Xie, you ought to be a little more careful in the bedroom. Even if you're in a bad mood, you shouldn't resort to such violent methods of destressing."

Xie Qingcheng's expression soured in an instant.

"I only noticed the marks on your body; I didn't look anywhere else. Don't overthink it." A beat of silence passed. The director cocked his head slightly and gestured at the doorway. "The one that just left—is he your boyfriend?"

"Just a friend."

He hadn't been very close to this director when he was a doctor, but for some reason, he always felt that the man looked a little familiar. Likely due to some subtle compatibility in their auras, the two of them had been capable of holding a conversation back when he was still at the hospital. But Xie Qingcheng felt extremely humiliated at the moment, so he kept his expression stretched taut and devoid of any emotion. He had absolutely no intention of explaining further.

But the director continued, "That's good. If it were a cop who had those kinds of violent tendencies, they ought to book an appointment with the psychiatric department."

This wholly infuriated Xie Qingcheng, so he eventually spoke up in a mild voice. "You've misunderstood, it was a woman."

"Ah...?" The director lifted his chin slightly in complete astonishment, but his eyes remained rather calm. It was quite evident that he hadn't taken Xie Qingcheng's nonsense as truth. "In that case, this woman needs to undergo some training. How could she be so feral?"

"If you could please leave, I would like to rest now."

"Very well then, have a good rest. You've probably had a lot on your mind these past few days and haven't been able to get a good night's sleep. I'm on shift tonight, so you can rest easy."

With that, the director walked over to the curtains, notebook in hand, and pulled them open.

As it turned out, there was someone standing outside.

It was Chen Man, who had returned from buying congee. He'd been standing beyond the curtains just now and heard a part of their conversation. Now he was staring at the director in a daze, his pale face gradually flushing so red that even his earlobes began to glow scarlet. After a while, his eyes moved involuntarily from the director and landed on Xie Qingcheng, who also looked rather taken aback.

This was wholly a coincidence; Chen Man had meant to come in as soon as he returned. But he had faintly heard them talking about the importance of restraint in the bedroom and promptly froze like he'd been electrocuted. The congee was dangling from his hand, but it seemed like there was more congee than brain in his head at the moment.

The director examined Chen Man's face. "What are you doing?"

Chen Man didn't know what to say. He bit his lips and kept mum.

Xie Qingcheng was equally speechless. But in the end, he had to cough lightly before the director let Chen Man off without further interrogation and walked away, minding his own business.

Only Chen Man and Xie Qingcheng remained on this side of the curtain.

Chen Man took a step forward but then froze, as if going any further would mean trampling over some boundary, as if he'd learned a truth capable of stabbing him.

"Ge. You...you've gotten a girlfriend?" Chen Man forced a smile. When Xie Qingcheng didn't reply, he added, "A new saozi?"

"No." Xie Qingcheng was beyond annoyed, but also embarrassed. He had no desire to speak anymore, since the more he said, the further he ended up from the truth. "I was just in a bad mood and hooked up with someone for fun."

But Chen Man didn't think Xie Qingcheng was that type of guy; he might've believed it from someone else, but Xie Qingcheng going out and hooking up for fun? Even if every man on Earth had one-night stands, Xie Qingcheng still wouldn't do such a thing. He was the most stubborn and responsible person. There was no way he'd cause such unnecessary hurt.

Seeing the disbelief written over Chen Man's face, Xie Qingcheng grew even more irritated. He was so frustrated that he craved a smoke. But of course he couldn't find one.

"Why would you..."

Xie Qingcheng glanced at him, unable to understand his hurt feelings. He assumed Chen Man simply felt he shouldn't be acting like this. "Right now, I'm single and without a wife or kids," he said calmly. "There's nothing wrong with what I did."

He brought a hand to his still-scalding temple as he spoke. Almost apathetically, he went on, "I've told you not to put me on too high of a pedestal. I'm just an ordinary person. I have all the desires any human should have."

Chen Man choked up and turned away abruptly. He sniffled as he lifted the pack of congee and put it on the bedside table next to Xie Qingcheng.

"Um... I-I just remembered I left something at the shop. I need to go get it." As soon as Chen Man finished speaking, he left without a backward glance, moving even more hastily than usual, as if he were fleeing.

After Chen Man fled to the main lobby of the night emergency department, he sighed deeply, eyes red-rimmed as he stood in a daze. His head was an absolute mess. What he'd overheard earlier kept echoing through his mind.

He knew Xie Qingcheng must have slept with someone. The thought made his heart throb with pain—but he didn't even have the courage to ask who Xie Qingcheng had slept with.

In Xie Qingcheng's eyes, he was forever a child. Xie Qingcheng would take care of him and protect him, but he'd never open his heart to him, let alone share his personal life with him. If Xie Qingcheng knew he actually had these kinds of feelings for him, Chen Man worried that he'd destroy their friendly relationship forever.

But right now, his heart was twisted up too tightly.

He wondered, *Who exactly* is *it... What kind of girl is she?*

Chen Man closed his eyes. It really was too painful for him; just because he wasn't a woman, he would never be able to confess his feelings to Xie Qingcheng, would he?

But what Chen Man didn't know was that at this very moment, that "girl," the primary culprit, the one he hated so much he could spit blood, was leaning against the wall in the corner with his hands in his pockets, watching from afar as Chen Man exited the emergency infusion room.

He Yu had followed Xie Qingcheng and Chen Man all the way here.

And it was only now that he got a clear look at the person scurrying about by Xie Qingcheng's side.

He Yu recognized Chen Man. He had eaten a meal with this guy, that time at the dining hall. He was very close to Xie Qingcheng.

As Chen Man stood in the light, his heart in distress, He Yu stood in the darkness, also a bit uncomfortable, with a heart that felt like it had been stuck through with thorns. But he wasn't sure why he felt that way.

Though he despised Xie Qingcheng, when he woke up, sobered up, and recalled the scattered fragments of those past incidents, he felt that it would be a bit much to allow Xie Qingcheng to meet with a truly terrible mishap. But in the end, after he followed Xie Qingcheng all the way back, all he got for his efforts was the opportunity to personally witness Chen Man half-carrying the unconscious Xie Qingcheng out of the medical school's faculty dormitory and into a car...

As He Yu watched these events unfold, he felt very, very uncomfortable.

It was his fault that Xie Qingcheng had fallen ill. He didn't fear anything and was willing to bear the consequences for all his actions. He wasn't ashamed of facing the doctor. He didn't need someone else to clean up the debts he incurred, especially since Xie Qingcheng had just today accused him of "running away after doing something wrong" back when he was still conscious.

I didn't run away, He Yu thought. Xie Qingcheng was the one who had way too many friends who were too young for him, friends who were always following him around at his beck and call, eagerly scrambling to clean up He Yu's messes.

He Yu had been standing outside the whole time Xie Qingcheng was hooked up to the IV in the infusion room. Although he wanted to know about Xie Qingcheng's current condition, there was no way for him to go in and ask with Chen Man present.

It was indisputable that he was the one who had given Xie Qingcheng a fever, but after all this time, he couldn't even enter the infusion room—until now, when Chen Man stepped out.

Watching from afar, He Yu noted the grim expression on the youngster's face; he looked like he thought the sky had fallen. A tendril of worry immediately unfurled in his heart. Was Xie Qingcheng really in terrible condition? He couldn't care less about Xie Qingcheng, but he was the one who fucked the man. Out of respect for his own dignity, he felt honor-bound to bear some of the responsibility.

Then, Chen Man walked closer. Now that He Yu could clearly make out the unexpected redness rimming his eyes, he was even more dumbfounded. He felt somewhat at a loss. What did this mean?

What exactly was wrong with Xie Qingcheng?

He Yu's face had turned slightly pale. He didn't realize it, but he was practically the spitting image of a young father-to-be waiting outside of a delivery room—barred from entering, unable to obtain any information, and desperately anxious. As He Yu was caught in the midst of his fretful hand-wringing, though, one of the nurses stationed in the emergency infusion room came running out, saying, "Sir, you're Xie Qingcheng's family, right?"

Briefly startled, Chen Man gave it a moment of thought and then nodded slowly.

"The results of the blood work covered by the patient's insurance should be out. You missed one when you were picking them up just now, so if you could, please go get it. There's also the medicine prescribed by the doctor. Please pay and pick it up as soon as possible."

"Oh... Okay."

Chen Man walked listlessly over to the reception window for the lab report and collected Xie Qingcheng's blood test results. Then he went to a different window to pay for the medicine. But he was truly in a terrible mood, his mind wandering as he went through the motions. As he was picking up the medicine and paying the bill, the blood test report that he had only just obtained floated from his pile of miscellany and onto the ground.

The flimsy sheet of paper fell like a snowflake onto the ice-cold tiles of the emergency room lobby's floor.

He Yu stared at it, transfixed.

That was Xie Qingcheng's lab report...

After a few seconds of indecision, he pulled the brim of his cap lower. Then, before Chen Man could notice, he walked over with an upright posture and picked up that snow-white sheet of paper.

In that moment, He Yu was struck by an exceptionally bizarre thought. It was as though he were a scumbag university student who, after having sex for the first time, was worried that he had accidentally gotten his girlfriend pregnant because he had been too hasty to put a condom on properly. And now he was sneaking a peek at his girlfriend's pregnancy test.

He Yu shook his head aggressively, trying to dislodge the ludicrous thought. He'd really gone mad. After so many momentous events these last few days, even his thinking process had become warped.

Lowering his head, He Yu carefully examined Xie Qingcheng's blood test report. Only his white blood cell count was elevated—

it seemed like he was suffering from inflammation. Everything else seemed to be within the normal ranges, so there was nothing seriously wrong with him.

Then what was that young guy crying about...?

Breathing a small sigh of relief, He Yu lifted his lashes slightly and his eyes fell on the words "Xie Qingcheng, Male, Age 32" written at the top of the report.

He stroked a finger over the line of fine print.

Hot off the press, the report still carried a hint of residual warmth from the printer.

Warm to the touch, just like that man's skin...

"Excuse me, buddy, but I believe that belongs to me."

After a round of bustling activity, Chen Man had finally come to his senses and realized that he had lost the blood test report. When he retraced his steps, however, he saw a young man about his own age carefully analyzing that very same report.

It was just a pity that Chen Man's mood was so poor, and with He Yu wearing his cap, Chen Man didn't get a very good look at his face and missed his opportunity to confront the primary culprit. Taking He Yu for an ordinary patient, he said, "Sorry, but could you please give that report back to me?"

He Yu didn't reply. With his eyes hidden in the shadow cast by the brim of his cap, a thought struck him for a split second: there was no way he would hand over the report. But an instant later, that thought seemed strange to him. Why didn't he want to hand it over? After all, it wasn't as if he was *actually* a scumbag university student holding the results of his girlfriend Xie Qingcheng's pregnancy test.

How utterly absurd.

Despite these thoughts, he still said in a chilly voice, "You're mistaken. This is mine."

Chen Man said, "I clearly… Please, can I just take a look?"

He Yu refused to give the paper back to Chen Man, tightening his pale, slender fingers on the lab report as he held it behind him.

"You can't. Patient confidentiality."

"I just want to see the name! Because I just dropped this sheet, right around here…"

"You want to see my girlfriend's pregnancy test results?"

Chen Man was speechless.

He Yu himself found it ludicrous the moment the words left his mouth, but perhaps because he had been thinking about all that nonsense earlier, *that* was the refusal that slipped out.

The deterrent those words posed was far too great. A naive young lad like Chen Man could never have the nerve to keep badgering He Yu after hearing the words "pregnancy test results."

Chen Man turned bright red and didn't dare look the boy standing before him in the eye, even though he found the entire situation rather preposterous. He hadn't taken a proper look at He Yu's face, but he was certain that the other party must be a student who was younger than him.

The things that college boys got up to these days were truly…

Chen Man stammered, "S-sorry, my mistake."

He Yu tucked Xie Qingcheng's blood test report into his pocket with a cold expression. "Yes, it was indeed your mistake."

"Then I'll keep looking…"

He Yu ignored Chen Man. That report was honestly of little use to him and could at most prove that he had fucked Xie Qingcheng for an entire night. Still, he stuffed it into his pocket with a chilly cast to his face and left without a backward glance.

Not a single person knew that he had been there.

APPENDIX

Characters, Names, and Locations

CHARACTERS

MAIN CHARACTERS

HE YU: 贺予: A nineteen-year-old university student with a rare mental illness.

XIE QINGCHENG 谢清呈: He Yu's former doctor, who currently works as a medical school professor.

SUPPORTING CHARACTERS

XIE XUE 谢雪: Xie Qingcheng's younger sister, and a lecturer at He Yu's university.

CHEN YAN 陈衍: A police officer and family friend of Xie Qingcheng. Nicknamed "Chen Man."

LÜ ZHISHU 吕芝书: He Yu's mother, a wealthy businesswoman.

HE JIWEI 贺继威: He Yu's father, a wealthy businessman who is often away from home.

LI RUOQIU 李若秋: Xie Qingcheng's ex-wife.

JIANG LIPING 蒋丽萍: The morality advisor in charge of He Yu's screenwriting/directing class.

QIN CIYAN 秦慈岩: Xie Qingcheng's former colleague, who was killed by the angry son of a patient.

ZHUANG ZHIQIANG 庄志强: A mentally ill homeless man.

JIANG LANPEI 江兰佩: The now-deceased patient who burned down Cheng Kang Psychiatric Hospital.

LIANG JICHENG 梁季成: The former director of Cheng Kang Psychiatric Hospital.

DUAN-LAOBAN 段老板: A mysterious figure working in the shadows.

WEI DONGHENG 卫冬恒: A senior drama student at Huzhou University.

ZHENG JINGFENG 郑敬风: A veteran criminal investigator and former colleague of Xie Qingcheng's parents.

NAME GUIDE

Diminutives, Nicknames, and Name Tags

DA-: A prefix meaning "big" or "elder," which can be added before titles for elders, like "dage" or "dajie," or before a name.

DI/DIDI: A word meaning "younger brother." It can also be used to address an unrelated (usually younger) male peer, and optionally used as a suffix.

GE/GEGE: A word meaning "older brother." It can also be used to address an unrelated male peer, and optionally used as a suffix.

JIE/JIEJIE: A word meaning "elder sister." It can also be used to address an unrelated female peer, and optionally used as a suffix.

LAO-: A prefix meaning "old." Usually added to a surname and used in informal contexts.

LAOSHI: A word meaning "teacher" that can be used to refer to any educator, often in deference. Can also be attached to someone's name as a suffix.

LAOBAN: A word meaning "boss" that can be used to refer to one's superior or the proprietor of a business. Can also be attached to someone's name as a suffix.

SAOZI/-SAO: A word meaning "elder brother's wife." It can be used to address the wife (or informally, girlfriend) of an unrelated male peer.

XIAO-: A prefix meaning "little" or "younger." Often used in an affectionate and familiar context.

XUEZHANG: Older male classmate.

XUEDI: Younger male classmate.

XUEJIE: Older female classmate.

XUEMEI: Younger female classmate.

APPENDIX

Glossary

GLOSSARY

EYES: Descriptions like "almond eyes" or "peach-blossom eyes" refer to eye shape. Almond eyes have a balanced shape, like that of an almond, whereas peach-blossom eyes have a rounded upper lid and are often considered particularly alluring.

FACE: *Mianzi* (面子), generally translated as "face," is an important concept in Chinese society. It is a metaphor for a person's reputation and can be extended to further descriptive metaphors. For example, "having face" refers to having a good reputation, and "losing face" refers to having one's reputation hurt. Meanwhile, "giving face" means deferring to someone else to help improve their reputation, while "not wanting face" implies that a person is acting so poorly or shamelessly that they clearly don't care about their reputation at all. "Thin face" refers to someone easily embarrassed or prone to offense at perceived slights. Conversely, "thick face" refers to someone not easily embarrassed and immune to insults.

JADE: Jade is a semi-precious mineral with a long history of ornamental and functional usage in China. The word "jade" can refer to two distinct minerals, nephrite and jadeite, which both range in color from white to gray to a wide spectrum of greens.

UNIVERSITIES AND CLASS STRUCTURE: In Chinese universities, students are assigned to a class of students in their major. Each class takes their major courses together for the duration of their university career.

WECHAT: A Chinese instant messaging, social media, and mobile payment app ubiquitous in modern Chinese society. People use its text, call, and voice message functions for both personal and business communications. Many vendors in China prefer its mobile payment capabilities to cash.

WEIBO: A popular Chinese microblogging social media platform similar to Twitter.

XUEBA: 学霸, literally "academic tyrant," is a slang term for high-achieving students. Usually complimentary.

Seven Seas

耽美Danmei
Seven Seas Entertainment
sevenseasdanmei.com

文學城
WWW.JJWXC.NET